Under the Ensign of the Rising Sun

A Story of the Russo-Japanese War

by

Harry Collingwood

Double9
BOOKS

Under the Ensign of the Rising Sun
A Story of the Russo-Japanese War
by Harry Collingwood

ISBN: 978-93-68097-64-8

Published by

DOUBLE 9 BOOKS

2/13-B, Ansari Road
Daryaganj, New Delhi – 110002
info@double9books.com
www.double9books.com
Tel. 011-40042856

ABOUT THE AUTHOR

Harry Collingwood (1851-1922) was an English author known for his adventurous novels and stories, particularly those set in maritime environments. Born in London, Collingwood was a prolific writer whose works often centered around themes of adventure, exploration, and nautical life. Collingwood's literary career was marked by his fascination with the sea and maritime adventures. His background and experiences as a sailor heavily influenced his writing, contributing to the authenticity and excitement of his stories. Some of his notable works include: The Pirate Island (1887): One of his most famous novels, it tells the tale of a group of pirates and their adventures. The book combines elements of high-seas adventure with thrilling escapades and daring heroism. His writing often reflects his enthusiasm for adventure and exploration, capturing the excitement of the unknown and the allure of the sea. Harry Collingwood's legacy lies in his ability to captivate readers with tales of adventure and exploration. His novels remain a testament to his passion for maritime life and his skill in crafting engaging and adventurous stories.

CONTENTS

Chapter One
Dismissed the Service

"Well, good-bye, old chap; keep a stiff upper lip, and hope for the best; the truth is pretty sure to come out some day, somehow, and then they will be bound to reinstate you. And be sure you call on the Pater, and tell him the whole yarn. I'll bet he will be able to give you some advice worth having. Also give my love to the Mater, and tell her that I'm looking forward to Christmas. Perhaps I may see you then. Good-bye again, and good luck to you."

The speaker was young Ronald Gordon, one of the midshipmen belonging to H.M.S. *Terrible,* and my particular chum; and the words were spoken as we parted company on the platform of Portland railway station, Gordon to return to his ship, while I, an outcast, was bound for London to seek my fortune.

Yes; after doing splendidly at Dartmouth, heading the list at the passing-out exam, and so at once gaining the rating of midshipman; doing equally well afloat during the subsequent three years and a half, qualifying for Gunnery, Torpedo, and Navigating duties, serving for six months aboard a destroyer, and everywhere gaining the esteem and goodwill of my superiors, here was I, Paul Swinburne, at the age of seventeen and a half, an outcast kicked out of the Navy with ignominy and my career ruined, through the machinations of another, and he my cousin!

He, Bob Carr,—like myself, a midshipman aboard the *Terrible,*—had committed a crime of a particularly mean and disgraceful character— there is no need for me to specify its precise nature—and with diabolical ingenuity, knowing that discovery was inevitable, had succeeded in diverting suspicion so strongly toward me that I had been accused, court martialled, and—although I had pleaded not guilty—found guilty and dismissed the Service.

Now, it is necessary for me to say here just a word or two in self-defence; for there is no reason whatever why the reader should be allowed to believe me guilty, although, for certain reasons of my own, I permitted the officers who tried me to think so.

I am an orphan, both my parents having died within a few months of each other when I was less than three years old, leaving me to the mercy of the world. My nearest relation was Aunt Betsy Carr, my father's only sister, and at my mother's death she and Uncle Bob adopted me as their own, although they had a baby boy of their own, at that time nearly two years old—the Cousin Bob who was responsible for my present trouble. They took me not only into their home but also into their hearts; they made not the slightest difference in their treatment of Bob and me; I was as much a son to them as he was; and the result was that I soon grew to love them both as much as though they had been my own parents.

At first, as children, Bob and I got on splendidly together; but later on, when we were respectively about seven and eight years of age, my cousin gradually developed a feeling of jealousy that at length became inordinate— although he was very careful to conceal the fact from his parents; so that when, in my second year at Dartmouth, the matter of sending him there also was mooted, I was exceedingly sorry, although I of course gladly promised to help him to the utmost, in the event of his being entered. And when in due time he turned up there, I redeemed my promise, so far as Bob would let me; and it cost me a good deal to do so, for he soon became exceedingly unpopular. But he managed to scrape through his final, and, some six months before the opening of this story, was appointed to the *Terrible*—to my great chagrin, for I had a presentiment that his coming meant trouble for me.

And now the trouble had come, with a vengeance. It was really Bob, and not I, who had committed the crime of which I was accused; and clever as the young rascal had been in diverting suspicion from himself to me, I could have cleared myself, had I so chosen, but only by fixing the guilt upon him. And that I could not bring myself to do, after all the kindness which I— had received at the hands of my aunt and uncle; for they not only idolised the lad but believed in him implicitly, and I knew that disillusion would simply break their hearts—they would never again be able to hold up their heads and look others in the face. Therefore when I was summoned to be tried by court martial, I simply pleaded Not Guilty—which was regarded as an aggravation of my offence—and did not attempt to defend myself, with the result that I was found guilty, and expelled.

Of course I knew that this would be a bitter blow to my uncle and aunt; but it would not be nearly so bitter as it would have been had the guilt been fixed upon Bob, therefore of the two evils I chose what I considered the least, although it involved the ruin of my career—a career which I loved and of which I was intensely proud.

And now I was not only without a career, but also without a home; for I simply could not endure the idea of going back to my aunt and uncle, and witnessing their grief as well as enduring their reproaches. I therefore wrote them a brief letter informing them of the misfortune which had befallen me, assuring them of my innocence, and announcing my determination to start afresh, fight my own battle, and rehabilitate myself as best I could.

In making my plans I was greatly helped by my chum, Gordon. He had been with me at Dartmouth, after that in the *Vengeance*, and now again in the *Terrible*; he therefore knew me well enough to implicitly believe me when I assured him upon my word of honour that I was innocent. He was a good chum; not only did he believe in my innocence but he also stoutly maintained it to others, whenever the matter was referred to, although the evidence so cunningly woven was strong enough to secure my conviction. And when the result of the court martial was known, he not only sat down and wrote a long account of the affair to his parents, but insisted—taking no denial—that, before doing anything else, I should call upon his parents and consult with his father, Sir Robert. And this I at length, somewhat reluctantly, agreed to do, although I was by no means sure that his people would be so ready as he was to take me upon trust. Yet, apart from my uncle and aunt, Sir Robert and Lady Gordon were the only friends I had; and now was the time when of all others I most urgently needed the help of friends. At first I permitted myself to entertain certain high-flown ideas of going out into the world and fighting my battle alone and unaided; but Gordon was a level-headed youngster, and although he was a year younger than myself I was fain to admit the wisdom of his assertion that no fellow is sufficiently independent to ignore the advice and help of friends. Besides, I had already met Sir Robert and his wife—had indeed on one occasion spent ten days' leave with Ronald under their roof; and more genial, kindly, warmer-hearted people it would be impossible to imagine; so I felt hopeful that, with Ronald for my sponsor and advocate, Sir Robert would not refuse to give me his best advice and assistance.

It was late in the afternoon when I arrived at Waterloo—too late, I knew, to catch Sir Robert Gordon at his office; I therefore slung my chest on top of a cab, and ordered the driver to take me to a certain quiet and unassuming but comfortable hotel near the Embankment, where I proposed to take up my quarters until I could see my way a little more clearly. Here I dined, took a walk along the Embankment afterwards, and turned in early, not feeling in cue for amusement of any kind.

On the following morning I rose late, of deliberate purpose, had my breakfast, and then sauntered along the Embankment toward Sir Robert's office, timing myself to arrive there about eleven o'clock, by which time

I calculated that Ronald's father would about have gone through his morning's correspondence, and would be able to spare me a few minutes of his time.

As it chanced, I could not have timed my movements better, for as I was shown up to Sir Robert's private room I encountered his secretary just coming out, with a notebook in one hand and a goodly batch of letters in the other.

I may here explain that Sir Robert Gordon was an official of high position and very considerable importance in the Foreign Office. He received me very kindly, bade me be seated, and then said:

"Well, Swinburne, here you are at last. From Ronald's letter I rather gathered that I might see you some time yesterday. And now, before we go any farther, let me say how exceedingly sorry Lady Gordon and I are to hear of your misfortune—for a misfortune it is, and not a fault, Ronald assures me. Now,"—looking at his watch—"I can spare you just a quarter of an hour; so go ahead and tell me as much of the matter as you can in that time."

Thereupon I proceeded to relate, in as few words as possible, the particulars of the whole affair, not concealing the fact that my cousin was the actual culprit—for I knew that my confidence would be respected, and explaining my reasons for taking the onus upon myself instead of allowing the real culprit to suffer. But a quarter of an hour soon passes, when one is talking of oneself and one's own misfortunes; and the announcement that a certain important personage had called by appointment gave me the signal that it was time for me to go, though as I rose to take my leave I had the satisfaction of knowing that I had succeeded in convincing my friend of my innocence, for as we shook hands, Sir Robert said:

"We must talk this matter over again at our leisure, Swinburne, possibly this evening. Now, before you go, let me say that my wife and I expect you to take up your quarters with us until your future is definitely arranged. No, we will take no refusal; you are Ronald's chum, and we should not think of allowing you to stay at an hotel while there is a spare room for you at Maycroft. So off you go; get your luggage at once and make the best of your way to Norwood, where Lady Gordon will expect you to arrive in time for luncheon at one o'clock. I shall 'phone to her that you are coming."

What could one do but gratefully accept an invitation proffered in such friendly terms? It would have been boorish to refuse. I therefore returned to my modest hotel, paid my bill, and made the best of my way to Maycroft, where I was received with such kindness and cordiality as I have no words to describe.

Lady Gordon was a fit mate for her distinguished husband; smart, clever, accomplished, of attractive appearance, and so irresistibly fascinating a manner that within two minutes she succeeded in not only making me feel absolutely welcome and at home in her house, but also in some subtle fashion imbued me with the conviction that, serious as my misfortune undoubtedly was, it was by no means irretrievable. We could not talk confidentially at luncheon, the servants being present, but afterward, the weather being fine and the air warm for the time of year—it was the first day of December 1903—we adjourned to the garden, and there I told my tale all over again, this time in full detail, and received all the sympathy that my aching heart craved for.

Sir Robert reached home that night only just in time to dress for dinner, so there was therefore neither time nor opportunity for the discussion of my affairs until the meal was over and we had adjourned to the drawing-room. Then, while we were sipping our coffee, my host turned to me and said:

"I have been thinking a good deal about you, to-day, between whiles, Swinburne; and at last I think I have discovered a way to help you. By a lucky chance it happens that Viscount Hayashi—the Japanese Minister to Great Britain, you know—with whom I have been brought into very close touch of late, is dining here, *en famille*, to-morrow night, in order to have the opportunity to discuss certain rather delicate matters in private with me; and when we have finished talking business together—which will probably not occupy us more than an hour—I will put your case to him, giving him all the details of it—for we must be perfectly honest with him, you know— and ask him whether, under the circumstances, there is any likelihood of your being able to obtain employment in the Japanese Navy. Things are looking very black in the Far East just now; war between Russia and Japan is practically inevitable; and although the Japanese have long been preparing for it, and seem confident of success, I should imagine that they would be only too glad of the opportunity to secure the services of a smart and specially qualified young officer like yourself."

Much more was said upon the same subject which it is unnecessary to repeat here, and I also completed the story which I had begun in Sir Robert's office that morning, with the result that I was able to make my innocence as clear to him as I had already done to his wife. Sir Robert expressed the opinion that my action in taking the blame upon myself had been somewhat quixotic; but when I explained my reasons in full for doing so, he admitted that it seemed to be the only thing possible, and was good enough to say that it reflected the greatest credit upon me.

On the following night the Viscount and Sir Robert arrived at Maycroft together in the latter's limousine; and after introducing his wife and myself our host excused himself and hurried away to dress, leaving Lady Gordon and me to entertain our distinguished guest.

The conversation before and during dinner was exceedingly lively and interesting, the Ambassador telling us many remarkable things about Japan. Then the talk veered round toward naval matters, and my kind hostess afforded me the opportunity to parade my special knowledge by asking me to explain the difference between armoured and protected cruisers, one question leading to another, until at length His Excellency, who had been listening most courteously and attentively, said:

"Am I mistaken, sir, in supposing that you are an officer in the honourable Navy of Great Britain?"

That was the opportunity for which Lady Gordon had been waiting, and she at once replied:

"Mr Swinburne was, until a few days ago, senior midshipman on the same ship as my son—the battleship *Terrible*. But a very exalted sense of gratitude on his part has resulted in a grave miscarriage of justice whereby, through accepting the blame for another's fault, he has been dismissed from the Service, to his great grief, for he was passionately devoted to his profession."

The Viscount rather raised his eyebrows at this, and regarded me keenly, as though seeking to read my character from my face.

"Really?" he said. "That is indeed a terrible misfortune, which I should scarcely have thought could possibly happen in such a Service as yours, where, I have always understood, such matters are inquired into with the most scrupulous fairness."

"So they are, Your Excellency," I replied. "But my expulsion was not in any sense due to remissness on the part of the officers who tried me. It was due to the fact that, for the reason named by Lady Gordon, I deliberately refrained from producing evidence which would have resulted in my own acquittal and the conviction of the actual culprit; and thus the members of the court martial were, in the course of their duty, compelled to find me guilty and to pass upon me sentence of dismissal."

"I see. Yes, I think I understand," observed the Viscount. "The feeling of gratitude which could induce you to take the extreme step of ruining your entire career must have been wonderfully strong. I find the incident remarkably interesting, Mr—er—Swinburne, so much so, indeed, that when my friend Gordon and I have concluded the business talk which has brought me down here to-night I should very much like to hear all the particulars of your story, if you will do me the favour to confide them to me."

I replied that I would do so with great pleasure; and then, the meal being at an end, our hostess rose from the table and retired to the drawing-room, while Sir Robert, apologising for leaving me alone, carried off the Ambassador to the study, where he had ordered coffee to be served.

Naturally, I did not linger at the table after the others had gone, but followed my hostess to the drawing-room, where I at once proceeded to thank her for the kindly tact with which she had made my case known to so influential a personage as Viscount Hayashi. On her part, she was just as pleased as I was that so exceptionally favourable an opportunity to restore my wrecked fortunes had presented itself, and for some time we sat talking the matter over. Then Lady Gordon insisted upon my singing to her while she played my accompaniments; and in this manner the time passed rapidly, and before we dared expect them her husband and the Viscount reappeared. But even then we did not stop at once, His Excellency being polite enough to beg us to continue. At length, however, our guest rose and, beckoning me to his side, said:

"Before I go, Mr Swinburne, let me say that Sir Robert Gordon has confided to me the full particulars of your remarkable story. And, having heard it, I should like you to know that, not only am I fully convinced of your entire innocence of the foul charge preferred against you, but also that I, as a native of a country in which filial affection is held in the highest honour and esteem, am full of admiration for your conduct. I am proud to have the honour of knowing a young man possessing the courage to act as you have done; and I have no hesitation in expressing the opinion that, in dispensing with your services, your country has lost a most promising and valuable servant. But if Great Britain is unable to appreciate your value, there are other countries which can, and Japan is one of them. You are doubtless aware that war between Russia and Japan is inevitable; it is merely a question of weeks, perhaps only of days; the Japanese naval service will afford many opportunities for an officer, qualified as I understand you are, to distinguish himself, and rapidly advance his fortunes. If you would care to enter that service I believe the affair might be easily managed, backed up as you are by the recommendation of a gentleman of Sir Robert Gordon's position. Think the matter over, will you? And when you have decided, call upon me at this address, and let me know." And he handed me his card.

On the spur of the moment I was very much inclined to close with His Excellency's offer there and then; but even as the words of acceptance leapt to my lips I bethought myself that it would only be courteous to wait and hear what my kind host and hostess had to say upon the matter before taking the irrevocable step. I therefore expressed my hearty thanks for the offer, and promised to give it my best and most careful consideration.

When the Viscount had gone, Sir Robert, his wife, and I formed ourselves into a little committee to discuss His Excellency's proposal. Of course there was never a moment's doubt as to the wisdom of accepting the offer, but Sir Robert expressed his satisfaction at my self-control. He and his wife were quite of one mind that there was nothing to be gained by my appearing to be too eager, and they strongly advised me to allow at least one whole day to pass before presenting myself at the Ambassador's residence; they also advised me not to accept any rank below that of a full lieutenant, which was quite in accordance with my own views.

Accordingly, on the day but one following that of His Excellency's visit to Maycroft, I journeyed up to town with Sir Robert and, upon parting from him at the Foreign Office, made the best of my way to Viscount Hayashi's residence.

His Excellency was at home, and I was at once received. He was polite enough to express extreme satisfaction when I informed him that I had definitely decided to accept his offer, provided that the conditions could be satisfactorily arranged; and within half an hour we had come to terms, the arrangement being that I was to enter the Japanese naval service with the rank of a full lieutenant, my commission to bear date of my landing in Japan; that a passage was to be provided for me; and that I was to hold myself in readiness to depart at twenty-four hours' notice. A letter to this effect was given me to hand to a certain subordinate official whose business it was to arrange all such details; and I then made my exit, the recipient of many good wishes on His Excellency's part for my success.

My next visit was to a Mr Yuri Kuroda, the subordinate official above mentioned, who, having read the letter of which I was the bearer, immediately became very polite, requested to be favoured with my honourable name and address, which he at once entered in a big book, and then proceeded to discuss the question of my passage out to Japan. It transpired that his Government was negotiating with the Argentine Republic for the purchase of two powerful armoured cruisers, built for the Government of the latter country at Genoa; and Mr Kuroda suggested that if the negotiations resulted successfully, it might suit me to go out in one of them as an officer, the date of my commission to be advanced accordingly. I asked for some particulars of the ships; and upon learning that they measured 7700 tons, that they were entirely sheathed amidships in 6 inches of Krupp steel, and that they were armed with four 8-inch guns in their turrets, with a central battery consisting of fourteen 6-inch guns, I quickly replied that there was nothing I should like better. And so it was arranged, Kuroda undertaking to inform me in good time when my services would be likely to be required.

Two days later, however, I received a telegram from Kuroda, requesting me to call upon him at the earliest possible moment. It came while we were sitting down to dinner, and Lady Gordon expressed the opinion that if I made my call on the following morning it would be early enough, and Sir Robert was rather inclined to agree with her. But the receipt of the telegram seemed to suggest that something unexpected had happened, and I therefore determined to obey the summons that night. I accordingly scribbled a reply saying that I would present myself at nine o'clock; and within ten minutes of that hour I was once more in the Ambassador's house. His Excellency was out; but Mr Kuroda was in and waiting for me; and he expressed his gratification at my prompt response to his summons. He then proceeded to inform me that certain news had arrived—he did not state the nature of it— which rendered it highly desirable that I should expedite my departure for Japan, instead of awaiting the issue of the negotiations for the purchase of the Argentine cruisers, and inquired when I could be ready to start. My reply that I could start on the morrow, if necessary, pleased him greatly, but he intimated that the earliest date upon which it would be possible to dispatch me would be the 8th of the month—it was then the 5th—and requested me to make my arrangements accordingly, and to call upon him again on the morning of the 7th, when he would give me my final instructions and hand me my credentials, with railway and steamer tickets, etcetera.

The Gordons received the news of my impending departure with mixed feelings. They were delighted that, through their help and influence, I had been able to so quickly find another opening for my energies, but were exceedingly sorry that I was to leave them so soon, as they had confidently reckoned upon my spending the Christmas holidays with them and Ronald. However, Sir Robert took me up to town with him, in his car, on the morning of the 7th, and Lady Gordon accompanied us, saying that she had some shopping to do. I left them at the entrance to Sir Robert's office, and in due time found myself once more in Mr Kuroda's presence.

It was easy to see that the little man was so busy that he scarcely knew which way to turn, but he was as smiling and polite as ever, and had everything ready for me, neatly enclosed in a stout official envelope, the contents of which he turned out for my inspection. There was my railway ticket from London to Dover, my steamer ticket from Dover to Calais, my railway ticket from Calais to Marseilles, *via* Paris, my steamer ticket from Marseilles to Yokohama, and my credentials, which were to be presented to a certain official in Tokio, who would hand me my commission and give me my final instructions. Everything was cut and dried, even to a travelling schedule giving me the train and steamer times of departure and arrival; therefore, having looked them through and satisfied myself that nothing had been omitted, I returned the several documents to the envelope, thrust the latter into my pocket, and bade Mr Kuroda farewell. He replied with hearty good wishes for my welfare and success, expressed his deep regret that he was not going with me instead of remaining in London, shook my hand with great fervour and friendliness, and, as he bowed me out, touched the bell which was the signal for another visitor to be ushered in.

When Sir Robert came home that night, he brought with him two parcels wrapped in stout brown paper, one of them being rather long and slim; but I thought nothing of it, as I knew that it was a custom, when things were urgently needed, to have them sent to his office, so that they might be brought home at night in his car. After dinner, however, the two parcels were produced, opened, and found to contain, the one a handsome oak case containing a pair of heavy and very business-like Colt automatic pistols, with all necessary tools, bottle of oil, and one hundred cartridges; while the other was a beautiful naval sword and sheath, the blade perfectly plain but of such exquisite temper that, by exerting my full strength, I was able to bend it until the point met the hilt. The pistols were a farewell gift to me from dear Lady Gordon, while the sword was from Sir Robert. The gifts were accompanied by the heartfelt good wishes of the donors for my welfare, happiness, and safety in the strenuous times that seemed to be looming ahead, and the hope that the weapons would prove useful to me in my new service. They were, as will be seen from the account of my adventures, set forth in the following pages.

Chapter Two
The Russian Destroyer

At a quarter to eleven o'clock on the morning of December 8, 1903, I stepped out of a cab at Charing Cross railway station, and forthwith proceeded to get my luggage properly labelled and checked through to Marseilles. While I was doing this, I became aware of some one by my side, and, looking up, saw a little man, the formation of whose features and the colour of whose skin at once apprised me that he was a Japanese. He was dressed in a neat travelling suit of tweed, and wore a bowler hat and brown boots. He was reading my name, legibly painted on my sea chest, and as I looked at him he turned to me and bowed.

"You are Mr Paul Swinburne, bound for Japan?" he said, putting the statement in the form of a question, and speaking in perfect English.

"I am," I replied. "And you?"

"I am Captain Murata Nakamura, of the Japanese army, in England on Government business, and now returning to Japan in the *Matsuma Maru*, the steamer in which I understand you are going out. Half an hour ago I was with Mr Kuroda, whom you know, and he told me about you, and bade me look out for you. I am pleased to make your honourable acquaintance, Mr Swinburne, and shall be happy to place my humble services at your honourable disposal."

"Gad! that's very good of you," I said. "Very glad to know you, Captain. Is your baggage ready? Then, let us try to secure a compartment to ourselves and travel through together."

"It will give me great pleasure to travel in your honourable company," replied my new acquaintance. "And I have already secured a compartment by, as you say, 'squaring' the guard. There he is now. Let us go and—how do you say? Oh yes, I remember—'interview' him."

We obtained a compartment to ourselves, and my new friend at once started smoking cigarettes and chatting in the most animated manner upon the prospects of war. He was in high spirits, and apparently had no doubts at all as to the outcome of the fighting—if fighting there was to be. And of this also he appeared to entertain no doubt, although there were people who still believed that either Russia or Japan would climb down and so avoid a fight.

By the time that the train reached Dover we were "as thick as thieves," for Nakamura's perfect frankness and his geniality of manner quickly conquered my insular aloofness toward the foreigner; and upon boarding the Channel steamer we at once went below and were busy with our luncheon almost before the boat had cast off from the pier.

At Calais, Nakamura, who seemed to speak every language under the sun, took charge of my baggage as well as his own, and by some mysterious process, probably not altogether unconnected with "backsheesh," managed to clear the whole through the Customs in about five minutes. Then he again "squared" the guard and secured our privacy as far as Paris, where we arrived about five o'clock in the evening. There was a train leaving for Marseilles at half-past seven, so we took a cab, drove across the city, and dined at the railway station in comfort before beginning the long night journey. Then, once more securing a compartment to ourselves, we settled down for our twelve hours' run to the shore of the Mediterranean.

I was very much amused at the naïveté of some of my companion's remarks. He asked the most intimate questions in the coolest possible manner, and if I had not already resolved to be absolutely frank with my new comrades in arms I should have been somewhat embarrassed to find replies for some of them. He was greatly surprised to learn that I was not yet eighteen years of age, and was still growing, for although he appeared to be not more than twenty-five, he informed me that he was actually thirty-three, and I was a head taller than he, the fact being that I had a natural tendency toward bulkiness which my passion for athletics had further encouraged. He jocularly remarked that he hoped the authorities would have sense enough to appoint me to a battleship, for he was sure that in no other quarters would I find room to stand upright.

We reached Marseilles without adventure at eight o'clock on the following morning, and, after breakfasting at the railway station, chartered a cab and drove down to the Joliet, where we found our ship, the *Matsuma Maru*, lying alongside a wharf piled yards high with crates, bales, and cases of all sorts and sizes waiting to be stowed in the ship's holds. The skipper was somewhere ashore, it appeared, but we hunted up the chief officer and introduced ourselves, upon which we learned that every effort was being made to have the ship ready for sea by three o'clock that afternoon, but that it would be impossible for her to get away a minute earlier than that; we therefore found the chief steward, got him to show us our cabins, and had our baggage carried aboard. Then we went ashore again and, Nakamura happening to learn that the place boasted a zoological garden, nothing would satisfy him but we must needs go there, which we did, afterwards finding our way to the handsome Museum. Then down into the town again to lunch, finally returning to the ship at a quarter to three. I had been accustomed to seeing work smartly done in our own navy, but I was amazed to see what a few hours of strenuous labour had effected upon that wharf. It was practically cleared, and even as we stood and watched, the last cases were slung aboard, and the first bell, warning visitors that the ship was about to start, was rung, whereupon we trotted aboard and took up a position on the poop, where some fifty or sixty other passengers, all men, with about half a dozen exceptions, were already congregated. Nakamura looked eagerly about him and quickly spotted at least a dozen acquaintances and fellow-countrymen, to all of whom he insisted upon introducing me; and his mention of the fact that I was *going* out for the express purpose of fighting for Japan at once ensured me a most friendly welcome among them. While this was going on, the ship was unmoored, and a few minutes later we were outside the harbour and shaping a course that took us at no great distance past the islet which Hugo has immortalised in his *Count of Monte Christo*.

Once clear of the harbour, the skipper rang for full speed; and the *Matsuma Maru*, a white-hulled, steel-built ship of some four thousand tons, rigged as a topsail schooner, soon showed that she was the possessor of a nimble pair of heels. She was loaded well down, yet an hour after the patent log had been put overboard it recorded a run of seventeen knots. The weather was gloriously fine and the sea glass-smooth, so that one had not much opportunity of judging her quality as a sea boat, but when I went forward and, duly paying my footing, looked over the bows and noted their outward flare as the sides rose from the water, I had not much difficulty in deciding that she would prove very comfortable and easy in a seaway.

Upon going below to dinner that night, a glance round the saloon tables showed that at least seventy-five per cent, of the passengers were Japanese, while, of the remainder, half, perhaps, were English, the rest being composed, in pretty nearly equal proportions, of French, Germans, and, somewhat to my surprise, Russians. These last, however, it eventually transpired, had booked only as far as Hong Kong, from whence it was probable that they intended to proceed to Port Arthur, although they said nothing to that effect.

We passed through the Straits of Bonifacio and Messina, and in due course arrived at Port Said without incident, except that, thanks to Nakamura, I soon became upon friendly and even intimate terms with all the Japanese passengers in the saloon, as well as the ship's officers. There was one old gentleman in particular, rejoicing in the name of Matsudaira Hashimoto, an ex-professor of languages at the Imperial College of Tokio, who, happening to hear that I was anxious to utilise the large amount of time occupied by the voyage in acquiring as much knowledge as possible of the Japanese language, at once came forward with an offer to gratuitously teach me, in order that, as he remarked, I might be equipped with a working knowledge of the language upon my arrival, and so be in a position to immediately render my services valuable. The old gentleman, it appeared, had been remarkably successful in his day as a teacher of languages, working upon a system which he had himself invented; and, luckily for me, his system was so excellent that, working with me for five hours daily, he actually succeeded in redeeming his promise so thoroughly that when we at length reached Yokohama I was able to manage quite fairly well without the services of an interpreter. This by the way.

It was a part of the skipper's plan to replenish his bunkers at Port Said, an operation involving a detention of three hours. We therefore all went ashore, and I posted a letter to my friends, the Gordons, attaching to it a number of stamps of different denominations, for the benefit of Ronald, who was an enthusiastic collector. We then roved about the town, but, finding nothing to interest us, soon returned to the ship, which we found enveloped in a cloud of coal dust which was playing havoc with her fresh white paint, despite the canvas screens spread to protect it.

We got under way again shortly after three o'clock that afternoon, two of our passengers—Russians who looked very much like military men in mufti—cutting things so fine that they were actually compelled to follow after us in a steam launch; and when at length they overtook us, scrambled aboard, and went at once to the cabin which they shared, the skipper, with whom Nakamura and I had become very chummy, caught our eyes and signed to us both to come up to his cabin on the bridge, the ship then being in charge of a canal pilot, with Sadakiyo, the chief officer, standing beside him on the navigating bridge.

Accordingly, we sauntered up in a nonchalant sort of way, as though intent upon watching the progress of the ship through the canal, for there had been something of furtiveness in the skipper's action which seemed to hint that he did not wish his sign to be observed by others, which led me at least to imagine that there might be something in the wind.

And so, apparently there was, for when we had entered the cabin, the skipper softly closed the door and drew the curtains across the two after ports, as though desirous of concealing the fact of our presence in his cabin.

Then, having produced whisky and soda and a box of cigars, he seated himself on the sofa, facing us, and said in English:

"You saw those two Russians come aboard, just now, after nearly losing their passage?"

And when we nodded affirmation he continued:

"I am wondering whether the circumstance means trouble for us. And for this reason. When I was ashore, about an hour ago, I had business that took me into McIntosh's store. Now, McIntosh is a very good fellow, whom I have known for some time. He is very friendly to us Japanese, and 'has his knife'—as you English term it—into the Russians. Well, after chatting together for a little while, he took me into his inner room and informed me that there is a steamer, flying the Russian naval ensign, and a Russian destroyer lurking near the southern extremity of the Red Sea, which seem disposed to give trouble to Japanese merchant craft. It appears that only last week, one or the other of these—McIntosh is not sure which—stopped and boarded the *Mishima Maru* and insisted upon examining her papers and inspecting her passengers, for what reason McIntosh could not say, as he had merely heard the bare facts of the case. And about a quarter of an hour later, shortly after I had left McIntosh's place, I saw those two Russians who nearly missed us enter the telegraph office, and I began to smell mischief. Of course it may only be imagination, but remembering what McIntosh had told me, I wondered whether by any chance they were wiring to Dgiboutil the news of our arrival, and warning their friends to be on the lookout for us."

"But why wire to Dgiboutil?" I demanded.

"Because," replied Kusumoto, "Dgiboutil belongs to the French, who are strongly pro-Russian; and those craft must have a sort of headquarters at which they may receive news and instructions, and where they can replenish their bunkers and storerooms, and I know of no place so likely for this as Dgiboutil."

"I see," said I. "Yes, you are most probably right, so far. But why on earth should those fellows interfere with Japanese ships? By what right do they claim to do it? The two countries are not yet at war, whatever may be the case within the next few months."

"That is true," agreed the skipper. "But the mouth of the Red Sea is a long way from Japan; we have no warships anywhere near there to protect us; the Russians are by nature a very high-handed people, and not too scrupulous when dealing with a prospective enemy; and perhaps they think that before Japan could make an effective protest, we may be at war, and have other things than pin-pricks to occupy our attention."

"Very true," I assented. "That may be so. But I should like to know upon what pretext they presume to molest and interfere with Japanese ships. Such action is contrary to international law, and in fact is closely akin to piracy, if indeed it is not piracy, pure and simple. Now, suppose these fellows attempt to interfere with us, what do you propose to do?"

"Ah!" ejaculated Kusumoto, "that is an exceedingly difficult question to answer. I do not want them to come aboard me, if it can be helped, for—to let you into a secret—our cargo consists of munitions of war of various kinds, and if the Russians should discover that fact, as they must if they board us and force me to show my papers, they may be unscrupulous enough to play some trick upon me, either jeopardising my cargo, or possibly detaining me in some way until war is actually declared, and then confiscating both ship and cargo. I must think the matter over, and try to hit upon some plan of 'besting' them, as you English say. And perhaps you two gentlemen will also give it a thought. I am only a mercantile shipmaster, and have had no experience in matters of this sort to guide me, but you are both military men, and out of your knowledge you may be able to suggest something helpful to me. Of course nothing may happen; we may not fall in with the Russians at all, which will be so much the better; but if we should encounter them, and they should attempt to interfere with me, I want to be prepared."

We continued to discuss the matter for some time longer; but it is not necessary to repeat more of what was said, sufficient having been already recorded to indicate the nature of the trouble that was possibly waiting for us.

The engines were only stopped long enough at Suez to enable us to land the pilot and the big searchlight which we had shipped at Port Said to help us through the canal; and, this done, we steamed on into the Gulf of Suez and the Red Sea.

Our passage down the Red Sea was quite uneventful until the Hanish Islands hove in sight over the port bow—uneventful, that is to say, with one exception only, but it was an exception which seemed to cause our two Russian passengers much perturbation of spirit. For the chat which Nakamura and I had had with the skipper, shortly after leaving Port Said, had been succeeded by another on the following day, the outcome of which was that Kusumoto, with the full approval of my friend Nakamura and myself, had resolved to take the very serious step of broaching cargo, with the result that, when the passengers came up on deck, on the morning which found us off Shadwan Island, they were amazed to discover two 1-pounder

Hotchkisses mounted, one on the forecastle-head and the other right aft over the taffrail, while a Maxim graced either extremity of the navigating bridge. The circumstance, with the reasons which seemed to make such a step necessary and desirable, was recorded at length in the *Matsuma Maru* official log, signed by the skipper and countersigned, at his request, by Nakamura and myself, as accessories, so to speak.

It was about three o'clock in the afternoon when the Hanish Islands hove up above the horizon, at which moment, as it happened, Nakamura and I were in the captain's cabin, where indeed we had spent most of the time of late, when we were not in our bunks. The Hanish Islands are, roughly speaking, within about one hundred miles of the Strait of Bab el Mandeb; and as we had not been interfered with thus far, we had practically made up our minds that if the Russians intended to molest us at all, it would be here, the back of the islands affording an excellent place of concealment from which to dash out upon a passing ship.

Nor were we disappointed in our expectations; for when we had brought the northernmost island square abeam, a long, black, four-funnelled destroyer suddenly slid out past its southern extremity, heading west, so as to intercept us. And, looking at her through our glasses, we saw that she was flying the International Code signal, "Heave-to. I wish to speak you."

"So! it's time for us to be making a move, Nakamura," said I. "You quite understand the line you are to take with those fellows, skipper? Good! Then, all that remains to be done is to get some ammunition on deck, and we shall be ready. Will you give the necessary orders?"

The skipper's response was to send for the chief officer, who, at least nominally, was off duty for the time being; and five minutes later I was on the forecastle-head, the Hotchkiss' tarpaulin jacket was off, a case of ammunition for the weapon stood conveniently at hand, and "All ready for'ard!" I reported. A minute or two later, Nakamura on the bridge was also ready, with a belt of cartridges in each of his Maxims, and more at hand, if required. Meanwhile, by the skipper's order, the answering pennant had been run up to our span, and dipped to show that the signal was understood, while the Japanese mercantile flag—white, with a red ball in the centre, which is also the Japanese "Jack"—was hoisted at our gaff-end.

Ten minutes later we were within hail of the destroyer, which, flying the Russian naval ensign, was lying motionless right athwart our hawse, broadside-on to us. Our engines were still running at full speed, and our safety valves were lifting, allowing a "feather" of steam to show at the head of our waste-pipe, while our quartermaster grimly kept our stem pointed fair and square between the second and third funnels of the Russian.

Then skipper Kusumoto raised his megaphone and hailed the destroyer, in Russian, with:

"Ho! the destroyer ahoy! Why are you lying athwart my hawse? Do you wish me to run you down?"

There were two officers on the destroyer's bridge, one of whom sprang to the engine-room telegraph and thrust it over to "Full speed ahead," while the other seized a megaphone and hailed back:

"Stop your engines instantly, sir! Did you not understand my signal that I wished to speak you? Starboard your helm, you confounded fool; hard a-starboard, or you'll be over us."

"Then get out of my way," retorted Kusumoto. "Starboard a little," (to the quartermaster), "and just shave his stern. I'll teach him to lay his tin kettle athwart a Japanese ship's bows."

The destroyer leaped from under our bows like a frightened thing, though not so quickly but that we caught her quarter with the rounding of our bows and gave her a pretty severe shaking up. Her skipper shook his fist at us and stamped on the bridge with fury. Then he raised his megaphone again and hailed:

"You infernal scoundrel, I'll make you suffer for that outrage! Heave-to at once, or I'll fire into you."

The boat was sweeping round on a starboard helm, and was now running practically parallel to us, at a distance of about a hundred feet.

"You will fire into me, if I don't stop, you say? Is Russia at war with my country, then?" hailed Kusumoto.

There was silence for a minute or two aboard the destroyer, during which the two officers on her bridge consulted eagerly together. We could see that her engine-room telegraph stood at "Full speed," yet, strange to say, she was only just holding her own with us. Then the commander of her again raised his megaphone.

"My instructions are that I am to examine the papers of all foreign vessels passing down the Red Sea," he shouted; "and I must insist that you heave-to and let me board you."

"I shall do nothing of the kind," retorted our skipper. "I do not admit your right to board me, so try it if you dare. I believe you are nothing less than a pirate masquerading as a Russian ship of war; and I shall treat you accordingly if you do not sheer off."

This defiance was more than enough for the proud and choleric Russian, accustomed to have his every order servilely obeyed. Such unparalleled insolence from a "little yellow-skinned monkey"—as the Russians had already begun to dub the Japanese—and in the presence of his own crew, too! It was unendurable, and must be severely punished. He called an order, and the Russian seamen, who had been standing about the deck, listening half-amused and half-indignant, to the altercation, made a move in the direction of the destroyer's 4-pounder and her port torpedo deck tube. But our skipper had been expecting and keenly on the watch for such a move, and he now hailed again:

"Destroyer ahoy! Keep away from the tube and the gun, you men! If I see a man attempt to approach either, I will sweep your decks with Maxim fire. Do you hear what I say?"—as half a dozen men continued to slouch toward the tube. "Open fire, there, the starboard Maxim!"

Nakamura was at the gun mentioned, which he was keeping steadily trained upon the tube. At the word, he fired a single shot, and the bullet spattered into a star as it struck the mounting. The Russians halted as if turned to stone, and glanced anxiously at their commander. Kusumoto raised his megaphone and hailed:

"Is that enough, or will you have more? Now, sheer off at once, if you please. If you don't, I shall fire again; and my next shots—with my Hotchkiss guns—will be at your waterline and your boilers."

The Russian commander was by this time literally foaming at the mouth; he seemed speechless and beside himself with rage, and there is no knowing what the outcome might have been, had not his second in command here intervened, and, forcibly seizing him by the arms, shook him violently as he said something which we were too far off to hear. Meanwhile, ever since the firing of the shot, the helmsman of the destroyer had been quietly edging away from us; and presently, at a sign, apparently, from the junior officer, he put his helm hard over to port, and the venomous-looking craft swung sharply upon her heel, listing heavily as she did so, and a few seconds later was speeding away in the opposite direction to ourselves. But even now we had not quite done with her, for almost immediately she swung round to cross our stern, and a moment later we saw the silvery flash of a torpedo as it left her tube. Kusumoto, however, was not to be caught unawares; apparently he more than half suspected something of the kind, and was on the watch. For an instant he watched the bubbles which marked the course of the missile, and then shouted an order to our helmsman; the *Matsuma Maru* swerved from her course, and the torpedo sped harmlessly past us, a hundred yards to port. I, too, had quite expected that the fiery Russian would not allow us to go scot-free if he could help it, therefore the moment that the destroyer swerved away from us I sprang off the forecastle and ran aft to the other Hotchkiss, which I reached too late to prevent the discharge of the torpedo. But I saw men clustering about her 4-pounder, as though about to bring it into action, and as I was more afraid of this gun than of the torpedoes, I unhesitatingly opened fire upon it, and at the fifth shot had the pleasure of dismounting it. This was enough for the Russians; they realised at last that they had caught a Tartar, and bore away for their lurking-place behind the Hanish Islands, where we eventually lost sight of them.

" I unhesitatingly opened fire upon it. "

As soon as the destroyer had disappeared, Kusumoto retired to his cabin and wrote a lengthy account of the affair in his official log-book, getting Nakamura and me to sign it, as before, in testimony of its veracity. This he did in order to justify himself for broaching cargo and temporarily mounting the Hotchkiss and Maxim guns; and it may be said here that not only was his justification accepted, but his conduct was highly commended by the authorities.

About four bells in the first watch that night, we passed through the strait, and shifted our helm for Cape Guardafui, not calling at Aden, since we had coal enough to carry us on to Colombo; and we saw nothing more of the Russians until after our arrival in Japan on 22nd January 1904.

Chapter Three
War!

On the morning of the day which witnessed my arrival in the Land of the Rising Sun, the berth-room steward who brought me my early cup of coffee informed me, with a broad grin of satisfaction, that we were in Sagami Bay; that it was a beautiful morning, but very cold; and that he would advise me to turn out at once if I desired to obtain the best possible view of Fujiyama, or Fujisan, as the Japanese love to call it. I took his advice, bathed and dressed with seamanlike celerity, and, donning a thick, warm ulster, made my way to the navigating bridge, catching my first glimpses of Japan—Shimoda, on the port, and the island of Oshima on the starboard quarter, as I went. And when I reached the bridge and took my stand beside Sadakiyo, the chief officer, I mentally returned thanks to that steward for his advice, and was glad that I had acted upon it, for the sight which met my gaze was beautiful beyond all power of description, and such as I shall never forget.

The air was clear as crystal, there was no wind, and the water was mirror-smooth, its surface dotted with fishing-boats, the unpainted hulls and white sails of which floated double, with nothing to show the junction of substance with reflection. Reflected, too, were the serrated ridges of Awa's and Kasusa's mountain-peaks and their ravines, dark and mysterious, with little villages of grey huts surmounted by high-pitched roofs of thatch clustering here and there along the beach to starboard, while, to port, dominating all else, towered high in air the majestic, snow-crowned peak of Fujisan, its summit blushing a delicate rosy pink in the first light of dawn. And, as I gazed, that beautiful rosy tint suddenly changed to gold as it caught the first rays of the rising sun, invisible to us, as yet, behind the high land to starboard, and as speedy as thought the light flashed down the mountain-side, revealing its matchless perfection of form, and bathing it in the glory of a hundred varied and beautiful tints.

Moving forward at reduced speed, to avoid the destruction of a few of the fishing-boats or junks that were ever becoming more numerous as the land closed in upon us on either side, we at length sighted and passed a lightship with, somewhat to my surprise, the words "Treaty Point" painted in large letters upon her red sides. If I had thought upon the matter at all, I should naturally have expected to see the name of the ship set forth in, to me, unintelligible hieroglyphics, but instead, there it was in plain homely English, and I comforted myself with the reflection that if the Japanese used British characters and words to distinguish their lightships, my as yet very imperfect knowledge of their tongue was not going to handicap me as heavily as I had feared.

In due time we arrived in the roadstead of Yokohama—not so very long ago a small fishing village, but now an important city—and made fast to our buoy. Instantly the ship was surrounded by sampans, and the occupants, not a few of whom were Chinese, swarmed aboard, eager to find buyers for the fruit, *sake*, and other articles which they had for sale. The jabber of tongues was incessant and deafening, and the importunities of the salesmen a trifle annoying; but Nakamura quickly sent them to the right-about, and inviting me to go up on the bridge with him—we were staying aboard to lunch with the skipper—we amused ourselves by watching the debarkation of the other passengers, my companion, between whiles, pointing out the various objects of interest visible from our standpoint.

I must confess that I was not very greatly impressed by Yokohama, as viewed from the roadstead. The most prominent object was the "Bund," or water-front, which is a wide wharf or esplanade, backed by gardens, hotels, and well-built dwelling-houses. Then there is the "Bluff," covered with fine villas and dwelling-houses, large and small, and of pleasing varieties of architecture; and, finally, there are the "Settlement" and the native town, about which I need say nothing.

After luncheon, by which time all the passengers but ourselves had gone ashore, we engaged a sampan, bade Kusumoto and the ship's officers farewell, and landed in the English "hatoba," which is a sort of floating basin, the shore end of which consists of landing-steps alongside which a whole fleet of boats can be accommodated at once. A word from Nakamura caused our baggage to be at once passed through the Customs with only the merest pretence at examination, and then, engaging rickshas, or "kurumas," as the Japanese call them, we wended our way to the railway station, and took train for Tokio.

The journey of eighteen miles was performed in an hour, in an exceedingly comfortable first-class carriage, upholstered in red morocco; and I noticed that the guard and engine-driver of the train were Englishmen— another good sign for me, I thought. Although the speed of the train was nothing to boast of, I found the journey interesting, for the scenery, with its little grey villages of thatched, wooden houses, and the temples with their quaintly shaped roofs on the one hand, and the sea on the other, with its islands, wooded gardens, and hundreds of fishing-boats, with Fujisan always dominating everything else, were all novelties to me.

The railway does not run right into the city of Tokio, but has its terminus at the village of Shimbashi, on the outskirts; here, therefore, we left the train and, engaging kurumas for ourselves and our baggage, drove to the Imperial Hotel, where Nakamura advised me to take up my quarters *pro tem*, and where he also intended to stay, that night. It was then six o'clock in the evening, and too late to transact our business, so, after a wash and brush-up, we sallied forth to see something of the city.

On the following morning, at ten o'clock, I presented myself before Vice-Admiral Baron Yamamoto, the Minister of the Navy, and handed him my credentials. He received me with great politeness, read a private letter from Viscount Hayashi, of which I was the bearer, asked me a good many questions as to the length and nature of my service in the British Navy, and my experiences therein, and finally handed me my commission as Lieutenant, together with a letter to Admiral Togo, which I was to deliver to him at Sasebo, without delay.

Now, Sasebo is situated on the north-western extremity of the island of Kiushiu, and is nearer seven than six hundred miles from Tokio; moreover, I found that during my voyage out to Japan, events had been progressing by leaps and bounds—so far at least as Japan was concerned. In diplomatic circles war with Russia was regarded as not only inevitable but imminent, and preparations for the struggle were being breathlessly pushed forward day and night. Of the evacuation of Manchuria by Russia, which should have been *completed* on the 8th of the preceding October, there was still no sign; on the contrary, everything pointed to a determination on the part of Russia to make her occupation permanent. Actions, it is said, speak louder than words, and while the diplomats on both sides were still engaged in an apparent endeavour to settle matters amicably, the action of those on the Russian side was characterised by systematic procrastination and delay which admitted of but one interpretation, namely, that Russia had no intention to quit Manchuria until she was compelled to do so by force.

This being the state of affairs, I interpreted Baron Yamamoto's order literally, leaving Tokio by the first available train. This took me back to Yokohama, where I only quitted it because I found I could proceed no farther until nine o'clock that night. At that hour, then, I made a fresh start and, not to dwell unduly upon this part of my story, reached Sasebo late in the evening of 26th January, having been delayed upon the road owing to the congestion of traffic caused by the war preparations.

Sasebo was a very hive of activity, to such an extent indeed that I had the greatest difficulty in finding quarters. All the hotels were packed to their utmost limit, and indeed I do not know how I should eventually have fared had I not luckily encountered an unmistakable Briton, whom I halted, and to whom I confided my plight, asking if he could direct me to some place where I could find accommodation for the night. He turned out to be a Scotsman named Boyd, in business at Sasebo, and no sooner had I made my situation plain to him than he took me by the arm in the most friendly manner and exclaimed:

"Come awa' hame wi' me, laddie. I'll pit ye up wi' the greatest of pleasure, and the gude-wife 'll be gey an' pleased to meet a body fresh frae the auld country."

It was easy to see that the fine fellow was absolutely sincere in his invitation; I therefore gladly accepted it, and, half an hour later, found myself comfortably housed in the bosom of a typically hospitable Scottish family, whom I found most delightfully genial, and from whom I subsequently received much kindness.

By my friend Boyd's advice I sallied forth early the next morning in search of Admiral Togo, who was of course up to his eyes in business, and who would be difficult to find unless I could catch him before he left his hotel. I was fortunate enough to arrive while he was still at breakfast, and, having sent in my card, was at once admitted.

I found him still seated at the table, in company with several other officers, all of them dressed in a naval uniform almost identical in cut and appearance with our own. Like every other Japanese I ever met, he received me with the utmost politeness, and, having read Baron Yamamoto's letter of introduction, again shook hands with me most heartily, expressed the pleasure it afforded him to welcome another Englishman into Japan's naval service, and forthwith proceeded to introduce me to the other officers present, one of whom, I remember, was Captain Ijichi, of the *Mikasa*, Togo's flagship. They all spoke English, more or less, Togo perfectly, for he had served as a boy aboard the British training ship *Worcester*, and later in our own navy. Also he had taken a course of study at the Royal Naval College, Greenwich. He was a typical Japanese, short and thick-set, with black eyes that seemed to pierce one through and through and read one's innermost thoughts. His hair, beard, and moustache were black, lightly touched here and there with grey, and though it is a little difficult to correctly estimate the age of a Japanese, I set him down at about fifty, which I subsequently learned was not far out.

Like Baron Yamamoto, the Admiral asked me quite a number of questions; and at length, when he found that I had qualified for gunnery, torpedo, and navigating duties, and had seen service in a destroyer, he said:

"You seem to have an exceptionally good record for a young man of your years, Mr Swinburne; so good, indeed, that I feel disposed to avail myself to the utmost possible extent of your services. I foresee that in the coming war the destroyer is destined to play a most important part, and while I anticipate that the service which that class of craft will be called upon to perform will be of the most arduous description, and of course exceedingly dangerous, it will also afford its officers exceptional opportunities to distinguish themselves. Now, it happens that I have one destroyer—the *Kasanumi*, one of our best boats—for which, thus far, I have been unable to find a suitable commander; your arrival comes therefore at a most opportune moment, for the perusal of your record convinces me that you are the very man for whom I have been looking. I rather flatter myself that I am a good judge of character, and I believe that you will do as much credit to the ship as she will to you. Now, what do you say? Will the command of a destroyer be satisfactory to you?"

"Indeed it will, sir," I replied, "and more than satisfactory. I have not dared to hope for such a big slice of good fortune, and I know not how to adequately express my thanks for the confidence you are reposing in me."

"Nay," answered Togo, "there is no need for thanks, at least in words. You can best show your appreciation by deeds, for which I promise you shall be afforded abundant opportunity. And now, if you are anything like what I take you to be, you will be all anxiety to see your ship; is it not so? Very well; you will find her in the small graving dock, where she is being scraped and repainted. Go down and have a good look at her, inside and out; and if you can offer any suggestions for improvements on board, I will give them my best consideration. Do you know your way to the docks? If not, I will find somebody to act as guide for you."

"I am very much obliged, sir," I replied, "but I should prefer to find my own way, if you please. I have been studying Japanese during the passage out, and I am anxious to make the most of every opportunity to increase my knowledge of the language."

"Good!" exclaimed Togo, in Japanese. "I believe you will do very well. Do you understand that?" he added, in English.

"Yes, sir," I replied, in Japanese; "and I am much obliged for your good opinion." My speech was a bit halting and my pronunciation by no means perfect, but it was evidently intelligible, for the whole party applauded me and shouted words of encouragement, some of which I understood, while others puzzled me. Then, as I turned to leave the room, the Admiral said:

"When you have had a good look at your ship, Mr Swinburne, come to me aboard the *Mikasa*, where I shall be all the morning."

I found the docks without difficulty, and in the smaller graving dock lay the *Kasanumi*, my first command! Seen thus, out of water, she looked a craft of quite important dimensions, as indeed she was, being more than two hundred feet in length. She had four funnels, the space between the second and third being only about half that between numbers one and two, and three and four. She had beautiful lines, and looked as though she ought to be an excellent sea boat. Her armament consisted of one 12-pounder, mounted aft, and five 6-pounders, all quick-fire guns capable of discharging ten shots per minute. She also mounted on the after-deck two 18-inch torpedo tubes, firing Whiteheads of an effective range of eight hundred yards at a speed of thirty knots, and carrying a charge of one hundred and seventy-one pounds of gun-cotton—enough to destroy a battleship, if it happened to hit the right spot. The dock foreman, who happened to be an Englishman, told me that she was British built—a Thorneycroft boat, he believed—and that, on trial, she had steamed as much as thirty-three knots! Here was a craft which any reasonable man might be proud to command, and I there and then registered a vow that it should not be my fault if she did not make a name for herself during the coming war.

She was painted white, with a lead-colour bottom, and her four funnels were white with black tops. But they were burning and scraping off all her outside paint, from the sheer-strake downward, and I asked the foreman what colour they were going to repaint her. He answered that this had not yet been decided, whereupon I requested him to provide me with three small pots of paint, white, black, and blue, and with these three I compounded a smoky-grey tint of medium depth which I believed would be practically invisible by day and quite invisible at night, and this tint I applied to a small piece of board which I requested the foreman to take care of for me.

Then I went aboard and had a look at the *Kasanumi's* interior arrangements. The engine and boiler-rooms, the torpedo room, and magazine naturally absorbed a large proportion of the interior space, but the accommodation for officers and crew, though a trifle cramped, was sufficient to ensure quite a reasonable amount of comfort. Everything of course was done to economise space, and the fittings were all quite plain, but the cabin which would be mine was a compact, cosy, little cubbyhole, with a tiny stove to warm it in cold weather, and I believed I could make myself very happy and comfortable in it, although the beams were so low that I should never be able to stand upright. The engines were superb pieces of machinery, as of course they had need to be, to drive the boat at a speed of thirty-three knots, and the working parts shone like burnished silver and gold, while the rest was painted green. I spent two hours aboard, making a few notes referring to suggestions which I proposed to make to the Admiral, and then started off to find the *Mikasa*.

This was not difficult, for the whole fleet—excepting one battleship and two cruisers in dry dock—were lying off the dockyard, while the *Mikasa* was easily distinguishable, even to a stranger, from the fact that she was flying the Admiral's flag. I noticed also that her stem-head was decorated with a gilded conventional representation of the open chrysanthemum, the Imperial crest. The Admiral was in his cabin, I was informed, when I got aboard, but I was kept waiting nearly an hour before I was admitted to his presence, for he was holding something very much like a council of war with the officers of his fleet when I arrived. But when at length—the council coming to an end—I was ushered into the cabin, I could not avoid being surprised at the wonderful courtesy and politeness which everybody exhibited to everybody else, notwithstanding that they were all evidently so full of business that they seemed scarcely to know which job to tackle first. As soon as Togo caught sight of me he beckoned me forward and introduced me to as many of those present as I had not already met, and, this done, he handed me my appointment to the *Kasanumi*, and requested me to at once take up my command. Then he asked me if I had any suggestions to make; and upon my answering that I had, he opened a notebook which lay upon the table, and jotted them down as I read them out to him, and promised to give them early consideration. As I bowed myself out of the cabin he called after me, advising me to see to the ordering of my uniforms at once, as events were progressing rapidly, and there was no knowing how soon it might be necessary for us all to go to sea. Stepping out on deck, I encountered Captain Ijichi, the skipper of the ship, in earnest converse with several of his officers, to whom he at once introduced me, whereupon the First Lieutenant invited me to dine that night, aboard the ship, as his guest, which invitation I naturally accepted.

A week of feverish activity now ensued, by the end of which time every dock in Sasebo was empty, and every ship in the harbour ready, down to the last ropeyarn, bunkers and magazines full, and even the fires laid under the boilers ready to light at a second's notice. War was by this time an absolute certainty, and the only question was when would it break out. The Japanese plan of campaign was ready cut and dried, and Togo, resolved to be in a position to act upon the instant of the receipt of his orders, had already dispatched the cruiser *Akashi* to sea, with instructions to ascertain the whereabouts of the Russian fleet and, after securing this information, to rendezvous at Mokpo, a port situate at the south-western extremity of the Korean peninsula. I had said farewell to my very kind friends, the Boyds, some days before, and had taken up my abode aboard the *Kasanumi*, which, with the *Asashio, Shirakumo,* and *Akatsuki,* constituted the 1st Division of the destroyer flotilla. Admiral Togo had approved my suggestion to paint the entire exterior of the boat a medium smoky-grey tint, and the effect had proved so satisfactory that the skippers of several other destroyers had followed my example.

At length dawned the eventful 6th of February 1904. A fresh north-easter was blowing, the sky was heavy and louring, and a fierce squall of snow and sleet was sweeping the harbour when a gun from the *Mikasa* caused all eyes to turn toward her, and the next moment there fluttered from her yardarms the signals commanding the fleet to light fires and prepare to weigh! So it had come then, that fateful moment for which we had all been waiting with bated breath, for a full week; and as the purport of the signals became known, a frenzied roar of "Banzai Nippon!" went up from ships and shore, a roar that sent a shiver of excitement thrilling through me, so deep, so intense, so indicative of indomitable determination, of courage, and of intense patriotism was it. Peal after peal of "Banzais" swept over the sullen, turbulent waters of the harbour, to be taken up and repeated by the thousands who thronged the wharves ashore, and who seemed to have sprung from nowhere in an instant; and before the shouts died away thin curls of light brown smoke were already rising from the funnels of the fleet and six fast transport steamers which were lying a little nearer the shore. Half an hour later, the blare of bands was heard ashore, one of the wharves was hurriedly cleared of people, and presently soldiers were seen marching down on to that wharf and aboard a whole fleet of lighters that were lying alongside. It was indicative of the thoroughness with which the Japanese authorities had thought out every minutest detail, that within three hours, three thousand troops, horse, foot, and artillery, with all their kit and camp equipment complete, were transferred from the shore to the transports, and the latter had signalled that they were ready to get under way.

It was not, however, until shortly before two o'clock in the afternoon that the signal was made for the fleet to weigh and proceed to sea, by which time every ship was under a full head of steam; and then the fleet, which up to then had lain quiescent, burst into strenuous but orderly activity. Officers on the several bridges seized megaphones and shouted orders through them; boatswain's whistles shrilled and boatswain's lungs bellowed, "Clear lower deck! Hands up anchor, ahoy!" the massive cables began to quiver and clank as they were hove in; the flagship became a very rainbow of rapidly changing signal flags; answering pennants appeared like magic and vanished again; hundreds of sampans and craft of every description— anything and everything that would float, apparently—loaded with men and women, all frantic with patriotic excitement, put off from the shore and formed a sort of lane for the fleet to steam through, the men yelling "Banzai!" until it seemed as though their throats would crack, while the women—many of whom were very pretty, while all looked charmingly demure—urged the boatmen to pull in as close as possible to the ships, that they might strew with artificial flowers the water through which we were about to pass. The military bands aboard the transports were playing what I supposed to be patriotic airs, from the applause which they evoked, steam was roaring from the safety valves, fussy little tugs were rushing hither and thither, and at the precise moment when the water under the *Mikasa's* counter broke into a sudden swirl and the ship began to move, a transient gleam of wintry sunshine burst through the clouds and fell full upon her! It was the finishing touch; everybody unquestioningly accepted it as an omen of victory and triumph, and the thousands afloat and ashore incontinently went mad with joy. And indeed there was every excuse for so much enthusiasm, for we presented a truly imposing sight as we swept out to sea, a fleet consisting of six battleships, six armoured cruisers, four 23-knot light cruisers, six protected cruisers, and eighteen destroyers, surrounding the six transports. The primary object of the expedition was to escort the transports to Chemulpo, where the troops were to be landed to effect the seizure of Seoul, the capital of Korea; and, this accomplished, Togo was to find and defeat the Russian fleet, which, so long as it existed and was free to roam the seas, constituted a most formidable menace to Japan.

Twelve knots was the steaming speed ordered for the fleet; and the course was due west for the passage between the islands of Gotoshima and Ukushima. As soon as we were clear of the harbour the destroyers, in five divisions, were ordered to take up scouting duty, which we did by arranging ourselves in a complete circle round the fleet, the boats being about a mile apart, thus forming a circle of eighteen miles in circumference.

The weather was vile, for after that transient gleam of sunshine which had marked the moment of our departure, the clouds had closed over us again in a compact mass, and pelted us with sleet and snow so thickly that it was only with the utmost difficulty we were able to see the next boat ahead and astern; also it was so piercingly cold that even the long lamb's-wool coat, with which I had taken the precaution to provide myself, seemed utterly inadequate. Fortunately, excitement and the joy of finding myself not only once more under a pennant but actually in command, with a war before me in which I felt convinced I should have ample opportunity to prove my mettle, helped to keep me warm. And there was pride, too; pride in my ship and pride in my crew; for there was not a better or faster little ship in the fleet than the *Kasanumi*, while my crew, officers, and men alike, were splendid fellows, fine sturdy men, with the courage of lions, the lithe, light-footed activity of cats, and respectfully and promptly obedient to an extent which left nothing to be desired. My "sub," a merry, light-hearted little fellow, named Ito, although more than a year my senior, displayed not an atom of jealousy, but carried out my every order with the same prompt, unquestioning alacrity as the men; he was keen as mustard, and his chief, indeed his only, recreation seemed to be the working out of battle problems.

For the first four hours of our voyage, while we were still well under the lee of the land, the water was moderately smooth; but when, about seven o'clock that evening, the negotiation of the passage between the islands had been successfully accomplished, and we found ourselves fairly out at sea, and shifted our helms to pass to the northward of Quelpart Island, we soon found that we were in for a regular "dusting." For we presently ran into a high, steep sea, which our shift of helm brought almost square abeam, yet just enough on our starboard quarter to set us all rolling and squirming most atrociously, particularly the "mosquito" division. Our every roll, whether to port or starboard, sent us gunwale under, so that it was only with the utmost difficulty we managed to retain our footing, while more than half my complement, on deck as well as below, suffered agonies of sea-sickness; yet they stuck to their work like heroes. The spray swept us continually from end to end, flying high over the tops of our low funnels, and freezing as it fell, so that the watch on deck were kept busy chipping the ice off our decks and shovelling it overboard; yet, wretchedly uncomfortable as was the weather, the destroyers, running at less than half-speed, rode the sea like gulls, and kept station with the utmost ease.

Shortly after eight bells in the middle watch, the weather cleared and the stars shone out with piercing brilliancy, enabling us to see the whole of the big ships and the transports, although we were all steaming with lights out, except for a solitary shrouded lantern carried by each ship right aft, to enable her next astern to keep station.

The night passed without incident, but shortly after sunrise, smoke was sighted broad on our port bow, the ship from which it proceeded evidently steering to the northward. We all seemed to see it at the same instant, for in less than half a minute the signal reporting the circumstance was flying aboard nearly every craft in the fleet. But the lookouts aboard the *Mikasa* were evidently as wide awake as any of us, for our flags were scarcely aloft when the flagship signalled the armoured cruiser *Asama* to chase in the south-western board; and in little more than an hour afterward she rejoined the fleet, accompanied by the Russian steamer *Argun*, as a prize. We flattered ourselves that the honour of capturing the first prize of the war had fallen to us; but, later on, we learned, to our disgust, that when the *Argun* was taken into Sasebo, there were already three more prizes there to keep her company.

We arrived off Mokpo about ten o'clock that morning, when the *Akashi* came out to meet us and make her report. We of the rank and file, so to speak, did not, of course, know at the time what was the nature of that report, which was for the Admiral's ear alone; but, later on, it leaked out that it was to the effect that the Russian fleet at Port Arthur had begun to move on the last day of January, by warping and towing certain of the ships out of harbour. This movement had continued on the first and second days of February, by the end of which time the entire fleet was anchored in the roadstead; and it seemed pretty evident that Admiral Alexieff was preparing to vigorously carry the war into the enemy's country, which was the great fear that had been haunting Togo from the moment when he received his instructions to put to sea. His dread was that the Russian fleet would forestall him by getting to sea first, steam to the southward, and, getting into touch with one or more of the craft which were certain to be watching the Japanese fleet, would lie *perdu* until that fleet had passed to the northward, and then fall upon and ravage the unprotected Japanese coast. And, at first sight, this seemed to be the Russian Admiral's intention, for, on the 4th of February, the fleet, having coaled, weighed and steamed out to sea, leaving only two battleships—the *Sevastopol* and *Peresviet*—in the harbour, where they had perversely stuck on the mud and refused to be got afloat again, for the moment at least. The Russians, twenty-six ships strong, inclusive of eleven destroyers, having cleared the roadstead, steamed slowly to the eastward, and were, that same day, sighted in the offing from Wei-hai-wei, apparently practising evolutions. But on the following day they all returned to Port Arthur, and anchored in the roadstead, under the guns of the batteries. The pith of the *Akashi's* report, therefore, was that there were two Russian ships—the new cruiser *Variag*, and the gunboat *Korietz*—at Chemulpo, four cruisers and an armed merchantman at Vladivostock, while the remainder of the Russian fleet was at Port Arthur.

Possessed of this knowledge, Togo issued orders to Rear-Admiral Uriu, in the *Takachiho*, to take command of a squadron consisting of, in addition to his own ship, the *Asatna, Chiyoda, Niitaka,* and *Miyako*, with eight destroyers, and with them to convoy the transports to Chemulpo, taking measures upon his arrival, to insure that the Russian ships should not interfere with the landing of the troops. Those were the only orders of which we were aware, but in the light of what occurred after Uriu's arrival at Chemulpo, it is probable that the Vice-Admiral was given a considerable amount of latitude with regard to his further proceedings.

It was about seven o'clock in the evening when the two fleets parted company, the *Mikasa* signalling: "I congratulate you in anticipation of your success," to which the *Takachiho* replied: "Thanks for your kindness." Then the signal was given by wireless for the main fleet to proceed on a north-westerly course, in an extended formation of line abreast, with the destroyers scouting on both wings, and a great shout of "Banzai Nippon!" went up, for everybody knew that north-west was the road to Port Arthur, where Togo fervently hoped and prayed he might find the Russian fleet still at anchor.

For, if not, it would certainly mean that Alexieff had proved himself the better strategist of the two, and had contrived in some subtle manner to slip past us to the westward, when any one or two of three terrible things might happen. He might realise Togo's original terrible fear of an attack on the undefended coast of Japan; or he might make for Chemulpo and destroy the Japanese squadron and transports upon their arrival there; or he might pass through the Korean Strait northward to Vladivostock and there unite his two forces, when he would be strong enough to give no end of trouble, if not indeed to defeat us out of hand and so decide the war at one fell stroke. It was exceedingly difficult to know what to do for the best, and our gallant little Admiral felt to the full the responsibility attaching to his momentous decision, as was made manifest when, about two bells in the first watch, the order was wirelessed to the fleet to alter the course twenty-two degrees to the northward, evidently with the object of falling in with the Russians, should they by any chance be making for Chemulpo. Our next order was to clear for action.

To further increase our difficulties and embarrassments, the weather had again changed for the worse. The sun had set in a wrack of wild, storm-riven cloud painted with the hues of fire and smoke, which, louring threateningly, had overspread the sky with incredible rapidity, completely obscuring the light of the stars; the wind, still icy cold, had breezed up again savagely, kicking up a tremendous sea, the spray from which quickly drenched us in the destroyers to the skin, despite our "oilies," sou'-westers, and sea boots; yet the staunch little vessels, though rolling and pitching in the most distracting manner, rode like gulls the seas which, to us, seemed to be literally running "mountains high." True, our speed was only about twelve knots; what the *Kasanumi's* behaviour would probably have been at double that speed, in such a sea, I shuddered to think. But I was destined to *know*, in the not-far-distant future.

When Ito, my lieutenant, called me at midnight to relieve him, he informed me that a wireless message had just been received from the flagship, ordering a shift of helm for the Elliot group of islands, distant some sixty miles from Port Arthur, and for the speed to be increased to sixteen knots, which order he had acknowledged and executed, as I discovered, the moment I tumbled out of my hammock; for the boat was kicking up her heels more madly than ever, while every few seconds there resounded a heavy thud on the deck overhead, and the craft shivered from stem to stern as she drove her sharp nose into the heart of a great comber, throwing the water in tons over herself. This was the rough side of work aboard a destroyer, with a vengeance, and I spent four miserable hours on the navigating bridge, drenched to the skin, and pierced to the marrow by the bitter cold. All things come to an end, however, sooner or later; and about two o'clock next day we steamed into the sheltered waters of the Elliot Islands and came to an anchor. This was the spot which the Admiral had selected to serve as a rendezvous and lurking-place from which he could sally forth with a good chance of cutting off the Port Arthur fleet, should it venture to stray far from the shelter of the fortress; and subsequently it was often referred to in his dispatches as "a certain place."

Chapter Four
The Council in the Mikasa's Cabin

As we entered the roadstead we found there, at anchor, a small Chinese junk of such a dilapidated and weather-beaten appearance that she seemed as though she might go to pieces at any moment. She was flying the Japanese mercantile flag, a white flag with a red ball in the centre—which is also the Japanese "Jack," and I soon learned that in her case, as in many others, appearances were deceptive, for I was assured that she was as staunch as staunch could be. She was officered and manned by a Chinese crew, and she was ostensibly loaded with bricks; but surrounded by these bricks, which were only a blind, was a sturdy little closed-in engine and boiler, the smoke from the latter issuing from the unusually big chimney of her galley stove, while the engine worked a small but powerful set of pumps which strongly sucked in water through her bows and discharged it equally strongly from her stern, under water, of course, giving her a speed of seven knots in smooth water. And when I sought further information with regard to this mysterious craft, I was informed by Ito, who seemed to know all about her, that she had been purchased by the Japanese Secret Service Department, fitted with her engine, boiler, and pumps by an ingenious Japanese engineer, and that her business was to go to and fro between Port Arthur and "a certain place," ostensibly as a trader, but in reality that her skipper, a particularly bold and clever spy, might obtain information for the Japanese.

The spy's name, it appeared, was Hang-won,—a rather ominous name, I thought, under the circumstances,—while the name of the junk was *Chung-sa*. She had arrived from Port Arthur about midday, and this was Hang-won's first essay in Japan's service. But he had brought from Port Arthur two items of news that were likely to prove most valuable to us; one of them being, that the Russian destroyers were being sent to sea every night to reconnoitre, and that upon their return they always showed a white light above a red, to indicate that they were Russian; while the second item was to the effect that that day, 8th February, happened to be the name-day of Madame Stark, the wife of the Russian Admiral, and that in honour of the day a great banquet was to be given at nine o'clock that night, at the

Admiral's house, which was to be followed by a special performance at a circus which chanced to be in the town.

The moment that this information was communicated to Togo, he recognised the magnificent possibilities offered by the occasion. For it was morally certain that, between the banquet and the circus, most of the officers, and possibly also a good many of the men, of the Russian fleet would be ashore, that night; and what better opportunity for an attack upon it was likely to offer? The chance was very much too good to be missed, and a signal was at once made for the captains of all craft, destroyers included, to repair on board the *Mikasa*.

I was one of the last to reach the flagship, for the destroyers were anchored outside the rest of the fleet, and when I arrived the Admiral's cabin was full of men, as many of them as could find room being seated round the table, while the rest were accommodated with chairs. All were talking indiscriminately together, for the council had not yet begun; but it was characteristic of Togo that he saw me the instant I entered the cabin, and rose to shake hands with me, exclaiming, "Ah! here comes our young British giant." Then, pointing to a chair near himself, he motioned me to be seated, saying as he did so with a humorous smile:

"Well, Mr Swinburne, I hope you find the *Kasanumi* a nice, steady, comfortable ship. Is there room enough in her for you to stretch yourself, or shall we have to lengthen her a few feet?"

"She is a splendid little craft, sir," I said heartily, "far better than the British boat in which I saw some service. She is a magnificent sea boat, and came through the wild weather of yesterday and last night without turning a hair. True, she is a bit cramped between the beams, and I have already raised a few bumps on my head while trying to stand upright in my cabin; but I'm ready to go anywhere and attempt anything in her."

"That's right," remarked Togo; "you show the true Nelson spirit, sir— the spirit which we expect to find in every Briton; the spirit which we so greatly admire, and which we are humbly striving to imbue our Japanese seamen with. So you are 'ready to go anywhere and attempt anything,' eh? Excellent! I hope to afford you the opportunity to show us what you can do before you are many hours older."

Then, turning to where Captain Ijichi stood near the cabin door, he said, in Japanese:

"Are all present, Ijichi?"

Some half a dozen officers had followed close upon my heels, and I noticed that, as each entered, the *Mikasa's* skipper had ticked off something on a list which he held in his hand.

"All present, sir," answered Ijichi, referring to his list.

"Good!" remarked the Admiral. "Then, be so good as to tell the sentry that we are on no account to be interrupted. Then close the door and find a seat for yourself."

With the closing of the cabin door the general conversation that had been proceeding came to an abrupt termination and a tense silence ensued. Togo looked round the cabin, as though taking stock of us all; then in a few terse words he communicated to us the information which he had just learned from Hang-won, who, by the way, was still in the cabin, ready to answer any questions that might be put to him.

"Now, gentlemen," he continued, "there is no need for me to enlarge upon the splendid opportunity which Madame Stark's celebration of her name-day offers us to strike a heavy blow at the enemy's fleet; I am sure that you will all see it for yourselves. The only question is: In what way can we best avail ourselves of the opportunity? What form is the blow to take?

"So far as we are concerned, we are seventeen ships strong, apart from our destroyers, while our friend, Hang-won, informs me that the Russian fleet consists of fourteen ships, again apart from destroyers. We are therefore three ships to the good. But, of those fourteen Russian ships, seven are battleships, while we muster only six; furthermore, the whole fleet is anchored under the protection of the Port Arthur batteries, a further tremendous advantage to them. Notwithstanding this, however, the opportunity is such a splendid one that, were my hands free, I should be strongly disposed to take my whole fleet into Port Arthur roadstead, engage the Russian ships at close quarters, trusting to find them unprepared; do them as much damage as possible with our heavy guns; and trust to our destroyers to complete their destruction while the confusion of the surprise was at its height. But, gentlemen, I cannot do this. My orders from the Cabinet and the Elder Statesmen are clear and precise, and under no circumstances whatever am I to disobey them. They are, that I am never to risk my ships, especially my battleships, by exposing them to the fire of the Port Arthur batteries; and if I do not myself obey orders, how may I expect that my orders will be obeyed? Strict and unquestioning obedience to orders is, as you all know, almost an article of faith with us; therefore, sorely tempted though I am, to disobey just this once, I dare not set an example which might be fraught with the most disastrous consequences. Hence, gentlemen, I have summoned you this afternoon, to assist me with your counsels. I may mention that, keeping in view the fact that my superiors, the Government, have given me certain orders which I must obey, the only thing I can see for it is to send in our destroyers, and let them do their best. Can any of you suggest a better plan?"

For a full minute or more a tense silence reigned in the cabin, everybody apparently waiting for somebody else to speak first. Then a young officer in lieutenant's uniform (whom I subsequently learned was no less a personage than Prince Kasho, one of the *Mikasa's* officers), rose and, bowing first to the Admiral and then to the rest of us, said, in Japanese of course:

"Do I understand, Admiral, that your question carries with it your permission to us to express our candid opinion?"

"Assuredly," answered Togo.

"Good!" returned the Prince. "Then, since no one else appears to have a suggestion to offer, perhaps I may be permitted to do so, though I happen to be the junior of most of the honourable officers present. You told us just now, sir, that, *were your hands free*, you would be strongly disposed to take your entire fleet into Port Arthur roadstead, where, I understand, almost every Russian ship of importance in Eastern waters now rides at anchor, and make an end of them."

The speaker was here interrupted by a low murmur of applause from many of the officers present, who seemed to have a shrewd suspicion of what was coming. Togo held up his hand for silence, the Prince bowed smilingly to his audience, who he felt he had with him, and resumed:

"But you tell us, sir, that you are not free to exercise your own discretion, that your hands are tied by certain orders which you have received; and you have reminded us that implicit obedience is the supreme virtue, almost an article of religious faith, with the Japanese.

"With that sentiment, sir, I am, I scarcely need say, in perfect, whole-hearted agreement. But there is a point which I wish to make, and it is this. The Cabinet and the Elder Statesmen are, as their designation indicates, *statesmen*; they are neither soldiers nor sailors. And while I will not attempt to dispute either their wisdom or their right to formulate certain general rules for the guidance of their Generals and Admirals, I feel that I should not be doing my full duty to my country, in the circumstances which now confront us, if I did not boldly declare my fixed conviction that such general rules as I have just alluded to ought to be regarded and accepted by us merely as guides, and not as definite, imperative orders which are under no circumstances whatsoever to be disobeyed."

Here another little murmur of applause, more general and decided than the first, ran round the cabin. As it died away, the speaker resumed:

"I cannot believe, sir, that the orders laid upon you were intended to deprive you of the power to exercise your own discretion under such exceptional circumstances as the present; and I therefore take upon myself the responsibility of saying, here in the presence of all your officers, that I believe you would be amply justified in acting in the manner that you indicated a few minutes ago."

There was no mistaking the meaning of the applause that rang through the cabin now; it was perfectly evident that—with the solitary exceptions of the Admiral and myself—the Prince had every man present heartily with him.

"I have but a very few more words to add, sir," the speaker resumed, when the applause died away, "and they are these. What you have told us concerning to-night's projected happenings in Port Arthur seems to indicate that an opportunity, such as may never occur again, now offers for us to strike such a blow at the enemy that it will be impossible for him ever to recover from it; and if the striking of that blow does indeed involve actual disobedience of precise orders, I venture to assert that the result will amply justify the deed."

The Prince resumed his seat amid thunders of applause which rang through the cabin for at least a couple of minutes. When at length it died down, Togo rose to his feet.

"Gentlemen," he said, "I gather from your plaudits that you all fully agree with Prince Kasho's honourable speech, for which I beg to most heartily thank him, although it places me upon the horns of a dilemma. Let that pass, for the moment, however. What I want, now, is that each of you should, in as few words as possible, express your opinion upon the Prince's suggestion that I should take the whole of my ships into Port Arthur roadstead and engage the enemy in a pitched battle."

In response to this appeal, the officers rose, one after the other, apparently in the order of their seniority; and each man expressed his hearty concurrence with Prince Kasho's proposal, the concurrence being accompanied in many cases by the expression of sundry lofty and beautiful sentiments extolling the virtues of patriotism and valour. At length everybody had spoken except myself, and I was heartily hoping that I should be passed over as a person of so little account that my opinion would not be considered worth having. Not so, however. The Admiral turned to me and said, with a smile:

"And now at last we come to our honourable English friend, the captain of the *Kasanumi*. What has he to say upon the matter? You have heard what has been said; and although you have perhaps been unable, through your restricted knowledge of our language, to grasp the full meaning of it all, you may possibly have understood enough to enable you to comprehend the way in which this momentous question appeals to the Japanese heart and intellect. Now, kindly favour us with the view which you, as a hard-headed Englishman, take of it."

"Really, sir," I said in English, springing to my feet in some confusion, "I would very much prefer to be excused, if you will kindly allow me. It would be the most rank presumption on my part to—"

"No, no," cried several voices, among which I distinctly recognised that of Prince Kasho; "let us hear what the honourable Englishman has to say."

"Quite right, gentlemen," said Togo. "I fully agree with you. I know something of the English; and even though Mr Swinburne may differ from us all, I'll warrant that he will not suggest any action that is not consonant with our honour, as seamen, or our loyalty to the Emperor. Pray proceed, Mr Swinburne."

"Very well, then, Admiral, and gentlemen, since you do me the honour to insist, I will," said I. "But you must permit me to begin by reminding you that I am only a boy, and that this is my first experience of actual warfare; therefore if I venture to express an opinion on what has been justly described as a most momentous question, I do so with the utmost diffidence. At the same time, although I have had no previous experience of war, I should like to say that I have studied the subject deeply and with intense interest. And it is with equal interest that I have listened to the expression of your views on the question now under consideration. I am filled with admiration of the noble and patriotic sentiments which have to-day been spoken within the walls of this cabin—sentiments with which I most cordially agree, since they happen to accurately coincide with my own.

"But, gentlemen, may I dare venture to remind you that patriotism and valour, splendid and admirable as they are, are not the only qualities that should distinguish the soldier or sailor who fights for his country? Inspired by them, a man may no doubt accomplish great things, wonderful things; but we Britons have a proverb which declares that discretion is the better part of valour, and in my humble opinion—which, I repeat, I advance with the utmost diffidence—the present is one of those occasions when valour, as heroic and self-sacrificing as you will, should go hand in hand with discretion.

"With your kind favour I will briefly mention the picture that arose in my mind while Prince Kasho was advocating the plan of taking the entire fleet into Port Arthur roadstead and engaging the Russians in a pitched battle.

"I readily grant you that the information communicated to the Admiral by Hang-won seems to indicate that to-night, or the small hours of to-morrow morning, will afford a magnificent opportunity for such a *coup*; but—let us consider all the consequences which that *coup* would entail. It may be that we should be able to take the Russians by surprise; it is exceedingly probable that some of the officers—perhaps a good many of them—will be ashore to-night; but, recognising the fact that Russia and Japan are at war, do you, gentlemen, as reasonable, sensible men, really believe for a moment that the Russian fleet will be left defenceless in an open roadstead, or that the vigilance of the lookouts will be relaxed? I do not. And, if not, the approach of such a formidable array as ours would assuredly be detected, and the alarm given, long before we could arrive within effective striking distance. Then what would be the ultimate result? I have not a doubt that we should be victorious, but at what cost? We must remember, gentlemen, that we should be not only engaging a fleet but slightly inferior in strength to our own, *but the batteries as well*; and it is in the batteries that our danger lies. I know not what the armament of those batteries may be, but I think we may safely assume that it will consist of weapons heavy enough to sink many of our ships while we are doing our best to sink theirs. With all submission, I think it would be the height of folly for us to assume that we could fight such a battle without serious loss to ourselves. And the point which I wish to emphasise is this: *How are we going to make good those losses?* The Russians can make good theirs by sending more ships out from Europe; but where are we to get more? I need not labour this question, gentlemen; I am sure you will all see what I mean, and therefore understand why I say that, altogether apart from the question of slavish obedience to orders, or otherwise, I think the Admiral is fully justified in his decision not to risk his ships in such an exceedingly hazardous enterprise."

"Thank you, Mr Swinburne," said Togo, offering me his hand as I sat down. "You have spoken pretty much as I expected you would." Then, turning to one of the officers who had been busily writing all the time that I was speaking, he said:

"Captain Matsumoto, am I correct in supposing that you have been taking down Mr Swinburne's remarks?"

"Quite correct, sir," answered the skipper of the *Fuji*.

"Then," said Togo, "do me the favour to read them over aloud, in Japanese, for the benefit of those officers who have been unable to closely follow Mr Swinburne's English."

This was done; and when Matsumoto sat down there was silence for a few moments, succeeded by a faint murmur of applause. Then the Admiral rose.

"Gentlemen," he said, "you have now all spoken; and I tender you my most hearty thanks for the frank expression of your several opinions. I have listened with the greatest interest and satisfaction to everything that has been said, but you must pardon me if I say at once, frankly, that you leave me as unconvinced as ever. Or, no; not unconvinced; on the contrary, I am more convinced than ever that, apart, as Mr Swinburne has remarked, from any question of slavish obedience to orders, I should be guilty of a serious, even disastrous, error of judgment, were I to take my battleships and cruisers into Port Arthur roads and give battle to the Russian fleet. The only alternative is to employ the destroyers; and I shall be glad of any suggestions you may be pleased to offer as to the best method of attack."

Nobody spoke. It was easy to see that the officers of the battleships and cruisers, deeply imbued with the somewhat fantastic and high-flown ideas of the Japanese with regard to the almost divine virtue of heroism and self-sacrifice, were profoundly disappointed that they were not to be afforded an opportunity to display their possession of those virtues.

"Has no one a suggestion to offer?" demanded Togo, in a tone of surprise. "What say you, Swinburne?" turning to me.

"It would greatly help us, sir," I said, "if Hang-won could give us even an approximate idea of the position of the Russian ships in the roadstead."

"You are right, sir; it would," answered the Admiral. And turning to the Chinaman, he addressed to him a question in what I imagined to be Chinese. The man was replying at some length when Togo interrupted him and turned to the skipper of the flagship.

"Captain Ijichi," said he, "a chart of Port Arthur, if you please."

The chart was brought, and Hang-won, after poring over it awhile, took a pencil and with meticulous care jotted down certain marks upon it. When he had finished, Togo turned to me and said:

"Here we are, Mr Swinburne. These marks indicate the positions of some of the Russian ships, as nearly as Hang-won can remember them. As you see, they are moored in wedge-shaped formation, the point of the wedge to seaward; and that point is occupied by the *Tsarevich*, a battleship. Next her, inshore, comes the *Poltava*, also a battleship, then the *Sevastopol*, another battleship, and abreast of her, in the second line, the battleship *Pobieda*. Of the positions of these he is certain, he says, having taken particular notice of them as he came out; but of the rest he is not so sure, except that there are thirteen of them, exclusive of the *Askold*, all anchored inside the *Tsarevich*. The *Askold* is a cruiser, and according to Hang-won she is performing patrol duty to and fro, outside the rest of the fleet. You will readily recognise her from the fact that she is the only craft with five funnels.

"There is another point in favour of our employing destroyers. It appears that Admiral Stark sends out a destroyer flotilla every night to patrol the coast as far as Dalny—there it is, about twenty miles north-east of Port Arthur. If, upon approaching the roadstead, our boats show the lights usually exhibited by the Russian destroyers—a white light above a red—on their return from Dalny, they ought to be able to get right in among the Russian fleet and do a tremendous amount of damage before their identity is discovered, and I shall confidently look for important results accordingly. Now, gentlemen, I have my own idea as to how the attack should be conducted; but I have heard it said that in many councillors there is wisdom, therefore I should be glad to have your views on the subject."

And, one after the other, the officers present gave them, the general opinion being that the destroyers ought to approach to within about five miles of the shore at a moderate speed, showing no lights; then dash in at top speed, discharging torpedoes right and left, and continue to do so, regardless of consequences, until every Russian ship was destroyed.

Finally, I was called for to give my opinion; and again I found myself obliged to differ from the others.

"If I were leading the attack, sir," I said, "I should time myself to arrive at about eleven o'clock, that being the time, I imagine, when the banquet and the special performance will both be at their height. At the distance of about five miles from the shore I should slow down, instead of increasing speed, because I should then have no fear of flames escaping from my funnels and so betraying my approach. I should then divide my force into two, one of which should sweep well away to the nor'ard, while the other sheered off toward the south, my object being to get my boats well into the concealment of the shadow of the high land east and west of the roadstead. Under the cover of this shadow I should creep close along shore until I was well inside the enemy's fleet, when I should wheel outward, get good way on my boats, and torpedo the enemy, ship after ship, as I came out. By this plan I should be heading seaward, ready to make good my escape as soon as the alarm was given, which I believe will be within a few seconds after the first torpedo is fired. Then I should run for it out to sea, at top speed; for

I am convinced that, once the alarm is given and the searchlights are turned on, we shall be afforded no further opportunity to do mischief; and I see no sense in sacrificing ships and lives uselessly. I have heard the remark made, more than once, that it is a glorious thing to die for one's country and one's Emperor. So it is—when the sacrifice of one's life is necessary to secure a certain object; but I maintain that it is still more glorious to *live* for one's country. One live man can render more useful service to his country than a hundred dead ones."

Again there was a little half-hearted murmur of applause.

But Togo expressed his approval in no half-hearted manner. Dashing his fist upon the table he exclaimed:

"By Hachiman Sama!" (the Japanese god of War), "you are right, Mr Swinburne. You told us, a little while ago, that you are only a boy, but you have the brains and wisdom of a man, sir. Your plan of attack is the right one—cannot you see that it is, gentlemen?—and it shall be followed. By attempting the other plan, we should in all probability lose every boat and every man, with no better result; while, by adopting Mr Swinburne's plan, we may save at least two-thirds of them. Now, gentlemen, before we terminate the council, has any one a better plan to propose?" And he glanced round the cabin, inquiringly.

No one answered. Then Captain Matsumoto, commanding the battleship *Fuji*, rose.

"As one whose knowledge of the august English language is perhaps superior to that of most present—your honourable self, sir, excepted," he said, addressing the Admiral, "I should like to say that I have listened to the remarks of the honourable commander of the *Kasanumi* with profound interest. His doctrine, that it is more glorious to live than to die for one's Emperor, is a new one to us Japanese, and I confess that for the moment it shocked me, as I saw that it shocked most of us. But, if one comes to reflect, one sees that there is sound sense in it; therefore I should like to record my entire approval of the projected plan of attack upon the enemy's fleet. For, by adopting it, there is a good prospect that many lives and many craft, which would otherwise be uselessly sacrificed, may be preserved to render further valuable service to Japan and its Emperor."

The applause this time was real and hearty enough, and several of the officers who were sitting near me offered me their hands and smilingly complimented me.

"Very well, then, gentlemen, that matter is settled, and most satisfactorily, too, in my humble opinion. And, now, as to details. Divisions 1, 2, and 3 of the destroyer flotilla will attack the fleet at Port Arthur; Divisions 4 and 5 will proceed to Dalny in quest of the Russian destroyers said to reconnoitre in that direction nightly; and all will inflict as much damage as possible upon the enemy. Captain Matsunaga of the *Asashio* will command Divisions 1, 2, and 3; while Captain Nagai will command Divisions 4 and 5. The flotilla will start at five o'clock this evening. You are dismissed, gentlemen. I thank you for your honourable attendance, and the assistance which you have rendered me."

Chapter Five
My "Baptism of Fire"

The weather had cleared somewhat during the afternoon, but when, at a few minutes before five o'clock, the *Mikasa* made the signal for the destroyer flotilla to weigh and proceed, the clouds had gathered afresh, and it was looking as wild as ever. It was exactly five o'clock when the *Asashio*, followed by the *Kasanumi*, led the way out to sea; and as we began to move, the Admiral signalled us: "Go in and sink the enemy's fleet. I pray for your success."

The Elliot group of islands, from which we started upon our great adventure, is situated some sixty miles north-east of Port Arthur, and within some seven or eight miles of the mainland. Our nearest and best way, therefore, under ordinary circumstances, would have been to creep down the coast close inshore. But this would have involved our passing Dalny on the way, and there were the Russian destroyers, which were said to patrol as far as that place every night, to be reckoned with. We did not desire to encounter them on the way, and so afford them a chance to slip back to Port Arthur and give the alarm; our object was to get in between them and Port Arthur, and so cut off their retreat. Also, we had decided to approach Port Arthur from the south-west, so as to give the idea that we were the Russian boats returning after a scouting excursion in the offing; we therefore headed due south at the start, our speed being fifteen knots, which was later increased to twenty-two, as the course which we had decided upon took us far out of our way and nearly doubled the distance to be run.

The sun disappeared beneath the horizon in a heavy squall of rain, the wind breezed up fiercely, and it was piercingly cold. The night shut down upon us dark as a wolf's mouth, the only relief to the intense blackness being the phosphorescence of the bow wave as it swept, roaring and scintillating away to port and starboard, and the faint gleam of a shrouded lamp which each vessel bore at her taffrail as a guide to the craft next astern of her. Well, so much the better; the darker the night, the better for our purpose; only I fervently wished that the water had not been so brilliantly phosphorescent, for in the intense darkness the gleam of it was visible for quite a considerable distance, and I feared that, if the Russians were keeping a sharp lookout, it would prematurely reveal our approach. We had cleared for action before getting under way, and each boat carried two torpedoes in her tubes, her guns loaded, and ammunition ready to pass up on deck at a moment's notice.

Hour after hour we steamed on, describing the arc of a big semi-circle as we altered our course from time to time, until at length we were heading west-nor'-west for Port Arthur; and during the whole time we had not sighted a craft of any description.

At length, about half-past ten, the darkness ahead seemed to grow blacker than ever, and turning to Ito, who stood beside me on the bridge, I said:

"Do you see that darkness ahead, Ito? Surely that is the loom of land."

"Yes," answered Ito, who spoke English excellently. "Without a doubt that is the high land on either side of Port Arthur; and—ha! there is the Pinnacle Rock light, straight ahead. By Jingo! as the honourable English say, Captain Matsunaga has 'hit it off splendidly.' And see there," —as a light began to wink at us from the bridge of the *Asashio* ahead—"there is the signal for the 4th and 5th Divisions to part company. Yes; there they go; and now, as again the honourable English say, 'we shan't be long.'"

I shivered involuntarily. A quarter of an hour more and that blackness ahead would be pierced by the blinding rays of the inexorable searchlights and stabbed by the fierce flashing of artillery, the glare of bursting shells, and the radiance of star rockets. And we should be in the midst of it. It would be my first experience of actual warfare, and I wondered how I should pass through the ordeal. I had already learned that the Japanese soldier or sailor is absolutely the most fearless creature in existence. He fears death as little as he fears sleep, provided that it comes to him in the service of his Emperor and his country. To die for his Emperor, indeed, who is to him as a god, is the very highest honour, the greatest glory, that the male Japanese can look forward to. He faces such a death with the same pure joy, the same exaltation, that the early Christian martyrs displayed when they were led forth to die for their faith. It was this spirit, this eagerness, this enthusiasm to die in battle, that caused the enormous losses suffered by the Japanese during the war; but it made them invincible! How was my conduct going to compare with that of men like these, I who was animated by no more lofty sentiment than the desire to do my duty to the best of my ability, to play my part as a man should, and, above all, to uphold the honour and dignity of my race? I was happy in the conviction that I should not disgrace myself by any exhibition of craven fear, but what I dreaded was that in the excitement of the moment I should get "nervy," lose my head (if only figuratively), and perhaps forget to do something that I ought to do, to miss some opportunity that I ought to see and seize. "Brace up, Paul!" I said to myself, "pull yourself together for the honour of the dear homeland; forget all about yourself, and think only of the work that lies before you." And I did. My thoughts went back to my talk with the Admiral in the *Mikasa's* cabin that afternoon; I suddenly remembered that the work in hand was to be carried out as I had planned it; and in a moment all my anxiety vanished, I was my own man again, mentally planning what I would do; and from that moment I felt as cool and collected and keen as was Ito who stood beside me.

As the tail lights of the 4th and 5th Divisions of the flotilla vanished in the darkness on our port quarter, the *Asashio's* signal lantern began winking again, and Ito read off and translated the message to me:

"Reduce speed to twelve knots. Be ready to show signal lanterns if required. When I starboard helm, Division one will follow me, while Divisions two and three will port helm and sheer off to the eastward."

A single flash from our own carefully shrouded signal lanterns informed the Commodore that the message had been read and understood, and all was opaque darkness once more. The rain had by this time cleared off and the atmosphere was much clearer, so clear indeed that the outlines of the hills ahead showed with tolerable distinctness, and the water was getting smoother.

The lighthouse light was showing very bright and clear by this time, and two or three other and much dimmer lights, like those of houses, showed here and there in the shadow of the hills. The gap between the hills which marked the harbour entrance was also visible, while a faint glare in the sky to the right of it showed that Port Arthur was still awake. But everything seemed absolutely peaceful, and there were no signs of that alertness which we had expected to find.

Suddenly the lighthouse light, upon which my gaze happened to be fixed, seemed to blink several times in a very curious manner; then it disappeared altogether for a moment, and I saw a great black shadow that seemed to rapidly increase in size as I stared at it. Then I glimpsed at the base of the shadow the ghostly gleam of phosphorescent foam, such as is piled up by the bows of a ship travelling at speed, and high above it a rolling, swirling cloud of blackness spangled with evanescent sparks which, a moment later, I saw was issuing from three of a group of five tall funnels.

"By Jove! Ito," I exclaimed, "here comes the patrol cruiser—the *Askold*—and she is heading straight for us! Gun and tube crews, stand by! Quartermaster, light those two signal lanterns, white above red, bend them on to the signal halliards, and stand by to hoist away when I give the word."

"Yes," agreed Ito, his voice tense with excitement; "she has seen and intends to speak us. See, she has stopped her engines, and is hailing the *Asashio*! What a jolly, bloomin' chance," (Ito was very proud of his command of English slang, and availed himself of every possible opportunity to air it) "to honourably torpedo her! Will the honourable Swinburne augustly grant the humblest of his servants permission to do so?"

"Heavens! no, man," I exclaimed, "not for worlds. And I pray that Matsunaga may also have the sense to refrain from doing so."

"But why, my honourable friend; why?" demanded Ito, literally dancing with eagerness and impatience.

"Because, don't you see, my honourable duffer, that if we did so the explosion would put all Port Arthur, and the fleet too, on the *qui vive* long before we could get at them, and thus spoil our chances of bagging the battleships?" I replied. "No, certainly not. Let the cruiser go; it is the battleships we want. There go the *Asashio's* lanterns. Hoist away, quartermaster!"

"Yes, yes; I see," replied Ito in crestfallen tones; "you are honourably right, of course. Aha! there goes the cruiser. The honourable Captain Matsunaga has evidently honourably satisfied her. He honourably speaks Russian like a native."

It was an exciting moment; but, tense as it was, I could not help being amused at the pertinacity with which Ito, like all the Japanese, dragged in the word "honourable" upon every possible and impossible occasion. It arises, of course, out of the desire, drilled into them, generation after generation, to be extremely polite; and doubtless when speaking in their own tongue, the word is never unsuitably used; but when they undertake to talk English, it is frequently pitchforked into the conversation in the most incongruous and even ludicrous fashion, and I decided that it would only be kind to give Ito a lesson upon the absurdity of employing it inappropriately. The opportunity came a few minutes later.

The *Askold*, apparently satisfied with Captain Matsunaga's explanation, put her helm hard a-starboard and swept on, presently vanishing in the darkness; and a minute or two later the *Asashio* made the signal for the Divisions to separate as arranged, starboarding her helm as she did so and leading Number 1 Division to the westward, while Divisions 2 and 3 ported and swerved sharply away to the eastward.

"The critical moment is at hand," said I. "Be so good, Mr Ito, as to go down on the main deck and assure yourself that everything is ready, and that the men are standing by the tubes and guns."

Then Ito turned upon me and poured out an impassioned entreaty that he might be "honourably" permitted to take charge of and fire the torpedoes himself. I considered for a moment. The man who might chance to score a hit in the coming attempt would gain immense kudos, I knew, and, in all probability, promotion also. By rights, of course, Ito's station should be by me, to take my place should I chance to be hit; but he was just as liable to be hit on the bridge as anywhere else; also it would be doing him a kindness to grant his request. So:

"Now, look here, Ito," I said, "it is of paramount importance that the men in charge of the tubes to-night should be first-rate shots, and as cool as cucumbers; for, hit or miss, I do not suppose we shall be afforded a chance to discharge more than the two torpedoes already in our tubes; therefore they must both hit. Now, are you a good shot with the torpedo?"

Ito solemnly assured me that there was not a better torpedo shot than himself in the whole Japanese fleet.

"And is your nerve all right? I mean, are you perfectly cool?" I demanded.

"As cool as the honourable cucumber," he asserted. "Feel my unworthy hand."

I could not help laughing. Here was the inevitable "honourable" being dragged in again. I seized his hand and held it loosely in mine for a few seconds. It was firm and steady as a rock.

"Good!" I said. "You will do, Ito. Go down and work the tubes, my boy, and see that you excel yourself to-night. And, Ito, if you love me, do not, for heaven's sake, forget to withdraw the honourable safety pin from the honourable fan before you honourably fire the honourable torpedo, or you will make no honourable hits this honourable night. Do you honourably take me?"

"A long, brilliant beam of intensely white light shot out."

" A long brilliant beam of intensely white light shot out. "

There! I had fired off my little joke on Ito; illustrated to him, I fondly thought, the absurdity of indiscriminately dragging in the word "honourable" in and out of season. How would he take it, I wondered.

"The august captain may honourably rely upon his unworthy lieutenant to do his honourable best," he gravely answered; and the next moment was "honourably" descending the bridge ladder to the deck. My miserable attempt at jocularity had absolutely missed fire; the dear, innocent fellow had accepted my speech as uttered in all seriousness.

It was at this moment that I first caught the loom of the Russian ships, showing up a deeper black against the black shadow of the frowning cliffs away to starboard; and a second or two later a long, brilliant beam of intensely white light shot out from one of the black shapes and slowly swept hither and thither, now striking the heaving surface of the black water, and anon vividly illumining one of her sisters. Our orders had been not to discharge at a higher range than five hundred metres.

Slowly, the beam swept round toward us until it halted and rested steadily upon a great lump of a craft that towered out of the water like a castle, almost immediately between itself and us. Luckily, the dazzling light itself was hidden from our eyes by the bulk of the ship upon which it rested, but it invested her with a sort of halo of radiance against which she stood out black and grim, a perfect silhouette. She was a big craft, evidently a battleship, with a lofty superstructure, three big funnels cased half-way up, a long overhanging bridge, and two stout military masts with fighting tops, and two yards across each. She was just within range, and, seizing a megaphone, I was in the act of raising it to my lips to order Ito to let fly at her, when I saw a long, silvery shape flash out from our after-deck, and a few seconds later a great cone of water leaped into the air and fell like a deluge upon the great ship, which seemed to lift half out of the water, as though hove up by a giant. A heavy *boom* followed, and I had the extreme gratification of knowing that the little *Kasanumi's* first Whitehead had got home.

The explosion was quickly followed by several others; and in the midst of them a sudden transformation took place. The pitchy darkness gave way to the glare of a perfect network of searchlight beams streaming out from ship after ship and from the cliffs above, sweeping here, there, and everywhere, lighting up the fleet, the cliffs, the channel leading to the harbour, the lighthouse, everything, in fact, except our destroyers, which they all seemed to miss in the most miraculous way. Excited shouts came pealing across the water to us from the decks of the various ships, boatswains' whistles shrilled, order after order was hoarsely bellowed, and with a rattling crash of gun-fire a perfect tempest of projectiles was sent hurtling out to sea from the now thoroughly awakened and panic-stricken Russians, not a solitary shot of which came anywhere near us; for the enemy seemed to have not the slightest idea of our actual whereabouts. And then, to add to the turmoil and confusion, the forts on the cliffs above opened fire with their heavy guns, and we heard the shells go muttering angrily far overhead, as the gunners ashore also fired into the offing.

The fleet as a whole now lay broad on our starboard beam, and we in the *Kasanumi* were crossing the bows of a two-funnelled battleship which, from her position as the outermost ship of the fleet, I knew must be the *Tzarevich*, when, out of the tail of my eye, so to speak, I again caught the flash of one of our Whiteheads as it leapt outward and plunged into the sea. Breathlessly I awaited the result, and presently, to my delight, I saw that our second torpedo had got home!

"Good old Ito!" I exclaimed aloud; and, as I spoke, the man himself stood beside me.

"Two hits!" he gasped, almost inarticulate with excitement and delight. "The *Kasanumi* has done her duty to-night."

"She has," I agreed; "and so have you, splendidly, old chap. This means immediate promotion for you, Ito; for you may rest assured that, if we get out of this alive, I will not fail to report to the Admiral what you have done. I don't see—"

"Ah, but," he interrupted me, "the real credit of it all belongs to you, not me. For if you had not warned me, I should certainly, in my excitement, have forgotten to withdraw the pins before firing the torpedoes. As it was, I very nearly did so when firing the first, but luckily your warning flashed into my mind at the very instant when I was about to fire. I am afraid that many of our men have forgotten that essential; for although all the torpedoes must be by this time discharged, I do not think that many ships have been hit."

I had noticed the same thing myself, and was about to say so, but at this moment the Russian ships opened fire with their heavy guns, and conversation, which up to now had been difficult enough, became quite impossible owing to the deafening din. But I observed that the ships and batteries were all firing out to sea, whereas our destroyers were by this time between the fleet and the land, completely absorbed in the deep shadow of the lofty cliffs, so that up to that moment I believed we had remained unseen. Then the *Asashio* flashed the signal for Number 1 Division to retire at full speed, putting her helm hard a-port as she did so, for by this time we were running parallel with the shore on the west side of the harbour, and a few minutes more would have taken us to the harbour's mouth, which was now brilliantly illuminated by the rays of some half a dozen searchlights, which it was essential for us to avoid if we wished to escape instant annihilation.

It was at this moment, when I was eagerly taking note of the most distinctive features of the harbour entrance, brought thus prominently into view—with the idea that such knowledge as I might then be able to acquire might prove useful at some future time—that three destroyers, coming out of the harbour at full speed, rushed across the illuminated area and, turning sharp round the Pinnacle Rock, headed almost directly toward us. A single glance sufficed to show that they were Russian craft, for they were of a different model from ours, and their four funnels were arranged differently from ours, being in pairs.

For a moment I believed that they saw and were about to engage us, I therefore laid my hand upon Ito's arm to attract his attention, pointed to the boats, and then yelled in his ear:

"Russians! Stand by to give them a broadside as they pass."

Ito nodded comprehendingly, and vanished from my side. A minute later, the leading Russian destroyer came abreast the *Asashio*, and Captain Matsunaga showed that he was as wideawake as the rest of us, by plumping a 12-pound and three 6-pound shells into her. Then came our turn, and we did the same, each of the four Japanese boats in turn firing all the guns that would bear upon each of the three Russian boats as they came up, without receiving a single shot in return; for, strange as it may seem, the Russians appeared to have no suspicion of our whereabouts until we actually fired upon them.

But perhaps we should have been wiser had we allowed our valour to be tempered with discretion, and refrained from attacking the enemy's destroyers; for the flashes of our guns, low down near the surface of the water, were instantly observed by a hundred sharp eyes, eagerly seeking the whereabouts of the elusive enemy, and almost immediately every searchlight on ship and shore swept round until it rested full upon us, thereafter inexorably following our every movement, while a perfect tornado of shell and rifle-fire hissed and whined about our ears. But for this, it might have been not very difficult for us to have inflicted further damage upon the battleships and cruisers; but as it was, there was only one thing to be done, namely, to effect our escape with the utmost expedition, if, indeed, escape were still possible; for to remain until fresh torpedoes could be got up on deck and placed in the tubes, would mean our swift and certain destruction before the opportunity came for us to work further mischief. As it was, it was simply miraculous that we were not instantly blown out of the water; for, with a dozen or more searchlights bearing full upon us, we were as plainly visible as though it had been broad daylight; yet, strange to say, not a shot struck any of us, a circumstance which can only be accounted for upon the assumption that the Russian gunners were so unnerved by our sudden and unexpected attack that, for the moment, they had completely lost the ability to shoot straight.

Through that frightful tempest of shot and shell we tore at top speed, the fragile hulls of the boats bucking and quivering to the impulse of their tremendously powerful engines, the water cleft by their sharp bows curling almost to the height of the navigating bridges and drenching the occupants with spray, while flames roared out of all four of their funnels as the stokers below toiled like fiends to feed the furnaces and maintain a full head of steam. To add to our difficulties, the glare of so many searchlights directed full upon us dazzled our sight to blinding point, so that it was only with the greatest difficulty we were able to find our way. The formation in which the Russian fleet was moored helped us, however, for we presently found ourselves rushing across the bows of their weathermost line, and we steered accordingly.

Then, quite unexpectedly, we came upon the three Russian destroyers again; and those of us who happened to be prepared—of which the *Kasanumi* was one—gave them a further peppering, to which, as before, they made no reply. And now, at last, we were reaching the end of the line, and the gauntlet was almost run, for as we drew out to seaward the inshore ships were compelled to cease fire for fear of hurting their friends instead of us. There was but one more ship to pass; and as we drew near to her I saw that she had a decided list to port, and was floating so deep aft that her "admirals' walk," or stern gallery, was very nearly submerged. Steam was roaring from her safety valves, and as we came up to her a small curl of water under her bows and a swirl at her stern showed that she was under way. It was the *Tsarevich*, heading for the harbour, evidently in a sinking condition, and we had the satisfaction of knowing that by that night's work we had put at least one of the Russian battleships *hors de combat*. Her crew were much too busy to pay any attention to us; and a quarter of an hour later we were beyond the zone of that awful, merciless fire, and were heading south-east for Mokpo, where we had been ordered to rendezvous.

We did not, of course, at that time know the extent of the damage that we had succeeded in inflicting upon the Russian fleet; but trustworthy information reached us later, that the *Tsarevich* had been struck aft, the torpedo blowing a big hole in her hull and flooding her steering compartment to such an extent that her captain had been obliged to beach her to prevent her from sinking. The *Retvisan* had been struck amidships, and a large hole blown in her pump compartment, rendering it necessary that she also should be beached in order to save her. Those two battleships constituted the *Kasanumi's* share of the bag; and very pleased we were with ourselves when the news became known, since those two ships were far and away the best in the Russian fleet, and the loss of them, even if it should prove to be only temporary, was a very serious matter for the Russians. But, in addition to these, the *Pallada*, cruiser, and the volunteer cruiser *Angara* were also hit, and were obliged to be beached to save them from foundering.

Thus we had done not at all badly; although some surprise was felt that, considering the favourable circumstances under which the attack was made—by which I mean our unsuspected approach, and the time which elapsed before the searchlights actually found us—we had not done a great deal more. For Divisions 1, 2, and 3, which had attacked the Russian fleet, consisted in all of ten destroyers, each of which had discharged two torpedoes—twenty in all. And of those twenty, only four, apparently, had got home. It was not a result to be proud of. But I had a suspicion that I could have put my finger upon the explanation, had I been asked to do so; and it would have been this: The night was bitterly cold; so cold, indeed, that the spray froze as it fell upon us, and the weather was simply atrocious; the result being that by the time the flotilla arrived in Port Arthur roadstead, the limit of even Japanese physical endurance had been almost, if not quite, reached. Most of our deck hands had been more or less severely frost-bitten, not only their bodies, but also their minds were benumbed by the arctic severity of the weather, and thus it came to pass (at least so I reasoned it out) that when the moment for action arrived their faculties, between physical suffering and mental excitement, became so confused that many of them made the mistake against which I had warned Ito, and failed to withdraw the safety pin before discharging their torpedoes, thus rendering the missiles ineffective. This was also Ito's opinion, you will remember.

By the time that we reached Mokpo we were all in a most deplorable condition, nearly half of the deck hands of the expedition being compelled to go into hospital suffering from frost-bite, a few of the cases being of so severe a character that the patients lost either their hands or their feet, while one man lost all four members, and narrowly escaped dying outright. Ito and I were somehow lucky enough to escape without serious injury, but we both developed virulent attacks of inflammation of the lungs, which put us *hors de combat* for nearly three weeks. But there is no doubt that our recovery was greatly facilitated by the intimation, which reached us while we were still in hospital, that we had both been promoted to the rank of Commander.

Meanwhile, things had been happening at Port Arthur and elsewhere. On the morning following our attack, Togo sent three fast cruisers in toward the fortress to reconnoitre; and these ships having discovered pretty much how matters stood there, and reported to the Admiral, the whole fleet stood in and engaged the ships and batteries at long-range, firing only their 12-inch and 8-inch guns, the range being too long for the others. The weather had changed, and was now bright and comparatively warm, the atmosphere so clear that even comparatively small objects were clearly visible.

The *Mikasa* opened the ball by firing a sighting shot from one of the 12-inch guns in her fore barbette, and at the same moment the Russian ships were seen to be getting under way. At low speed the Japanese fleet steamed past the port in "line ahead," firing as they went, and after an engagement lasting some forty minutes, drew off, hoping that the Russian fleet would follow them, but in this they were disappointed. Our ships were hit several times and sustained a certain amount of damage, but, luckily, not of a serious character. It was reported that we lost four killed and fifty-four wounded, none of the wounds being serious enough, however, to necessitate the men being sent ashore to the hospital. It was some time before reliable information reached us as to the extent of the damage sustained by the Russians, but when it came it was to the effect that several of our shells fell in the town, scattering the piles of coal on the wharves and creating general panic; the *Poltava* was so badly hit that she could not move, a shell blowing her bows open; the *Petropavlosk* and *Pobieda* were also hit, though not seriously; our old friend, the *Askold*, was hit on the waterline and set on fire, as was also the *Diana*; while the *Novik*, which had steamed out toward our fleet, was sent flying back with her rudder damaged, so that they had to steer her with her propellers. This affair caused Admiral Stark to be superseded; his successor being Admiral Makarov, said to be the finest seaman Russia then possessed. At the same time General Kuropatkin was appointed commander of the Russian land forces.

Two days later, the Russians lost the mine-layer *Yenesei* in Dalny Bay. This was a particularly hard bit of luck for them, inasmuch as that she had practically completed her work when the disaster happened. Her mission was to sow Dalny Bay with four hundred contact mines, in order to prevent the Japanese from using the bay as a landing-place for troops. She had successfully laid all but two of the four hundred mines; but when the three hundred and ninety-ninth mine was launched overboard, it floated, instead of sinking to its prescribed depth. The captain of the ship is said to have opened fire upon it with his light guns, to explode it; and in this he appears to have been only too successful, since it not only exploded but also blew up the ship, which sank almost immediately, most of her crew going down with her. And on the following day the small cruiser *Boyarin* went ashore in Dalny Bay, and became a total wreck. Thus in less than a week the Port Arthur fleet had become reduced in strength by no less than three battleships, five cruisers, and one mining ship, exclusive of the cruiser *Variag* and the gunboat *Korietz*, destroyed at Chemulpo.

Encouraged by the success of the first destroyer attack upon Port Arthur, Admiral Togo arranged for a repetition of the experiment on the night of 13th February, and the attempt duly came off, the 4th and 5th Divisions of the destroyer flotilla being this time told off to conduct the attack. These divisions, consisting of eight boats, had not participated in the previous attack, and Togo no doubt wished to give them an opportunity to acquire *kudos*, and, at the same time, by arousing their emulation, spur them on to outvie our performance.

Unfortunately, however, for the expedition, the weather was even worse than that with which we had had to contend: the cold was intense, a gale was blowing, a tremendously heavy sea was running, and, to cap it all, a terrific snow blizzard was raging. The result of this combination of adverse conditions was that the destroyers very soon lost touch with each other, and only two of them succeeded in entering the harbour, the *Asigiri* preceding the *Hayatori* by nearly two hours. The *Asigiri* entered the harbour unseen, discharged two torpedoes—both of which her captain, Commander Isakawa, believed had got home—and then fled, encountering an enemy's launch on the way, and sinking her. The explosion of the *Asigiri's* torpedoes of course raised an alarm, searchlights flashed wildly hither and thither, gunners blazed away madly, and so great was the panic that several of the Russian destroyers opened fire upon each other and did a lot of damage.

When Commander Takanouchi, in the *Hayatori*, arrived two hours later, the confusion was still at its height, and taking advantage of it, he, too, slipped in unnoticed and, as he believed, successfully torpedoed a cruiser before he fled. But it seemed very doubtful whether, after all, either of the Japanese boats did much damage; for when the Japanese cruisers reconnoitred next day, none could be detected.

Then, on the night of 23rd February, all the Russian ships being inside Port Arthur, Togo sent in five steamers, under Commander Arima, whose instructions were that they were to be sunk across the harbour entrance, in such positions as would effectually block the passage. But their approach was prematurely discovered, and so terrific a fire was opened upon them from the batteries that two were sunk, while the other three, their steering gear being shot away, went ashore outside. The attempt was consequently a failure, while ten men lost their lives in making it.

On the night of 24th February and the morning of the following day, the Japanese fleet made a second attack upon Port Arthur, bombarding the town and fleet for twenty-five minutes. The Russian cruisers *Bayan*, *Novik*, and *Askold* were hit, some shells exploded in the batteries, and the town was set on fire in two places, but the damage done was inconsiderable; and at length, in accordance with his instructions to on no account risk his battleships by engaging the forts, Togo felt himself obliged to retire.

Chapter Six
"Sealing up" Port Arthur

Our gallant and indefatigable little Admiral seemed to spend all his spare time in scheming out plans for the discomfiture of the enemy; and about this time he evolved one which seemed to possess all the elements of a brilliant success.

Knowing that Russian spies swarmed everywhere, he prepared an elaborate scheme to sow Port Arthur roadstead, in front of the harbour entrance, with electro-mechanical mines, with the ostensible object of preventing the Russian fleet from coming out. These mines were stated to be of a peculiarly dangerous and deadly character, invented by Captain Odo. With great ingenuity the details of the scheme were permitted to gradually leak out, so that in due time they came into the knowledge of the Russian spies and were promptly transmitted to Port Arthur. As a matter of fact, however, the mines which were proposed to be, and actually were, sown, were of a very innocuous character, Togo's object being to imbue the Russian mind with the idea that the Japanese mines were so useless that they might be safely disregarded. Then, when this object had been achieved, genuine Odo mines would be sown, with disastrous results to such Russian ships as might chance to run foul of them.

The task of sowing the innocuous mines was entrusted to two divisions of destroyers, consisting of five craft; the first division being composed of the *Asashio, Kasanumi,* and *Akatsuki,* while the *Akebono* and *Sazanami* constituted the second division. Ito and I had both happily recovered from our indisposition by this time, and were able to rejoin the fleet in time to participate in the projected operation. Although promoted to the rank of Commander, I was left in command of the *Kasanumi;* but Ito got a step up the ratlines, being given the command of the *Akatsuki,* while a youngster named Hiraoka was given me in his place.

On 9th March we were busy all day shipping our harmless mines; and at eight o'clock in the evening we weighed and, under easy steam, proceeded from our base at the Elliot Islands, bound for Port Arthur roadstead, accompanied by the fast cruiser squadron, the duty of which was to support us in the event of our being attacked, and cover our escape.

By 11:30 p.m. we were within ten miles of the roadstead; and at this point we parted company with the cruisers, who now hove-to for half an hour, to allow us time to reach our destination. At the expiration of that time, a light or two were "accidentally" revealed on board the cruisers for a few seconds, just long enough to give the Port Arthur lookouts an opportunity to detect them, when they were extinguished. But the ruse was successful, the attention of the lookouts had been attracted, and instantly the searchlights from the station on the cliff to the eastward of the harbour were turned upon the cruisers and kept steadily bearing upon them. They were, of course, so far away that they were only dimly descried, and too far distant to make it worth while to open fire upon them, but their movements were—of set purpose—of so suspicious a character that, having once detected them, the Russians were determined not to lose sight of them again. The attention of the lookouts having thus been attracted to our cruisers in the offing, we in the destroyers were able to slip into the roadstead undetected.

Arrived there, we lost no time in sowing our mine-field right athwart the harbour's mouth, and, had we been so minded, could have finished our work and retired before daylight. But to render the Admiral's scheme successful, it was necessary that we should be seen, and the nature of our work recognised; the 2nd Division therefore reserved a few mines to be dropped after daylight, and when that came they were at once discovered dropping mines, in a state of apparently feverish haste. The forts, of course, at once opened fire upon them; but before they could get the range, our destroyers launched their remaining mines overboard, and took to their heels, their task being accomplished. And now, all that remained was to patiently await the course of events, and thus see how far this part of Togo's plan had been successful.

The game, however, was not yet finished. While we had been busily dropping our mines, what I thought a rather brilliant idea had occurred to me; and, ceasing work for a while, I steamed up alongside the *Akebono*, of our 2nd Division, and imparted my idea to Commander Tsuchiya, who was pleased to very heartily approve of it. In accordance with my scheme, therefore, the 1st Destroyer Division completed its task before daylight, and quietly steamed off round to the westward of Liau-ti-shan, where we remained snugly concealed, close in under the cliffs.

My idea was that if our 2nd Division were discovered—as it was necessary it should be, the Russians would probably send out a few destroyers to attack it; and the event proved that my surmise was correct.

Six Russian destroyers were dispatched from the harbour, presumably with instructions to wipe the *Akebono* and *Sazanami* off the face of the waters; and as soon as the latter saw the enemy approaching, on a course intended to cut off their retreat to the eastward, the two boats swerved sharply away to the westward, with their funnels belching great clouds of smoke, and every indication that their crews were in a terrible state of fright—but with their engines working at only about three-quarter speed. The Russians, stimulated by our 2nd Division's apparent terror, and finding also that they were steadily gaining upon the chase, strained every nerve to overtake them, and at length came pounding round the point in great style.

Meanwhile, the two retreating Japanese destroyers had already swept past us—thus giving us the signal to be on the lookout—and, veering round, in a wide semi-circle, formed up in our rear, we of the 1st Division having already started our engines as soon as they hove in sight.

On came the Russian destroyers, rolling and pitching on the long swell, with the water spouting and curling under their sharp bows to the height of their bridges; and the moment that the first of them swung round the point, over went the indicators of our engine-room telegraphs to "Full speed ahead!" Our gun crews had been standing to their guns for some time past, all ready for action, and as we swept out to seaward, crossing the Russians' bows, we let fly at them with our twelve-pounders and as many of our six-pounders as could be brought to bear, concentrating our fire as much as possible upon the enemy's guns, several of which we succeeded in dismounting.

I feel bound to admit that, taken by surprise though they were, the Russians put up a splendid fight; but although they were superior to us in numbers, our men would not be denied, they worked their guns as coolly and with as deadly precision as though they had been at target practice, and the Russian boats were hulled again and again, clouds of steam arose from them, fires broke out aboard some of them, and so closely were we engaged that we could occasionally hear the cries of the wounded that arose as our shot swept their decks. The fight, which was a very hot one, lasted some twenty minutes, by which time the Russians had managed to get back round the point and under the cover of the batteries. We followed them to the very mouth of the harbour, fighting every inch of the way, but, at length, with heavy shells falling all round us, in some cases dropping so close that our decks were drenched with spray, it became imperative for us to be off, and we accordingly ported our helms and made off, followed by salvos of shot, big and small, until we were out of range.

Then we slowed down our engines and proceeded to take stock of our injuries.

So far as the *Kasanumi* was concerned, we had got off pretty lightly, although there was a period of about three minutes when we were hotly engaged by two Russian destroyers at the same time. Our decks were rather severely scored by flying fragments of shells, we had three shot-holes in our hull, we had one man killed and two wounded, one of them being our chief engineer, who, although severely wounded by a fragment of a shell which burst in the engine-room, gallantly stuck to his post until the fight was over, when he was able to turn the engines over to his second. The *Akatsuki* had received the severest punishment, one of her steam pipes being severed, and four of her engine-room hands scalded to death. In all, we lost in this fight seven killed and eight wounded; but none of the boats was very seriously damaged.

Meanwhile, our 2nd Division, consisting of the *Akebono* and *Sazanami*, had vanished, without leaving a sign of their whereabouts. It was now daylight, and the weather tolerably clear, yet, although Hiraoka and I swept the whole surface of the sea with our glasses, we entirely failed to pick them up. The *Asashio* and *Akatsuki* were within hail, both of them engaged, like ourselves, in temporarily patching up the holes in their thin steel sides, through which the water was pouring in whenever we rolled extra heavily; and I hailed them both, inquiring whether either of them had seen anything of the missing craft. An affirmative reply came from my friend Ito, aboard the *Akatsuki*, who informed me that shortly after the fight began, on the other side of the promontory, he had momentarily caught sight of them both, steaming hot-foot after a destroyer which was in full flight, heading toward Pigeon Bay.

Scarcely had this reply been given when the sounds of light gun-fire faintly reached our ears from the direction mentioned, and a few minutes later two destroyers, flying the Russian flag, came foaming round the point, firing as they came, while close behind them appeared our two missing boats, also firing for all they were worth. The Russian boats were running in "line ahead," and it seemed to me that the skipper of the leading boat was manoeuvring her in such a manner as to keep his consort as nearly as possible between himself and the pursuers; at all events the sternmost boat seemed to be getting the biggest share of the pursuers' fire.

At once I shouted an order for the men engaged upon our repairs to hasten their work and bring it to some sort of finish, at the same time signing the quartermaster to put his helm hard over, my intention of course being to go back and render such assistance as might be required, while the

Asashio kept on and stood by Ito, who had his hands full with his severed steam pipe.

But it was impossible for us now to steam at a greater speed than about three knots, for had we attempted to do so, we should have washed overboard the men who were making the repairs, as well as washed the repairs themselves away, in their uncompleted state; consequently, long before we could get near the scene of action, the fight was over. One of the destroyers—the leading one—managed to get safely into the harbour, while the other, which turned out to be the *Stercguschtchi*, riddled with shells, lost speed to such an extent that at length the *Sazanami* was able to run alongside and throw a boarding party upon her deck. They found that deck a veritable shambles, no less than thirty dead being counted upon it. Naturally, they took the craft without any resistance worth mentioning, for there were very few left to resist, while, of those who remained, the greater number jumped overboard rather than surrender. Of these, only two were picked up, while two others, too badly wounded to either fight or take to the water, surrendered.

At once the *Sazanami* took her prize in tow; but the craft was so seriously damaged that, despite all efforts to save her, she rapidly filled and sank, the towing hawser parting as she foundered.

Meanwhile the *Akebono* was in a somewhat parlous condition, for during the fight she had been struck on the waterline, and was now limping along as best she could, with two compartments filled; when, therefore, the Russian boat foundered, the *Sazanami* went to her consort's assistance and took her in tow, for two Russian cruisers, identified as the *Novik* and *Bayan*, were now seen to be coming out of Port Arthur harbour, and it was high time for us all to be off. Happily for us, by the time that the Russian cruisers were fairly out of harbour, five of our own cruisers had hove up above the horizon, steaming rapidly shoreward to our support, whereupon the Russians turned tail and retreated.

As our cruisers came up, their flagship signalled us to proceed to our rendezvous, after ascertaining that we could look after ourselves and needed no assistance; and shortly afterward we fell in with our main fleet, under Togo, bound for Pigeon Bay, whither the Admiral was proceeding for the purpose of testing his theory that the fortress could be successfully bombarded by high-angle fire projected over the high land between Pigeon Bay and the town. The signal was made for Commander Tsuchiya and me to proceed on board the *Mikasa*, where we jointly made our report, with which the Admiral was pleased to express his satisfaction. He, too, was anxious to know whether we required any assistance, and finding that we did not, ordered us to proceed to our rendezvous and get our repairs put in hand without a moment's delay. We arrived safely at our destination early in the afternoon, and within the next hour our damaged craft were in the hands of strong repairing gangs, so prompt were the Japanese to act.

The main fleet arrived at the rendezvous shortly before sunset, and anchored. I looked keenly at ship after ship, as they steamed in, but could detect no signs of injury to any of them; so after dinner I took our dinghy and rowed across to the *Mikasa*, with several of the officers of which I was by this time on quite intimate terms. The first man I happened to run into, however, upon passing in through the gangway was Captain Ijichi, commanding the ship; and he, as anxious to hear my yarn as I was to hear his, instantly pounced upon me and marched me off to his own cabin, where we were presently joined by Lieutenant Prince Kasho, for whom Ijichi had sent.

Here I was made to start the proceedings by spinning, at considerably greater length, the yarn which I had related to the Admiral earlier in the day, and which I was now able to supplement with the additional information that our 2nd Division had chased the Russian destroyer, of which they had started in pursuit, into Pigeon Bay, where they had sunk her. The honours of the day were of course with them, for they had accounted for two Russian destroyers, whereas we of the 1st Division had only given five of the enemy a very severe mauling; nevertheless, my little audience were good enough to stamp our performance with their marked approval.

Then the skipper of the *Mikasa* related his story. The long-range bombardment of Port Arthur was not a very exciting affair, it seemed, but it was successful in so far that it proved the correctness of the Admiral's theory that it could be done by firing over the high ground and dropping shells upon an unseen mark on the other side.

The attempt was of a twofold character, one part of which was to test the above theory, while the other was to destroy the Russian signal station upon the island of Sanshan, off Dalny, from which spot the enemy were able to observe and report to Port Arthur the movements of our fleet. This task was successfully accomplished by a detachment of our cruisers.

As regards the long-range, high-angle bombardment of the fortress, it was accomplished in the following fashion. Our battleships proceeded round to the westward of the promontory of Liau-ti-shan to a spot where the high land hid them from the sight of the Port Arthur batteries, and, elevating the muzzles of their 12-inch guns to the required extent, they discharged five rounds each from their four guns—one hundred and twenty shots in all, one shot at a time, while our first cruiser squadron, stationed off the port, to the south-east, carefully noted the spot where each shell dropped, and reported the result by wireless to the battleships, thus enabling them to adjust their aim and rectify any inaccuracies. The result was that one of our shells hit the Golden Hill fort, exploding a magazine and doubtless doing a considerable amount of damage to the structure, while the Mantow Hill fort, on the west side of the harbour, was hit several times and considerably damaged. Several shells fell in the New Town of Port Arthur, setting fire to a number of houses there and causing a tremendous panic and great loss of life. The fifth shell fired by our battleships struck the Russian battleship *Retvisan*, while another fell aboard the *Sevastopol*, exploding on her armoured deck. Yet another of our shells struck a train which happened to be just entering Port Arthur station, destroying the locomotive and, as we subsequently learned, killing the engine-driver and severely wounding the fireman. Finally, the *Retvisan* adopted our own tactics and retaliated by firing her heavy guns over the intervening high ground, while some of the forts did the same, a party of signallers being stationed on the crest of the hill to direct their aim. As a result of this, shells at length began to drop near our ships; whereupon the Admiral, in obedience to his instructions not to risk his battleships, hauled off; the fleet, as it went, observing three dense columns of smoke rising from the city.

Seeing that our ships were retiring, the Russian Admiral led out to sea such of his ships as were fit for service, with the evident intention of luring our ships into the zone of fire of the forts; but he might as well have saved his coal, for Togo was much too wary a bird to be caught with that kind of chaff.

On the following day we learned by wireless, from one of our cruiser scouts, that the Russian fleet was being cautiously taken out to sea through our mine-field off the harbour's mouth, the innocuous character of which they had already ascertained, —as intended by our Admiral, —and, later on, the further information reached us that the fleet was at sea and carrying out evolutions while cautiously working its way southward. Later still, we were informed that the Russians, learning from their scouts that none of our ships were in the vicinity, had proceeded as far as the Miao-tao Islands, off the Shan-tung peninsula, which they subjected to a careful examination, under the impression, as we subsequently learned, that those islands were being used by our destroyers as a hiding-place from which to make our raids. All hands of us immediately made our preparations to weigh at a moment's notice, fully expecting that the Admiral would seize what seemed such a splendid opportunity to intercept the enemy and give him battle in the open sea. But no orders were issued; and we were given to understand that there were certain good and sufficient secret reasons why the opportunity must be permitted to pass. A great deal of surprise, not to say dissatisfaction, was caused by this strange decision; but discipline was so strong, and the idea of implicit, unquestioning obedience had been so thoroughly instilled into the Japanese mind, that not a word of grumbling passed any of our lips.

On the night of 21st March the tactics of the 9th of the same month were repeated, including the laying of harmless mines off the mouth of the harbour, and the high-angle bombardment of the fortress by the *Fuji* and *Yashima* from Pigeon Bay; but the affair was uneventful; it may therefore be dismissed with the bare mention of it. The Russian ships again came out of harbour and ranged themselves in battle formation in the roadstead, but no wiles of ours could tempt them to leave the protection of the forts, so we drew off and returned to our rendezvous among the Elliot Islands.

During the night of 22nd March, four merchant steamers, purchased by the Japanese Government, arrived at our rendezvous from Sasebo, in response to a request from Togo; and the Admiral, with characteristic energy, at once proceeded to prepare them for the task of making a second attempt to bottle up the fleet in Port Arthur harbour.

They were the *Fukui Maru, Chiyo Maru, Yoneyama Maru,* and *Yahiko Maru*—all old craft, practically worn-out, and of very little value. These ships, like those used in the first attempt, were loaded with stones and scrap iron consolidated into a mass by pouring liquid cement over it, thus converting it into a sort of reinforced concrete, underneath which was buried the explosion charges destined to blow out the bottoms of the ships and sink them upon their arrival at their destined stations.

Hirose, now promoted to the rank of Commander for the gallantry which he displayed upon the occasion of the first attempt, was given the command of the largest ship, the *Fukui Maru*, while, to my intense surprise and gratification, I was given the command of the *Chiyo Maru*, a craft of 1746 tons. The expedition was in charge of Commander Arima, who went with Hirose. The ships were armed with a few old Hotchkiss quick-firers, for use against torpedo craft, should any attack us.

Our preparations were completed late in the afternoon of 26th March; and we immediately weighed and proceeded to sea, escorted by a flotilla of destroyers and torpedo-boats, among which was the *Kasanumi*, temporarily under the command of my subordinate, young Hiraoka, who had already proved himself to be a very capable, discreet, and courageous lad.

The weather on this occasion was everything that could be desired, perfectly clear, with no wind and a sea so calm that the veriest cock-boat could have safely ventured upon it. The only drawback was that there was a moon, well advanced in her first quarter, floating high in a sky dappled with light, fleecy cloud through which enough light percolated to render even small craft distinctly visible on the horizon. But, after all, this would not greatly matter, indeed it would be an advantage to us, always provided, of course, that we were not prematurely sighted by some keen-visioned, swift-steaming Russian scout; for the moon would set about midnight, while two o'clock in the morning was the time set for our attempt.

The run to the offing of Port Arthur was like a pleasure trip; our fleet of old crocks pounded along steadily, with a soft, soothing sound of purling water rising from under their bows, dominated from time to time by the clank of our crazy engines, which our mechanics had doctored up as thoroughly as time permitted, in order to ensure that they should outlast the run across. There was nothing for us to do but follow our leader, so I spent an hour of the time in making sure that our solitary boat should reach the water with certainty and on a level keel when the time should come to launch her, taking the turns out of the davit tackles, well greasing the falls, oiling the block sheaves, and rigging up a device of my own contriving whereby the necessity to unhook the blocks could be avoided when the boat touched the water.

At eleven o'clock Commander Arima signalled the destroyer flotilla, and five of the fastest of them at once went full speed ahead, spreading out in a fan-shaped formation ahead of us and on either bow to reconnoitre the roadstead. At ten minutes to midnight the moon, a great golden half-disc, swimming in a violet sky flecked with great islands of soft, fleecy cloud, touched the high land of Liau-ti-shan; and as she sank behind it, the order was given to stop our engines and lay-to for a short while, as we had made a good passage and were somewhat ahead of our scheduled time; also to await the return and report of the destroyers. We were now about twelve miles off Port Arthur, and far enough beyond the range of the searchlights to ensure our presence being undetected.

With the setting of the moon, the clouds seemed to bunch together and acquire a greater density, and it fell very dark, such starlight as filtered through the canopy of cloud only barely sufficing to enable us to detect our next ship ahead and astern. The land about Port Arthur loomed up in the darkness like a shapeless black shadow, stretched along the horizon to the west and north, pierced only by the long beam of the searchlight on Golden Hill, sweeping slowly to and fro at intervals. Watching this, for want of something better to do, we presently noticed that, for some reason not explicable to us, the beam never travelled farther south than a certain point, where it invariably paused for a few seconds, and then slowly swept round toward the north again.

Wondering whether Arima also had noticed this, I rang our engines ahead for a revolution or two, and hailed the *Fukui* to inquire. It appeared that he had not; and I was in the middle of a suggestion, the observance of which would, I believed, enable us to get close in, undetected, when our destroyers came rushing back with the information that everything was clear ahead, and that the prospects of success looked exceedingly promising. Whereupon Arima, hailing me, directed me to take the lead in the *Chiyo*, steering such a course as seemed desirable, and the rest would follow. Accordingly, we in the *Chiyo* went ahead, the *Fukui* falling in next astern, and the other two retaining their original positions.

We started at a speed of six knots only, to give our stokers a chance to get their boilers into the best possible trim and to raise a good head of steam for the final rush, and as soon as our safety valves began to blow off, we increased the number of our revolutions until, when we arrived within four miles of the harbour's mouth, we were racing in, as though for a wager. At this point the destroyers stopped their engines and lay-to. They had done the first part of their work, and must now wait until we had done ours.

Meanwhile, I had quite made up my mind as to the proper thing to do, and accordingly shaped a course by which, instead of running straight in, and so crossing the track of the searchlight beam, we edged away to the southward and westward, traversing the arc of a circle, and so just keeping outside the range of the beam. But of course this sort of thing could not go on indefinitely; to enter the harbour we must, sooner or later, get within the range of the light; and when we arrived within two miles of the harbour's mouth further concealment became impossible. But we had done not at all badly, for a ten minutes' rush would now see us where we wanted to be, if in the meantime we were not hit and blown out of the water.

As we came within reach of the searchlight, I called down to the engine-room, enjoining those below to give the old packet every ounce of steam they could muster; and the engineer responded by calmly screwing down the safety valves, ignoring the fact that, by doing so, he risked the bursting of the boilers. This was no time for caution, and if the worn-out kettles would only stand the strain for another ten minutes, all might be well.

Slowly the searchlight beam came sweeping round toward us, until it rested fully upon us. It swept on for a yard or two, switched back, paused for a few seconds, and then began to wave wildly to and fro, seemingly by way of a signal, while a solitary gunshot pealed out upon the air. Then the light came back to us, fully revealing the four steamers making their headlong rush for the harbour entrance.

Following that solitary gunshot there was a tense silence, lasting for perhaps half a minute, while searchlight after searchlight was turned upon us from the heights and from every ship so placed that they could be brought to bear. Then, as though at a preconcerted signal, the batteries on the heights and two gunboats anchored at the harbour entrance opened fire upon us, and the darkness of the night was stabbed and pierced by jets of flame, while the air became vibrant with the hiss and scream of projectiles of every description, which fell all round us, lashing the surface of the sea into innumerable jets of phosphorescent foam. The crash of the heavy gun-fire, and the sharper crackle of the quick-firers, raised such a terrific din that it quickly became impossible to make one's voice heard; but my crew had already received their orders, and the moment that we got within range they opened a steady fire with our two old Hotchkisses upon the gunboats at the harbour's mouth, while our destroyers, pushing boldly in after us, opened fire upon the searchlights, hoping to destroy them, and endeavouring by every possible device to distract the attention of the gunners and to draw their fire from us. But in this they were unsuccessful; the Russians at once divined our intention to seal up the harbour, and recognised that it was vastly more important to them to frustrate our purpose than to waste their fire upon our elusive destroyers; and I doubt whether a single gun was turned upon them.

On through the tempest of projectiles we rushed, our old and patched-up engines rattling and clanking and groaning as they worked under such a pressure of steam as they had not known for many a long day; the stokers, after a final firing-up, came on deck, by order of the engineer, and went upon the topgallant forecastle to assist with the guns; and I took up my station by the wheelhouse to con the ship to her appointed berth, which was immediately under Golden Hill, and about a hundred yards from the shore. One of the two gunboats that were guarding the entrance was anchored so nearly in our way that I was sorely tempted to give her the stem and sink her where she lay. But I successfully resisted the temptation, for, had we sunk her, she was too far out to have become an obstruction, while we should probably have smashed in our own bows and gone to the bottom before arriving at our station. As we surged past her, however, within twenty fathoms, we peppered her smartly with our quick-firers, receiving in return a ragged discharge from her entire battery, including a shell from her 6-inch gun which happily passed through our starboard bulwarks and out through our port without exploding. Our foretopmast was at this moment shot away, and fell on deck, but hurt no one, our funnel was riddled with shrapnel, and a bridge stanchion, within a foot of where I was standing, was cut in two; but none of us was hurt. The next moment a shell struck our mainmast and sent it over the side, luckily severing the rotten shrouds and stays also, so that it fell clear and did not foul our propeller. A few seconds later a shell dropped upon our after-deck and exploded, blowing a jagged circular hole of some twenty feet diameter in it, and setting the planks on fire; but a few buckets of water promptly applied sufficed to extinguish the blaze.

Meanwhile we were plugging along in grand style and drawing so near to our destination that I called to the men to cease firing, and for two of them to stand by to let go the anchor while the rest came aft and held themselves ready to jump into our solitary boat when I gave the word. It was wonderfully exciting work, for as we drew nearer in we came into the range of fire of other forts and ships, and the air seemed to be thick with missiles, while shrapnel was bursting all round us, and the water was torn by flying shot to such an extent that our decks were streaming, and all hands of us were wet through with the thrown-up spray.

At length our appointed berth was so close at hand that I rang down to stop the engines and signed to the helmsman to put his helm hard a-port, while I stationed myself close to the electric button, pressure on which would fire the explosives in our hold and blow our bottom out. We were now so close in under the cliffs that the Golden Hill guns could no longer reach us, also we were out of range of the great searchlights, consequently we were enshrouded in darkness, yet the forts on the west side of the harbour still maintained their fire upon us; but we were now lost in the deep shadow of the cliffs, and the shots flew wide.

Half a minute later, I called down the tube to the engineer to send his engines astern to check our way, and then come on deck; and he was still ascending the engine-room ladder when I shouted to the men forward to let go the anchor. It fell with a great splash, and as we had snubbed her at a short scope, she quickly brought up in the exact spot destined for her.

"Lower away the boat, and tumble in, men," I shouted; and the words were hardly out of my mouth when I heard the murmur of the falls through the blocks, and the splash of the boat as she hit the water. A few muffled ejaculations followed as the men slid down the falls, then came the rattle of oars as they were thrown out; and finally a voice crying:

"All ready, Captain, we only wait for you."

"Good!" I ejaculated, and rammed down the button. A tremendous jolt that all but flung me off the bridge, accompanied by a not very loud explosion, followed, the ship trembled as though she had been a sentient thing, and the sound of water, as though pouring through a sluice, reached my ears. Down the ladder I rushed, on to the main deck, seized one of the davit tackles and slid down into the boat; and as the men replied to my question that all were present, the bowman thrust the boat away from the sinking steamer's side, and the oars churned up the water as we pulled away.

"Give way, lively, lads," I cried, as I seized the tiller; "we'll get close inshore, where nobody can see us, and save our skins in that way. We have happily escaped thus far; and it would be a pity for any of us to get hit now. There goes the old *Chiyo*! she hasn't taken long to sink, bless her! She is worth a lot more where she is, at the bottom of Port Arthur harbour, than she was when afloat."

Chapter Seven
The Koryu Maru

Meanwhile the *Fukui Maru* had also reached her destination, and as we pushed off in the boat from the side of our own sinking ship, we heard, through the din of firing and the explosions of bursting shells, the roar of her cable as her crew let go her anchor. I was sitting with my back turned toward her, intent upon getting our boat as close inshore as possible, when the engineer, who was sitting beside me, touched my arm and pointed.

I turned and looked, to see Hirose's ship brought up right in mid-channel—the berth assigned to her; and, bearing down upon her, a Russian destroyer, her funnels and guns spouting flame and smoke as she tore furiously through the water. Another instant, and the destroyer swerved, just clearing the stern of the *Fukui*; there was the flash of a torpedo from her deck tube, a terrific explosion, and the *Fukui* seemed to be hove up out of the water on the top of a great cone of leaping sea intermingled with smoke and flame. The ship had been torpedoed, quite uselessly, indeed worse than uselessly, for the Russians had simply saved our people the trouble of sinking her.

The destroyer passed on, and we temporarily lost sight of her in the darkness and wreathing smoke. We saw the *Fukui's* boat lowered, and the crew get into her; but she remained alongside so long that she only got away barely in time to avoid being dragged down with the ship. Meanwhile, shells were falling not only all round but also aboard the *Fukui*, and we presently saw that she was on fire, as well as sinking. Nearly or quite a dozen shells must have struck her before she finally foundered; but it was not until the next day that we learned the full extent of the tragedy. It then appeared that the explosion of the torpedo had either disconnected or shattered the wires connected with the explosives in the *Fukui's* bottom, and a petty officer named Sugino had gone below to explode the charges. It chanced that this man was a blood-brother of Hirose, and, not returning to the deck as he was expected to do, Hirose went in search of him, after ordering the boat to leave the ship. A few seconds later a shell was seen to strike Hirose on the head, of course killing him instantly. Later on, we heard that his floating body had been picked up in the harbour by the Russians, who, to do them justice, buried it with military honours.

A small air of wind at this time came breathing down the harbour, momentarily dispersing the thick veil of smoke that overhung the water, and we were thus enabled to see that our third ship, the *Yahiko Maru*, had also succeeded in reaching the berth assigned to her, and was at that moment in the very act of sinking, close to the Pinnacle Rock, a great monolith which rose high out of the water on the western side of the harbour's mouth. Thus far, therefore, everything had gone well with the expedition; and now all that remained was for the fourth ship, the *Yoneyama Maru*, to close up the gap that still remained.

I looked round to see if I could see anything of her, and presently the shifting of the searchlight beam from the *Yahiko* revealed her coming along in fine style, and heading straight for her appointed berth. Hitherto, the Russian batteries had been too busy, attending to us others, to take much notice of her, and she appeared to be all ataunto and quite uninjured. I felt curious to see what was going to happen to her, and gave my crew the order to "Easy all, and lay on your oars!"

As I did so, a Russian destroyer—I could not tell whether it was the craft that had torpedoed the *Fukui*, or another—emerged from the darkness, heading straight for the *Yahiko*, as though to run her down! Would they dare? I wondered. Surely not. But if they did not, there was no reason why the *Yahiko* should not; she was a stout-built, merchant steamer, and, old as she was, would shear through the destroyer's thin plating as though it were brown paper. If I had been in charge of the *Yahiko*, I would not have hesitated an instant, indeed I would have jumped at the chance, and in my excitement I leaped to my feet and, making a funnel of my hands, yelled frantically:

"*Yahiko* ahoy! Give her the stem, man; give her the stem!"

But at that precise moment the Russian guns opened again, this time directing their fire upon the *Yahiko*, and my hail was effectually drowned by the crash of the explosions.

I am of opinion that, a moment later, the commander of the *Yahiko* saw his chance, just too late to fully avail himself of it, at all events the bows of the steamer suddenly swept round, and although the destroyer instantly shifted her helm, she was too late to entirely avoid a collision; the rounding of the *Yahiko*'s bow struck her and roughly shouldered her aside, both craft reeling under the impact; and at that instant the destroyer let fly every gun that would bear, the fire from them actually scorching the Japanese crew, who were at that moment preparing to lower their boat. The *Yahiko* passed on, and so did the destroyer, the latter vanishing in the darkness to seaward, while the *Yahiko*, the centre of a very galaxy of bursting shells, staggered on in a sinking condition, and went down at the very moment when, with astounding skill and coolness, her skipper had brought her to the exact spot for which she was intended.

Then it was seen that, either through some miscalculation or, more probably, because the Russians had widened the channel, there still remained an unfilled gap, wide enough for a single ship to pass through! It was a most vexatious thing, after all the trouble that we had taken and the ordeal which we had passed through; but it could not be helped; it was the fortune of war.

Stay, though! Why should it not be helped? All that was needed was another steamer—or perhaps two steamers—to fill the gap, and the thing was done. And, hang it all! I was game to do the job myself to-morrow night, when the Russians would least expect me.

But, to do the job effectually, it was highly necessary to know the exact width of the gap, and the depth of water in it; and now was the time to ascertain those particulars, while we were on the spot. I would do it!

Then came the very practical question: How? What means had we to take soundings, or to measure the gap between the sunken *Fukui* and the *Yoneyama*? I looked about me, and found that all we had with us was the boat's painter, a piece of rope some seven or eight fathoms long, which might serve as a sounding-line, if only we had a sinker of some sort, which, unhappily, we had not. Then one of the men in the boat, realising what I wanted, informed me that, while preparing the boat for lowering, he had chanced to glance into the locker in the stern-sheets, and had noticed a fishing-line there. Would that be of any use? Of course it would; the very thing for sounding, at all events. We had that line out in double-quick time, cut away the hooks, and then proceeded to knot it at exact intervals corresponding with the length of the boat's after-thwart. Precisely what that length might be, we could ascertain afterward.

But, how to measure the width of the gap? There seemed to me to be but one way to do it, and that was by taking the length of our boat herself as a unit of measurement; not a very satisfactory method, I admitted, yet better than nothing. So thereupon we set to work.

Starting at the *Fukui's* mainmast, we dropped the sinker of the fishing-line over the stern and paid out until it reached her deck. Then, giving way with the oars, we felt our way along her deck to her taffrail, lifted the sinker, and dropped it again, clear of the wreck, until it touched bottom. Then, noting the depth as so many knots and fractions of a knot, I jotted the result in my notebook while, the oarsmen keeping the boat in position, another cast was made at the bow end of the boat. Proceeding in this manner, and taking the utmost care to obtain accurate results, we accomplished our task in about half an hour, under a heavy fire from the Russians on the heights, which, strange to say, injured none of us.

This done, we pulled out to sea, and were soon afterward sighted and joined by the *Tsubame* and *Aotaka*, Japanese torpedo-boats, which took us aboard, and exultingly informed us that, a quarter of an hour or so earlier, they had engaged and driven ashore a Russian destroyer, which afterward proved to be the *Silny*, the craft which had torpedoed the *Fukui*, and had narrowly escaped being run down and sunk by the *Yahiko*.

The torpedo-boats' crews made much of us and, I believe, would have given us everything they had, if we would have taken it; but I contented myself with a pannikin of *saki*, to counteract the cold of my drenched clothing, and then asked them to run me off alongside my own ship, the *Kasanumi*, which was hove-to about a mile further out. My crew received me back with literally open arms and loud shouts of "Banzai Nippon!" when I allowed it to be known that we had succeeded in doing all that we had been ordered to do. Young Hiraoka was disposed to regard me as a hero, and to treat me as such, commencing a long complimentary speech of homage and congratulation; but I cut him short by remarking that I was perishing of cold, and dived below to give myself a good rough towelling and to change into dry kit.

When I went on deck again, the dawn was just brightening the eastern sky, and I then noticed that we seemed to have more than our proper complement of men aboard. Inquiring the reason, I learned that the *Kasanumi* had picked up the crew of the *Fukui Maru*, poor Hirose's ship; and they furnished me with the particulars of the gallant fellow's heroic death. I also learned that while we had been engaged in the endeavour to block the harbour, our destroyers had been busily employed in sowing further harmless mines, in accordance with the Admiral's plan to convince the Russians that Japanese mines were useless and need not be feared.

As the daylight strengthened, it revealed our fleet, strung out along the horizon, the Admiral having followed the blocking ships and destroyers upon the off-chance that the Russians might be tempted to come out and attack them, in the event of our failing in our mission.

And at first it appeared as though that chance might be afforded us. For, as we steamed away to the eastward, we saw smoke rising from the funnels of some of the ships in the harbour, and shortly afterward the cruisers *Bayan*, *Novik*, and *Askold* came steaming out, with the battleships following. But it was no go; the Russians opened a long-range fire upon us, to which we gave no reply, slowly retiring instead, in the hope of enticing the enemy's ships to follow us beyond the cover of their batteries. The Russian Admiral, however, was too wary, refusing to be drawn, and, putting up his helm, he returned to the harbour. Nevertheless, the event was not altogether unprofitable to us, for as the Russian ships re-entered the harbour, the *Petropavlosk* ran foul of the *Sevastopol* and damaged her so severely as to render her unfit for further service until she could be repaired.

Meanwhile, the destroyers being no longer required, I devoted myself to the task of reducing to an intelligible state the soundings and measurements which I had that morning taken; and by the time that we were back at our rendezvous I had a little sketch plan of the harbour's mouth ready for the Admiral, showing the exact width of the gap and the depth of water in it, thus enabling him to determine the precise size of the craft required to fill it. I also volunteered to return and fill up the gap that very night, if he could let me have a ship of the required dimensions. But it appeared that he had no ship that could at that time be spared; consequently the job had to wait.

But Togo was profuse in his thanks for my offer; and was pleased to be exceedingly complimentary in his remarks touching my "gallantry" in the matter of taking the soundings, as also upon our conduct generally in taking in the blocking ships under such a terrific fire and sinking them exactly in the required positions. He expressed great grief at the loss of poor Hirose, who was, without doubt, a remarkably promising officer, and would assuredly have further distinguished himself and gone far, had he lived.

Just before we arrived at our rendezvous that night, our high-pressure cylinder developed a bad crack, possibly through some unsuspected flaw in the casting; and as there were no means of repairing it, except temporarily, where we were, and as in the meantime the boat was useless, I received orders to have the crack patched-up as far as possible, and then to proceed to Sasebo, to have a new cylinder fitted. This mishap involved an absence of the *Kasanumi* from our rendezvous for ten days; but, as events proved, it did not matter in the least; for the Admiral, doubtless for good and sufficient reasons, now permitted a period of inaction to occur, during which nothing happened beyond the usual watching of Port Arthur harbour. I availed myself of the opportunity thus afforded to have my little ship docked, scraped, and repainted; while my engineer took his engines entirely to pieces, subjected them to a thorough overhaul, and replaced a few brasses and other matters that were showing signs of wear. He also overhauled the boilers, and fitted quite a number of new tubes; so that when at length the boat left the dry dock she was in first-class condition, and ready for any service that could be reasonably asked of her.

I found awaiting me at the post office quite a nice little batch of most cheering and encouraging letters from my friends, the Gordons, to which I duly replied at considerable length, giving them—and especially Ronald— full particulars of my adventures up to date; and the receipt of their letters made me feel that while a man had such staunch friends as they had proved to be, the world was not such a bad place, after all.

We got back to our rendezvous at the Elliot Islands on the afternoon of 9th April, the little *Kasanumi* looking as smart and spick-and-span as a new pin, her hull, funnels, mast, guns—everything, in fact, except her deck— painted that peculiar tint of medium smoky-grey which experience had proved to render her almost invisible, even in daylight, and absolutely so at night; and the moment that our anchor was down I proceeded aboard the flagship to report myself, and also to deliver mails for the fleet and dispatches for the Admiral, which I had brought with me.

There did not seem to be very much doing at the rendezvous when I arrived, beyond the rebunkering of such craft as needed it; but I noticed a rather smart-looking steamer of about four thousand tons, fitted as a mine-layer, with lighters on both sides of her, out of which a number of very business-like-looking mines were being hoisted.

But when I got aboard the *Mikasa*, and was shown into the Admiral's cabin, I found the little gentleman up to his eyes in business, as usual. He dropped his work, however, when I was announced, and, rising from his chair, greeted me in the most hearty and friendly manner; then, bidding me be seated, he asked me how I had spent my time at Sasebo. He expressed the utmost satisfaction with everything that I had done; and presently, when the orderly brought in a bundle of letters and papers from the mail which I had brought, he opened the latter and, selecting from it a particular sheet—the Tokio *Asahi*, I believe it was—opened it, glanced eagerly at a particular column, and then, with a smile and a pointing finger, handed the sheet to me. It had been opened at the page containing naval intelligence; and glancing at it, I perceived, to my amazement and delight, that I had been gazetted to the rank of Captain, "as from 27th March, in recognition of conspicuous gallantry in connection with the second attempt to close Port Arthur harbour." The two other surviving skippers had also been similarly promoted.

I scarcely knew how to find words eloquent enough to thank Togo for his generous recognition of my services, such as they were; but he would not listen to a word of thanks, insisting that I had honestly earned the promotion, and thoroughly deserved it.

"And now," he concluded, "I am going to give you a further opportunity to distinguish yourself. I have in hand some work, the successful execution of which demands a man who can be depended upon to keep his head and his nerve under the most trying conditions, such as those which existed when you took those soundings and measurements, under, fire, the other day; indeed it was that piece of daring which caused me to select you for the work. You may perhaps have observed a steamer shipping mines— You did? Yes, I thought you would. Well, that steamer is the *Koryu Maru*, a very smart boat, steaming twenty-two knots, which I have had fitted as a mine-layer. The Russians have passed to and fro over our mine-field off Port Arthur, and have had full opportunity to learn that our mines are so harmless that they may be regarded as negligible, so, now, I propose to teach them a new lesson. The mines which the *Koryu* is shipping are not harmless; on the contrary, they are exceedingly formidable affairs, containing charges ranging from one hundred to two hundred pounds of Shimose explosive, and they are arranged to automatically adjust themselves to varying depths of water. The ship which strikes one of them will be done for! Having told you so much, you will readily understand that they are ticklish affairs to handle, particularly when it comes to laying them; hence my choice of you, Captain Swinburne, to supervise and execute the task. I shall be glad if you will go aboard, at your earliest convenience, and make yourself thoroughly acquainted with the mode of handling them, which is essentially different from that of handling the mines to which you have been accustomed."

I thanked the Admiral for this fresh manifestation of his trust in me, and took my leave, pausing only for a few minutes, on my way to the gangway, to exchange greetings with some of the officers of the ship, and reply to their congratulations upon my promotion, the news of which had already got abroad. Then I went down the side, got into my boat, and was pulled across to the *Koryu*, where I found the delicate operation of shipping and stowing the mines in brisk progress. I introduced myself to the officer in charge, who at once proceeded to explain to me the structure and mechanism of the class of mines being dealt with; thus enabling me to understand the danger to be guarded against while handling them; after which he conducted me to my cabin, perched high on the boat deck; and I immediately took possession, sending my boat back to the *Kasanumi* with a note for young Hiraoka, requesting him to take charge during my absence, and another to my steward, instructing him to send me across such things as I immediately needed. The change was greatly the better for me; for whereas my quarters aboard the *Kasanumi* were cramped and of Spartan simplicity, the captain's cabin of the *Koryu* was a spacious and almost luxurious affair, handsomely and comfortably furnished, with all the accommodation that a reasonable man could wish for.

Two days later our fleet weighed and proceeded to sea, leaving the *Koryu* at anchor, with our fourth and fifth destroyer flotillas and fourteenth torpedo-boat flotilla—twelve craft in all—to protect her. My orders were to proceed to sea in time to reach Port Arthur roadstead at midnight of the 12th, sow the harbour approach with mines according to a certain plan, and then retire, with the assurance that, if attacked, there would be a force of ample strength lying in wait to protect me.

One part of my duty—after laying the mines—was to endeavour to entice the Russian fleet to come out in pursuit of me. Experience had taught us that, for some reason with which we were unacquainted, the Russian ships invariably followed a certain course when leaving the harbour, while, when returning, they as invariably followed another; my instructions, therefore, were to sow my mines over the area by which the ships returned to port, while leaving free that area traversed by them when coming out; the reason of course being, that as many ships as possible should be enticed to come out, in the hope that many of them would be destroyed upon their return.

The night of the 12th was a wretched one in some respects for our purpose. The weather was thick; a strong breeze was blowing from the southward, kicking up a nasty sea; it was bitterly cold; and a thin drizzle of fine snow made the thick atmosphere still thicker; so that it was impossible to see farther than a ship's length in any direction. I foresaw, therefore, that I had a very difficult task before me, not only in getting the little torpedo-boats across in the heavy sea, but in depositing the mines in the right place after we should arrive.

To spare the torpedo-boats as much as possible while making the passage against a heavy head sea, I decided to proceed at a speed of ten knots; and we accordingly got under way at five o'clock in the evening, leaving ourselves an hour in hand to cover any delay which we might meet with. I had very carefully studied the tides and the current charts during the afternoon, taken careful note of the strength of the wind, and, taking these matters into consideration, had worked out a course that, unless some of the conditions changed, should take me to the exact spot I wished to reach, at eleven o'clock.

Punctual to the moment we started, "in line ahead," each vessel towing a fog buoy behind her to serve as a guide to the next astern, and these buoys I had at the last moment caused to be coated with luminous paint, to make them visible in the intense darkness.

All went well with us; the destroyers rode the seas like gulls, while, at the moderate speed of ten knots, the torpedo-boats were not only able to keep station perfectly but also avoided washing their crews overboard. At ten-thirty I made the prearranged signal, and my escort hove-to, leaving me to finish my journey and carry out my perilous task alone.

I knew exactly where I was—or rather, where I ought to be—for I had kept a careful reckoning of our progress from the moment of starting, and, unless something had gone wrong, we were then exactly two miles south-east of the Pinnacle Rock lighthouse. But it was necessary to make sure, otherwise I might lay my mines in the wrong place, and all my labour would be useless; I accordingly shaped a course for the lighthouse and cautiously stood in, with a leadsman stationed at each extremity of the overhanging navigating bridge. These took continuous casts of the lead and reported the result to me through my "Number 1," who stood outside my cabin and called to me through an open window, while I stood at the table, with the chart spread open before me, pricking off our position minute after minute, and comparing the leadsmen's results with those shown on the chart, the two agreeing accurately.

At length we reached a point beyond which it would be dangerous to go, and I ordered the engines to be stopped and reversed, at the same time stepping out on to the bridge, to ascertain if anything could be seen. But it was as thick as a hedge, the lighthouse lantern was unlighted, and there was not even a gleam from the searchlight on the cliffs above to enable us to verify our position. True, the roar of breakers close at hand told us we were not far from the shore; but that was all we had to guide us; there was nothing for it, therefore, but to go ahead and do the best we could.

There is no need for me to enter into a detailed and technical description of the operation of laying mines; I will therefore merely state that, despite the adverse conditions, we succeeded in accomplishing our task and withdrawing without mishap. But we were not a moment too soon, for the light of dawn was filtering through the haze as we dropped our last mine and moved cautiously away from the completed field.

The next thing was to find our escort, which we had left two miles out at sea. We were groping our way slowly seaward through the fog, keeping a sharp lookout for the destroyers, when all in a moment the mist lifted, and we sighted them about half a mile distant. And at the same instant, some four miles away to the north-east, appeared a squadron of five destroyers, which we at once identified as our second destroyer flotilla. And yet—no that could scarcely be right, for our "second" consisted of only four boats, while yonder were five—with—yes—a sixth close inshore. I turned to get my binoculars out of the case, in order to investigate a little more closely, and even as I did so the five destroyers became suddenly enveloped in a wreathing cloud of powder smoke, while the sharp, angry bark of quick-fire guns broke the morning silence. The five destroyers were unquestionably engaged in a fight among themselves. The firing continued quite briskly for about five minutes; then there pealed out a sharp, violent explosion, a great cloud of smoke shot into the air; the firing abruptly ceased; and the smoke cleared away just in time to show that one of the destroyers—the craft which we had been unable to identify—was sinking, a shattered, shapeless wreck.

At this moment a cry from my "Number 1" distracted my attention from the interesting little drama which I was eagerly watching, and, turning toward the harbour's mouth, in response to his pointing finger, I saw a big, four-funnelled, two-masted cruiser, which I instantly recognised as the *Bayan*, coming foaming out of harbour, evidently intent upon driving off our destroyers, which were now busily launching their boats to save the crew of the destroyer, which had by this time foundered. I was in the very act of issuing an order for one of our Hotchkisses to be fired, to warn the destroyers, when the *Bayan* opened fire upon them with her light guns, and they were obliged to retreat, double-quick.

Of course the *Bayan* was no match for them in the matter of speed, so after covering the retreat of the second destroyer, which was creeping along close inshore, and pausing to pick up the survivors of the sunken destroyer, the cruiser turned her attention—and her guns—upon us. But we were out of range of her light guns, and for some unknown reason she did not open fire upon us with her heavy weapons, we therefore quickened up to about her own speed, or a trifle less, hoping we might be able to entice her out to where we knew our own cruiser squadron was waiting to cover our retreat. Unfortunately for the success of my scheme, Admiral Dewa, who commanded the squadron, no sooner heard the firing than he put on speed and rushed to our rescue, emerging from the mist and becoming visible while still some three miles away. The instant that they were clear of the fog bank, and could see what was happening, the squadron opened fire upon the *Bayan* with their heavy guns, when that ship was in turn compelled to up helm and beat a hurried retreat, to my intense disgust; for I felt confident that if our cruisers had only lain doggo in the fog bank, I could have cajoled the Russian ship into following me so far out to sea that her retreat could have been cut off, and we should have nabbed her. As it was, the *Diana* and

Novik came rushing out to her rescue; whereupon Dewa, who by this time recognised the mistake he had made, turned and retired, apparently in a panic, for great clouds of smoke were presently seen to be pouring from the funnels of all his ships. But before ten minutes were over it became perfectly evident that the Admiral was "playing foxy," for despite the clouds of smoke, his ships were barely holding their own, if indeed they were doing as much as that. Naturally, we in the *Koryu* at once took our cue from the Admiral, and stoked up for all we were worth, using as much small coal as we could scrape together, in order to increase the volume of smoke pouring from our funnel, while we allowed the *Novik* to gain upon us a trifle from time to time, and then, by an apparently desperate effort, drew away from her again. And this time it really looked as though our ruse was going to prove successful, for the three Russian cruisers continued to chase us with the utmost pertinacity and determination.

Chapter Eight
The Petropavlosk lured to her Doom

The explanation of the Russian cruisers' pertinacity was soon made plain to Admiral Dewa by a wireless message which he picked up, addressed to the captain of the *Novik*, which, decoded, ran thus: "Keep in touch with enemy but do not attack until I join you. Two battleships and *Askold* following to support you. Signed Makarov."

Of course I did not know anything about this until afterward, the *Koryu* not being fitted with a wireless installation; but Dewa at once made a code signal to me instructing me to continue my present tactics; and while this was being done his wireless operators were busily engaged in transmitting a code message to Admiral Togo, who was at that moment lurking, enveloped in mist, some thirty miles away, near the Miao-tao Islands, with his whole battle squadron and the new cruisers *Nisshin* and *Kasuga*.

Makarov, however, was evidently ignorant of that fact; the atmosphere in the neighbourhood of Port Arthur was now quite clear, and to the lookouts on the highest points about the fortress no Japanese ships were visible, save the cruiser squadron, which was undoubtedly in full retreat from the pursuing Russian ships, which it was perfectly evident they were afraid of. It was the moment and the opportunity for which the Russian Admiral had long been pining, the moment when a weak Japanese force, entirely unsupported, lay at his mercy, and now he would smash them!

Accordingly, he hurried aboard the *Petrofiavlosk* and signalled the *Poltava* and *Askold*—both of which, like the flagship, had steam up—to weigh at once and proceed to sea. This was done, with marvellous smartness, considering that the craft were Russian, and presently out they came, their funnels belching immense volumes of black smoke and the water leaping and foaming about their bows as they pounded after us at their utmost speed, which, after all, was only about fourteen knots.

Meanwhile, Dewa, who was bringing up the rear in the *Asama*,—by the speed of which ship the rest of the squadron regulated theirs,—was very cleverly allowing the Russians to slowly overtake him, while the Russians were straining every nerve to do so, stoking up furiously and wasting their coal in the most reckless manner.

Then came an order from the Admiral to me to increase speed and pass ahead of the squadron, out of harm's way, as he was about to open fire upon the Russians. Of course there was nothing for it but to obey, which I did forthwith; but when I had got about a mile ahead, I gradually slowed down again; if there was any fun toward, I was not going to miss it. Besides, it was just possible that I might be of use, for, following the Russian battleships and cruisers, there was now coming up, hand over hand, a crowd of destroyers, against which the *Koryu's* Hotchkisses might be brought into play.

Admiral Dewa only allowed me just bare time to get ahead of his squadron, when he made the signal to open fire upon the pursuers with our cruisers' 8-inch turret guns; and the signal, which had been awaited with the utmost impatience, was promptly responded to with a steady and deadly deliberate fire upon the *Bayan*, which was leading the Russian line. Before her officers had time to realise what was happening, shells were hurtling all about her and raining against her bows and upon her deck, punishing her so severely that they had to stop her engines and allow the rest of the fleet to pass ahead. The Russian fleet, which had thus far been coming on in line ahead, now hurriedly formed line abreast, the two battleships opening fire upon our cruisers with their 12-inch guns. Luckily for us, although the water was smooth the Russian aim was bad, and their shells flew over and on either side of us, but none hit us. Then Dewa, who was far too good a tactician to pit his cruisers against battleships, gave the order to increase speed, and we ran out of range, undamaged.

But only just out of range; for we wanted to draw the Russian ships so far away from Port Arthur that Admiral Togo might have a chance to come up, slip in between them and the fortress, cut off their retreat, and force them to fight. And without a doubt we should have been successful, had not the capricious weather played us a scurvy trick at a critical moment when the Russians were some eighteen miles off the land in a south-easterly direction from Port Arthur. For it was at this moment that the fog, which had hitherto hidden Togo's approaching fleet, suddenly cleared, revealing to the Russian lookouts on the Liau-ti-shan heights, the Japanese warships, racing up from the south-west.

The approach of the Japanese was instantly frantically signalled to the wireless station, which in turn wirelessed the alarming intelligence to the Russian Admiral. A few moments' study of the chart revealed to Makarov the precariousness of his situation. If he turned and retreated at once, he might possibly escape by the skin of his teeth and get back into harbour before Togo's ships could get up to cut him off, and he did not hesitate a moment. Up went the signal to retire, over went the Russians' helms, and away they scuttled back toward their lair, even faster than they came out, while our cruisers, keenly on the watch for some such movement, also wheeled sharply in pursuit, keeping up a steady fire upon the *Bayan* and the *Novik*, the rearmost ships in the Russian line. Naturally, the *Koryu* turned when our cruisers did, following them up at full speed until we were close in their rear, while Dewa was far too busy attending to the pursuit to spare any attention to me and my doings.

It was at this juncture that the Russian destroyers made a gallant effort to check our pursuit by distracting our attention from their big craft to themselves. Believing that they held an important advantage over us in point of speed, they boldly slowed down, dropped astern, and, in two divisions, made a determined demonstration on our two flanks, repeatedly threatening to make a dash, close in, and use the torpedo.

There was one exceptionally audacious craft, the pertinacity of which caused me to take particular notice of her, and keep a specially watchful eye upon her, because I speedily came to the conclusion that she was doing more than merely demonstrate, she was bent upon mischief. She was making a dead set at the *Asama*, our most valuable ship, getting right to windward of her, and pouring dense volumes of black smoke from her four funnels, so forming a screen for herself, under cover of which she was evidently trying to edge in to within effective torpedo range. Of course the *Asama* and one or two of the other cruisers opened fire upon her with their light guns, but we, who had crept up to windward, saw that the smoke screen was serving its purpose admirably, and that although the projectiles were falling all round her, she was not being hit. It occurred to me that now was the time when we in the *Koryu* might be able to render a little useful service, our own destroyers having been unfortunately ordered to return to their rendezvous, some time before, and were now out of sight. Accordingly I gave orders for the gunners to stand by their Hotchkisses, and rang for full speed, also calling down to the engineer for the very last ounce of steam he could get out of his boilers.

Like an arrow shot from a bow, the *Koryu* started forward and, edging well out to windward of the destroyer, opened a brisk fire upon her with our Hotchkisses, aiming at her deck tubes, round which I had seen some men busily clustering. And it was well that I did so, for the Russians were in the very act of launching a torpedo at the moment; indeed they actually *did* launch it, but by one of those extraordinary flukes that sometimes happen, and are so difficult to describe convincingly, one of our shots struck the weapon at the instant that it issued from the tube, wrecking its propeller and rudder and sending it to the bottom.

Evidently the destroyer's crew had been so completely absorbed in their attempt upon the *Asama* that they had been oblivious to our approach; but now, seeing us bearing menacingly down upon her, her skipper suddenly shifted his helm and would fain have beaten a retreat. As it happened, however, we had by this time drawn up abreast and were between him and his friends, so he evidently came to the conclusion that there was nothing for it but to fight his way out; accordingly he made a dash to cut out across our bows, at the same time turning his whole battery of guns upon us. I instantly ordered my men to leave their guns and get away aft, out of the way of the shot, dismissing the quartermaster also, and taking the wheel in his stead.

" Then there arose a sudden outery as the crew forsook their guns. "

At such short range, his shots could not possibly miss, and in less than a minute our bows and fore deck showed a very pretty "general average," a 6-pound shell blowing a hole through our plating and wrecking the topgallant forecastle, while several 4-pound projectiles pierced our funnel, blew away our fore topmast, and knocked one corner of the wheelhouse to smithereens. But I did not care; the purpose which I had in mind was fully worth all the damage and more, and I knew now that unless I personally was hit and disabled, I should be able to accomplish it. For I meant to give that impudent destroyer the stem, to run her down and sink her, knowing that our stout bows would shear through her thin plating as though it were paper. And the *Koryu* had the speed to do it, the destroyer having lost much of her speed by the barnacles and weed on her bottom, which she exposed at every roll.

Evidently the Russian did not realise my purpose until it was too late; he seemed to think I was a fool who was giving him a chance to inflict a deadly raking upon me as he crossed my bows; and it was not until I suddenly shifted my helm, rendering a collision inevitable, that what was going to happen dawned upon him. Then there arose a sudden outcry as the crew forsook their guns and made a mad dash at the two small boats slung to the davits, there was a frantic jangling of bells down in the destroyer's engine-room, an officer on her bridge snatched a revolver from his belt and snapped off five shots at me in as many seconds—none of which took effect—and then we were upon her. With scarcely any perceptible shock we struck her fair and square amidships, right in the wake of where I judged her boiler-room would be; there was a horrible crackling and rending of wood and iron as our stem sheared into and through her deck, a clamour of yells from the crew as they fought with each other in their mad haste to lower the boats, and the destroyer heeled over until she was almost on her beam-ends, a volleying succession of deep, heavy *booms*, accompanied by a tremendous outburst of steam, proclaimed that her boilers had burst, and at the same instant she seemed to crumple up and break completely in two, her bow-half sweeping along our port side, while her stern-half drove past to starboard, the crew, unable to get the boats afloat, leaping desperately overboard. A moment before striking the craft, I had rung down an order to the engine-room to stop the engines, and shouted for my crew to stand by with ropes' ends; and now several of these were hove, by means of which we managed to drag three Russians up on to our deck; and then we backed astern and fished up eight more, all of whom we marched below and locked up securely. The other poor fellows, including the captain of the boat, must have gone down with her, for we saw nothing more of them. But we had taught the destroyers a lesson, for thenceforth they kept their distance.

Examining into our own condition, we discovered that our injuries arising out of the collision amounted to about as much paint scraped off as might be replaced by the contents of a 10-pound tin, while all other damage was so high above the waterline as to make it of no practical account. And we had not a man injured; so I considered that we had emerged from the encounter very cheaply.

It was just half-past nine o'clock, by my watch, when, bursting through the curtains of haze, our battle fleet hove in sight in the south-west quarter, with flags flying, the water leaping and foaming about their cutwaters, and a fine "white feather" of steam playing on the top of their waste-pipes, indicating that the stokers were maintaining a full head of steam in the boilers. But—Japanese luck again—they were just too late; for at that moment the Russian fleet entered the protective zone of their shore batteries and, with a very poor attempt at bravado, slowed down to a speed of about six knots, while the *Sevastopol, Pobieda,* and *Peresviet* came steaming out to meet them. They had managed to escape by the skin of their teeth; and now, in accordance with the instructions given to the Admiral not to risk his ships by pitting them against the shore batteries, we also were obliged to slow up, and finally to stop our engines. As a matter of fact, the time had come for us to retire; but evidently everybody was curious to see what would be the result of my mine-laying operations of the preceding night, and by common consent we all lay-to.

We had not long to wait. We saw some signalling going on between the flagship and the three craft that had come out to meet the fleet; saw the trio fall into line in rear of the retreating fleet; and then, while our glasses were glued to our eyes as we watched the procession of great ships sweeping majestically toward the harbour's mouth—from which they were then little more than a mile distant—we suddenly beheld a tremendous flash of fire envelop the bows of the *Petropavlosk,* the flagship, which was leading the way into the harbour. The flash was accompanied by the upheaval of a gigantic cone of water and an outburst of thick yellow smoke which at once told us that one of our mines had got in its deadly work. Instantly a great exultant roar of "Banzai Nippon!" burst forth from the throats of the eagerly watching Japanese, but it was as instantly checked when they began to realise the full magnitude of the disaster that had befallen their enemy. For even before the sound of the shattering explosion reached our ears we saw her fore topmast fall, saw long tongues of flame leap up from her decks, saw her-two funnels whirl over and fall, one after the other, while her bridge, pilot-house, and foremast soared high into the air; and so tremendous was the force of the explosion that actually one of her 6-inch gun turrets was torn bodily from its strong fastenings and hurled some twenty feet aloft, to crash downward again upon the hapless ship's deck, while a great burst of flame, probably due to the explosion of her boilers, shot up where her two funnels had stood a moment before. A series of heavy explosions followed, seeming to indicate the explosion of her magazines, and then the doomed ship became enveloped in a thick haze of green smoke, in the midst of which played great streams of fire. Through that terrible green haze we were just able to see that she had taken a heavy list to starboard; then her bows dipped, her stern rose until her two propellers were lifted out of the water, a great mushroom-shaped pillar of smoke shot up from her, and—she was gone! And all this had happened in the short space of two minutes, during which shells from our battleships were falling thick and fast about the Russian ships, which had stopped their engines when the explosion occurred, while some of them lowered boats, in the hope of being able to render assistance to the unfortunate flagship.

"—the doomed ship became enveloped in a thick haze of smoke—"

The doomed ship became enveloped in a thick haze of smoke- "

With the disappearance of the flagship, the Russian fleet resumed its way toward the harbour, the *Pobieda* now being at the head of the line. But scarcely had she started her engines when an enormous pillar of flame, water, and smoke enveloped her amidships. She, too, had come into contact with one of our mines, but, fortunately for her, with much less disastrous results than those attending the destruction of the *Petropavlosk*. She instantly listed, showing that she was severely damaged, but beyond that nothing further happened, so far as we could see, except that the second explosion appeared to have created a perfect panic among the Russians, who immediately opened a terrific fire with every gun, big or small, apparently at random, for we could see the shots throwing up great jets of foam in the water all round them. Later, we learned that when the second explosion occurred, some one aboard one of the ships yelled that the fleet was surrounded by Japanese submarines, discharging torpedoes; hence the frantic firing at the water. Of course the assertion was groundless, since, as a matter of fact, the Japanese had no submarines; but it is not very surprising that, with two disasters, one following so closely upon the heels of the other, the Russians should jump to the conclusion that they had been attacked by submarines; for it must be remembered that we had carefully educated them into the belief that our mines were quite harmless.

The loss of the *Petropavlosk* was a terrible misfortune for the Russians, for she was one of their most formidable ships; being armed with four 12-inch guns of the most recent design, mounted in pairs in her two big turrets; with, as a secondary battery, twelve 6-inch quick-fire guns, eight of which were mounted in pairs in four small turrets placed, two on either beam, behind 5-inch steel armour, while the other four were in casemates similarly protected. She had six torpedo tubes, and we conjectured that she probably had a torpedo in each tube which exploded at the time of the disaster.

As for the *Pobieda*, our spies were able to ascertain that the mine which damaged her had breached three of her big compartments and some smaller ones, so that it was only with the utmost difficulty she was got into harbour and beached in time to save her. Also one set of her Belleville boilers was so severely damaged as to be rendered useless. Consequently she, too, was put out of action for a considerable period.

Thus, at one fell swoop, the Russian fleet was reduced in strength by two battleships. But their worst loss was their Admiral; for it is indisputable that Makarov was the most able, energetic, and enterprising naval leader they possessed.

Two days later, more mines were laid in Port Arthur roadstead, and another attempt was made to entice the Russian fleet to come out and fight us; but the attempt was a failure. As a matter of fact, it afterwards transpired that, upon receipt of the report announcing the loss of the *Petropavlosk* and the damage to the *Pobieda*, the authorities at Petersburg had telegraphed orders to the effect that the Port Arthur fleet was on no account whatever to leave the harbour until the arrival of Admiral Skrydloff, Makarov's successor.

Failing in this, Admiral Togo dispatched the cruisers *Nisshin* and *Kasuga* to Pigeon Bay, to make a high-angle fire attack upon the fortress and the ships in the harbour. I was not engaged in either of these attempts, the Admiral considering that I had well earned and was deserving of a few days' rest. Besides, he very properly wished to give some of his other officers a chance to distinguish themselves. But I understood that, with the exception of silencing a new battery which the Russians had built commanding the bay, the bombardment was not attended with any very important results.

On the following day our little Admiral, whom some have named the Japanese Nelson, dispatched a squadron of ten cruisers, accompanied by a torpedo flotilla, to attempt to bring the Vladivostock squadron to battle. This squadron was accompanied by a cargo steamer named the *Kinshiu Maru*, loaded with coal and spare stores for the use of the squadron while away from its base; and the expedition was placed under the command of Vice-Admiral Kamimura, with the cruiser *Idzumi* as his flagship. I had now had a little rest, and as there seemed to be no immediate prospect of serious fighting at Port Arthur, I volunteered for the expedition, and was temporarily attached to the *Idzumi* as a supernumerary.

We left our base among the Elliot Islands on the 16th of April; and after an uneventful cruise of a week's duration arrived at the port of Gensan, on the eastern coast of Korea, about two-thirds of the distance from the Elliots to Vladivostock.

There was a Japanese consul at this place, and upon our arrival off the port he and the Commandant came off in a steam launch and, boarding the *Idzumi*, requested an interview with the Admiral, which was at once granted, and the pair were conducted to Kamimura's cabin, where they remained for the best part of an hour. At the close of the interview the visitors entered their steam launch and returned to the shore. Some ten minutes later, Kamimura sent for me; and when I entered the cabin I found him poring over a chart of the east coast of Korea. He welcomed me with the usual elaborate courtesy of the Japanese in their intercourse with each other as well as with strangers, and invited me to approach the table.

"I am particularly glad that it is my good fortune to have the pleasure of your honourable company, Captain Swinburne," he began; "for an occasion has just arisen upon which I think your services may prove of the utmost value. You see this little place—Iwon—on the chart. The two honourable gentlemen who have just visited me—the Commandant of Gensan and our Japanese consul stationed here—inform me that rumours have reached their ears of certain suspicious occurrences at Iwon which seem to point to the possibility that the Russian Government may be contemplating the dispatch of a large body of troops to Vladivostock by rail, their embarkation there for Iwon, at which spot they may land, march across Korea, and take our troops at Port Arthur in the rear. To tell you the truth, I have not much faith in the idea, the only point in its favour being that such a movement would be wholly unanticipated by us. But in view of the information which I have just received, it is my bounden duty to investigate the matter; and I therefore propose to dispatch the *Kinshiu Maru* on a reconnoitring expedition to Iwon, to ascertain what foundation, if any, there may be for the suspicion. As of course you are aware, she carries a small detachment of troops, who may be very useful, should any opposition be met with. These troops will, of course, be commanded by their own officers, while Captain Yago will continue to command the ship. But, being a merchant seaman, he has had no experience of landing troops; and that is where your services will prove of value, especially should any resistance be offered. I therefore want you to change over temporarily to the *Kinshiu*, still as a supernumerary, but with my authority for you to take charge of and superintend the landing and subsequent embarkation arrangements. I am afraid this will mean a certain amount of disappointment for you, since as soon as you have started I shall proceed in search of the Vladivostock fleet. But you must endeavour to console yourself with the reflection that I may not find them, or be able to entice them to come out and fight me."

It was true, I certainly did feel a bit disappointed, for I most earnestly desired to see what it was like to be engaged in a regular pitched battle, even though it were only between a couple of hostile squadrons; but I was where I was, to lend a hand where required, not to pick and choose what I would or would not do; in any case I was not going to make occasion for it to be said that an Englishman had unwillingly accepted any duty offered to him; therefore with as much cheerfulness as I could muster, I expressed my perfect readiness to do my best; whereupon Kamimura gave me my written instructions and dismissed me to pack up such few of my belongings as I thought I might need. However, as I had only brought a very limited kit aboard the *Idzumi*, I decided to take everything, since it would all go into a small portmanteau.

Meanwhile, the skipper of the *Kinshiu* had been signalled to have a cabin prepared for me, and for him and Captain Honda, the officer in command of the troops, to repair on board the *Idzumi* to receive their instructions. They of course came at once, had a short interview with the Admiral, and we all left together, Honda doing the honours of the ship, welcoming me on board the transport, and introducing his fellow-officers, all of whom seemed very jolly fellows, with but one desire, namely, to get to grips with the Russians.

We left Gensan that afternoon, escorted by the 11th torpedo-boat flotilla under the command of Commander Takebe; the cruisers weighing at the same time and heading east, in the hope of seeing or hearing something of the Russians.

Unfortunately for us, we had not been under way a couple of hours before we ran into a dense fog which delayed our progress to such an extent that we did not reach Iwon until the morning of the 25th. We found there a long, roughly constructed wooden jetty running far enough out from the shore to give a depth of about six feet alongside its head, at low water, which greatly facilitated our landing; and, ashore, we discovered certain artfully concealed field-works of such a character that, armed with a few heavy guns, they might have pretty effectually covered a landing, unless interfered with by a very powerful force. But our visit was evidently quite unexpected, for we only found a small body of Russian troops—about a hundred or so, with a squadron of Cossacks—in possession; and a few shells from our torpedo-boats sent them to the right-about in double-quick time. We destroyed the earthworks, and the jetty, as a precautionary measure, and, having reconnoitred the country for several miles in every direction without discovering anything very alarming, returned to the ship the same night, without casualties of any kind.

It was now about six o'clock in the evening. During the greater part of the day the weather had been beautifully fine; but toward three o'clock in the afternoon a heavy bank of dark, slate-coloured cloud had gathered in the eastern quarter of the sky, so quickly rising and spreading that, by five o'clock, the entire firmament had become obscured, the wind dropped to a dead calm, the light dwindled to a murky, unnatural kind of twilight, there were a few flickerings of sheet lightning, low down on the horizon, occasionally accompanied by a low muttering of distant thunder, and the mercury was dropping with rather ominous rapidity.

I confess that, for my own part, I felt a bit puzzled; I did not quite know what to make of the weather indications. It might be that nothing worse than a violent thunderstorm was brewing; but against this theory there was to be set the sudden and ominous decline of the barometric pressure. We had fulfilled our task, and were preparing to get under way, when Takebe, who was in command of the torpedo flotilla, came aboard to consult with our skipper as to the advisability of going to sea, in the face of such threatening conditions.

Unfortunately, our escort was composed entirely of torpedo-boats; and although they were staunch enough little craft of their kind, they were nothing like such good sea boats as our destroyers. The latter were, under able management, capable of riding out practically any weather, but with the torpedo-boats it was rather a different story. Some of those that we had with us were small and rather ancient, their engines were not to be too implicitly relied upon, and their boilers were nearly worn-out; indeed, they would never have been detailed for the service, had it been thought that there would be any likelihood of real righting. If by any chance they should happen to be caught at sea in anything like a heavy gale, and anything should go wrong with either their engines or their boilers, the probability was that they would founder, taking all hands with them.

It was these considerations that were weighing upon Commander Takebe's mind when he came aboard the *Kinshiu* to consult with Captain Yagi; and it was evident from his first words that he was all in favour of adopting the prudent course, and staying where we were until it could be seen how matters were going to turn out. But Yagi and he looked at things with different eyes. In the first place, Yagi did not believe that the portents indicated anything more serious than, at worst, a sharp thunderstorm, while at the same time his instructions from Kamimura were that the reconnaissance was to be executed with the utmost dispatch, and that, this done, he was to immediately return to Gensan, so that he might be on the spot in the event of the cruisers needing to re-bunker. And in any case, should it come on to blow, as Commander Takebe seemed to fear, he had no apprehensions concerning the *Kinshiu*; she was a good sturdy little ship, and would weather out the worst that was at all likely to happen.

The two discussed the matter together for quite half an hour, occasionally referring to me for my opinion; but both of them were considerably older than I, and had had a much more varied experience than myself of the somewhat peculiar weather conditions of the Sea of Japan; I therefore said as little as possible, and did not attempt to offer a word of advice to either of them. Finally, the matter ended by each of them having his own way—that is to say, Yagi decided to leave for Gensan forthwith, unescorted, taking such trifling risk as there might be—which, they both agreed, amounted practically to none at all—while Takebe determined to study the safety of his command by remaining where he was and awaiting developments. Accordingly, as soon as the Commander had gone, the order was given to get the anchor; and about seven o'clock we steamed out to sea.

Chapter Nine
The Adventure of the Kinshiu Maru

By the time that we were fairly out at sea, it was pitch dark, not a star to be seen, and to add still further to the obscurity, a light mist gathered, as it so often does in the Japan Sea, so that by eight o'clock it was only with the utmost difficulty that we were able to discern a small junk which we had in tow, and which had been employed by us to facilitate the landing of the troops. The weather still continued overcast, and the play of sheet lightning gradually grew more vivid and frequent; but there was no wind, and not much sea; and as time went on I began to think, with Yagi, that Takebe's apprehensions had been groundless, and that we were in for nothing worse than, may be, a thunderstorm, after all.

I spent a couple of hours in the saloon that night, watching the infantry officers, of whom there were six, playing some wonderful game of cards, of which I could make nothing, and then strolled up on the bridge to see what the weather was like, and to have a yarn with Yagi, before turning in for the night. It was still hazy and very overcast, but there was not a breath of air save the draught created by the motion of the ship, and there was a very beautiful display of sheet lightning, almost continuous, which lighted up the clouds, the mist, and the sea in the most marvellous manner.

The ship was then heading south-east, with all her lights burning brightly, as in duty bound, and I was sitting astride a camp-stool, with my shoulders resting against the port rail of the bridge, while Yagi, also occupying a camp-stool, sat facing me. He was spinning some yarn—a sort of Japanese fairy tale, it seemed to be—about a geisha, while I was staring contemplatively into the darkness over the starboard bow, watching the wonderful play of the lightning, when suddenly, as a flash lighted up the gloom, I thought I caught a momentary glimpse of three or four dark shapes, about a mile away, broad on the starboard bow. If I had really seen those shapes, they could only be ships, *and they were showing no lights*; I therefore ruthlessly cut into the skipper's yarn by directing his attention to the point where the momentary vision had revealed itself.

"What is that you say?" he exclaimed. "Ships without lights? Then it must be our Admiral, still hunting for the Vladivostock squadron. Well, we have not seen them, and we had better tell him so, and at the same time inquire whether he has any fresh orders for us. Mr Uchida,"—to the chief officer,—"our squadron is away out there, somewhere on the starboard bow. Have the goodness to honourably make our night signal, as I wish to speak the Admiral."

Uchida hurried away and, the signal lanterns being always kept ready for immediate use, in less than a minute they were hoisted. Meanwhile there had been no further lightning flashes to illuminate the darkness, and I rose to my feet, for we were still steaming ahead at full speed, and I had a feeling that we must be drawing pretty close to the strangers. As I did so, our signal was answered by the imperative order: "Stop immediately!" And at the same instant a brilliant and protracted flicker of sheet lightning revealed four large ships, not more than three cables' lengths distant. The leading ship was a big lump of a four-funnelled cruiser, the funnels coloured white, with black tops, and she carried three masts. The second craft was very similar in general appearance to the first, also having four white, black-topped funnels, and three masts. The third was a two-masted, three-funnelled ship; while the fourth was of distinctly ancient appearance, being of the period when sails were as much used as steam. She had two funnels, and was barque-rigged, with royal yards across, but she was now under steam, with all her canvas furled. We had no such ships in our fleet, while I instantly identified the barque-rigged craft as the Russian cruiser *Rurik*, of the Vladivostock squadron! That squadron, then, for which Admiral Kamimura was especially hunting, was actually at sea, and we had fallen in with it!

There was not the least doubt about it. In every wardroom and gunroom of every Japanese warship there was an album containing a beautiful, complete set of photographs of every ship in the Russian navy, each ship being pictured from at least four different points of view; and it was a part of every officer's duty to study these photographs until he had acquired the ability to identify at sight any Russian warship he might chance to encounter. Thus, in the leading ship of the squadron in sight, a moment's reflection enabled me to recognise the *Rossia*, with, astern of her, the *Gromoboi*, then the *Bogatyr*, and finally the *Rurik*.

"Jove!" I exclaimed. "We've done it now, with a vengeance, Yagi. Those four ships comprise the Russian Vladivostock squadron; and we are right under their guns! Stop her, man, for heaven's sake. It is the only thing you can do. If you don't, the beggars will sink us out of hand."

"They will probably do that in any case," growled Yagi, as he laid his hand on the engine-room telegraph and rang down an order to stop the engines. "But, as you honourably say, Captain, it is the only thing to be done, although it means the interior of a Russian prison for all hands of us."

As the *Kinshiu's* engines stopped, the *Rossia* turned her searchlights upon us, brought her guns to bear, and lowered two boats, the crews of which we could see were armed to the teeth. And at the same moment two destroyers loomed up out of the darkness, one of which stationed herself on our port bow, while the other placed herself upon our starboard quarter, each of them with their tubes and guns manned. Evidently, the Russians did not mean to leave us the smallest loophole for escape.

The six Japanese infantry officers, noting the stoppage of our engines, came rushing up on deck to learn what was the matter; and upon hearing that the strange ships which had stopped us were Russian warships, hurried away below again, presumably, I thought, to give orders of some sort to the troops under their command.

The *Rossia*, with the way she had on her, had by this time closed to within about twenty-five fathoms of us; and at this juncture an officer on her bridge hailed, ordering our skipper to send a boat.

"Good!" ejaculated Yagi. "We will do so. But we will not go aboard the *Rossia*. Oh, no. We will slip away in the darkness and make for the land. And you will honourably accompany us, will you not, Captain? A Russian prison has no attractions for you, eh?"

"You are right, my friend, it has not," I answered; "for which reason I must decline to accompany you. Because you will never get away, Yagi. How can you, with those searchlights turned full upon us, and those destroyers where they are?"

"Nevertheless, I shall try," answered the skipper; and he turned away to bellow an order to the crew to clear away and lower the port lifeboat, the port side being shielded from the glare of the searchlights. Then I heard him order the chief officer to superintend the lowering of the boat, and at the same time to smuggle an extra breaker of water and a bag or two of biscuits into her.

Then he turned again to me. "If you will not come with us, what will you honourably do, my friend?" he demanded.

"Oh," said I, "I shall join the infantry officers below, and see what they are going to do." And without further parley, I ran down the ladder and made my way below to the saloon, where I found the six officers sitting at the table, looking very pale and grave.

"Well, gentlemen," I cried, "here we are, in a nice little Russian trap. What do you propose to do?"

"We thought at first of performing hari-kari," said one of them. "But Captain Nagai, with whom you were discussing the subject of hari-kari, only the night before last, appears to have come round to your way of thinking that it is better to live for the Emperor than to die for him. He argues—as you did—that a dead man can do nothing for his Emperor, whereas a living man may be able to do many things; in which statement there is truth. Therefore we propose to surrender to the Russians, in the honourable hope that we may be able to effect our escape, sooner or later, and return to fight for Nippon. What do you honourably propose to do, Captain?"

"Oh," said I, "to surrender seems the most sensible thing to do, and doubtless I shall do it—eventually. Meanwhile, however, I think I will toddle up on deck again, and see how Yagi and the ship's crew are getting on. They are going to try to slip away in the ship's lifeboat, you know?"

"Banzai!" cried one of the officers. "I hope they will honourably succeed. But, having decided to surrender, I think the safest place is down here. Doubtless we shall soon see you again."

"Y-e-s,—possibly," I replied. "But I shall not surrender until the last moment; so, if you do not see me again, you may conclude that I have found some means of effecting my escape, and have seized them."

Saying which, I shook hands with them all round, and returned to the deck. During my brief visit to the saloon, Yagi and his men had got their boat into the water, and were now pulling boldly for the *Rossia*; but I noticed that directly they passed out of the area of radiance cast by the searchlight, they shifted their helm sharply and, crossing the cruiser's bows, were evidently endeavouring to slip past her in the gloom of her own shadow.

Then, suddenly, an idea occurred to me. The *Kinshiu Maru* had in tow a small junk, or lighter, which we had used to facilitate the landing of the soldiers at Iwon. Where was she now?

Crouching low under the cover of the bulwarks, to avoid being seen by those aboard the *Rossia*, I slipped aft and, cautiously peering over the taffrail, saw that she had drifted right in under the *Kinshiu's* counter, where she was momentarily threatening to bilge herself against the steamer's iron rudder, as the two craft ground against each other on the swell. The forward half of her lay in the deep shadow of the *Kinchiu's* stern—a shadow rendered still deeper and more opaque by the vivid brilliance of the searchlight beam that covered the stern-half of her, and it immediately occurred to me that if I could but climb down into her, unobserved, and cut her adrift, I might possibly contrive to avoid entering a Russian prison after all.

No sooner thought of than done; the moment was propitious, the towing hawser lay under my hand, and in another moment I was down upon her tiny forecastle, hacking away at the grass rope with my pocket-knife. The blade was keen, as a sailor's knife should always be, and with a few vigorous slashes the hawser was severed and I was adrift. Then, taking advantage of the heave of the two craft, I managed to move the junk until she lay entirely in the shadow cast by the *Kinshiu's* hull.

At this juncture I heard the gruff voices of Russians overhead, on the transport's deck, and, thinking discretion the better part of valour under the circumstances, dropped off the junk's short fore deck into her shallow hold and there concealed myself, lest any inquisitive Russian should peer over the bulwarks, catch sight of me, and order me up on deck again. I don't know whether it occurred to any of the enemy to look over the side, but I do not think so; at all events, if they did, nobody took the trouble to come down and search the junk; and in a few minutes the voices ceased; I took it that the visitors had gone below to search the ship. If they had, what would happen to them, with over a hundred armed Japanese soldiers down there?

I had not long to wait for an answer to this question. About two minutes of silence succeeded to the sudden cessation of the Russians' voices on deck, and then the muffled crack of a pistol-shot rang out from the *Kinshiu's* interior, instantly followed by a shout of "Banzai Nippon!" and the crack of several rifles; there arose a sudden outburst of yells and execrations in Russian, a stampede of many feet along the deck, the sounds of a scuffling hand-to-hand fight, a volley of orders from the Russian officer in command of the boarding party, a hoarse hail from one of the warships, and then the rattle and splash of oars hastily thrown out. Evidently, the Japanese soldiers had given the intruders a warm reception.

The hurried departure of the boarding party was quickly followed by a rolling volley of rifle-fire from the *Kinshiu*, apparently directed upon the retreating boats, for I heard cries and groans which seemed to proceed from them. Then, from the *Rossia* came the sudden, snapping bark of her quick-firers and machine-guns, and a storm of missiles crashed through the transport's thin bulwarks or flew whining overhead, intermingled with shrieks, groans, and excited shouts from the Japanese soldiers, who had evidently resolved to die fighting, rather than surrender. The sounds awakened the fighting instinct within me; I felt that, let happen what would, I must be among those gallant fellows, doing my share of the work; and I nipped out from under the junk's short deck, intent upon climbing aboard the *Kinshiu* again. And then I found that during the short period of my seclusion, the junk had parted company, and was now a good twenty feet distant from the transport. True, I might jump overboard and swim the intervening space, and I was actually poising myself for the dive when the question flashed into my brain: How was I to get aboard, how climb the vessel's smooth iron side. There were no ropes hanging overboard, save the severed towing hawser, and I had cut through that so high up that even when the steamer's stern dipped, the end did not reach within a couple of feet of the water. I recognised that whether I would or not, I must now stay where I was, for return to the steamer was impossible. And while I stood there on the junk's short fore deck, watching the scene with fascinated eyes, that awful, unequal duel went on between the Japanese rifles and the *Rossia's* machine-guns; the soldiers frenziedly yelling "Banzai Nippon!" between each volley, while the Russian gunners plied their pieces in grim silence. The *Kinshiu's* deck, I knew, must be by this time a veritable shambles, for the Russian cruiser lay close aboard, and her machine-guns could sweep the transport's decks from stem to stern; moreover, the rapid and ominous slackening of the rifle-fire testified eloquently to the frightful carnage that was proceeding. The cries of "Banzai Nippon!" were no longer thundered forth in a defiant roar, but were raised by a few voices only, which were almost drowned by the dreadful shrieks and moans of the wounded and dying.

Then, suddenly, there occurred a frightful explosion, the *Kinshiu Maru* was hove up on a mountain of foaming water which belched forth fire and smoke, the air became suddenly full of flying splinters and wreckage, a heavy fragment of which smote me full upon the forehead and knocked me back into the junk's hold, and as my senses left me I was dimly conscious of a wailing cry, pealing out across the water, of "Sayonara!" (Farewell for ever). It was the last good-bye to Emperor, country, and all who were nearest and dearest to them of that heroic little band of Japanese infantry-men who preferred to die fighting gloriously, rather than win inglorious safety by surrender. The Russians had made an end of the affair by torpedoing the transport, and she must have sunk within a very few minutes.

When I recovered my senses it was broad daylight. For a few moments I knew not where I was, or what had happened to me, but I was conscious of the most splitting headache from which I had ever suffered in my life. The next thing that dawned upon me was that I was lying in the bottom of a small craft of some sort, which was rolling and plunging most atrociously on a short, choppy sea, that I was chilled to the very marrow, and that water was washing about and over me with every motion of the boat. I was wet to the skin and, although shivering with cold, my blood scorched my veins as though it were liquid fire.

I sat up, staring vaguely about me, and then became aware of a curious stiff feeling in the skin of my face. Putting my hands to my head, to still the throbbing smart of it, I found that my hair was all clogged with some sticky kind of liquid which, upon looking at my hands, I found to be blood, evidently my own. This at once explained the curious stiff feeling of my face; it was probably caused by dry caked blood. But, to make sure, I sprang open the case of my watch—the polished surface serving well enough for a mirror—and gravely studied my reflected image. I must have presented a ghastly sight, for my whole face was a mask of blood, out of which my eyes glared feverishly. Then, as I continued to stare at the interior of my watch-case, wondering what it all meant, my memory of the events of the preceding night—I knew it must be the preceding night, because my watch was still going—all came back to me, and I understood where I was.

Scrambling giddily to my feet, I looked about me and saw a bucket rolling to and fro on the junk's bottom-boards. The sight suggested an idea to me and, taking the bucket and the end of a small line which I bent on to the handle, I somehow managed to hoist myself up on to the small foredeck and, lying prone—for I dared not as yet trust myself to stand—I lowered the bucket, and drew it up again, full of clean, sparkling salt-water. Into this I plunged my head, keeping it immersed as long as my breath would allow, meanwhile removing the blood from my face and hair as well as I could. The contact of the cold salt-water made my lacerated forehead and scalp smart most atrociously, yet it relieved my headache and greatly refreshed me. Then, stripping off my wet shirt, I tore a long strip from it and, thoroughly saturating it in the clean salt-water, bound up my wound as best I could, after which I felt distinctly better.

Then, sitting on the little deck, I looked about me to see if I could discover any traces of last night's horror; but there was a moderate breeze blowing, and I instantly recognised that the junk must have drifted several miles from the spot where the disaster had occurred. There was nothing to be seen, no, not so much as a solitary scrap of wreckage, within the radius of a mile, beyond which everything was blotted out by a curtain of haze.

By this time I had pretty completely recovered my senses, and was able to fully realise my situation. I was wet, cold, feverish, and horribly thirsty, and was the sole occupant of a small, leaky junk of about twenty-five tons, without masts or sails, these having been removed in order the better to fit her for the duty of carrying troops. She had a pair of sweeps aboard, it is true; but they were so ponderous that each demanded the strength of four men to work it; they were therefore quite useless to me, even had I known precisely where I was, which I did not. All I knew was that I was some fifty miles, or thereabout, to the southward and eastward of Iwon; but I might as well have been five hundred miles from the place, for all the means I had of returning to it, or even of making a shot at Gensan. The fact was that I was adrift in a hulk; and the utmost that I could do was to keep her afloat, if possible, and patiently wait for something to come along and take me off her.

Realising this, I proceeded to overhaul the junk, with a view to ascertaining what were her resources. I remembered that a cask of fresh water had been put aboard her for the use of the troops while landing and embarking; and I soon found this, still more than half-full, snugly stowed away under her foredeck, with a lot of raffle consisting of odds and ends of line of varying sizes, a fragment of fishing-net, a few short lengths of planking, and other utterly useless stuff. I drank dipper after dipper of water, until my raging thirst was quenched, and then stripped off my clothes, wrung them out, and spread them to dry in the wind while I rubbed my body dry with my hands, employing a considerable amount of exertion, in order to restore warmth to my cramped limbs. In this effort I was at length successful; and my next business was to search the other end of the junk, in the vague hope that I might find something in the way of food; but there was none; therefore I had to go hungry. I had a bucket, however, and with this I bailed the hooker practically dry, as much to pass the time and keep myself warm, as for any other reason. Then, having done everything that I could think of, all that remained for me was to wait as patiently as might be for something to come along and rescue me.

My position was by no means an enviable one. I had no food; but, for the moment, that did not greatly matter, since the smart of my wound had made me feverish, and I had no appetite. On the other hand, I suffered from an incessant thirst, which even the copious draughts of water in which I frequently indulged did little to allay. The weather was overcast, and there was a thin mist lying upon the surface of the grey sea which circumscribed my view to a radius of less than a mile, and the air was keenly raw. I recognised that it was necessary to keep myself constantly active, to counteract the effect of the chilly atmosphere, and this I did, bustling about, overhauling the raffle in the junk, and executing a good deal of utterly useless work, which I varied from time to time by taking long spells of watching, in the hope of sighting some craft to which I might signal for assistance. Also I repeatedly bathed my head in sea water, which did a little toward reducing the feeling of feverishness from which I was suffering.

Toward the afternoon the conditions became more favourable. The clouds broke, the sun came out and took the feeling of rawness out of the air, so that I no longer suffered from the cold, and the mist melted away, affording me a clear view to the horizon. But the sea was bare; there was not even so much as a blur of steamer's smoke staining the sky in any direction; and I began to wonder how long it might be before I should be picked up, or whether indeed I should be picked up at all. I knew, of course, that the non-arrival of the *Kinshiu* at Gensan would give rise to speculation, and that probably a search for her would be instituted along the course which she might be expected to steer, but I was already several miles from that course, and hourly drifting farther from it. The question of importance to me was whether the search would extend over a sufficiently wide area to take me in.

The remainder of that day passed uneventfully for me; I could do nothing beyond what I have already indicated; no craft of any description hove in sight; and toward sunset the pangs of hunger began to manifest themselves. I watched the sea until night closed down; and then, when it became so dark that further watching was useless, I crept in under the fore deck among the raffle and turned in upon such a bed as I had been able to prepare for myself during the day, in anticipation of the possibility that I might be obliged to pass the night aboard the junk.

As might be supposed, under the circumstances, the earlier part of the night at least was full of discomfort for me; but somewhere along in the small hours I dropped off to sleep, and eventually slept soundly, to be awakened by the noise of steam blowing off, close at hand. I started up, listened for a moment to assure myself that the sound was not an illusion, and, satisfied that it was real, scrambled up on the junk's deck, to be greeted with the sight of several ships of war close at hand. A single glance sufficed to assure me that my troubles were at an end; for the ships in sight were those of Admiral Kamimura's squadron, the *Idzumi* being hove-to at less than a cable's length distant, in the very act of lowering a boat. There were several officers on her bridge, and she was close enough to enable me to see that they were all scrutinising the junk through their glasses; I therefore waved to them, and was waved to in reply. A few minutes later the boat, in charge of a lieutenant, dashed smartly alongside and the officer scrambled nimbly up the junk's low side.

I think he had not recognised me until then, although we knew each other very well. He gazed at me dubiously for a moment, then his hand shot out to grasp mine as he exclaimed:

"Hillo! my dear Swinburne, what does this mean; what are you doing here? And are you all alone?"

I answered his question by informing him, in as few words as possible, of what had happened to the ill-fated *Kinshiu Maru*, and then we got down into the boat and pulled across to the *Idzumi*, where Kamimura and his officers were impatiently awaiting us. They gave me the warmest of welcomes, and would not even permit me to tell them my story, the lieutenant who had rescued me assuring them that he had already obtained all the particulars and could tell it as well as I could. I was accordingly at once turned over to the care of the ship's surgeon, and made comfortable in the sick bay, the squadron immediately resuming its cruise.

Now that the tension of looking after myself was relaxed, a reaction set in, with high fever, and for the next four days I was really ill, with frequent intervals of delirium. But there were no complications of any kind, and by the end of the sixth day I was so far recovered as to be able to dress and sit up for an hour or two. Everybody aboard the *Idzumi* was exceedingly kind to me, as kind indeed as though they had been brothers; and this fraternal feeling of kindly interest was not confined to the *Idzumi* alone, Kamimura himself informing me, with a smile, that it had become quite a habit for the other ships to signal an inquiry as to my condition, every morning. As the officers of the ship came off watch, they came tiptoeing along to inquire after me; and if I happened to be awake, and the doctor permitted it, they would sit and chat with me for half an hour or so before retiring to their cabins, by which means I gradually acquired all the missing links in the story of the squadron's abortive cruise.

From these conversations I gathered that after the squadron and the *Kinshiu* parted company off Gensan, while we in the transport headed for Iwon, the squadron proceeded toward Vladivostock, being much delayed by a dense fog, through which it steamed at half-speed, each ship towing a fog buoy as a guide to the ship immediately following, though, even with this assistance, keeping touch was only accomplished with extreme difficulty. Thus they proceeded until, by dead reckoning, they arrived at a point seventy miles south of Vladivostock, when, the weather being much too thick to permit of fighting the enemy, even should the two fleets blunder together, Admiral Kamimura decided to retrace his steps, arriving at Gensan two days later. Here the Japanese consul boarded the *Idzumi* and imparted to the Admiral the startling information that on the previous day four strange warships, accompanied by a couple of destroyers, had appeared off the port, the warships being later identified as those constituting the Vladivostock squadron. The destroyers had entered the harbour, boarded a small Japanese craft loaded with fish, ordered her crew to get into her boat and go ashore, and had then torpedoed her; the expended torpedo being probably at least as valuable as the ship which it sank! Later on, the Russian cruisers had entered the harbour, but had left again without doing any damage. In reply to an inquiry concerning the *Kinshiu Maru*, the consul replied that neither she nor her escort had yet returned. This information caused Admiral Kamimura some uneasiness, since there had been time for us to do all that we had been ordered to do, and to get back to Gensan; and the squadron was actually getting its anchors, preparatory to its departure to hunt for the transport, when Commander Takebe with his torpedo-boats arrived. Questioned as to the whereabouts of the *Kinshiu*, he expressed surprise at her non-arrival, briefly relating particulars of the discussion which had resulted in the transport leaving Iwon, unescorted, while he remained in harbour to see what the weather developments were going to be.

This was enough for Kamimura. Takebe's story, in conjunction with that of the consul at Gensan, convinced the Admiral that something very serious had happened; and he at once gave orders for the torpedo flotilla to proceed along the coast to hunt for news of the transport, while he, with his squadron, started off in chase of the Russians.

It was on the morning following this second departure of the squadron from Gensan, that they sighted the junk from which I was rescued. It is possible that, in his eagerness to overtake the Russians, he might have pushed on without pausing to examine a small, apparently derelict junk, but for the fact that, fortunately for me, two or three of the *Idzumi's* officers recognised her as the junk which the *Kinshiu* had taken with her to facilitate the landing operations at Iwon.

After they had taken me off the junk, the Japanese had pushed ahead direct for Vladivostock, in the hope of arriving there before the Russians. But in this hope they were disappointed. Upon their arrival, the Russian cruisers were seen to be already back in harbour; and all that was accomplished was to drive precipitately back into the harbour two Russian destroyers which had the impudence—or the courage—to come out and threaten them; and also to exchange a few shots with the Russian forts.

Chapter Ten
Ito's Yarn

We arrived at our rendezvous among the Hall Islands on the afternoon of May 3rd, and found the place practically deserted, those who were left behind reporting that Admiral Togo and the fleet had left for Port Arthur, the previous day, for the purpose of making a third attempt to seal up the Russian fleet in the harbour. I was by this time making excellent progress toward recovery, but the *Idzumi's* surgeon considered that I should do still better in the hospital ashore; I was therefore landed within half an hour of the ship's coming to an anchor, and that evening found me comfortably established in the roomy convalescent ward, in charge of an excellent and assiduous medical and nursing staff. The latter was composed of young Japanese women, than whom, I think it would be impossible to find more gentle, attentive and tender sick-room attendants. I don't know whether they were more than usually kind to me because I happened to be a foreigner who was helping to fight Japan's battles in her hour of need, but it appeared to me that they were vying with each other as to who should do the most for me. Had I been a king, they could not have done more for me than they did.

On the following morning, having been assisted to rise and dress by the two nurses whose especial charge I was, and established by them near an open window overlooking the roadstead, I was making play with a particularly appetising breakfast when, glancing out of the window, I saw a big fleet of transports arriving—there were eighty-three in all, for I had the curiosity to count them; and while they were coming to an anchor another fleet appeared, consisting of the warships which had been to Port Arthur to assist in the attempt to seal up the harbour. So interested was I in these arrivals that, in watching them, I allowed my breakfast to go cold, and nothing would satisfy my nurses but that they must get me another breakfast, which they did.

I had scarcely finished my belated meal and been attended to by the surgeon, when the door of the ward was thrown open, and in rushed my former lieutenant, Ito, now captain of the destroyer *Akatsuki*. He had volunteered for service on the 2nd, it appeared, and upon his return had encountered the *Idzumi's* Number 1, who had related to Ito my adventure aboard the junk, and the good fellow had straightway come to the hospital to see me "and pay his respects." Also, I shrewdly suspected, to spin me the yarn of his own adventures. But he insisted upon hearing my story first; and when I had told it, in the fewest words possible, he told me his own, which, stripped of his somewhat peculiar modes of expression, ran somewhat as follows:

"Two days ago," he began, "the news reached here that our soldiers had crossed the river Yalu; and thereupon the Admiral made up his mind that the moment had arrived for a further attempt to be made to seal up the Russian fleet in Port Arthur harbour.

"As you are aware, Togo has for some time been quietly making preparations for this attempt, the twelve steamers that have been lying at anchor here having been provided especially for that purpose. You know also that of those twelve, eight have been prepared in the usual manner, by placing heavy charges of gun-cotton in their bottoms, connected with the bridge by electric wires, so that the officer in command might be able to explode the charges and sink his ship at the proper moment, while, on top of these charges, the hull of the ship was converted into a solid rock-like mass by filling her with concrete made of stone, old railway metals and other iron, and cement. Five of the ships were also fitted with searchlights, so that we might not again have to contend with the difficulty of finding the harbour entrance.

"Commander Hayashi, whom I believe you know, was appointed to command the expedition; and volunteers were called for in the usual way. Of course I offered myself; and Togo was good enough to appoint me to the *Totomi Maru*, a small craft of some nineteen hundred tons, under a splendid fellow named Honda.

"We left here at noon of the 2nd, escorted by the gunboats *Akagi* and *Chokai*, the second, third, fourth, and fifth destroyer divisions, and the ninth, tenth, and fourteenth torpedo-boat flotillas.

"When we started, the weather was everything that could be desired; there was no wind, and the water was like glass, while, for a wonder, the air was crystal clear; also there would be a good slice of moon to light us on our way after sunset. But the weather was too fine to last; you know how it is in these seas, my dear chap. Toward sunset the barometer began to fall very rapidly, and about eight o'clock a fresh south-easterly breeze sprang up quite suddenly; it became hazy, the sea got up rapidly, and by six bells in the first watch it was blowing hard, and the weather became so thick that we lost sight of each other. I heard to-day that Hayashi, seeing what was coming, made the signal to postpone the attempt; but we never saw the signal, and went on, rolling and plunging through the short, choppy seas in the most uncomfortable manner.

"It appears that the alarm was first given to the Russians, about two o'clock next morning, by the appearance of what looked like a searchlight, far out at sea, directed full upon the mouth of the harbour. Of course the searchlight on Golden Hill was at once brought into play, and it chanced that as the beam swept the sea, five of our torpedo-boats were sighted, attempting to slip into the harbour. It was a thousand pities that they were prematurely discovered, for their skippers had formed a bold plan to enter the harbour and torpedo every ship they could find, taking their chance of being able to get away afterward. But of course their discovery frustrated that plan, for so hot a fire was opened upon them by three Russian gunboats which were guarding the harbour's mouth, that to have persisted would have meant their destruction. So they were obliged to retire; for the Admiral would not have thanked them for throwing away their boats uselessly.

"Then the searchlight picked up the *Mikawa Maru*, which was leading three other explosion ships straight for the harbour, and a terrific fire was opened upon her, the Russians evidently recognising her as a merchant ship, and guessing at her business. From Sosa's report it appears that, having seen the flashes of the guns, firing upon our torpedo-boats, he was under the impression that certain of the explosion ships had already entered the harbour and were being fired upon by the Russians; but, as he drew nearer in, his searchlight revealed his mistake, showing him that instead of being one of the last, he was the first to arrive; therefore he called down into the engine-room for every ounce of steam they could give him, and went, full pelt, for the harbour, through a perfect tornado of projectiles, great and small, few of which, however, touched the ship, though they were lashing the sea into spray all round her.

"Without sustaining any serious damage, the *Mikawa* charged right into the narrow channel at top speed. At this point she came into violent collision with something that afterward proved to be a 'boom,' constructed of stout balks of timber, steel hawsers, and ponderous chain cables, all strongly lashed together and stretched right athwart the channel, from shore to shore. But she was of nearly two thousand tons measurement, and, with the way that she had on her, she went through that boom as though it had been a thread! On she went, until not only the searchlight but also Golden Hill fort was on her starboard quarter, and she had penetrated farther than any other Japanese ship had done since war was declared, when, having reached the point where the channel is narrowest, Sosa, her skipper, swung her athwart the fairway and, amid the cheers of his crew and the deafening explosions of guns and shells, coolly blew her bottom out and sank her, he and his crew just having time to scramble into their two boats as the steamer foundered. Wasn't that fine?"

"Splendid!" I agreed, heartily. "And what became of that fine chap, Sosa, and his crew? Did they manage to escape?"

"Sosa and three men of his boat's crew contrived, although they were all wounded, to pull out to our torpedo-boats, and were picked up," replied Ito. "But the Russians fired upon the other boat and destroyed her and her crew, despite Sosa's desperate efforts to save them.

"The next ship to arrive was the *Sakura Maru*. She was about a mile and a half ahead of us in the *Totomi*, and we were able to see everything that happened to her.

"I believe it was her opportune arrival that gave the gallant Sosa and his companions the chance to escape; because of course as soon as the *Sakura* was seen, the Russian gunners gave all their attention to her.

"It was a grand sight to see her—she was more than a thousand tons bigger than the *Mikawa*—rushing straight for the harbour's mouth at her utmost speed, with the water foaming about her bows, a thin stream of smoke and sparks issuing from her funnels, her whole hull, spars, rigging, and funnels standing up, a black silhouette, between us and the white beam of the searchlight, with shells exploding all about her, deluging her with foam, but apparently doing her no harm. She stood on, evidently under a full head of steam, for we could see 'the white feather' at the top of her waste-pipes, until she reached the Pinnacle Rock; and there they anchored and sank her. She was manned almost entirely by cadets; and as an illustration of the consummate coolness with which they behaved, let me tell you that when the ship went down, they actually had the presence of mind to take flares aloft with them, which they burnt from the crosstrees, to guide us into the channel!

"Of course the Russians fired upon them, and shot away first one mast and then the other. Then they were called upon to surrender, some of the Russians actually launching boats to take them off the floating wreckage; but the cadets were imbued with the true Samurai spirit, they preferred death to surrender, and they defended themselves with their revolvers from all who approached them, until every Japanese was slain.

"Then came the turn of the *Totomi Maru*, we being the third ship to arrive. Well, I have not much to say about what we did, or what happened to us; it would be merely a repetition of what I have already described. Like our predecessors, we went in at full speed, struck some floating object two terrific blows just as we entered the channel, swept on, amid a hurricane of shells and bullets shrieking and whining about our ears, until we came to the wreck of the *Mikawa*, and there Honda—who is about as cool a chap under fire as you are—stopped and reversed his engines, swung the ship athwart the channel, with our bows as close as we could guess to the *Mikawa's* taffrail, let go two anchors, one ahead and one aft, and calmly sank the craft.

"The Russians kept their searchlight upon us, and peppered us well with rifle-fire, until the *Totomi* went down; and then they had other fish to honourably fry, as you English say; for the *Aikoku Maru* was now racing in toward the harbour's mouth, and it was high time for them to attend to her. They turned the searchlight upon her, opened fire upon her with every weapon that would hurl a shot, and presently, when she was within about a thousand yards of the entrance, they fired an observation mine as she passed over it, and down she went, taking her engine-room and stoke-hold crew with her.

"Then there ensued a 'spell'—as you, my dear Swinburne, honourably call it—an interlude; possibly it was the end, for there were no more ships in sight; the firing died down, the searchlight beam stared steadily out to seaward, and we who had survived that saturnalia of slaughter had an opportunity to slip out and rejoin the torpedo-boats which were lurking close in under the shadow of the cliffs, waiting to pick us up.

"Honda commanded the leading boat in which our party were making their escape, and I the other. We were both creeping along as close as possible to the foot of the cliffs under Golden Hill, in order to elude the notice of the Russians above; and Honda, with fourteen men, was about a quarter of a mile ahead. I had eleven men with me.

"We had arrived at a point which I believed to be, rightly as the event proved, immediately beneath the fort, and I was staring contemplatively up at the face of the cliff which towered above us, when we came abreast of a sort of cleft in the rock, at the foot of which lay several big boulders in a great pile, some of which were in the water. Suddenly, the idea occurred to me that it might be possible for active men to climb that cleft; and acting upon the impulse of the moment, I put the boat's helm hard a-starboard and, giving the word 'Easy all!' headed in toward the boulders.

"A minute later, we found ourselves in a miniature harbour, just large enough to receive the boat, the big boulders forming a sort of breakwater.

"'Men,' I said, 'have all of you your revolvers and cutlasses with you?'

"They answered that they had. 'Then,' said I, 'let us give those Russians, up above, a little surprise. I believe we can climb that cleft, and I, for one, am determined to try. Who goes with me?'

"As I had quite anticipated, they all agreed to join me in the attempt; so, making fast the boat's painter to a rock, and leaving her to take care of herself, we scrambled out, and I honourably taking the lead, as was my right, up we went. It was a very difficult climb, in the semi-darkness, for the moon was hidden by clouds, and the way was so steep that we were obliged to push and pull each other up; but at length we reached the top, and then lay down in a little hollow to recover our breath.

"The fort crowned the summit of a steep hill immediately in front of us. For fully five minutes I patiently examined it, and at the end of that time came to the conclusion that only by the rear could we hope to approach it undiscovered. Accordingly, I led my men round to the land side of the fort and, taking our time, that we might save our breath, we crept slowly up the slope until we reached not only the summit of the hill but actually the parapet of the fort itself. Peering over this, I was able to see that it was armed with eight 11-inch Canet guns; and there were, including the gun crews, at least a hundred men in the place, all of them intently staring out to seaward, evidently in momentary expectation of seeing more explosion ships arrive.

"Had it been possible for us to have entered that fort at that moment, I would have led my men in, and we would have honourably died for the glory of Nippon, destroying as many of the enemy as we could before 'going out' ourselves. But entry, at least swiftly enough to take the Russians by surprise, was not possible, the parapet being protected by substantial *chevaux de brise* which we could neither have surmounted nor broken down without attracting attention; I was therefore obliged to content myself with giving them what you call a 'scare.' Ranging my men in open order along the rear parapet, so that only their heads and their levelled revolvers could be seen, I loudly called upon the Russians to surrender!

"My dear Swinburne, it was worth all the toil of that climb up the cliff, and up the steep slope of the hill, to behold the blank dismay of those Russians. It did not last long, though; to give them the credit due to them, they were brave fellows, and the moment they realised the situation, they simply laughed at us, regarding our exploit as a joke—as indeed it was, more than anything else.

"But the joke had its grim side, too; for the commandant immediately ordered his men to cover us with their rifles, and then ordered us to surrender.

"'How are you going to take us?' I asked.

"'Throw your revolvers over here to me,' he ordered; 'and I will send out some men to conduct you to the town.'

"'No,' I said.

"'If you do not, I shall be compelled to shoot,' he said.

"'Then, shoot, and be hanged to you,' I replied; and giving a sign to my men, we opened fire with our revolvers at the same moment that the Russians blazed away at us with their rifles. And not until every chamber of our revolvers was empty did we turn and race down that hill toward the head of the cleft by which we had ascended."

"Did you suffer any loss?" I asked.

"None at all," was the cheerful answer. "The bullets hummed about our ears like mosquitoes in the summer-time, but not one of us was even touched. On the other hand, I saw several Russians fall before our fire, and I think that at least thirty of them must have gone down before we turned and honourably 'hooked it,' as you would say."

I smiled. Good old Ito! He was a splendid fellow, honest as the day, utterly unassuming, brave as a lion, everything in short that a shipmate should be; but it was evident that the habit of introducing that favourite expression "honourable" in conjunction with a bit of British slang, was inveterate with him, and I felt that it would be a long time before he would be able to recognise its incongruity.

"Well," I said. "What happened next?"

"Oh, nothing, so far as we were concerned," he replied. "We scrambled down the cleft into our boat and pushed off, still keeping quite close to the foot of the cliffs, although there was a heavy sea rolling in and breaking upon them. And indeed it was high time for us to be off, for when we pulled out of our little harbour at the base of the cliff, the first light of dawn was showing along the horizon to the eastward.

"Suddenly, the cannonading, which had completely died away, broke out furiously again from the heights above, and from the new batteries which have been built on the low ground higher up the harbour. At first we thought we had been seen, and that they were firing at us; but presently a steamer hove in sight to seaward, and we saw that the firing was directed at her and three others which followed her. These we presently recognised as the remaining explosion steamers, which had lost their way in the fog of the night before.

"On they came, rushing toward the harbour at top speed, with a hurricane of shells of all sizes falling upon and about them, and the full glare of the searchlights shining full upon them.

"The first of them to come I recognised as the *Edo Maru*, under the command of Commander Takayagi. She looked frightfully battered as she swept past us, yet she kept afloat and reached the spot for which she was aiming. Her engines stopped and reversed, and she was evidently preparing to anchor, when a shell struck poor Takayagi, who was standing on the port extremity of the bridge, and, almost cutting him in two, hit the funnel, and exploding blew a tremendous hole in it. Nagata—you know Lieutenant Nagata, I think—the second in command, who was also on the bridge, immediately took charge, anchored the ship, exploded the charges down in her hold, and, ordering away the boats, left her, just as she was sinking, the crew bringing away poor Takayagi's body with them. He is to be buried ashore here, this afternoon, with full military honours, of course.

"The next steamer to come was the *Otaru Maru*. I think the fire directed upon her was even hotter than that which greeted the *Edo*. Shells fell all round her, but none of them seemed to hit her; and meanwhile she was replying briskly with her Hotchkisses. The din was terrific, for every battery that could bring a gun to bear was blazing away at her, while troops made their appearance on the cliffs above and rained bullets upon her deck; indeed a sort of panic seemed to have seized the Russians, for not only were they hurling hundreds of shells at the devoted *Otaru*, but were exploding observation mines everywhere, in the most reckless manner. But their most deadly weapon of all was their searchlight beam, which they directed right into the eyes of the helmsman and the officers on the bridge. Dazzled by its blinding brilliance, our people could not see where they were going; and instead of reaching her appointed station in the harbour, the *Otaru* dashed at full speed upon the rocks. The crew, of course, took to the boats, but they were unfortunately in the full glare of the searchlight, and the Russian troops shot every one of them.

"We were by this time about a mile out at sea, when we suddenly caught sight of a torpedo-boat hove-to, without lights, and rolling and pitching furiously not far away. Feeling sure that she must be Japanese, I hailed her, got a reply, and five minutes later was following my crew up the side of Number 65, being warmly welcomed by my friend, Lieutenant Taira, who was in command.

"And now came a misfortune; for as I made a spring from our boat to the deck of the plunging Number 65, the sweeping ray of the Russian searchlight passed over us, returned, and rested inexorably upon us. Taira instantly gave the order to the engineers to go full speed ahead; but even before the engines could be started, a number of shells came hurtling about us, and one unfortunately passed through the boat's thin side and, without exploding, cut the steam pipe of Number 3 boiler. Of course the stoke-hold was instantly filled with high-pressure steam, and before the stokers could escape, three of them were scalded to death. It was horrible to hear their screams and at the same time to realise the impossibility of doing anything to save them. Luckily for us, Number 75, lying at no great distance, saw that we were in difficulties, and pluckily came to our rescue, taking us in tow and, despite the tremendous fire directed upon us both, dragging us out of range.

"I was too busily engaged in helping to save Number 65 to see much of what further happened in connection with the attempt to 'bottle up' the Russian fleet; but I have since learned that the *Sagami Maru*, which followed the *Otaru Maru*, was peculiarly unfortunate, in that she struck a mechanical mine, just outside the harbour, and went down with all hands. The last ship, the *Asagao Maru*, was scarcely less unfortunate; for a shell struck her rudder as she neared the harbour, and rendered her unmanageable, so that she went ashore close under Golden Hill, and her crew, refusing to surrender, were killed, to a man.

"Just after this last happening, a fog came driving in from seaward and swallowed us all up, so that the Russians lost sight of us; and then the firing ceased. Shortly afterwards, our fast cruisers came looming up through the fog, to cover our retreat; and about nine o'clock in the morning Togo himself joined us with the battle squadron. He was most anxious to know the result of the night's operations; but, unfortunately, none of us could afford him more than mere disconnected snatches of information. I think I possessed more information than anybody else; but of course mine was by no means complete, and the Admiral was most anxious to know exactly how matters stood, for great things hinged upon the measure of our success; I therefore offered to take in a picket boat and attempt to obtain all the information required, and my offer was accepted. I steamed in under cover of the fog, which was so thick that it was impossible for us to see more than a few yards in any direction; so thick, indeed, that we actually found ourselves among the masts of the sunken craft before we really knew where we were. There were two or three shore boats groping about the wreckage already, but they took no notice of us, imagining, perhaps, that we belonged to one of their own ships; and we were therefore able to complete our examination and to definitely satisfy ourselves that at last the harbour was entirely blocked. Learning this, the Admiral wirelessed a message to General Oku, informing him that he could safely move, since the Russian ships were now effectually bottled up; and the result of that message is the fleet of transports that you see yonder. And now, my dear chap, I must be off; the doctor told me that I must on no account weary you by talking too much; and here have I been yarning for the last half-hour or more. Good-bye! Hope to see you about again soon."

"Here, stop a moment, old chap," I cried. "Having told me so much, you may as well tell me the rest. Where is Oku going?"

"Ah!" answered Ito. "That is a secret. But I think many of us could make a good guess, eh?"

"If I were asked to guess, I should say, Pi-tse-wo," answered I.

"And very probably, my dear Swinburne, you would be honourably correct," answered Ito, as he waved his hand and smilingly bowed himself out.

A little later I was honoured by a visit from Togo himself, with whom I believed myself to be something of a favourite, although Togo's favouritism never took the form of sparing the favoured one, or giving him easy work to execute; on the contrary, the most infallible sign that a man was in the Admiral's favour was the assignment to him of some exceptionally difficult, arduous, or dangerous task. He had, of course, already heard of my adventure from Kamimura, but he wanted to hear the story from my own lips, and he also had several questions to ask me. He remained with me nearly an hour, and was most friendly and kind in his manner, expressing regret at my sufferings—such as they were—and the hope that I should soon be well enough to resume duty.

To my surprise, the Admiral called again, somewhat late in the afternoon. He was very busy, he said, being engaged on the task of arranging for the convoy of General Oku's Second Army, consisting of 70,000 men, the task of whom was to assist in the reduction of Port Arthur. He expected to be away a full week, at least, possibly longer, and the object of his visit was to explain to me that, aboard the transports in harbour were all the materials for the construction of a great "boom," eight miles long, to be carried from the island of Kwang-lung-tau, the most westerly of the Elliot group, to the mainland. Similar booms had already been run from island to island of the group, and the new, big boom would render the rendezvous immune to attack from the land to the northward. His object in looking me up, now, was in connection with the construction of this new, big boom. It appeared that, after leaving me that morning, he had encountered the physician who had charge of the hospital, and that official had expressed the opinion that, in the course of the next three or four days, I might probably be sufficiently recovered to be discharged from the hospital, and be employed upon light duties, such as those of superintendence, or anything which did not involve personal exertion.

That remark had suggested an idea to Togo, the result of which was his second call upon me, to inquire whether I knew anything about the construction of protective booms. As it happened, I did, having once been actively employed upon the construction of an experimental boom which was afterward stretched across the mouth of Portsmouth harbour. When, therefore, I told the Admiral this, with his usual directness of purpose he at once appointed me to superintend the construction of the long boom; his orders being that I was to remain in hospital until the doctors should discharge me; when I was to resume the command of the *Kasanumi*, and with her as flagship, proceed to the Elliot Islands, in charge of the torpedo flotilla which he would leave behind for that purpose, escorting the steamers into which he would tranship all the materials necessary for the construction of the long boom. And upon our arrival there, I was to discharge the steamers— or, rather, supervise the discharge of them, landing the materials at the most suitable spot I could find; and then, still supervising only, proceed with all celerity upon the construction of the boom. He briefly gave me his own ideas as to how the boom should be constructed, but left me with an entirely free hand to introduce any improvements that might suggest themselves to me, so far as the materials at my command would permit. The task was one that strongly appealed to me, for it gave some scope for the employment of a certain inventive faculty which I believed I possessed; and I undertook it with avidity.

That evening, about half an hour before sunset, the transhipment of the materials for the boom having been effected, the transports containing Oku's Second Army got their anchors and started for Pi-tse-wo, escorted by a portion of the fleet under Togo, while the remaining portion, consisting of the light, fast cruisers and a detachment of destroyers, proceeded to Port Arthur, to make assurance doubly sure by keeping an eye upon the Russian ships there. I subsequently learned that the latter appeared to be quite inactive, although the sounds of frequent loud explosions proceeding from the harbour indicated that the Russians were already busily engaged upon the task of attempting to blast a passage through the obstructing wrecks.

Chapter Eleven
The Russian Submarine

By dint of wheedling entreaty and the most lavish promises on my part that I would on no account attempt to do any actual work, I succeeded in inducing the doctor to discharge me from the hospital on the second day after the departure of the Admiral, with General Oku's transports, to Pi-tse-wo.

I was discharged shortly after eleven o'clock in the morning, and was conveyed in a hand ambulance down to the landing-place, where my boat was waiting for me, having been semaphored for, the instant that I obtained my discharge. I was glad to find myself aboard my own little ship once more; and the crew seemed to be as glad to see me as I was to see them; for it appeared that during my absence the *Kasanumi* had been employed upon nothing but patrol work, which was not at all to the taste of my lads. Young Hiraoka, my lieutenant, seemed keenly disappointed when he learned that our most exciting work, for some time to come, was to be the construction of the long boom; but philosophically remarked that no doubt as soon as the Russians learned what we were about, we should have a few of their destroyers paying us a call, when we might hope for a little fun.

By the time that I got aboard, it was noon; and I at once signalled the transports, asking how soon they could be ready to start. The reply was that, not expecting to be called upon to go to sea so soon, their fires were all out—but boilers were full and fires laid, and they could have steam in three hours; whereupon I made the signal to light fires at once, and report when they were ready to move. Then I got into a reclining chair under the awning aft, and, having partaken of a hasty luncheon, treated myself to a snooze, since I expected to be up all night.

We all got under way shortly after three o'clock in the afternoon, and, having cleared the harbour, headed away north-west for the Elliot group. The weather was, for a wonder, beautifully fine, no fog, very few clouds, brilliant sunshine, very little wind, and the water as smooth as a mill pond; consequently we made very good progress, although the speed of the slowest transport was only ten knots, and of course the rest of us had to regulate our pace by hers. Had the weather been threatening I should of course have been anxious, but the barometer stood high, and as even at ten knots the passage would only occupy about thirteen hours, I felt quite easy in my mind.

The trip across the Yellow Sea was made without mishap or adventure until we arrived within about twelve miles of our destination. The night was still gloriously fine, the water smooth, the stars brilliant, and the moon, within about an hour of setting, hung in the western sky, spreading a broad path of silver on the surface of the gently heaving sea. It was a few minutes after four bells in the middle watch when, having been dozing for some time in my chair, which had been taken up to the bridge for my convenience, I scrambled to my feet and began to pace to and fro, for I was feeling somewhat chilly, although wrapped in a good warm ulster.

The beauty of the night fascinated me. It was so calm and peaceful, and the air, although a trifle cool, was yet bland, as though it were a breath of the coming summer; and, looking back upon what we had been called upon to endure of storm and darkness, and bitter, numbing cold and wet, I rejoiced that summer was at hand, hoping that, before winter came again, there would be peace, and that our nightly buffetings by arctic winds, hail, snow, and icy seas would be at an end.

As these thoughts passed through my mind, my gaze fixed itself contemplatively on the broad path of silver—now imperceptibly changing to liquid gold—cast upon the surface of the sea by the setting moon; and, as I gazed, I gradually became aware of a tiny black object, about a mile away, on our port bow, rising and falling with the lazy heave of the swell. In that mine-strewn sea the smallest and least conspicuous floating object demanded one's instant and most careful attention, and whipping my binoculars out of the case, strapped to the bridge rail, I quickly focused them upon it. Through the glasses it looked very like the top of a ship's galley funnel, though not quite so stout, and it was moving as though to cross our hawse, for with the help of the glasses I could see the little ripple of scintillating foam it piled up before it.

I knew in an instant what it was, for I had seen submarines before, and at once recognised the slender object forging through the water out yonder as the upper portion of a submarine's periscope.

Of course she had seen us, probably a good half-hour before, or she would not be submerged; and the course she was steering indicated that she was bent upon mischief.

I congratulated myself upon having sighted her in good time before entering her danger zone, for the *Kasanumi* was about a mile ahead of the main body of our little fleet, and I felt that I should have time to deal with her before the others came up. The question was: would she attack the destroyer, or would she allow us to pass and reserve her energies for the transports, under the impression that they were carrying troops? It was impossible to guess, and it would never do to take any chance; I therefore pointed out the periscope to young Hiraoka, told him what it was, and then ordered him to go down quietly, have the hands called, and get all guns loaded. The thought of trying to get in a torpedo before the Russian discharged hers, occurred to me; but I decided against it, as some of our torpedoes had a trick of running erratically.

Meanwhile, we continued to potter along at ten knots, as though we had seen nothing and had not so much as the ghost of a suspicion that submarines were in our neighbourhood. There was but one, so far as I could see; and indeed until that moment we never suspected the Russians of having any in those seas, although vague rumours—which we had never been able to substantiate—had reached us of submarines having been brought overland to Port Arthur from Petersburg in sections.

With my eyes glued to my binoculars, and my binoculars focused steadily upon that small pole-like object protruding a bare two feet above that shimmering, silvery sheen of water, I directed the signalman near me to ring down the order to the engine-room to "Stand by"; and then to fetch our wireless operator to me. In a few words I explained the situation to this youngster, when he came, and gave him his orders, while the sounds of Hiraoka's preparations came to my ears.

Suddenly, as I watched the periscope every moment becoming more distinct, I noticed that the ripple of foam about it was steadily lessening, and presently it disappeared altogether. The submarine had evidently stopped her engines, and was lying in wait, either to torpedo us as we passed, or to permit us to pass on unsuspecting, and then get in her work upon the transports. It was a bit of luck which I had not dared to hope for, and I instantly made my plans. Steadily the *Kasanumi* held on, as though utterly unsuspecting, steering a course which, if continued, would take us athwart the submarine's hawse at a distance of about three hundred yards, or less than half the effective range of her torpedo.

Was she stealthily altering her position under water, turning her bows toward us, so as to torpedo us the moment we should arrive within range, or was she trusting that her presence was undetected, and waiting patiently for the moment when we should cross her bows as she lay? The latter, I believed, for she could not cant toward us without going either ahead or astern, and she could not do either without her periscope raising a ripple;

and I was certain that nothing of that sort had happened. I determined to risk something, after all, to put that submarine out of action, and so held steadily on. At length we arrived so close that I could see the periscope almost as distinctly without the glasses as with them, and still intently watching it, I laid my hand on the engine-room telegraph, carefully estimating the steadily decreasing distance which separated us from moment to moment.

Six hundred yards. Five hundred. Four-fifty. Four hundred. I crashed the telegraph handles over to "Full speed ahead!" on both engines, and never moving my eyes for an instant from the periscope, directed the helmsman to steer straight for it. The submarine was lying motionless and inert there, some fifteen feet beneath the surface; and I calculated that it would take the Russians at least half a minute to realise that they were discovered, and to get way upon their craft; and by that time we should be so close to them that it would be impossible for them either to dive or to turn the submarine bows on to us, much less to escape. Then, as I felt the destroyer leap forward beneath me, like a spirited horse at the cut of a whip, I blew my whistle, as a signal to "Sparks," who instantly wirelessed back to the main body to stop until further orders, and to keep a sharp lookout for submarines.

Like a greyhound slipped from the leash, the *Kasanumi* rushed at that luckless periscope, about which a few bubbles of foam were just beginning to gather at the moment when our stem, towering over it, hid it from my sight. The next instant our hull swept over it and of course snapped it clean off, although we felt no shock whatever, for our draught of water was too light for our keel to reach the submarine's conning tower. But by the loss of her periscope the craft was effectually blinded, and now she was at our mercy, for she *must* come to the surface, sooner or later, while, so smooth was the water, the swirl or wake of her as she forged ahead was clearly perceptible, and all we now had to do was to follow her until she rose, and then take or sink her.

As I lost sight of the periscope, I rang down to stop and reverse both engines, at the same time ordering our helm hard a-port. Then, as we checked and lost way, we went ahead, first on our port engine and then on both, at the same time shifting our helm, so as to get into the wake of the submarine. We managed to do this before quite losing sight of the disturbance made by her passage through the water; and, this done, we regulated our pace by hers, maintaining a distance of about fifty fathoms between her and ourselves. She shifted her helm several times in an evident attempt to baffle pursuit; but, thanks to the tell-tale swirl she raised, we were able to follow her; and at length, after a chase of about three-quarters of an hour, she rose to the surface, the watertight door of her tower opened, and a man's head appeared.

He looked greatly astonished to see us within a biscuit-toss of him, and instantly ducked out of sight, leaving the hatch open, however, and we heard him shouting something to some one in the boat's interior. A few seconds later another head appeared, stared at us fixedly for a few seconds—during which young Hiraoka, who had a very fair knowledge of Russian, hailed him to surrender—and he, too, disappeared. Then, while we were patiently awaiting further developments, the submarine, which was still going ahead, suddenly inclined her bows and, before we could do anything, *dived with her hatch open*! The brave fellows who manned her, evidently taking a leaf out of their opponents' book, had chosen death rather than surrender, and had deliberately plunged to the bottom rather than yield their vessel to us! For, of course, the craft was never seen again, nor did any of her crew come to the surface, although we hove-to for an hour or more, and got our boat out in readiness to pick up any one who might escape from that steel coffin.

I was quite prepared to hear a loud cheer of exultation burst from the lips of my crew when they realised what had happened. But no. There is nothing that the Japanese admire more than courage; and such a deliberate act of devoted self-sacrifice for the honour of one's country and flag as they had just beheld, called forth merely a low-spoken murmur of intense, almost envious praise.

We arrived at our destination without further adventure, and dropped anchor in the roadstead just as the sun rose above the horizon, flooding the rocky shores of the Elliots with gold, and were heartily greeted by the few craft which we found lying at anchor there.

Looking back upon our adventure with the Russian submarine, I could not help regarding it as almost providential that we had encountered her; for I think there can be very little doubt that when we fell in with her she must have been on her way to the Elliot archipelago, where, had she arrived safely, she might have found more than one spot in which she could have lain *perdu*, to emerge at a favourable moment and destroy at least one, if not more, of our most precious battleships.

Giving orders for the immediate discharge of the materials for the boom, at a spot which I selected immediately after we had come to an anchor, I turned in and slept soundly until past midday, resting again all the afternoon; so that when evening came I had quite recovered from the fatigue of the previous night, and was pronounced by the doctor in charge of the hospital ashore to be progressing toward complete recovery quite as rapidly as could be reasonably expected, while my wound was healing in fine style. About four o'clock that afternoon, word was brought to me that the whole of the materials intended for the construction of the boom had been landed; and I went ashore to inspect them. They consisted for the most part of enormous balks of timber and massive cables; but there were also immense quantities of chain to serve as lashings, stout staples, iron bars, innumerable bundles of long, massive, pointed spikes, and thousands of empty casks, stoutly hooped, without bung-holes, and coated with pitch to ensure permanent watertight-ness. Commander Tsuchiya, whom I had placed in charge of the discharging operations, had done his work well, stacking the various items each by itself, and keeping a careful account of the quantities of each. He handed me a copy of his list, and after I had inspected the whole of the material, I returned to my ship and sat down to plan out the details of the construction of the boom, which, with the list of the quantities before me, was a comparatively easy task.

Dawn of the following day found us all ready to make a start, and with Tsuchiya again as my principal *aide*, we quickly got to work, pressing every available hand into the service. Many hands make light and quick work, especially where those hands are willing, but I was astonished at the ardour and zest which those handy little Japanese seamen manifested; they toiled untiringly all through that long, hot day, with the result that, when we knocked off at nightfall, we had considerably more than half a mile of that boom put together and secured in position by ponderous anchors and stout chain cables.

We were hard at work upon the boom again when, during the afternoon of the following day, our battle fleet returned from Pi-tse-wo, after covering the landing of General Oku's army. The fleet steamed in between the islands and Cape Terminal on the mainland, toward which we were running the boom; and my friend Ijichi, the skipper of the *Mikasa*, told me, with a laugh, that when the little Admiral first saw the boom and made out what it was, he could hardly credit his eyes. He had been under the impression that I was still in hospital, and would probably not be able to get to work for a week or more. Yet there I was, as large as life, in a picket boat, with my head still swathed in a bandage, superintending operations, and clearly recognisable with the assistance of a pair of binoculars. And when at the close of the day I went aboard the flagship to report myself, Togo did not hesitate to let me understand how intensely gratified he was at the progress which we had made.

Meanwhile, I was fast progressing toward complete recovery; and on the day following the return of the fleet to the Elliots, the bandage was removed from my head, and I was pronounced to be practically all right once more. And, to add to my gratification, a destroyer arrived from Sasebo, bringing mails for the fleet, among which were no less than three delightful letters from my friends the Gordons, at home, and two, equally delightful, from my Sasebo friends, Mr Boyd and his wife. Those from the Gordons were full of congratulations; for I gathered from them that a long and circumstantial account of our second attempt to seal up Port Arthur harbour had appeared in the home newspapers, in which somewhat conspicuous mention was made of my doings, and my friends were delighted to learn that I was "so successfully maintaining the finest traditions of the British Navy," as they were kindly pleased to put it. My chum, Ronald, was particularly chirpy about it, expressing in no measured terms the wish that he could have been with me, while he informed me that, notwithstanding the painful circumstances under which I had left the *Terrible*—and the British Navy—the officers of that ship, with only one or two exceptions, had expressed their gratification, while several of them, whom he named, had desired him to convey to me their congratulations and good wishes.

During the next day or two excellent progress was made with the construction of the long boom; and then came a spell of bad weather which, although it did not hinder the putting together of the sections of the boom, in the smooth water of the anchorage, rendered it impossible for us to tow them out and splice them to the portion already in position. But although the bad weather greatly delayed us in this way, we did not altogether regret it, for the heavy sea kicked up by the gales afforded a splendid test of that portion of the boom already in place, and we were greatly gratified, as we steamed out day after day to examine it, to find that it had not been damaged or displaced in the smallest degree.

It was toward the end of the third week of May that the Admiral signalled me to proceed on board the flagship. It was late in the afternoon of a thoroughly wretched day; the wind had been blowing hard from the south'ard for the past three or four days, with almost incessant rain, and there was a very heavy sea running between the islands and the main. I had just returned from my second inspection of the boom that day, and I naturally thought that the signal indicated a desire on the part of the Admiral to question me in relation to the stability of the structure. And when I entered his cabin, and he greeted me with the question:

"Well, Captain Swinburne, how is the boom standing the sea, out yonder?" I was confirmed in my opinion. But I presently found that I was mistaken; for when I had told him all that there was to tell about the boom, and he had expressed his satisfaction, he said:

"By the way, it is Commander Tsuchiya who has been your chief assistant in this work, is it not?"

I replied in the affirmative.

"And I suppose he understands the whole business pretty well by this time, eh?" the Admiral continued.

"Every bit as well as I do, sir," I answered, seeming to scent other work for myself at no great distance.

"That is good," commented Togo. "Do you think he would be capable of completing the work without further assistance from you?"

"Undoubtedly he would, sir," I replied. "Indeed, I think it right to say that, after the first day, Commander Tsuchiya required no help or suggestion of any kind from me at all. He seemed to perfectly understand the principle of the boom's construction, almost from the very beginning; and after the first day's work upon it he took the entire supervision into his own hands, leaving me nothing whatever to do but merely to look on and satisfy myself by personal observation that the work was being properly done."

"Which it was, I presume?" remarked the Admiral.

"Which it certainly was, sir," I replied.

"Good!" said Togo. "That being the case, you are free for another service. How would you like the chance to get a little fighting ashore, by way of a change?"

"Jove!" I exclaimed, "that would be splendid, sir. Are you going to land a naval brigade anywhere?"

"Well—no," answered the Admiral, "hardly that, I think; at least, that is not my present intention, although circumstances may possibly render it desirable, eventually. The matter stands thus," —turning to the table where a map of the Liaotung peninsula lay unfolded upon it.

"This," —pointing to a certain spot on the map—"is where General Oku landed, the other day, with his army. And this," —pointing to another spot—"is where he is now. His object of course is to march south and lay siege to Port Arthur. But at this point, some two and a half miles south of Kinchau, which, as I suppose you know, is a Chinese walled city, the isthmus is only about two miles wide; and in and about the city the Russians have established themselves in force, prepared, apparently, to dispute Oku's passage of the isthmus to the last man.

"This mountain, so prominently marked on the map, is Mount Sampson. It is more than two thousand feet in height and, as you will readily understand, dominates the entire district. Upon this mountain the Russians very strongly established themselves, scarping the heights and constructing formidable breastworks behind which to shelter themselves. Of course it was necessary for our troops to take this mountain, since, until that could be done, to pass the isthmus would be impossible. I am glad to learn that the mountain is now in our hands.

"But here, just to the south of Kinchau, is another range of hills, known as the Nanshan Heights. They form a sort of backbone to the isthmus, and occupy almost its entire width, their crests completely commanding the narrow strip of low ground on either side. On these heights, too, the Russians have very strongly established themselves; so that although Mount Sampson is in our hands, the isthmus remains impassable. The unfortunate fact, so far as we are concerned, is that General Oku has no heavy artillery with him, otherwise he would be able to shell the Nanshan Heights from Mount Sampson, and drive the Russians out. But he has only field and mountain guns, of a range insufficient for that purpose; therefore he has requisitioned help from me, and I propose to send some craft round to Kinchau Bay, to shell the Russian positions from the sea."

"Kinchau Bay, sir?" I interrupted. "Pardon me, but the water in Kinchau Bay is so shallow, according to the chart, that I am afraid any of our craft capable of carrying guns heavy enough to be of service would have very great difficulty in approaching the land near enough to be of any real use. Why not Hand Bay, sir, on the eastern side of the isthmus?"

"For the very good reason, my dear fellow, that not only is Hand Bay mined, but it would also be impossible for us to clear it, the bay being completely commanded by works which our craft could not face for five minutes. No, it must be Kinchau Bay; there is nothing else for it," answered the Admiral.

"That being the case," he continued, "it is my intention to dispatch thither the *Akagi, Chokai, Hei-yen*, and *Tsukushi* to afford the assistance required by General Oku; and those ships will be accompanied by a torpedo flotilla, the duty of which will be to take soundings, lay down a line of buoys inside which the ships must not pass, and search for and clear the bay of mines, as well as to render such further assistance as may be possible to the land forces.

"I anticipate that the work required of the torpedo flotilla will be of an exceptionally arduous and hazardous character; and for that reason, Captain Swinburne, I am going to place it under your command, with the *Kasanumi* as your flagship. I have been keeping my eye upon you, sir, and I will take this opportunity to express my very high appreciation of your conduct. You have manifested all the dash, the fertility of resource, and the cool courage under exceedingly trying conditions which we have grown to look for as a matter of course from Englishmen; and to that you add an element of caution which I fear we Japanese have not as fully developed as we ought to have done; I therefore regard you as the fittest man I could possibly select for the service upon which I now propose to employ you.

That also is the reason why I have so fully explained to you the situation at Kinchau, for it is very necessary that you should clearly understand all that may be required of you.

"We have, of course, any number of Japanese officers whose courage would be quite equal to the task I am assigning to you, but they unfortunately lack that element of caution which you possess, in proof of which it will be my painful duty to presently announce a series of terrible disasters, news of which has just reached me, and three of which, at least, I am afraid I must attribute to a lack of caution."

"Indeed, sir," I said; "I am exceeding sorry to hear that. Is it permissible to ask particulars?"

"Oh yes," answered the Admiral, with a heavy sigh. "I should not have mentioned the matter to you at all, but for the fact that it must very soon have come to your ears in any case. Within three days, sir, we have lost six war vessels, while a seventh, the *Kasuga*, has been temporarily put out of action. And of the six lost ships, Captain, two are battleships, the *Hatsuse* and the *Yashima*!"

"The *Hatsuse* and the *Yashima*! Good heavens! sir. Is it possible?" I exclaimed.

"It is more than possible," answered Togo, with another heavy sigh, "it is a disastrous fact. And in addition to those two ships, we have also lost the *Yoshino*, fortunately not one of our best fast cruisers. Oh! it is terrible, terrible! And all three disasters have occurred to-day, within a very short space of time. The news reached me by wireless in the interval between my sending for you and your arrival.

"It appears that while the *Yoshino*, *Takasago*, *Chitose*, *Kasagi*, and *Kasuga* were to the westward of Port Arthur this morning, just after dawn, they ran into a patch of dense fog, while steaming through which, the lookout aboard the *Yoshino* sighted a floating mine a short distance ahead. Thereupon the officer in charge seems to have temporarily lost his presence of mind, for instead of sheering out of the line, as it seems to me he might have done, and so avoided the mine, he instantly stopped and reversed his engines, without warning the *Kasuga*, which was his next astern. The inevitable result of course was that the *Kasuga* struck the *Yoshino* heavily, making such a terrible rent in her side that, in spite of collision mats, she speedily filled, capsized, and sank, drowning over two hundred of her crew. The *Kasuga*, badly damaged, is on her way hither, and may be expected to arrive some time to-night.

"That disaster, however, serious as it is, is nothing compared with the loss of the *Hatsuse* and *Yashima*, which occurred shortly after midday. Little did we dream, as they steamed away from here, this morning, that we should never see them again! It happened about ten miles south of Port Arthur, the two ships striking mines within a few minutes of each other. The *Hatsuse* appears to have struck two mines, the second of which completed her destruction, for she foundered in less than two minutes after the second explosion occurred. I understand that considerably more than half her crew have gone down with her.

"There were hopes at first that the *Yashima* might be saved, as collision mats were got over her damaged bows and the steam pumps were started, while she headed for here under her own steam, with the rest of the squadron in company; but the latest news is to the effect that she cannot possibly be kept afloat, and that her crew are being taken off. Well, it is the fortune of war, I suppose, and it is useless to murmur; we cannot hope to always have things go well with us, reverses *will* happen occasionally; and I am afraid that we have been growing just a little too careless and over-confident of late. We must take the lesson to heart and see that it does not again happen. But it is a paralysing blow for us.

"And now, to return to the matter which more immediately concerns you, Captain. I have given you the earliest possible warning of what I am going to ask you to do, in order that you may have an opportunity to think over the situation and make your plans. I want you to be ready to start at practically a moment's notice; but I shall not dispatch the squadron until I have further news from Oku, which may arrive at any minute."

As it happened, however, although a communication arrived from Oku the next day, it was a full week before we got our orders; for a careful reconnaissance revealed that very important preparations would be necessary before it would be possible to take Kinchau, or storm the Nanshan Heights.

Just about sunset the *Shikishima*, with her attendant cruisers, hove in sight, and before they were hull-up it was possible for us to distinguish that the *Yashima* was not among them. She had gone down off Dalny—in shallow water, fortunately—but not until every man had been safely taken out of her.

The other losses to which the Admiral had referred were torpedo-boat Number 48, and the dispatch boat *Mikayo*, both of which had come to grief, the one on 12th May, and the other two days later, through striking mines in Kerr Bay, some thirty miles to the north-east of Port Arthur. Torpedo-boats Numbers 46 and 48, it appeared, were engaged in sweeping for mines when the accident happened. They had already found and destroyed three mines, and had discovered a fourth, which they fired several rounds at without result. Then Number 48 imprudently approached the mine with the intention of securing it, when it exploded, blowing her in two, and killing or wounding fourteen of her crew of twenty-three.

It was two days later when the *Mikayo*, believing the bay to be clear, entered it to make sure. She was passing in through the channel supposed to have been cleared by our torpedo-boats, when she, too, struck a mine; there was a terrific explosion, and she went to the bottom, with eight casualties in her crew of two hundred. She was a useful little ship, having a speed of over sixteen knots when she was destroyed, although she had been known to achieve as much as twenty. She mounted two forty-sevens and ten 3-pounders, and was therefore not a very formidable fighting craft.

The story told by the Russians concerning her destruction was to the effect that she fell a victim to a mine, placed overnight, in the channel previously cleared by our boats, by a young Russian naval officer, who stole out from Port Arthur in a small steam launch, under the cover of night. Whether the story is true or not, I cannot tell, yet there is nothing very improbable about it, for it is indisputable that many of the Russians displayed as fine a courage as even the Japanese themselves.

Chapter Twelve
At Work in Kinchau Bay

Meanwhile, I was spending my days poring over the maps and charts of Kinchau and its neighbourhood with which I had been supplied, leaving Commander Tsuchiya to carry on the work of constructing the long boom, and merely visiting it in a picket boat at the close of each day, to see how the work was progressing. My study of the maps and charts had reference to a scheme which had come into my head whereby it might be possible to determine the ranges of the several Russian positions from certain fixed points in the bay with the utmost accuracy, thereby greatly increasing the effectiveness of the naval fire when our flotilla should be called into action. The map in particular which had been issued to me was drawn upon a scale so large that even comparatively insignificant distances could be closely measured upon it, and it was so full of detail that apparently every building, however unimportant, was marked upon it; also it was "contoured"—that is to say, it was covered all over with wavy lines, each of which represented a definite height above sea-level. With such a map before me it was of course the easiest matter imaginable to determine the position of all the most salient points of the landscape, of which there were several, and— assuming the map to be correctly drawn—to measure the distances of these from one another.

With such a bountiful fund of at least approximately accurate information for a starting-point it was a simple matter for me to fix upon a number of points in the bay—as many as I chose, in fact—which could be clearly indicated by buoys bearing different coloured flags, the positions of which could be accurately determined by cross bearings; and my plan was, first to lay down these buoys and determine their positions, and then mark them on maps, a copy of which would be handed to each captain, from which, by the employment of a scale and a pair of dividers, he could immediately measure off with precision the exact range of any object desired.

Having at length arranged my scheme on the map to my liking, I proceeded with it aboard the *Mikasa*, and submitted it to the Admiral, who, with Captain Ijichi, the Commander, and several of the officers of the ship, examined it with the utmost interest, asking me several questions in connection with it. When I had fully explained the scheme, they all agreed that it was an admirable idea, and would undoubtedly be of the utmost value—if it could only be carried out. Togo was of opinion that it could not; I, on the contrary, was convinced that it could; and at length I managed to get the Admiral's somewhat reluctant consent to make the experiment.

Armed with this, I went ashore and, making my way to the carpenter's shop which formed part of our shore establishment among the islands, ordered a certain number of small triangular rafts to be made, of a size just sufficient to support a bamboo staff ten feet long, to the top of which a flag six feet long by three feet wide was to be firmly lashed, the flags to be of different colours, arranged in pairs. The rafts were constructed merely of rough timber stoutly nailed together, while the flags, being only required to last a day or two, as we hoped, were made of coloured calico, the edges turned over and hemmed with a sewing-machine, that they might not fray or tear. A couple of hours' work sufficed to complete my small requisition, with which I returned to the *Kasanumi*.

It was within half an hour of sunset when I got aboard with my boatload of miscellaneous paraphernalia; and as the torpedo flotilla always kept steam while at the Elliots, excepting when it became necessary to clean flues or boilers, we at once got our anchor and proceeded to sea at a speed of twenty knots. I was bound round to Kinchau Bay, the distance of which from the Elliot group, by sea, was about one hundred and thirteen sea miles; I therefore reckoned on arriving at my destination about midnight, which would suit me admirably. The moon was in her third quarter, and was due to rise, that night, at a few minutes after one o'clock, which would also suit me excellently.

For a wonder, the night was fine, with a light air out from about south-east; there was no sea, and not much swell, and as the destroyer was running well within herself, we went along quite easily and comfortably, and I seized the opportunity to snatch a few hours' sleep, leaving the navigation of the boat to my chief officer, who was quite equal to the task.

The trip was uneventful, and at midnight Lieutenant Hiraoka aroused me with the intimation that we were standing into Kinchau Bay, and were already near enough to the land to enable the watch-fires on the hills to be made out; I accordingly turned out and went on deck to take a look round. I had studied my maps so exhaustively that, dark though the night was, I was able without difficulty to identify the various heights in sight, of which Mount Sampson was by far the most conspicuous; the general appearance of the land, indeed, was remarkably like what I had already mentally pictured it to be, and I seemed to be gazing on quite familiar ground. We were of course running without lights, and there was hardly a ghost of a chance of our being seen, but I eagerly searched the bay for craft, and was gratified to find that it was empty.

But if there were no craft, there might be a good many mines; therefore in order to avoid all possible risk we crossed the bay to its northern shore, keeping well out, and then, going dead slow and feeling our way with the lead, we hugged the northern shore line as closely as the depth of water would permit, until we arrived abreast a little indentation, or cove, when the engines were stopped, the boat lowered, and, with my revolvers in my belt, but no sword, a pocketful of cartridges, a water bottle, a wallet of provisions, an azimuth compass, and a box sextant, I was pulled ashore and landed in the cove, the boat immediately returning to the destroyer, which soon vanished in the darkness, making for the offing.

There were some half-dozen small, crazy-looking fishing-boats drawn up on the beach of the cove, and, groping about, I presently found a footpath leading somewhere inland. This I cautiously followed for a little distance until the crow of a wakeful cock and the bark of a dog warned me that I was at no great distance from a human dwelling of some sort, when I struck off the path and waded through a field of millet, heading north-west for the summit of a hill which I easily recognised, even in the dark, as one of the points from which I purposed to take my set of observations. My more immediate anxiety, however, was to get away from the neighbourhood of all human habitations, for although I knew pretty well, in a general way, where the Russians might be expected to be found, there was always the possibility of running unexpectedly into a small detachment of them, or of encountering some Korean peasant who might be disposed to betray me, upon the off-chance of securing a reward for so doing.

The low ground at the foot of the range of hills for which I was heading was all cultivated, as well as the lower slopes, but, higher up, the ground was covered pretty thickly with scrub, with here and there a few patches of fir trees; and when once I got among these I felt that I was fairly safe, for I imagined that nobody would be likely to have any business up there, while in the disturbed state of the country nobody would be likely to wander there for pleasure.

By the time that I reached the lower margin of the belt of scrub, the moon, one-half of her in shadow, had crept up above the crest of Mount Sampson, and the whole of the country round about me was flooded with her dim, ghostly light, with the help of which I was able to make out the small walled city of Kinchau, planned in the form of a square, each side measuring about half a mile long; the Japanese position in the valley to the south of it; and a few of the Russian positions on the Nanshan Heights; I was also able to definitely reassure myself as to my own position.

The point for which I was aiming was about three miles north of the little cove in which I had landed, and the intervening ground was rugged, with many outcrops of rough, jagged rock, and much overgrown with thick, tangled scrub; the "going," therefore, was a bit toilsome, but that did not greatly matter to me, for the night air was distinctly raw, I was none too thickly clad, and the exertion kept me warm. When I reached the belt of fir wood that seemed to completely encircle the range of heights which I was climbing, the obscurity was such that it was only with the utmost difficulty I was able to make any headway at all; and at length, coming to a spot where the grass was exceptionally thick and dry, feeling somewhat fatigued with my unwonted exertions, I flung myself down for a short rest, and before I knew what was happening, fell fast asleep.

I awoke, chill and cramped, at the sound of a distant bugle call, to find that the sky over the summit of Mount Sampson was just paling to the approach of dawn. I therefore scrambled to my feet, much refreshed by my nap, and resumed my climb, eager to get a glimpse of my surroundings with the first of the daylight; for I had a great deal to do, and not very much time in which to do it.

A quarter of an hour of brisk walking brought me to the upper edge of the fir wood, and there before me, scarcely a mile distant, stood the peak which I had chosen as the starting-point for my operations. I had been guided by the map in my selection of it, for the contours showed me that, apart from Mount Sampson, it was one of the most lofty elevations in the neighbourhood, and also that it rose somewhat abruptly to a small, well-defined point. My first glance at it assured me that, so far at least, my map spoke truly, for the summit appeared to consist of a rocky knoll, the highest point of which was a short, stunted, conical mass, the top of which seemed scarcely capable of affording standing room. Nothing could possibly have been better for my purpose, and I hurried forward and upward, eager now to get at my work.

I will not afflict the reader by attempting to describe in detail my plan of operations, for it involved a mathematical problem of some complexity, only interesting to and comprehensible by a mathematician. Suffice it to say that what I had undertaken to do was to make three separate sets of observations from as many chosen points, consisting of carefully observed compass bearings, and angles taken with my pocket sextant; and the taking of these observations, and the travelling from one point to another, kept me so busy all day that I was scarcely able to find time to snatch a couple of hurried meals while walking from one point to another. I was not interfered with by anybody, for, with two opposing armies facing each other at close quarters, the population seemed scarcely inclined to venture out of doors. Of course I saw plenty of armed men, both Russians and our own troops, moving about in the plain which surrounds Kinchau, and there was a considerable amount of desultory firing going on; but it was not until well on in the afternoon that I came into close proximity of any of the troops, and that was when it became necessary for me to cross a road leading into Kinchau from the north. Along this road armed Russians, singly, in twos and threes, and often in large bodies, were passing to and fro; and I lost nearly an hour of valuable time waiting for an opportunity merely to cross that road unseen. However, I managed it at last, and reached my final observation point just in time to satisfactorily finish my work before night fell and the light failed me.

And now my next task was to somehow make my way back to the cove in which I had landed some eighteen hours earlier. To do this it was necessary for me to recross the road where I had been held up during the afternoon; but now the darkness was in my favour, and I succeeded in getting across with scarcely any delay, arriving at the cove safely, with a good hour to spare.

It was a weary waiting for the boat which was due to come for me at midnight, for I was very tired after my unusual exertions throughout the day, and would gladly have slept. But that would not do; for to have slept would have exposed me to the double risk of being surprised, and of missing my boat; I was therefore by no means sorry when, about midnight, I heard the low whistle which announced her arrival. To step lightly into her and murmur the order to shove off was the work of a moment, and half an hour later I was again safely aboard the *Kasanumi*, to the great joy of young Hiraoka, who, it appeared, had been all day haunted with the fear that I might fall into the hands of the Russians.

And now, weary as I was, there were at least two hours' work before me, with pencil, paper, protractor, parallel ruler, and scale, making calculations and laying down upon map and chart the result of my observations. This result was, on the whole, eminently satisfactory, for although I discovered a few trifling errors in the map, here and there, my observations enabled me to correct them; and when I had at length finished, map and chart were in a condition which would enable me to proceed with the second part of my task with the assurance of success. This accomplished, I retired to my cabin with an easy mind, and slept the sleep of the just until midday.

A salt-water douche on deck for a few minutes, skilfully administered by a laughing Japanese seaman, and a brisk rub down with a rough towel left me fresh and invigorated, quite ready for a meal and the work which still lay ahead of me. The first part of this consisted in laying down upon the chart a number of positions corresponding with the varying draughts of water of the several units which the Admiral was detailing to assist General Oku in his operations against the Russian forces who were barring his passage of the Kinchau isthmus. The laying down of the positions above referred to was a task demanding a considerable amount of thought and care, for it was important that the ships should approach the shore as nearly as possible, otherwise their guns might be out-ranged, while, on the other hand, they must not be permitted to approach too near, or they would be exposed to the risk of being left aground on a falling tide. Also it was imperative that the berths chosen for them should be so situated as to enable them to afford the maximum amount of possible assistance. I devoted the entire afternoon to the consideration of this question, and at length fixed upon a series of positions which seemed to me to answer all requirements as nearly as the tidal conditions would allow. My next task was to accurately fix these several positions by as complete a series of cross bearings as possible; having accomplished which, there was nothing more to be done until after midnight. Meanwhile, the *Kasanumi*, with her engines stopped, was lying hove-to some sixty miles to the westward of Kinchau, in the Gulf of Liaotung, waiting for nightfall.

At four bells in the first watch we got under way and started to run east at a speed of twenty knots, for I had now to complete my entire plan by placing the buoys, or triangular rafts which I had provided for the purpose, in the positions in Kinchau Bay which I had already selected for them and marked upon the chart.

Too anxious for the complete success of my scheme to be able to sleep, I had ordered a deck chair to be brought up from below, and was sitting in this on our little navigating bridge, with a midshipman named Uchida, who had been detailed for service with me, pacing softly to and fro from port to starboard, keeping the lookout; and the cold night air was beginning to produce a pleasantly drowsy effect upon me when, as the boy halted for a moment in turning on his march, he suddenly stiffened, and stared intently out upon our starboard beam. He stood thus, like a figure suddenly turned to stone, for the space of a full minute or more, then came softly to my side and saluted.

"Three craft on our starboard beam, sir, coming up from the south-west," he reported.

"What do they look like?" I demanded, rising to my feet and staring out in the direction toward which the boy pointed.

"I cannot yet say, sir," he replied. "At present they are too far off to reveal their character; indeed, I doubt if I should have seen them so soon, but for the fact that I glimpsed the flames issuing from one of their funnels."

"Yes," I said. "Thanks, Mr Uchida, I see them too. Have the goodness to bring me the night-glass from the chart-house. They appear to be steaming with lights out."

The lad hurried away, and quickly returned with the night-glass, which I focused and applied to my eye. The night was overcast, but there were a few stars blinking out between the clouds, which were flying fast up from the westward, and by their feeble, uncertain light I was presently able to distinguish a little more clearly the three small, shapeless blurs that Uchida's keen eyes had detected. They were little more than shapeless blurs still, even when viewed through the powerful lenses of the night-glass; but I was able to distinguish that one of them was considerably bigger than the other two, which were much of a size. It was the funnel of the big fellow that was showing the flames, which seemed to indicate that she was being driven, while the other two appeared to be running easily. Yet all three were in company. The appearance of the two smaller craft seemed to suggest to me that they might possibly be destroyers; but what the other was, I could not guess. She was not big enough for a cruiser or a transport; and the fact that she was evidently being hard driven to enable her to keep pace with her consorts—or, possibly, escort—led me to doubt whether she was a warship of any kind. One thing was pretty clear, which was that, like ourselves, they were evidently bound for Kinchau Bay. Were they enemies or friends? If the former, it was eminently undesirable that they should be permitted to arrive, and it was for me to look into the matter.

"How's her head?" I demanded of the helmsman.

"East, three degrees south," he replied.

"Shift your helm to east, twenty-five degrees south," I ordered; and the bows of the destroyer swung round until she was heading for a point at which we could intercept the strangers. Then: "Mr Uchida," I said, "pass the word to prepare to make the private night signal."

The signal was presently hoisted to the yard-arm and displayed for fully five minutes without evoking a response; and then I knew that the strangers were enemies. We accordingly hauled down the signal again and cleared for action, loading both torpedo tubes as well. This done, we quickened up our pace to full speed; for if we were going to have a fight, I wanted it to be out there in the open, so far away from the shore that the sounds of firing would not reach the Russians about Kinchau, and so apprise them of the presence of an enemy in the adjacent waters.

As we rapidly neared the enemy I made them out to be two destroyers, evidently escorting the third craft, which was a single-funnelled steamer of apparently about eighteen hundred tons. She sat deep in the water, as though loaded to her full capacity, but she was much too small for a transport, and for the life of me I could not imagine what her character might be. But there could be no doubt whatever concerning the destroyers; they were self-evident Russians, for they were four-funnelled, the funnels arranged in pairs, which was distinctly characteristic of a certain class of Russian destroyer.

Neither side wasted any time upon useless preliminaries; but it was the Russians who opened the ball by both craft firing, almost simultaneously, every gun they could bring to bear upon us. But their aim was nothing to boast of, for although we heard the shells screaming all about us, we remained untouched. Twice they fired upon us before I would give the word to our gun-layers, and both times ineffectively; then I gave the order to commence firing; and no sooner had the words passed my lips than our 12-pounder spoke, and a moment later there occurred two distinct explosions aboard the nearest Russian boat, which instantly became enveloped in a great cloud of steam. Apparently that first shot of ours had struck and exploded one of her boilers, for almost immediately she slackened speed and began to drop astern. This mishap, however, did not seem to in the least discourage her consort, which, putting on full speed, now dashed at us in the most determined and gallant manner, firing as she came, and receiving our fire in return. And then, for some ten minutes, we found ourselves engaged in a regular ding-dong fight, we and our antagonist closing to a distance of less than two hundred yards, and hammering away at each other as fast as the guns could be served.

But it very soon became apparent that our fellows were much the better and cooler gunners of the two; for whereas the Russians seemed to ram in their charges and let fly on the instant that their guns were loaded, our men waited, watching the roll both of their own ship and that of the enemy, and firing at her waterline as she rolled away from us, with the result that within the first five minutes of the fight a lucky shot from our 12-pounder sent a shell through her upturned bilge a foot or so below her normal waterline, blowing a hole through her thin plating that admitted a tremendous inrush of water every time that she rolled toward us. Her crew at once got out a collision mat and made the most desperate efforts to get it over and stop the leak; but our 6-pound quick-firers peppered them so severely that, after struggling manfully for two or three minutes, they were obliged to let the mat go, and lost it. Then they launched a torpedo at us, which missed us by inches only, whereupon I ordered our men to cease fire, and hailed the Russian to ask if she would surrender. But, not a bit of it; their reply, as translated to me by Hiraoka, who was an excellent Russian linguist, was, that they knew how to die, but not how to surrender; and the reply was accompanied by another salvo from every one of their guns that would bear. And this, too, at a moment when it became only too apparent that the boat was rapidly sinking. Since, therefore, it was evident that they were resolved to fight to the last, there was nothing for it but to open fire upon them afresh, much as I regretted it, as they obstinately persisted in keeping up a fire upon us.

The end, however, was nearer than even I thought, for we had fired but a few more shots at our opponent when there occurred a terrific explosion aboard her, instantly followed by several others, her deck opened up like the lid of a box, a great sheet of flame leapt up from her interior; and, seeming to break in two, the dismembered hull rapidly disappeared, the bow and stern portions rearing themselves out of water for a few seconds ere they plunged to the bottom, leaving nothing to show where the boat had been, save a great cloud of acrid smoke and steam, a few fragments of wreckage, and some half a dozen men struggling in the water.

Of course we instantly stopped our engines and launched a boat; but we only found and saved three men out of the boat's total complement of forty-seven. We learned that the name of the lost destroyer was the *Beztraschni*, and that all of her officers had perished with her.

We now had leisure to attend to the other two craft, which were by this time some three miles astern, having apparently stopped their engines to await at a safe distance the course of events. Swinging round, we headed for them at full speed, with all guns loaded, and a torpedo in each tube, ready to open fire as soon as we got within effective range. As we drew nearer, however, it became evident that there was something very seriously wrong with the destroyer which we had first fired upon, and which had dropped astern, disabled, for there were boats in the water about her, seemingly passing between her and the other craft, boats going to her with only two or three hands in them, and leaving her loaded. By the time that we had arrived within a mile of her we could see that the destroyer was in a sinking condition; and a minute later we lost sight of her altogether: she had gone down.

The boats were still in the water alongside the surviving craft, and men were climbing up her side from them as we arrived within some thirty fathoms of her and hailed, demanding her surrender. A reply instantly came from her to the effect that she surrendered; whereupon I dispatched Hiraoka on board, in charge of an armed boat's crew; and some ten minutes later the youngster hailed, informing me that our prize was named the *Vashka*, of seventeen hundred and sixty tons register, originally a cargo steamer, but now adapted for mine-laying; and that she was from Dalny, bound for Kinchau Bay for the purpose of sowing the bay with mines, in anticipation of the probability that some of our ships would be sent to participate in the attack upon the isthmus. He added the information that the vessel, hoping to escape the notice of Japan's warships by taking a roundabout route, had been escorted by two destroyers only, the *Beztraschni* and the *Storozhevoi*, the latter of which we had seen go down a few minutes before as a result of injuries inflicted upon her by our 12-pounder, the shell from which had not only blown a great rent in her bottom, as it burst, but the fragments of which had pierced two of her boilers.

It was evident that we had made a capture of considerable importance, I therefore proceeded on board the prize, with an armed reinforcement, and after going carefully into the matter with Hiraoka, arranged with him to take the *Vashka* to the Elliots, in charge of a prize crew, there to act according to the Admiral's orders.

This matter arranged, I returned to the *Kasanumi*, and we resumed our voyage while the prize headed away south-west, on her way round to the Elliot Islands. We now had leisure to look into the extent of our own injuries. These, it proved, were by no means so serious as might have been expected, having regard to the fierceness and closeness of the fight. Our casualties amounted to two killed and five wounded, one of them seriously; while the top of the aftermost of our midship pair of funnels had been blown away, the rail of the navigating bridge smashed and doubled up in a most astonishing way, the pilot-house roof torn off, our topsides pierced in no less than five places, and a very pretty general average made of my cabin, in which a shell had evidently burst. Luckily, none of these injuries seriously affected the craft's safety, while most of them could be at least temporarily patched-up in a few hours; also, very luckily, all the navigating instruments, the chronometer, my sextant, the nautical almanac, and my book of logarithmic and other tables had almost miraculously escaped all injury.

We steamed into Kinchau Bay, with all lights out, about an hour later than I had arranged for, but still in sufficient time for the work which lay before me; and when we arrived off the cove where I had previously landed, our largest boat was lowered, the buoys or rafts which I had caused to be prepared were placed in her, each having attached to it a very light chain of just sufficient length to securely moor it with the aid of a good grapnel; and, accompanied by two men, I then jumped in, and we pulled ashore, while the *Kasanumi* turned tail and steamed off to sea again at full speed, so as to be out of sight from the shore before dawn.

Arrived in the cove, we secured our boat, and then settled down as comfortably as was possible to await the dawn. It came at last, and, as I had expected, there very shortly afterwards arrived some forty Manchurian fishermen from a little village, about half a mile distant. At first they were somewhat alarmed to find the cove, and their boats, apparently in possession of Japanese men-o'-war's-men; but I had taken the precaution to ensure that one of my men should be capable of playing the part of interpreter; and before long I was able not only to reassure them but also, by a judicious admixture of cajolery and threats, to secure their assistance in the completion of my scheme. Money appeals to the Manchurian fisherman just as powerfully as it does to most other people, more powerfully than it does to many, for he sees so little of it; consequently when I intimated that I was prepared to pay the magnificent sum of ten yen for a few hours' use of one of their boats, with a crew of four men, the whole crowd came tumbling over one another in their eagerness to secure the prize. I chose the boat most suitable for my purpose, transferred my rafts and gear to her, leaving our own boat in charge of a man who undertook to guard her with his life for the sum of one yen; and then, in company with the other boats, which were going fishing in the bay, we shoved off and pulled out of the cove. By a stroke of the greatest good fortune, the day was beautifully fine and clear, so that I was able without the slightest difficulty to get every one of my bearings with the most absolute accuracy, and to place my several buoys on the prearranged spots with perfect precision. The work was successfully and most satisfactorily accomplished shortly before noon; and now all that remained to be done was to affix the different coloured flags to the buoys. But that part would have to be deferred until our ships should actually come into action; otherwise our sharp-sighted enemies might prematurely catch sight of them, and, guessing their purpose, destroy them.

Chapter Thirteen
I go ashore

" We made out the dark form of the destroyer. "

An hour before midnight, launching our own boat, my crew and I pushed out of the cove into Kinchau Bay, in readiness to board the *Kasanumi* immediately upon her arrival from the offing.

Toward the close of the afternoon the weather had undergone a change, becoming overcast and hazy, with a drizzling rain.

The wind, too, had shifted, and, as we pushed out of the cove, was blowing fresh from the westward, knocking up a short, choppy sea that threatened soon to become dangerous to such a small boat as ours. Luckily for us, however, Hiraoka was a bit ahead of time that night, the barometer having warned him that bad weather was brewing, with the result that in little more than half an hour after leaving the cove we made out the dark form of the destroyer, hove-to and waiting for us, within fifty fathoms of our boat. And now it was that I had practical experience of the value of a suitable colouring as an aid to concealment; for although the *Kasanumi* had been where we found her for a full quarter of an hour, and although we had been keeping a sharp lookout for her, she remained invisible until we were close aboard of her, thanks to the peculiar shade of grey with which I had caused her to be painted. We scrambled aboard gladly enough, hoisted the boat to the davits, and at once started back for our rendezvous at the Elliot group, where we arrived without adventure shortly after sunrise on the following morning.

When, a little later, I went aboard the flagship to report myself and the result of my expedition to the Admiral, I learned that I had only got back just in the nick of time, for at last a communication had been received from General Oku, announcing that his preparations were now complete, and the squadron detached to assist him was under orders to leave for Kinchau Bay that very night. This squadron consisted of the *Tsukushi*, a light cruiser, armed with two 10-inch and four 47-inch guns, and the old ironclad *Hei-yen*, once belonging to the Chinese navy, but captured by the Japanese at the first battle of the Yalu. She mounted one 10-inch Krupp which had formed part of her original armament, and two 6-inch modern guns. Also the *Akagi*, another survivor of the Yalu battle, armed with four 47-inch guns; and the *Chokai*, carrying one 8-2-inch and one 47-inch gun. These were the craft destined to bombard the Nanshan Heights from the sea while the Japanese infantry and artillery attacked them from the land side; and they were the only craft we had at the time at all suitable for the purpose, while even they were incapable of rendering such efficient help as might have been desired, the fact being that the shallow waters of Kinchau Bay compelled them to keep at so great a distance from the shore that they could only use their guns at extreme ranges. Accompanying these four ships was a flotilla consisting of ten torpedo-boats under my command, their duty being to lend a hand generally in any manner that might be required.

There was just comfortable time for us to re-bunker the *Kasanumi* before six o'clock, at which hour we got under way, the expedition as a whole being under the command of Rear-Admiral Misamichi, who knew the locality well, having carefully reconnoitred the whole of the western coast of the peninsula a week or two earlier. I had by this time completed all my calculations, laid down upon the chart the positions of my series of buoys, and indicated in figures the exact measurements in yards from the lines which they marked to a number of points ashore, and a copy of this chart had been handed to each captain; they were therefore now in a position to steam in and open fire forthwith, with the absolute certainty of landing their shots upon the spots aimed at.

We were rather a slow-going lot, our speed of course being regulated by that of the slowest craft of the bunch, which happened to be the old *Hei-yen*; and our progress was further impeded by the circumstance that, upon rounding Liao-ti-shan promontory we ran into a westerly breeze and sea that flung our torpedo-boats about like corks and necessitated our slowing down to a speed of about eight knots; in consequence of which it was late the next night when we arrived and came to an anchor well out in deep water.

And now arose a little difficulty. We started to communicate by wireless to General Oku the fact of our arrival in the bay, by code of course; but such was the Russian keenness and activity that the moment their own wireless picked up our message,—as, of course, it was bound to do,—finding that it was in a code which they could not decipher, they immediately proceeded to "mix" it so effectually that the reading of it became impossible. The first word or two, however, reached Oku, and he at once, shrewdly surmising that the message was from us, proceeded to signal us by searchlight, using an adaptation of the Morse Code. The conversation thus carried on was a lengthy one, occupying more than an hour, when it suddenly ceased, and almost immediately afterward the Admiral signalled me to proceed on board the flagship. This was much more easily said than done, for by this time it was blowing a moderate gale, and the sea was running so heavily that it was as much as my boat could do to live in it, while as for getting alongside the cruiser, that was quite out of the question, and they were obliged to hoist me aboard in a standing bowline at the end of a whip.

Upon being shown into Admiral Misamichi's cabin, I found its occupant somewhat ruefully contemplating the rather voluminous communication from the shore which he had just received. He welcomed me with much cordiality, and then passed the document over to me.

"Be so good as to read that, Captain," he said, "and then kindly tell me what you make of it. It purports to be General Oku's instructions for to-morrow; but so dense is my stupidity that I am compelled to confess my inability to understand it."

I read the communication carefully through from beginning to end three times, and was then obliged to admit that I had only been able to glean a very hazy, imperfect notion of what the General required. I gathered that he desired the squadron to concentrate its fire from time to time upon certain points, as directed by signal; but the mischief of it was that we out there in the bay had no means of identifying the points named by the General; in other words, he gave them designations of which we were completely ignorant. We produced the chart of the place, likewise the map, and studied them both intently, with Oku's message beside us, and finally came to the conclusion that it was incomprehensible. Then the Admiral sent for the captains of the other ships, and they had a shot at it, with a similar result.

At length I said:

"It appears to me, sir, that there is but one thing to be done, namely, for me to go ashore, find General Oku, explain to him our difficulty, and *get* him to mark on the map the several points mentioned here," — touching the dispatch. "As you are aware, I have already been ashore here; I spent a whole day among the hills, reconnoitring the ground and making observations. I therefore know the country well, including our own and the enemy's positions; and probably half an hour's conversation with the General will enable me to identify the points mentioned in this dispatch with some of those already marked upon my chart. Thus, for example, this point, the position of which we are wholly unable to identify, may be the position which I have marked 1, or 3, or 7, or, in fact, anything; but it *must* be one or other of those which I have numbered, for I numbered every one of them."

"Yes, yes," agreed the Admiral, "that is all quite comprehensible; and, if you could only get ashore, the matter could very soon be adjusted. But how are you going to get ashore; and—still more difficult—how are you going to get off again? From what I know of this bay, I am prepared to say that there is a surf breaking on the beach at this moment which no boat of ours could pass through and live. Listen to the wind, how it howls through our rigging!"

True! that was a point which had entirely escaped me, in my eagerness. How was I to get ashore? Or rather, how was I to get off again? I was pretty confident of my ability to get ashore, for surf-swimming was a favourite pastime of mine; but as to getting off again—well, I doubted whether even my strength was equal to the task of struggling out through the long lines of surf which I knew must now be thundering in upon Kinchau beach.

The difficulty was finally overcome by the Admiral consenting to my attempting to get ashore, upon condition that I would not attempt to swim off again unless I felt absolutely convinced of my ability to accomplish the feat. If I could not, I was to remain ashore with Oku, helping him in any manner that might suggest itself, but especially by signalling off to the fleet, from time to time, the numbers of the several positions which they would be required to shell.

This matter settled, I made my way back to the *Kasanumi*, and there prepared for my somewhat hazardous adventure by carefully tying up a marked and figured copy of the map of Kinchau and its surroundings in a piece of thin sheet rubber, to protect it from the wet. Next, I divested myself of all clothing except a pair of swimming drawers and a pair of thin canvas running shoes. Then, tying the map, in its rubber case, round my neck, I signalled our smallest torpedo-boat to look out for me and haul me aboard—for by this time the sea was running so heavily that it was impossible to launch a boat; when, having received a reply to my signal, I simply dived overboard and swam down to leeward to where the torpedo-boat lay. Her crew were, of course, keenly on the alert, and as I came driving down toward them, only visible in consequence of the phosphorescence of the water, they flung me a lifebuoy bent on to the end of a line, and so hauled me aboard.

We were anchored at a distance of about four miles from the shore, which was, of course, much too great a distance for me to attempt to swim in the sea that was now running, especially as I should need every ounce of strength to fight my way through the long stretch of surf that I knew must now be breaking all along the shore. I therefore briefly explained to the skipper of the torpedo-boat the mission upon which I was bound, and what I wished him to do, and then, while he saw to the doing of his part, I retired to his little cabin, stripped off my wet swimming kit, and gave myself a vigorous towelling to banish the cold of even the brief swim I had already undertaken. Meanwhile, the boat was got under way and taken in toward Kinchau, with the lead going all the time; and when at length she was as near the shore as it was at all prudent for her to approach, she was turned with her head to seaward, and the skipper came down to apprise me of the state of affairs. The boat had taken about twenty minutes to feel her way in, and during that time I had been assiduously practising gymnastics; I was therefore now not only dry but also in a pleasant glow of warmth, and quite ready to undertake the really formidable part of the task that still lay before me.

My swimming kit had meanwhile been taken down into the stokehole, so that when it was handed to me it was not only nearly dry but, what was very much more to the purpose, comfortably warm. Donning it and a fine warm boat cloak, I accompanied the skipper to the deck and walked aft to take a look at the task before me. I found that they had taken the boat in to the very edge of the outer line of the surf, which stretched away inshore of us, line after line, in an apparently interminable procession of breakers, like lines of infantry rushing forward to the assault, vaguely visible in their pallid phosphorescence against the blackness of the starless night. To fight my way to the shore through that wide area of roaring, leaping, and seething breakers promised to be a task that would tax my strength and energy to their utmost limits; but it was a case of necessity, and I had undertaken to do it; therefore, throwing off the borrowed boat cloak, with a word of farewell to the skipper of the boat, I waited for the next oncoming breaker, and dived overboard at the precise moment when it would catch me up in its mighty arms and sweep me, without effort on my part, a good twenty fathoms toward the shore.

B-r-r-r! The water struck icy cold to my warm skin as I plunged deep into the heart of the great arching mass of water, which caught me just as I was rising to the surface and hurled me shoreward with irresistible force, rolling me over and over like a cork as it broke into a long line of hissing, pallid foam. But I knew exactly what to expect, and was fully prepared for it. I therefore allowed it to do with me just what it would, holding my breath and waiting until the breaker had passed ahead and spent its force. Then, striking out strongly as I came to the surface, I swam on toward the next line of breakers, where the same thing was repeated, but each time a shade less violently, until at length, after what seemed like hours, but which, as a matter of fact, could not have been more than about forty minutes of battling with the breakers, my feet touched ground, and a moment later the last breaker, a very mild and harmless one compared with those in the offing, lifted me up and almost gently deposited me on the beach.

Upon hands and knees I crawled up above watermark and then rose to my feet to look about, recover my breath, and get my bearings. After the stinging cold of the water, the air felt quite pleasantly warm, but I knew that I should soon get chilled if I did not keep moving briskly; so, seeing a line of watch-fires about half a mile away, which, from their position, I guessed must be Japanese, I set out toward them at a brisk walking pace, and, the ground being fortunately open in that direction, it was but a few minutes before I found myself unexpectedly halted, with the point of a Japanese sentry's bayonet gently pressing against my breast. Of course I hadn't the countersign; but my appearance, and particularly my unconventional garb, must have convinced him of the truth of my story that, being unable to get ashore in any other way, I had swum in from the fleet, with a communication from the Admiral for General Oku, for he passed me on to the next sentry without hesitation; and thus in the course of another ten minutes I found myself in the tent of a certain colonel who not only had heard of me but had also seen me and now recognised me. From him I learned that the general staff quarters were situated about a mile farther inland, on one of the lower slopes of Mount Sampson, to which he very kindly offered to conduct me. But of course I could not present myself before General Oku in bathing rig, and it was not without difficulty that a suit of clothes was at length found into which I could get; but it was managed at last, and off we went, the colonel and I, my companion seeming to be greatly impressed with my swimming feat. "I wonder," he remarked, "if there is *anything* that an Englishman would not at least *attempt* to do!"

Our way led through the Japanese camp, so I had a very good opportunity to observe what the domestic life—if I may so term it—of the Japanese soldier was at the front; and I was surprised to see how thoroughly every possible contingency had been foreseen and provided for, and how many ingenious little devices had been thought out and included in his kit with the object of adding to his comfort.

In due time we arrived at headquarters; and late though the hour was, the General and his staff were all not only awake and on the move, but were holding a sort of council of war, for the purpose of making the final arrangements for the morrow. As it happened, my arrival was most opportune, for the staff were planning the details of an assault that could by no possibility be successful without the assistance of the navy, upon which they were all confidently reckoning, whereas it was my duty to inform them that, unless there came a very quick change of weather, it would be impossible for our ships to co-operate, and I had to explain at length why. This caused an immediate change of plan, the grand assault being provisionally postponed, since there was no prospect whatever at that moment of a change of weather occurring in time.

I delivered my message and produced my map, explaining the various markings upon it and describing the work upon which I had been engaged during the past few days; and I was exceedingly gratified to learn that it would greatly simplify and assist the general's plans.

It was also satisfactory to know that the Japanese had never had the slightest suspicion of what I was doing, which was tantamount to an assurance that the Russians were equally ignorant. It was amazing to see the facility with which Oku altered his plans. No sooner did he understand that the chances were all against the fleet being able to help him on the following day than he was ready with an alternative scheme; and in a quarter of an hour he had everything cut-and-dried, every officer present was given clear and concise instructions relative to his duties on the morrow, and we were all dismissed with a hint to get what rest we might, as the morrow was to be a busy day. General Oshima, who was in command of the 3rd Division, constituting the Japanese left, very kindly took me under his wing, and found me sleeping quarters in a tent, the occupants of which happened to be out on duty.

Being greatly fatigued after my swim, I slept soundly that night, but was awakened at dawn by the bugle calls, and turned out to see what the weather was like. To my disgust, and doubtless that of everybody else, it was worse than ever; the sky was overcast and louring, with great rags of dirty grey scud flying athwart the face of the heavens from the westward, while the top of Mount Sampson was completely enveloped in mist, which, notwithstanding the gale, clung to the rugged peak and ribs of the mountain very much as the "tablecloth" does to the summit of Table Mountain. There was no fog down where we were, but, what was even worse, we were smothered with blinding and suffocating clouds of dust, for it was a dry gale, and all hands were devoutly praying that the louring sky would dissolve into rain, if only for half an hour, just to lay the dust and so save us from the unpleasantness of being blinded and suffocated. As for the bay, it was just one continuous sheet of foam, while the breakers leapt and boiled for a space of a full mile from the beach. A single glance at it was sufficient to make it clear that it would be impossible for the fleet to co-operate so long as the gale lasted, even if the tossing masts and spray-enveloped hulls of our craft in the offing had not told a similar tale. General Oshima and I walked a couple of miles to the northward along the slopes of Mount Sampson, in order to get a good view of the bay, clear of the northern spur of the Nanshan Heights, just to make assurance doubly sure; but it was scarcely necessary to point out to him the wildly plunging hulls of our ships to make him understand the hopelessness of the case, and that once clearly established, we hurried back to Headquarters to make our report.

Oku, however, was not the man to be deterred by weather, or indeed anything else. Finding that the projected assault was impossible for the moment, he resolved to begin the bombardment with his own guns, doing the best he could with them, unaided, and accompanying the bombardment with what he termed "a demonstration in force," in order to bring out the Russians and compel them to man their defences while exposed to the fire of our guns. Thus, by a curious combination of circumstances, it appeared that at last I was to be afforded the opportunity of seeing what a land battle was like.

Naturally, I volunteered my services in any capacity where I could be made useful, and the general eagerly closed with my offer. He was particularly anxious to obtain the exact range of certain of the Russian positions without being obliged to fire any trial shots, and he asked me if I could do this for him, seeing that I had already done similar work quite recently; and I told him that I could, and would, with pleasure, if such a thing as a box sextant or an azimuth compass was to be found in camp. Somewhat to my surprise it turned out, upon inquiry, that no such things were to be had. I therefore had recourse to what is known among engineers as a "plane table," which I was obliged to extemporise; and with this apparatus, used in conjunction with a carefully measured line, three hundred yards in length, I was soon able to supply the information required. The whole device was, of course, of a very rough-and-ready description, but I was greatly gratified when the first shots were fired, to see the shells drop upon the exact spots aimed at.

The task which General Oku had undertaken, and which he must accomplish before an advance could be made by him upon Port Arthur, was an exceedingly difficult one. As has already been said, he effected a landing at a point near Yentoa Bay, distant some sixty miles north-east of Port Arthur as the crow flies. From thence he must needs make his way to Port Arthur overland, since there was no such thing for him as getting there by sea. About half-way on his journey occurred the isthmus of Kinchau, which is only about two miles wide, and which he must traverse on his way. A neck of land two miles wide is no great matter to fortify, a fact which the Russians speedily demonstrated. To march along such a narrow strip of land, with sixteen thousand resolute armed men saying you Nay, would be difficult enough, in all conscience, were that strip of land level; but unhappily for the Japanese it was not so, the Nanshan Heights running through it from north to south, like a raised backbone, leaving only a very narrow strip of low ground on either side of it. Nor was this the only difficulty which the Japanese had to contend with, for, some three miles north-east of the narrowest part of the isthmus, towered Mount Sampson, over two thousand feet in height, commanding the entire neighbourhood and affording an ideal position for the Russian batteries. Then, at the foot of Mount Sampson lay the walled city of Kinchau, which the Russians had seized and fortified; and, finally, there were the Nanshan Heights, upon the crest of which the Russians had constructed ten forts, armed with seventy guns, several of which were of 8-inch or 6-inch calibre, firing shells of from two hundred to one hundred pounds weight.

To attempt to pass these several positions while they were in the hands of the Russians would have been simply courting annihilation; the first task, therefore, was to capture them. This, so far as Mount Sampson was concerned, had been done when I arrived upon the scene; but there still remained Kinchau and the Nanshan Heights to be taken; and each of these threatened to be an even tougher piece of work than the storming of Mount Sampson; for the Russians, after their experience of the extraordinary intrepidity of the Japanese when storming the mountain, had adopted every conceivable means to make the heights impregnable.

First of all, there were the ten forts with their seventy guns lining the crest of the heights, in addition to which the Russians had two batteries of quick-fire field artillery and ten machine-guns. Next, in front of the forts, all along the eastern slope of the heights—which was the side from which attack was possible—there was row after row of shelter trenches, solidly roofed with timber covered with earth, to protect the occupants from artillery fire. Below these again the Russians had dug countless circular pitfalls, about ten feet deep, shaped like drinking cups, with very narrow bottoms, each pit having at its bottom a stout, upright, sharpened stake upon which any hapless person, falling in, must inevitably be impaled. They were, in fact, an adaptation of the stake pitfalls employed by many African and other natives to capture and kill big game. These pits were dug so close together that, of a party of stormers rushing up the slope, a large proportion must inevitably fall in, or be unwittingly pushed in by their comrades. Passages between these pits were purposely left here and there, but they were all mined, each mine being connected to one of the forts above by an electric cable, so that it could be exploded at any moment by merely pressing a button. And that moment would of course be when the passage-way was crowded with Japanese. And, lastly, at the foot of the hill there was a great maze of strongly constructed wire entanglements, during the slow passage of which the hapless stormers would be exposed to a withering rifle and shell fire. Thus the task which the Japanese had to perform was, first to pass through the wire entanglements at the foot of the hill; next, to achieve the passage of the staked pits and the mined ground between them—exposed all the time, be it remembered, to a terrific fire from the forts and trenches above; next, to take line after line of trenches; and, finally, to storm the forts on the crest of the heights—a task which, I frankly admit, seemed to me impossible.

I must confess that my first impressions of a land battle were disappointing. I had expected to see the Japanese march out and storm the heights under cover of the fire of their own guns. And, as a matter of fact, they did march out, but there was no storming of the heights; I had momentarily forgotten that what I was witnessing was merely a "demonstration." I presume it served its purpose, however, for the General and his staff seemed to be perfectly satisfied with the result; and in any case it had the effect intended of compelling the Russians to man their trenches under the fire of the Japanese guns, which, feeble though they were as compared with those of the enemy, must have inflicted severe punishment upon the packed masses of infantry who swarmed into the trenches to repel what they had every reason to suppose was a genuine attack. But the Japanese—closely watched by a Russian captive balloon, which was sent up directly our troops were seen to be in motion—having compelled the Russians to turn out and expend a considerable quantity of ammunition in comparatively innocuous long-range shooting, calmly marched back again about three o'clock in the afternoon, about which time the firing ceased. While it lasted, however, it was hot enough to bring on heavy rain, and the day ended with a tremendous downpour, which converted the hillsides into a network of miniature cascades, and must have been exceedingly unpleasant for any of the Russians whom expediency and watchfulness compelled to remain in the trenches.

With nightfall the gale increased in fury; but the rain had produced at least one good result; it had laid the dust most effectually while it had made but little mud, for the thirsty earth seemed to absorb the water almost as fast as it fell; also it cooled the air considerably, which was all to the advantage of the Japanese, who would have the strenuous work of climbing the hill, while it would tend to chill and benumb the Russians, who would be compelled to remain comparatively inactive in the sodden trenches. Whether it was this consideration, or the fact that the barometer was rapidly rising, or a combination of both, I cannot say, but about ten o'clock that night the word went round that a general attack upon the Russian works was to be made as soon as possible after midnight.

Chapter Fourteen
The Storming of Nanshan Heights

By midnight a change of weather had occurred; the wind, which at ten o'clock in the evening had been blowing harder than ever, suddenly subsided, the air grew close, almost to suffocation, and an immense black cloud settled down upon the summit of Mount Sampson, where it rested broodingly, the sure precursor of a thunderstorm, if I was any judge of weather lore.

The first troops to move consisted of a detachment of the 4th Engineers' Battalion, who were assigned the perilous duty of blowing down the gates of Kinchau, of which there were four, corresponding to the four cardinal points of the compass. I volunteered to accompany this party, for the task which devolved upon them was one that rather appealed to me; but Oku was most emphatic in his refusal, explaining that he would more than probably require my services at daylight, or shortly afterward, to communicate with the squadron in the offing. Accordingly, I had to stand aside, somewhat unwillingly, and see them march off without me; which was perhaps just as well, for the attempt resulted in failure, and every man who participated in it was killed.

Just as the Engineers marched out of camp on their way to Kinchau, the brooding cloud on the summit of Mount Sampson began to send forth flash after flash of vivid lightning, green, blue, and sun-bright, which lighted up not only the rugged slopes of the mountain itself, but also those other and more deadly slopes of the Nanshan Heights, while peal after peal of thunder crashed and rolled and reverberated among the ravines which scored the sides of the mountain. It was a weird enough scene of itself, but its weirdness was intensified by the Russian searchlights, which were turned on with the first crash of thunder, which the Russians appeared to mistake for the roar of Japanese guns. As a matter of fact they appeared to be a bit panicky that night, for not only did they turn on the searchlights at the first sound of thunder, but the occupants of the forts and trenches on the crest and side of Nanshan Heights at once opened a terrific fire from every piece, great or small, that could be brought to bear upon the foot of the slope, which was instantly swept by a very hurricane of shrapnel and rifle bullets, while the Japanese, safely under cover, looked on and smiled.

For two hours that storm raged with such fury that the volleying peals of thunder quite outroared the booming of the Russian artillery and rifle-fire, which gradually died down as the Muscovites began to realise that there was no attack; and about two o'clock in the morning the storm passed away, still rumbling and muttering, to the eastward. But during that two hours of elemental fury, a Chinese village in the neighbourhood was set on fire and practically destroyed, while several Japanese soldiers were struck by lightning, and either killed outright or more or less seriously injured.

With the passing of the storm a thick, white mist arose from the low ground, completely blotting out everything beyond a few yards distant; and under the cover of this mist the Japanese made their dispositions for the coming battle, entirely unseen by the enemy, and probably unheard also, for it was a revelation to me to see how quietly large bodies of men could be moved when the necessity for silence had been fully impressed upon them.

As the dawn gradually brightened the sky behind the ridge of Mount Sampson, the Russians again became uneasy, and their rifles once more began to speak from the trenches, a shot here, then another shot yonder, followed by quite a spluttering here and there all along their front; but their artillery remained silent, for the fog was still so dense that nothing could be seen at which to aim.

Protected by the cover of the fog, the Japanese soldiers went to breakfast, fortifying themselves with a good meal, in preparation for the arduous labours of the day that lay before them; and I did the same, for I knew not how long it might be before I should again have the opportunity to eat or drink; also, following the example of several of the officers and men, I filled my jacket pockets with biscuit, and provided myself with a good capacious flask of cold tea, having done which, I felt ready for anything.

We had barely finished breakfast when the sun showed over the ridge of Mount Sampson; and almost immediately the thick curtain of fog, which had thus far so effectually hidden the movements of the Japanese troops from the enemy, began to lift and thin. This was the signal for the final movement prior to the storming of the Nanshan Heights; and that movement was directed against the city of Kinchau, it being known by this time that the devoted band of engineers who had been dispatched at midnight to blow in the gates of the city must have failed in their mission, otherwise some of them at least would have been back to report.

To the 1st Division was assigned the task of taking the city; and they did it in brilliant style. Marching upon the southern gate, a party of four engineers was sent forward to blow in the massive barrier, which was protected by steel plates and bands, secured by heavy steel bolts, and loopholed for musketry. The devoted quartette succeeded in placing their blasting charges and igniting the fuses under a heavy fire, not only from the loopholed gate, but also from the walls, but in so doing they were so severely wounded that after they had lighted the fuses they were unable to effect their escape, and received further severe injuries when the explosion occurred and the gate was blown off its hinges. Then the waiting 1st Division, straining like eager hounds held in leash, rushed forward through the thick, acrid smoke, with levelled bayonets, yelling "Banzai Nippon!" as they ran; and as they charged impetuously in through the south gate, the enemy went streaming as impetuously out through the west gate, about half a mile away.

Kinchau was now in the hands of the Japanese; but this was not sufficient for them, they must needs pursue the flying Russians; and they did so with such furious impetuosity that they literally drove them into the sea—that is to say, into the waters of Kinchau Bay, where the luckless Russians, to the number of five hundred, were either shot down or drowned, almost to a man, only ten of them surviving and being taken prisoners. I had a distant view of the whole affair from a knoll on the northern spur of the Nanshan Heights, where I had taken up a position which commanded a view, not only of practically the whole of the ground over which the stormers would have to pass, but also of the bay and our fleet, to which I should probably be required to signal from time to time as the fight progressed.

Meanwhile, the mist had by this time lifted, revealing a flotilla of our torpedo-boats and destroyers feeling their way into the bay and keeping a bright lookout for possible mines. Well astern of them came the *Akagi* and *Chokai*; and still farther out were the old *Hei-yen* and the cruiser *Tsukushi*, cautiously creeping in, with leadsmen perpetually sounding on either beam. The bottom, about where they were required to be, was flat, and the tide was on the ebb, the great fear of the skippers of those two craft, therefore, was that they might touch the ground and hang there, left by the tide, exposed helplessly to the fire of the Russian guns. Thanks, however, to my labours of a few days earlier, they were all able to get close enough in to open upon the Russian works at extreme range, although, until the tide should rise, they could not bring a thoroughly effective fire upon the Russian batteries and so put them out of action.

But if we had ships, so, too, had the Russians, in the shape of the gunboat *Bobr* and five small steamers in Hand Bay, on the side of the isthmus opposite to Kinchau Bay, the Nanshan Heights being between them, so that each was hidden from the sight of the other. The *Bobr* was likely to prove a very awkward customer for us; for she mounted one 9-inch and one 6-inch gun, which, although they were a long way from being up-to-date, were still quite good enough to out-range the Japanese field-guns and severely pepper our left, which occupied the ground at the head of Hand Bay. The steamers which accompanied her were, our spies discovered, fitted up expressly for the purpose of quickly ferrying troops across from one side of Hand Bay to the other, according as they might be wanted, instead of being obliged to march round the head of the bay in the face of our troops. Thus the Russians were in a position to either harass our left flank and rear, or to rush reinforcements across the head of the bay—a distance of about a mile—as circumstances might require.

The *Bohr* began the day's proceedings by opening fire with her 9-inch gun upon the artillery of our 3rd Division, which had taken up a position upon the lower slopes of Mount Sampson, from which it could reach the Russian batteries established upon the crest of the Nanshan Heights. The gunboat's fire did very little mischief, but it seemed to be regarded by both sides as a signal to begin the fight, for at once our batteries got to work, their shells dropping with most beautiful precision upon the guns and trenches of the Russians. I was so stationed that I had a most excellent view of practically the entire scene of operations, and no sooner did our artillery open fire than the Russian batteries replied with a crash that seemed to make the very air quiver.

A land battle is a very different spectacle from a sea battle, in this respect: that, in the latter, a shell either hits or misses its mark, and if it misses there is a splash or two and that ends the matter, so far as that particular shell is concerned. But ashore, every shell, whether or not it finds its mark, hits something, though it be only the ground, and immediately there is a violent explosion, a flash of fire, a great cloud of smoke, and a violent scattering of dust, clods of earth, and stones—if nothing worse. Thus, I must confess that for a few seconds I was perfectly amazed to see the slopes of Mount Sampson, on the one hand, where our artillery was placed, and the Nanshan Heights, on the other, where were situated the Russian batteries, suddenly burst into great jets of flame, clouds of smoke, and flying débris, as the shells showered down upon them. The explosions of shrapnel were easily distinguished from those of common shell, for the former almost invariably burst in the air, the smoke from the explosions standing out against the background of sky or hill like tufts of cotton-wool that had suddenly sprung into existence from nowhere.

Very shortly after the artillery duel began, I saw the Japanese infantry moving out to storm the Nanshan Heights, and I smiled to myself at the acuteness of their leaders, for the men began their advance in such open formation that a shrapnel shell seldom succeeded in accounting for more than one man, and often enough it failed to do even that. Of course they were seen from the trenches, and a terrific rifle-fire was opened upon them, but for the same reason it was very ineffective—at the outset at least, for a rifleman had to be a crack shot to bowl over his man at a distance of close upon a mile. And if one wished to get his man, he had to aim at him, and correctly judge the distance too. This, of course, was at the beginning of the attack; later on, matters became a good deal more favourable for the defenders and correspondingly adverse to the attacking force.

I was interestedly watching the development of the attack upon the heights, when a galloper dashed up to me with a message from the General requesting me to signal our ships in the offing to concentrate their fire upon the Nanshan ridge; and so smart were our men, and so keen a lookout were they maintaining aboard our ships, that within three minutes of the receipt by me of the order, their 10-inch, 5-inch, and 6-inch shells were dropping all along the ridge, busily searching it for the Russian batteries, the positions of which, unfortunately, could not be seen from the western side.

For the next half-hour I was kept incessantly employed in signalling our fleet, directing their fire; but the shoal water of Kinchau Bay was all against us, and although our ships drew in so close that they touched the ground several times, they were still too far off to actually silence the Russian batteries, although they contrived to give them a very severe punishing and, to some extent, distract their attention from the stormers. Unfortunately, they could only muster six heavy guns between them, and these, at the extreme range at which they were obliged to fire, were not nearly enough, though they certainly helped.

When at length I was once more free to turn my attention to what was happening on the eastern side of the heights, I saw that our foremost line of skirmishers had reached a spot about a mile distant from the first Russian defences, consisting of a perfect maze of wire entanglements, and were signalling back to the main body. Almost immediately a detachment of Cossacks appeared, advancing at a gallop toward the signallers, from the direction of Linshiatun, a village on the shore of Sunk Bay, and as the horsemen appeared every Japanese soldier vanished, as if by magic, having flung himself down upon the ground and taken cover. On swept the Cossacks, yelling, lashing their horses with their whips, and brandishing their long lances. Suddenly, down went a horse and rider, the next instant a Cossack flung up his arms and collapsed inert upon his horse's neck, then another reeled and fell, then two or three went down almost at the same instant, then half a dozen. And the curious thing about it was that there was nothing, no sudden spurt of flame, no smoke wreath, no crack of a rifle, to account for these casualties. That is to say, I could neither see nor hear anything; but the fact was that those Cossacks were going down before the calm, deliberate rifle-fire of the concealed Japanese infantry-men. Then a flash from one of the field-guns of our 3rd Division caught my eye, and before the sharp bark of it reached my ear, a white tuft of cotton-wool-like smoke suddenly appeared in the air above the galloping Cossacks, and more of them went down. Another flash, and another, and another, more tufts of cotton-wool leaping into view, tremendous disorder and confusion among the Cossacks, men and horses falling right and left, and then the survivors suddenly wheeled outward and galloped back at headlong speed, leaving behind them a mangled heap of men and horses, the greater number dead, but here and there a prostrate, kicking horse might be seen, or a wounded Cossack crawling slowly and painfully away from the scene of carnage.

The flight of the Cossacks was the signal for the resumption of the advance by the Japanese, whose skirmishers reappeared, still in very open formation, a man here and a man there showing for a few seconds as, in a crouching attitude, he rose to his feet, scurried forward a few yards, and then again took cover, while the fire of the Russian guns swept the ground over which he was passing. As yet, however, there appeared to be very few casualties among our men; here and there I noticed a prostrate form lying motionless, while others crept up and scuttled past him; he had been found by a shrapnel shell, and his share of the work was done; but even shrapnel cannot do much harm if the formation is kept sufficiently open. And as man after man pushed forward, others crept out, following, until the whole of the ground between our lines and the base of the heights was dotted with Japanese infantry-men creeping ever closer up to the first line of the Russian defence, the terrible maze of barbed wire entanglements.

Meanwhile, the whole of the Japanese field artillery, as well as that of our ships, was concentrating its fire upon the crest of the heights, covering the advance of the stormers; and now my attention was once more diverted from that advance by the necessity for me to signal directions to the fleet. And now it was that the full value of my previous labours began to be manifested; for I had but to signal the ships to direct their fire upon such and such a point—wherever, in fact, a Russian battery was proving especially troublesome—and all that the gun-layers had to do was to refer to the maps with which I had supplied them, and they were at once informed of the exact range of that point, with the result that a hail of shells instantly began to fall upon that particular battery with the most deadly precision. Thus, after a little while, every battery on the heights became in turn the focus of a terrific crossfire from the ships and the field batteries, the effect of which soon became manifest in the silencing of several of the Russian guns, either by dismounting, or, as we afterwards discovered, by the complete destruction of the men working them.

With the guns of our fleet playing such havoc among the ten forts which crowned the heights, it now became possible for our field artillery to turn its attention upon the trenches, tier after tier of which lined the eastern slope of the heights, up which our stormers would have to pass. Those trenches were quite formidable works, roofed over with timber and earth to protect the occupants from artillery fire, and loopholed for rifle-fire; yet, thanks again to my labours of the previous day in determining the exact range of them, our guns were able to search them from end to end, blowing the parapets to dust and matchwood, and hurling the wreckage among the gunners who were working the Russian quick-firers and machine-guns, many of whom were thus killed or wounded. The carnage must have been—indeed was, as we later saw for ourselves—frightful, yet the Russians maintained a most gallant defence, and clung to their trenches with unflinching determination. A lucky shell from one of our field-guns fell upon and exploded one of the many Russian mines which were scattered pretty thickly over the hillside, and the explosion blew a big gap in one of the lines of wire entanglements, a circumstance which without doubt resulted subsequently in the saving of many lives.

Hour after hour the artillery duel proceeded, our gunners doing their utmost to cover the slow advance of the stormers, while the Russian artillery systematically swept with a crossfire every inch of the ground which our men would have to traverse. The crash of the artillery was continuous and most distracting, and the effect was intensified by the incessant scream of the shells and the sharp thud as they burst, interspersed with the everlasting hammering of the machine-guns and quick-firers; Nanshan was ablaze with the fire of the Russian guns and the bursting of our shells, and the entire hill was enwrapped in fantastically whirling wreaths of smoke which were every moment rent violently asunder by the explosion of bursting shells.

Thus far I had occupied my position undisturbed, but about mid-morning certain Russian sharpshooters chanced to detect me and my assistant in the act of signalling to our ships, and they at once favoured me with their undivided attentions, to such purpose that I was compelled to beat a hasty retreat. The change of position which I was compelled to make was, however, advantageous rather than otherwise, for I found a perfectly safe spot behind two tall boulders standing close together, which, while effectually shielding me from the Russian bullets, still enabled me to see all that was happening.

Yet, that "all" might be summed up in a very few words—just incessant flashes of fire, great volumes of smoke, and, interspersed with the smoke, patches of flying débris. Very little else. No great masses of troops advancing in serried lines, column after column, with colours proudly flying, and burnished bayonets glistening in the sun; none of the old-fashioned pomp and circumstance of war when the opposing armies marched toward each other with bands playing, discharged their muskets when they were near enough to see the whites of their opponents' eyes, and then charged with fixed bayonets, fighting it out hand to hand. That sort of battle went out of fashion with the introduction of the breech-loading rifle and the machine-gun; and now, with between fifty and sixty thousand men in action, there were periods when not a solitary human being could be seen. And when any did appear, which was only at intervals, they were but few in number—just a man here and a man there dotted about sparsely over a large area of ground, visible for perhaps half a dozen seconds, and then lost again, hidden behind cover of some sort.

It was getting well on toward noon when a message reached me from the General to the effect that two batteries of Russian quick-fire field-guns had been discovered on the summit of Nan-kwang-ling—a hill some eight hundred feet high, about a mile to the westward of the Nanshan Heights—and requesting me to signal our ships in the bay to give their whole attention to those two batteries. Unfortunately for us, the tide in the bay was now on the ebb, and the *Hei-yen* and *Tsukushi* were obliged to haul off to avoid grounding; but the *Akagi* and *Chokai* responded nobly to the call, creeping in until they actually felt the ground, and enveloping Nan-kwang-ling knoll in flame and smoke.

I had scarcely finished signalling to the ships when a stir on the plain immediately below me indicated that the General considered the artillery "preparation" complete, and that the actual storming of the Russian position was now to be attempted. A battalion of our 1st Division, situated in the Japanese centre, suddenly deployed into the open, and commenced its advance by making a series of short rushes through some fields of green barley, on the opposite side of the road from Kinchau to Linshiatun, dashing forward a few yards, and then, as the machine-guns and rifles in the Russian trenches were turned upon them, sinking from view into the barley, through which they crept on hands and knees until the whistle of the leader or the call of a bugle gave the signal for another dash. The heroism of those devoted Japanese infantry was something to send a thrill through the heart of a man; no sooner did they show than the whole of the ground which they occupied and that in front of them was swept by a devastating crossfire from the whole line of the Russian trenches, which beat down the young barley as a heavy shower of rain might level it. To me, unaccustomed to this style of fighting, it looked as though nothing might venture upon that shot-swept zone and live; yet time after time the intrepid Japanese rose to their feet and, crouching low, made yet another short rush forward, though with sadly diminished numbers. The uproar was deafening; the crash of the heavy guns upon the crest of the heights and from Fort Hoshangtao, near Linshiatun, which now joined in the fray, mingled with the hammer-like thudding of the machine-guns and the continuous rolling crackle of rifle-fire from the trenches, was frightful. And then, as though this were not enough, the Russian gunboat *Bohr* turned her 9-inch guns upon the advancing Japanese and, quickly getting the range, began to drop shells right among them. The slaughter, one understood, must be awful; yet, prepared as I was in a measure for what followed, I stood aghast when finally, out of that whole battalion, a mere handful of men, numbering perhaps some fifty or sixty, emerged from the growing barley and made a staggering rush toward the first line of wire entanglements, which they at once proceeded to attack with nippers, fully exposed all the while to the concentrated fire of the whole body of defenders. It was a forlorn hope of the most desperate description, and one after another the gallant fellows collapsed and died, pierced by innumerable bullets. The first assault had resulted in failure, and those who took part in it were wiped out!

And now it was that the Russians deemed the moment suitable for a counter-demonstration. The *Bohr*, doubtless in obedience to some signal from the shore, steamed up toward the head of Hand Bay as far as the shoaling water would permit, the five steamers loaded with troops closely following her and making as though it was their intention to land the troops upon a small promontory jutting out into the head of the bay. This was a distinct menace to the Japanese left, and although it might be merely a demonstration, it was imperative to meet it, or it might develop into a serious and most embarrassing attack; therefore, badly as it could be spared from the task of shelling the heights and the Russian trenches, a battery of our field-guns placed on the south-western slope of Mount Sampson was turned upon the gunboat and her accompanying flotilla of steamers, the latter being compelled to hastily retire, while several of our shells struck the *Bohr*, and temporarily silenced her fire. Judging from appearances generally, the gunboat appeared to have been rather severely punished; and about a quarter of an hour later she slowly retired to her former position, farther down the bay, and re-opened her fire, although with considerably less vigour than before.

The fire from Fort Hoshangtao, occupying the promontory which separates Sunk Bay from Hand Bay, was a most galling factor in the fight, for its guns had a range which enabled them to drop their heavy shells right upon our left and centre, while it was out of range of our own guns. Therefore our men had to stand motionless, hour after hour, and endure the pitiless shelling of the Russian gunners, with the bitter knowledge that to silence the fort was quite out of our power.

The utter annihilation of the first battalion of stormers warned General Oku that to advance comparatively small parties was but to sacrifice them uselessly, while it also indicated that the task of artillery "preparation" had been by no means as complete as he had judged it to be; he therefore sedulously continued the work of preparation all through the afternoon until five o'clock, when a message from the artillery commander warned him that the crisis was at hand. The message was to the effect that he had fired away practically his entire supply of ammunition, only his reserve rounds remaining. What was he to do?

Situated as I was at a distance of more than two miles from headquarters, upon an outlying spur of the Nanshan Heights, and quite alone, save for the companionship of a solitary assistant signaller, with only occasional curt orders from the General in reference to the signals which he wished me to transmit to our ships in the offing, I was naturally ignorant as to the critical pass at which we had arrived, and could only draw my conclusions from what I actually saw happening. What occurred at staff headquarters during this momentous day, and especially at this momentous hour, I did not learn until several hours later, but, so far as is possible, I propose to relate events in their chronological order, that the proper continuity of my narrative may be maintained; I will therefore briefly state here that when the General received the artillery commander's message that his ammunition was practically exhausted, he summoned a few of his principal officers, and held a brief council of war. What was to be done, under the circumstances? It was now five o'clock in the afternoon, and the bringing up of further supplies of ammunition would involve a delay of at least two hours, and probably more, while to suspend all action meanwhile would practically be to defer the assault until the next day. Certain of the officers present strongly advocated this postponement, giving it as their opinion that to attempt to storm the heights unsupported by adequate gun-fire was merely to make a useless sacrifice of whole brigades of sorely needed men; one or two officers, indeed, ventured to express their conviction that the heights were impregnable.

The discussion lasted about a quarter of an hour, at the end of which time General Oku, who had been listening but saying nothing, abruptly broke up the council by announcing his determination to risk everything upon a single cast of the die; the gunners were to expend their reserve rounds of ammunition upon a slow, carefully considered, deadly bombardment of the heights, while the entire infantry force was to move forward simultaneously to the assault. The officers who had ventured to advise delay shook their heads doubtfully, but at once proceeded to their stations, fully prepared to loyally support the General to their last breath.

When the news of the General's decision was communicated to the troops, it was only with the utmost difficulty that they could be restrained from cheering, and so putting the Russians on the *qui vive*, although they had been warned beforehand to maintain strict silence.

The first step in the proceedings was for the officers commanding the various regiments to call for volunteers prepared to undertake the task of preceding the main body of the stormers in order to cut a way through the lines of wire entanglements, and to sever the electric cables connecting the innumerable ground mines with the forts. Volunteers were invited to step six paces to the front, and in the majority of cases the entire regiment appealed to advanced six paces with the precision and promptitude of a parade evolution. Under such circumstances there was, of course, but one thing to be done, and that was for each captain to choose a certain number of men—those he considered best adapted for the work—and detail them for the duty.

These men, a veritable Forlorn Hope, discarding knapsacks, greatcoats, everything in the shape of impedimenta, even their weapons, and armed only with a stout pair of wire-cutting nippers, dashed out of the ranks like unleashed greyhounds at the word of command, and with a great shout of "Banzai Nippon!" went running and leaping through the fields of young barley, each eager to outdistance all the others. And as they went, the crash of their own and the enemy's artillery, the fire of which had been languishing, burst forth afresh, mingled with the hammering of machine-guns and the rolling volleys of rifle-fire. In a moment the whole of the ground over which the pioneers would have to pass was being swept by a crossfire of lead in which it seemed impossible that anything could live. Man after man was seen to go down, yet still his comrades pressed on, in ever-diminishing numbers, until at length a mere handful staggered up to the first line of wire entanglements, and there fell, riddled with bullets, their task unaccomplished.

But not for a moment did their fate discourage those who were detailed to follow them. Like racers they dashed forward, in widely extended order, now leaping high in the air and anon crouching almost double in a vain effort to dodge that terrible inexorable hail of bullets, and again man after man went crashing to the ground while other panting, gasping, breathless men staggered and stumbled past the prostrate figures, intent upon one purpose only, to reach that line of wire and sever a few of the entanglements before yielding up their lives. And a few of them actually contrived to accomplish their purpose before they died, although the damage which they were able to do was quite incommensurate with the frightful sacrifice of life which it cost.

In accordance with Oku's plan, the main body of the stormers followed closely upon the heels of the volunteer wire-cutters. The 1st Division led the way, dashing forward and losing heavily, until they arrived within a few yards of the foremost line of Russian trenches, and here they were brought to a standstill by the wire entanglements, while the Russian rifle and machine-gun-fire played upon them pitilessly, mowing them down in heaps. In desperation some of them seized the firmly rooted posts to which the wires were attached and strove to root them up by main force, while others placed the muzzles of their rifles against the wires and, pulling the trigger, severed them in that way. Some attempted to climb over the wire, others to creep through; but where one succeeded, twenty became entangled and were shot dead before they could clear themselves. Those, however, who contrived to get through at once gave their attention to the mines, the positions of which were clearly indicated by the settlement of the ground caused by the rain of the preceding night, and thus it became possible to sever several of the electric cables which connected them with the forts.

But those awful entanglements still held up the main body of the stormers, keeping them fully exposed to a murderous fire from the trenches as they desperately strove to break through, and things were beginning to look very bad indeed for our side when I chanced to notice that the Russian lines on their left were weak, the bulk of the men having been rushed toward the centre, where the attack was being most fiercely pressed. In an instant I recognised that here was our opportunity, our only opportunity perhaps, to retrieve the fortune of the day. Turning to my companion, I said:

"I dare not leave my post here, for at any moment I may receive a message to be signalled to our ships. But I can—I *will*—manage single-handed for the next quarter of an hour or so if you are game to sprint across the open to carry a message from me to General Ogawa. You will find him somewhere yonder, in command of the 4th Division; and if you run hard you can cover the distance in five minutes. Are you game to try it?"

"I am honourably game, illustrious captain," replied the man, standing at the salute.

"Good!" I said. "Then make your way as quickly as possible to General Ogawa, and when you have found him, say you come from me, Captain Swinburne. Explain to him where I am posted, and tell him that from here I can see that the Russian left has been so greatly weakened that a surprise attack on his part would certainly turn it, and thus very materially help the frontal attack. Tell him it will be necessary for him to lead his troops along the shore of the bay in that direction," —pointing; "say that it may even be necessary for his troops to enter the water and wade for some distance, since the tide is rising; but that if he will do that, I am certain he can retrieve the day. You understand? Then, go!"

With a salute, the man swung round upon his heels and sprang away down the hill, running like a startled hare, and in less than five minutes I saw him rush into the lines of the 4th Division. Then, feeling pretty confident that Ogawa would recognise the opportunity and seize it, I snatched up the signal flags that my assistant had dropped and proceeded to call up the fleet. After calling for about a minute, I dropped the flags and placed my glasses to my eyes. It was all right, they were keeping a bright lookout afloat, and the *Tsukushi* was waiting to receive my message. I therefore at once proceeded to signal them to be ready to support the anticipated movement with their gun-fire; and by the time that I had done, the men of the 19th Brigade were proceeding at something a bit faster than the "double" toward the shore, while every gun in the squadron opened in their support. As I had anticipated, the troops were obliged to actually enter the waters of the bay, which in some places rose breast-high; but they pushed through, losing rather heavily, and hurled themselves upon the Russian flank and rear, while the others, getting an inkling of what was happening from the sounds of heavy firing on the other side of the hill, pressed home the frontal attack, thus keeping the Russian main body busily engaged.

With yells of "Banzai! Banzai Nippon!" the men of the 19th Brigade fought their way forward, foot by foot, using rifle and bayonet with such furious energy that suddenly the Russians broke and fled before them, and with howls of exultation the victorious Japanese scrambled forward and upward until their figures became visible to their comrades below, still fighting desperately in the effort to break through the Russian lines. Thirty engineers of the victorious 4th Division were now detailed to cut a path through the wire entanglements that still protected the Russian trenches;

and they did it, lying flat upon the ground without attempting to raise their heads. Twenty-two out of the thirty were killed in the accomplishment of the task, but a way was made, and through it poured Ogawa's gallant brigade, the 8th Regiment taking the lead, and the next moment they were in the Russian trenches, fighting desperately, hand to hand, the Japanese determined to drive out the Russians, and the Russians equally determined to hold their ground at all costs.

And now the stormers of the 1st and 3rd Divisions, seeing the success of their comrades, were stung into the making of a further effort, and, hurling themselves bodily upon the entanglements, actually broke them down by sheer physical force, although hundreds were horribly mangled in the process, and despite the awful fire from rifles and machine-guns that mowed through them, up they swept irresistibly until, with deafening yells of "Banzai!" they joined their victorious comrades on the crest and planted the banner of Japan upon the topmost height of Nanshan. For a few brief, breathless minutes the members of the staff, watching from below, beheld the glint and ruddy flash of bayonets in the light of the setting sun as the Russians made a last desperate effort to hold their ground; but the Japanese infantry, intoxicated with their success in the face of stupendous difficulties, would take no denial: they had conquered wire entanglements, braved machine-gun-fire, and now mere flesh and blood was as powerless to stop them as a thread is to stop a battleship. The Russians simply had to fly or die; and they chose the former alternative, retreating in disorder upon Nankwang-ling, while the Japanese, whose turn it was now to take revenge for the losses so pitilessly inflicted upon them all through the hours of that terrible day, rained shot and shell without mercy upon the flying foe.

The weather had been improving ever since morning, and now, as the firing gradually died down, the sun sank into the waters of the Gulf of Liaotung in a blaze of purple and golden splendour. As the palpitant edge of his glowing upper rim vanished beneath the long level line of the western horizon, the firing on both sides suddenly ceased altogether, and a great, solemn hush fell upon the scene, that was positively awe-inspiring after the continuous, deafening roar all day of the cannonade, and the crash of bursting shells. And then, as the ear accustomed itself to that sudden silence, it became aware of a low but terrible sound breaking it, the moaning of hundreds of mangled, suffering, and dying men, the ghastly fruits of that ferocious struggle for the possession of a few barren acres of rough, hilly country.

Suddenly the fast-gathering dusk of evening became illuminated; the station buildings in the little village of To-fang-shan were ablaze, doubtless purposely set on fire by the Russians to hinder possible pursuit—and were soon a mass of flame, the flickering light from which luridly illuminated the scored and gashed sides of the neighbouring hills. Finally, with a terrific roar, a Russian magazine exploded, sending up a great column of flame and smoke; and as the reverberations of the explosion rumbled and echoed again and again until they finally died away among the gorges and ravines of the surrounding elevations, silence again sank upon the scene, the victorious Japanese being so utterly exhausted by their Herculean labours that pursuit of the flying Russians became impossible, the conquerors flinging themselves down on the positions which they had gained, and instantly sinking into a kind of lethargy, their fatigue being so great that they were unable to remain awake long enough to partake of the food that was quickly prepared for them.

Chapter Fifteen
I am thanked in Presence of the Army

The Japanese loss, incurred in the struggle for possession of the Nanshan Heights, amounted to over four thousand, killed and wounded. What the Russian loss in killed and wounded totalled up to I do not think we ever knew, excepting that, by the evidence of the captured trenches alone, it must have been tremendously heavy. Their material losses, however, amounted to sixty-eight guns, many of which were of 8-inch or 6-inch calibre, ten machine-guns, three searchlights, a dynamo, and a considerable quantity of ammunition and food; while the victory gave to the Japanese the complete command of the isthmus, by enabling General Nakamura to seize Linshiatun, and Fort Hoshangtao, in its immediate neighbourhood, thus opening the way to the occupation of Nan-kwang-ling and Dalny, and the advance of Oku's army upon Port Arthur.

As soon as it became evident that fighting was over for the day—by which time it had become too dark for me to signal to our squadron in the offing—I made my way down the hillside to the spot where the headquarters staff was established and, seeking General Oku's tent, entered and reported myself. The General received me very kindly and courteously, but I could see in a moment that he was tremendously busy, the tent being full of officers to whom he was rapidly issuing orders. Having therefore reported myself and received orders to remain in camp for the night, I withdrew and sought the hospitality of my hosts of the previous night, who accorded me a very warm and cordial welcome. But there was none of that joyousness, that exaltation of spirits that I had expected to see as a result of the brilliant victory which we had gained; our numbers were less than they had been on the previous night, the absentees were lying out under the stars, either dead or wounded, somewhere yonder upon those shot-scored, blood-drenched slopes of Nanshan, and the joy of victory was quenched in sorrow for the fallen. We snatched a hasty, almost silent meal, and then those of us who had not to go forth on duty rolled ourselves in our cloaks and sought the relief of sleep.

For my own part, I slept like a log, and only awoke when the bugles sounded the reveille. Our little party turned out, tubbed, took breakfast, and then, at the sound of the "assembly," sallied forth to see what was to be the next item on the programme.

Strong ambulance parties had been busily engaged all through the night, collecting the wounded and bringing them in to the hospital tents, but that work was now practically finished, and the preparations for the disposal of the dead had not yet been begun. The still weary troops were falling in, under arms, and in the distance I recognised General Oku, surrounded by the members of his staff, already on the ground. The commanding officers were at their posts, the non-commissioned officers were busily engaged in seeing that the troops were all in order for inspection, and a few minutes later the roll call was being gone through. This done, the troops were put through a few simple evolutions which terminated in their being drawn up in close formation constituting three sides of a hollow square, with the men all facing inward. General Oku then summoned an aide-de-camp to his side, gave him a brief order, and the aide, saluting, turned away and glanced rapidly about him, finally making his way toward where I now stood alone, at no great distance.

He halted within about six paces of me, saluted, and said:

"The Commander-in-Chief desires your immediate presence, most honourable Captain. He stands yonder."

"Right!" I said. "I will join him at once. Have you any idea what he wants me for?"

"I think I can guess," replied my companion, as he fell into step beside me, "but I am sure that the General will prefer to make that known to you himself."

I said no more, and a couple of minutes later we halted before the general staff, and Oku took and returned my salute. Then he shook hands with me with much cordiality, and requested me to take up a position alongside him, on his right hand. This done, he proceeded to make a little speech to the closely packed troops. Shorn of the rather strange—to Western ears—flowery phraseology peculiar to the Japanese, his speech ran somewhat as follows:

"Soldiers of the Second Japanese Army, I gladly seize the first available opportunity that presents itself to tender you, on behalf of our august Emperor and the people of Japan, my most heartfelt thanks for the glorious victory which, by your indomitable courage and self-sacrifice, you so nobly achieved yesterday. The difficulties which you were called upon to surmount were so stupendous and the valour of the enemy so great, that there was a moment when I almost became persuaded that the position which you were attacking was impregnable, and that all the courage and devotion which you had displayed had gone for nothing. Yet I could not quite bring myself to believe that soldiers of Japan would ever permit themselves to be beaten, under any circumstances, however adverse; I therefore called upon you again for one last, supreme effort, and the valour and devotion with which you responded to my call is attested by the victorious presence of our glorious flag upon the heights to-day."

Here the General was interrupted by a soul-stirring shout of "Banzai!" from the exultant troops. The echoes of the shout had not died away among the surrounding hills before the serried masses of infantry were once more silent and motionless as statues, and Oku resumed:

"I am proud, your officers are proud, and I am sure that you yourselves are proud, of your glorious achievement. Yet we soldiers must not arrogate to ourselves the entire credit of so magnificent a victory. Without the assistance of the navy, that victory—I say it frankly—would have been impossible. The sailors therefore are entitled to an equal share of the glory which we yesterday reaped on the slopes of those terrible heights; and I rejoice that chance has afforded me so early an opportunity as this to tender my personal thanks, the thanks of my officers, and the thanks of every soldier in the ranks, to the navy, here represented by the noble and gallant Captain Swinburne."

Here there were further shouts of "Banzai!" even more enthusiastic, if that were possible, than those which preceded them. The General raised his hand for silence, and presently proceeded:

"We are, however, indebted to Captain Swinburne, not only as representing the navy, but also in a purely personal form. All through the trying hours of yesterday he stood on the slopes of those heights, alone save for the companionship of a solitary signaller, exposed, during some part of the time, to the pitiless fire of the enemy, and in constant danger of being captured; and during the whole of that time he devoted himself unsparingly to the task of directing the fire of our ships to the spots where from time to time it was most urgently needed; crowning this great service by sending a communication to the commander of the 4th Division which enabled that officer to effect the diversion which resulted in our hard-won victory. I have, therefore, now in the presence of you all, the honour to tender to Captain Swinburne, on behalf of our august Emperor, thus publicly, heartfelt thanks for the inestimably valuable services which he yesterday rendered to the cause of Japan."

So saying, General Oku turned to me and gave me a hearty handshake, an example which was immediately followed by the officers of the staff, while the troops put their caps upon their bayonets and waved them enthusiastically, yelling "Banzai!" until I am sure they must have felt as hoarse as crows.

This little ceremony over, I received the General's permission to rejoin my ship as soon as he had penned a dispatch to Admiral Misamichi, who was in command of the squadron, and which he requested me to deliver. This dispatch I received about half an hour later, from Oku's own hands, whereupon I bade him and the members of his staff farewell, wished them the best of luck in their further encounters with the enemy, and then hurried away to the little cove on the north side of the bay, which I had used on two or three previous occasions, and where I had a shrewd suspicion that I should find my boat awaiting me. I was not mistaken, and shortly after six bells in the forenoon watch I was aboard the *Tsukushi*, handing over General Oku's dispatch to the Admiral. The latter at once read it, and seemed much gratified at its contents, which, however, he did not communicate to me. But I shrewdly surmised that it was a letter of thanks for the services rendered by the squadron and an intimation that our presence was no longer needed. And, so far as the latter part of my assumption was concerned, I was doubtless right, for after a little chat, during which I briefly related my experiences of the previous day—learning in return that the *Chokai* had lost her commander and two men killed, with two lieutenants and five men wounded—I received instructions to return to my ship, as the squadron would presently proceed to rejoin Admiral Togo at his base. And an hour later we were all steaming out of the bay.

Two days after our arrival at the base, the destroyer *Kagero* arrived with mails for the fleet, and, to my great surprise, she brought for me a letter from my Uncle Bob, as well as one from my chum, young Gordon, and another from Sir Robert.

Naturally, I first opened the letter from Uncle Bob, for not only was it the first letter which I had received from any of the family since my "disgrace," but also the envelope was deeply edged with black, and my first fear was that it might contain the announcement of the death of dear Aunt Betsy. But upon extracting the contents of the envelope I was at once reassured, for I saw that it really consisted of two letters, one from Uncle Bob, and the other from my aunt. There had been a death in the family, however, that of Cousin Bob, the author of the trouble which had resulted in my dismissal from the British Navy. It appeared that while engaged in battle practice there had been a bad accident on board the *Terrible*, one of her quick-firers having burst, killing two men and wounding five others, one of the latter so seriously that he had subsequently died. That one was Bob; and when informed by the ship's surgeon that he had but a few hours to live, he had sent for the chaplain and to him had made a full confession of his crime, declaring that he had been spurred to it by blind, unreasoning jealousy of me. The chaplain, horrified at what he heard, took down the confession in writing, and poor Bob had signed it after the chaplain had added, at the dying lad's request, an expression of deep contrition for his misdeed and a prayer to me for forgiveness of the wrong which he had done me. The two letters were sad reading, for they had been penned by heart-broken people who had not only lost their only son, but had learned, at the very moment of their loss, that all their pride in him had been misplaced, and that he had been guilty of a deliberate, despicable, cruel crime. Their shame and sorrow were patent in every sentence of the letters, indeed they made no effort to conceal them, and they finished up by saying that, Bob being gone from them, and gone so tragically, they hoped I would forgive them for any hard thoughts they may have had of me, and would be a son to them in place of the one they had lost. They further begged that, my innocence now being established, I would lose no time in hastening home to them, to comfort them in their bitter bereavement, and to take steps to procure my reinstatement in the British Navy, which, they had been informed, might probably be accomplished without much difficulty under the circumstances.

The letter from Sir Robert Gordon was also chiefly in reference to Bob's death, the particulars of which, and of his confession, he had learned from his son Ronald. He also was of opinion that, in view of Bob's confession, it ought not to be very difficult to secure the cancellation of my expulsion, whenever I might choose to return to England. But he said no word suggesting that I should return at once; on the contrary, he offered his own and Lady Gordon's very hearty congratulations upon the frequency with which my name had been mentioned in the papers as having been specially referred to by Togo in his dispatches, and they both expressed the hope that before the end of the war I should have many further opportunities to distinguish myself.

The letters from my aunt and uncle moved me profoundly; their grief for the loss of their only son, and, even more, their shattered faith in him, was pathetic in the extreme, while it was easy to see how yearningly their hearts turned to me for comfort and consolation in their bitter bereavement. They were smarting with shame at the thought that it was *their* son, the lad of whom they had been so proud and upon whose future they had built such high hopes, who was the author of my undeserved disgrace and ruin, so far as my career in the British Navy was concerned; and they wanted me at home in order that they might have the comfort of doing what they could to make up to me for their son's treachery. And in the plenitude of my affection I was, for the moment, more than half inclined to yield to their entreaties, resign my commission in the Japanese navy, and go home to them forthwith. But in the course of an hour or two calm reflection came to my aid; I would certainly return to England and endeavour to secure reinstatement in the navy of my own country, but not until after the war was over, if I lived so long. I had put my hand to the plough, and I would not turn back, although, of course, I knew that there were plenty of Japanese officers quite as good and useful as myself, and quite ready to step into my place, should I choose to vacate it. I came to the conclusion, however, that, let the authorities at home be ever so ready to remedy what had proved to be a miscarriage of justice, I should in nowise help my case with them by forsaking the cause which I had espoused, at the moment when the decisive events of the war were beginning, as we all then believed, to loom faintly upon the horizon. No, I told myself, if I wished for reinstatement—and I wished for nothing else half so ardently—I must remain until the issues of the war were decided, when I could go back home with a good grace, taking with me a fairly creditable record with which to back up my application. Meanwhile, I sat down and wrote a letter to my aunt and uncle, excusing myself for not at once acceding to their request to forthwith return to England, explaining the reasons which had urged me to that decision, and pouring out in a long, passionate declaration all the pent-up affection of my heart for them, and my sympathy with them in their bitter sorrow. I also wrote to Sir Robert Gordon, telling him that my aunt and uncle had expressed the desire that I should return to them forthwith, and reiterating the reasons which impelled me to decline.

On the following day my signal was made from the flagship; and upon proceeding on board I was informed by the Admiral that General Oku's report as to the assistance rendered by the ships during the battle of Nanshan, and especially of the important services which I personally had rendered on that particular day and those which immediately preceded it, had been particularly gratifying to him, and that it had afforded him the utmost satisfaction and pleasure to forward that report to Baron Yamamoto, the Minister of the Navy, with a covering letter from himself which he hoped would be of service to me. Meanwhile, I was instructed to proceed forthwith to Port Arthur with my ship, to assist in the blockading of the port.

We filled our bunkers and replenished our stock of ammunition during the afternoon, and steamed out of Tashantau harbour, with all lights out, as soon as darkness fell, steaming dead slow all night, and keeping a sharp lookout for enemy ships, as a rumour had reached the Admiral that the Russians were planning another raid upon the Japanese coast by the Vladivostock fleet, which might be expected to put to sea at any moment. But we saw nothing, and arrived off Port Arthur at daybreak on the following morning without adventure of any kind. Here we fell in with the cruisers of the blockading fleet, to the admiral in command of which I forthwith reported myself, and delivered over the mail bags for the blockading ships, with which I had been entrusted. My instructions were to remain with the blockaders during the daytime, while at night the *Kasanumi* was to take part in the mine-laying operations in the roadstead of the beleaguered fortress, which were nightly conducted with untiring pertinacity. Shortly after my arrival, the destroyer flotilla which had been engaged in these operations during the night came steaming out, and among the approaching craft I recognised with pleasure the *Akatsuki*, still commanded by my former lieutenant and staunch friend, the enthusiastic Ito. That he had by no means forgotten me was quickly made manifest, for no sooner was he near enough to identify the *Kasanumi* than his semaphore started work, signalling that he wished to communicate, and upon my signalman responding, his first question was whether I was still in command. Receiving a reply in the affirmative, he forthwith invited me to go on board his ship to take breakfast with him, and when I moved an amendment to the effect that the process should be reversed and that, instead, he should come and breakfast with me, upon the ground that, coming fresh from the rendezvous, my larder was probably better stocked than his, he at once joyously accepted the invitation, and a quarter of an hour later I had the very great pleasure of welcoming him on my own quarter-deck. The dear chap was just as enthusiastic, just as keen, just as full of life as ever, and seemed unfeignedly glad to see me. Of course we had a tremendous lot to say to each other, and I was most eager to learn what he had been doing since we parted company; but when he learned that I was fresh from Kinchau, and had actually assisted at the battle of the Nanshan Heights, he positively refused to say a single word about himself until I had given him a full, true, and particular account of all the happenings of that terrible yet glorious day. His enthusiasm and delight, as I endeavoured to describe the final irresistible rush of the Japanese up those heart-breaking, shot-swept slopes, were supreme; he seemed to literally swell with pride; and when I spoke of the thrilling Japanese cheer as his fellow-countrymen finally carried the last line of the Russian defences and routed the defenders, he leaped to his feet and repeated the shout of "Banzai!" again and again, while his eyes shone like stars, and tears of joy and pride rolled down his cheeks.

It was some time before I could turn his mind away from the events of that strenuous day; and when at length I succeeded in doing so, and could get him to talk about himself, it appeared that, stirring though the events seemed to be which were nightly happening before Port Arthur, they were all flat, stale, and unprofitable, compared with such an event as the storming of the Nanshan Heights. And so, as a matter of fact, they were, as I soon discovered for myself; for the duty of our destroyer flotilla consisted simply in steaming inshore every night industriously laying mines in the roadstead and at the harbour's mouth, which the Russians as industriously strove to remove next day. True, the sameness of this work was occasionally relieved by a more or less exciting episode, as when, for instance, the Russians would suddenly turn their searchlights upon us and all their batteries would open fire. Then we simply had to scuttle for our lives, for, of course, the shore batteries mounted very much heavier and longer range guns than any that a destroyer could carry; and there was no sense in attempting, as a general rule, to oppose our 12-pounders and 6-pounders to their 6-inch and 11-inch guns.

Yet we by no means allowed the Russians to invariably have it all their own way. There were times when, under cover of the darkness, one or two of us would creep right into the harbour entrance and, getting so close under the cliff that it became impossible for the Russians to depress their heavy guns sufficiently to reach us, would boldly engage the forts with our quick-firers, and even with rifle-fire, picking off any gunners that were foolhardy enough to expose themselves, and not unfrequently dismounting or otherwise putting out of action a few of their lighter guns. It was the good fortune of the *Kasanumi*, on one occasion, very shortly after our return, to strike one of the Russian 11-inch Canets, mounted in the fort between Golden Hill and the inner harbour, fair and square upon the muzzle and blow it clean off, with a shell from our 12-pounder; but such successes as these were of course very rare. These engagements between our destroyers and the Russian forts were immensely exciting, and afforded a most agreeable and welcome change from the monotony of mine-laying, for when we undertook such an adventure we never knew whether or not we should emerge from it scatheless. The operation of getting in close under the cliffs, undetected, was of course hazardous enough to make the attempt irresistibly fascinating; but it was the getting away again after the alarm had been given and all the enemy's searchlights had been turned upon us, when the excitement reached its height; for, of course, the moment that we were far enough away from the shelter of the beetling cliffs to enable the Russians to train their big guns upon us, they would open fire upon us for all that they were worth, and then it became a case of dodging the shells. It was then that our ingenuity was taxed to the very utmost, twisting and turning hither and thither as we ran at full speed into the offing, always endeavouring to make a turn in the most unexpected direction possible at the precise moment when we anticipated that the guns were being brought to bear upon us. And that, on the whole, we were fairly successful was pretty conclusively evidenced by the small amount of damage which we sustained. Indeed, our most serious mishap about this time in those waters arose from a totally different cause. One of our officers, a certain Commander Oda, had invented a particularly deadly kind of mine, which the Japanese Government adopted, and which they named after the inventor. A few days after my return to the waters of Port Arthur, Oda himself was engaged upon the task of laying some of his mines in the outer roadstead, when one of them somehow exploded, killing the captain of the ship and eighteen men, and wounding Oda himself and seven others. Strangely enough, however, the ship herself was only very slightly damaged. Less fortunate were the Russians; for, only a day or two later, two of their gunboats, while engaged in the attempt to remove some of our mines, came in contact with them, and both craft immediately went to the bottom, taking most of their men with them.

Chapter Sixteen
The floating Mine

It is a true saying, that "the pitcher which goes too often to the well gets broken at last;" and thus it came about with me, or rather with the *Kasanumi*.

As the days passed, we became aware of greatly increased activity on the part of the garrison of Port Arthur. Cruising in the offing during the daytime, well beyond the range of the Russian's biggest guns, yet near enough at hand to make sure that our blockade of the port was effective, the sound of violent explosions came floating off to us all day long, telling us in unmistakable language that strenuous efforts were being made to clear the channel of the sunken steamers wherewith we had blocked it, at such heavy cost to ourselves. There could be but one reason for such tremendous activity: it was doubtless that the enemy had it in contemplation to send his fleet to sea, probably with the object of finding a more secure shelter in the port of Vladivostock, a surmise which was confirmed by our spies in Port Arthur.

If still further confirmation of this intention were needed, it was to be found in the increased efforts which the Russians put forth to hamper our mine-laying operations in the roadstead; for about this time it became the practice of the enemy to send out a ship, sometimes two, or even three, to lie at anchor in the roads all night. The ship, or ships, always anchored well under the cover of the heaviest guns of the fortress, yet so far out that her, or their, own heavy guns completely commanded the waters of the roadstead, thus tremendously increasing the difficulty of sowing those waters with mines.

Naturally, the presence of these ships in the roadstead offered an almost irresistible temptation to our destroyers to essay the task of sinking them, or at least putting them out of action; and this desire on our part was smiled upon by Togo, to put the case mildly, for information was now continually reaching us to the effect that the formidable Baltic fleet was being rapidly prepared for sea, and that its departure on its long voyage to the Far East was imminent; while Togo was naturally anxious that the Port Arthur fleet—and the Vladivostock fleet also, if possible—should be effectually disposed of before the arrival of so powerful a reinforcement in Japanese waters. Therefore, great as was the risk attending the attack of a powerfully armed ship at anchor under the cover of several formidable forts, and careful as our Admiral was, both of his ships and of his men, no attempt was made to discourage us of the torpedo flotilla when our desire to attack was made known; on the contrary, the desire was smiled upon, as I have said, and nothing more than a word of caution was given against the incurring of unnecessary risks.

Perhaps I ought to explain precisely what I mean by saying that the desire of the commander of the torpedo flotilla to attack these ships was "smiled upon" by the Admiral. He had not only "smiled upon" but had given imperative orders that the torpedo fleet was to be employed upon every possible occasion for the harassing and discomfiture of the enemy; but hitherto the tactics employed had been for the destroyers and torpedo-boats to attack in numbers, a division or even two or three divisions being sent in at a time. It was due to my initiative that these tactics were now to be altered, and that attacks were now to be permitted by as few as two boats only. Up to now it had been our regular practice for a large number of craft to creep in toward the roadstead at a low speed until discovered by the enemy's searchlights, and then dash in upon the foe at our utmost speed, through a hail of shells, discharge our torpedoes as we circled round our quarry, and then dash out again, trusting to our speed to carry us back into the zone of safety. Of course this plan had its advantages, inasmuch as that the more there were of us, the greater—in theory—the chance that some of us would score a hit. But against this there was the fact that during the final rush of the torpedo craft upon the enemy, the necessity to maintain our highest speed throughout the entire period of the attack involved forced draught, and consequently flaming funnels, which latter of course immediately attracted the attention of the enemy and nullified all our efforts to take him by surprise.

Now, I had by this time gained a considerable amount of experience of torpedo warfare, and I had not failed to observe that in the majority of cases where our attacks had failed, the failure had been due to the above cause, combined with the fact that ten or a dozen craft ran a much greater risk of being picked up by the enemy's searchlights than would one or two. It had therefore seemed to me that, taking everything into consideration, the prospects of successful attack by two craft—one to support and assist the other in case of need—were as good as those of a dozen craft, while the risk would be very much less, provided that the attack were made coolly and circumspectly in accordance with a plan which I had worked out. This plan was, in brief, to run for the harbour at normal speed until we were practically within effective range, and then, instead of dashing in at full speed, to stop our engines—the throb of which was loud enough to be heard at a considerable distance on a quiet night—and head directly for our quarry, discharging our torpedoes when the momentum or "way" of the boat had carried her as far as she would go, trusting to the subsequent confusion to enable us to escape unscathed. I had fully explained this view of mine to the Admiral, and had obtained his sanction to put my plan to the test. Accordingly, on a certain night toward the middle of June, after the Russians had been let severely alone for some forty-eight hours, the *Kasanumi*, accompanied by the *Akaisuki*, my friend Ito's ship, left the rest of the blockaders, with the object of putting my theory into practice.

It was a splendid night for our purpose; there was a breathless calm, the water was smooth as oil, and although there was certainly a moon, she was in her last quarter, and did not rise until close upon one o'clock in the morning. Moreover, the sky was overcast by a great sheet of dappled cloud through which only a solitary star here and there peeped faintly; it was consequently dark enough to afford us a reasonable chance of getting within striking distance of our quarry undetected.

When the Russians sent their ships out of harbour to lie all night in the roadstead, as they did pretty frequently now, it was their custom to get them out early in the afternoon, after their destroyers had carefully swept the anchorage in search of mines; and it was my hope that—we having left them alone for the preceding two days—they would by this time be getting suspicious of such unwonted inactivity on our part, and consequently would send out one, or perhaps even two ships, to guard against a possible *coup* on our part.

Our mine-laying craft very rarely got to work before one or two o'clock in the morning, that being the hour when human vigilance is popularly supposed to be least active; I therefore planned to arrive in the roadstead about midnight, hoping that I should then catch the enemy off his guard, snatching a rest in preparation for the moment when our activities usually began.

Now, the thing which we had most to fear was a long-distance searchlight established in a station on Golden Hill, at a height of some two hundred feet above the sea-level. This searchlight was generally turned on at dusk, and was kept unceasingly playing upon the anchorage and its adjacent waters all through the night. It commanded the entire roadstead, from a point three miles east of the harbour's mouth, right round to the south and west as far as the Pinnacle Rock; and the difficulty was how to avoid being picked up by it before we had delivered our attack. But by this time I knew the seaward surroundings of Port Arthur almost by heart. I knew, for instance—and this was most important—that the searchlight station was placed so far back from the edge of the crumbling cliff that the water immediately at the foot of the latter, and for a distance of perhaps a hundred yards to seaward, could not be reached by the beam of the light, and was therefore enveloped in darkness, rendered all the deeper and more opaque by the dazzling brilliance of the light; and I also knew that along the outer edge of this patch of darkness there was a sufficient depth of water to float a destroyer, even at dead low water. My plan, therefore, was to make a wide sweep to seaward upon leaving the blockading squadron, gradually turning east and north, and thus eventually to get into Takhe Bay, some five miles east of Port Arthur anchorage, and from thence creep along the shore to the westward, keeping as close in as the depth of water would permit. There was only one difficulty about this, which was that at a certain point not far from where the searchlight station stood, there was a gap in the line of cliff where the ground sloped steeply down to the water's edge for a short distance, and here of course the beam of the light had uninterrupted play right up to the beach; but I believed I could overcome this difficulty by simply watching my opportunity and slipping past the gap when the searchlight was not playing upon it.

All went well with us until about seven bells in the first watch (half-past eleven o'clock) when a great bank of fog, for which those seas are notorious, came driving in from the south-west, and in a moment we were enveloped in a cloud so thick that, standing upon the bridge, I could scarcely distinguish our aftermost funnel, and could not see our taffrail at all. We were then about three miles from the shore, with the indentation of Takhe Bay straight ahead of us, and near enough the anchorage for a man on our signal yard to make out—before the fog enveloped us, of course—that there were two ships at anchor in the roadstead, one, a five-funnelled craft which I knew could only be the *Askold*, while the other, showing four funnels, I gathered from his description must be the armoured cruiser *Bayan*. The searchlight had of course been in action ever since we had made the land, and as its beam swept slowly over the ships it had revealed enough of their details to enable us to easily identify them.

It was most exasperating that the fog should have swept down upon us just when it did. Had it come an hour, or even half an hour, later, I would have welcomed it, for we should then have had time to get up within striking distance of the ships and, under cover of the fog, could have approached them closely enough to have made sure of both, while now! Well, it was useless to cry over what could not be helped; the only thing to do was to make the best of things as they were, and to hope that the fog might yet prove a friend in disguise, after all.

Fortunately, as the fog came sweeping up to us, I had the presence of mind to hail the man on the yard—who was at that moment describing the ships he saw riding at anchor in the roads—asking him to tell me exactly how they bore from us. His reply was:

"They are square abeam, honourable Captain."

I immediately put my head in through the window of the wheelhouse and demanded of the helmsman how we were at that moment heading. He answered that we were then steering north forty degrees west, by compass.

"Then," said I, "alter the course at once to west forty degrees south. That," I added, addressing young Hiraoka, who was standing beside me, "ought to take us to them, or near enough to enable us to sight them. Kindly go aft, Mr Hiraoka, and hail the *Akatsuki*, telling her of our shift of helm."

The youngster ran aft to do my bidding, the fog at that moment being so thick that it was impossible to see one's hand before one's face, even the beam of the distant searchlight being so effectually obscured that it might have been extinguished for all that we knew to the contrary. I had rung down for our engines to stop, so that we might not run away from the *Akatsuki*, after shifting our helm, without informing her of the alteration in our course, and everything was now so still that I had no difficulty in distinguishing young Hiraoka's hail, and the reply from the other destroyer, breaking through the soft swish and lap of water under our bows. It was the *Akatsuki's* lieutenant who was answering our hail, and he had just acknowledged the intimation of our altered course, and was ordering his own helmsman to make a like change, when, without the slightest warning, I experienced a terrific shock which felt exactly as though the ship had been smitten a savage blow from below by a giant hammer. So violent was it that I was flung high in the air and over the rail of the bridge on to the steel turtle-back deck beneath, upon which I landed head-first with such violence that I immediately lost consciousness. But before that happened I was sensible of two things; one of them being a blinding flash of flame, coincident with the shock, in which our bows, for a length of some ten or twelve feet, seemed to crumple up and fly to pieces, while the other was that, as I was tossed high in the air, I sustained a violent blow on the chest from some heavy object which seemed to sear my flesh like white-hot iron. Then down I came upon my head, and knew no more.

My first sensation, upon coming to myself, was that of a violent aching all over my body, as though every bone in it had been broken. But the aching of my head was even worse than that of my body, while as for my chest, it smarted and throbbed as though the blade of a burning knife rested upon it. I next became aware that I was in bed; and finally, opening my eyes, I saw that I was the occupant of one of many beds in a large, airy room which somehow seemed familiar to me, and which I presently identified as the ward which I had once before occupied in the hospital at our base among the Elliot Islands.

It was broad daylight, and the sun was shining brilliantly into the room through the widely opened windows, which admitted a gentle, refreshing breeze, pleasantly charged with ozone. Two dainty little women nurses were doing something at a table at the far end of the room, which happened to come within the range of my vision, and presently I heard the gentle splash of water in that direction, which immediately brought home to me the consciousness that my mouth and throat were parched. I opened my mouth to call to the nurses that I was thirsty, but it was only the very faintest of whispers that escaped my smarting lips. It was enough, however, to immediately produce a gentle rustle on the other side of my bed, and the next moment a pretty face was bending over me and a pair of soft, dark, almond-shaped eyes were gazing sympathetically into mine.

"Ah!" exclaimed the owner of those eyes, "at last the illustrious Captain is himself again. Are you suffering very acutely, noble sir?"

"Suffering?" I whispered. "*Rather*! I ache as if I had been beaten to a jelly, and I am as thirsty as a—as a limekiln. Can you by any chance get me something to drink? A bucketful will do to start with."

"A bucketful!" she murmured, looking anxiously down at me as she laid her long, slender, pointed fingers upon the pulse of my left hand where it rested outside the coverlet. "But no," she continued, evidently speaking to herself, "his pulse is almost normal, and there is no trace of fever. A bucketful! Oh, these English!"

She shook her head, as though giving up some problem that she found too difficult for solution, and shuffled off, with the curious gait peculiar to Japanese women, without saying another word to me. She approached the other two nurses, at the far end of the ward, and said something which caused them both to turn and stare in my direction. Then the senior of the party, accompanied by the girl whom I had so tremendously astonished, came up to my bedside, looked at me, felt my pulse, and shuffled away again, presently returning with one of those cups with a spout, from which one can drink while in a recumbent position. She placed the point of the spout between my lips, and the next moment I was aware that I was imbibing some delicious broth. But the cup! It was only about the size of an ordinary breakfast cup, and its contents were gone before I could well taste them. I asked for more, and got a second cupful; and then, as I was asking for still more, the Medical Staff of the hospital entered the ward, and the whole crowd turned with one accord and grouped itself around my bed.

The Chief, a keen, clever-looking little fellow, whose age it was impossible to guess at since he was clean shaven, turned to the nurse who was feeding me, and sharply demanded what it was that she was administering. She explained, adding in all seriousness the information that I had demanded a bucketful, whereupon he turned and regarded me with upraised eyebrows, and laid his fingers upon my wrist.

"So you are suffering from extreme thirst, Captain, eh?" he demanded.

I nodded emphatically.

"Ah!" he said, "yes; that was only to be expected. Well—" He turned to the head nurse and gave her certain instructions in so low a tone of voice that I could not catch what he said. Then, drawing a notebook from his pocket, he very carefully and with much consideration wrote what I imagined to be a prescription, tore out the leaf, and handed it to the nurse, with instructions to have it made up. Then, turning again to me, he inquired how I felt. I described my symptoms as well as I could, wondering all the while how it was that I was only able to speak in the merest whisper.

The members of the staff, including the Head himself, could not have listened with more rapt attention, had I been communicating to them some item of intelligence of the most tremendous import; and when I had finished, the Head drew away from my bed to the far end of the room, where for some minutes he appeared to be delivering a lecture to the members of his staff, who had followed him. Then, the lecture being finished, they all came back to the side of my bed, and one of the nurses having carefully folded back the covering as low as my waist, the Head proceeded to deftly loosen the fastenings of an enormous bandage which I now discovered enveloped my chest. This done, I was very tenderly raised to a sitting posture—an operation which gave me excruciating pain, by the way—and the endless turns of the bandage were deftly unwound, one of the nurses seating herself upon the bed and supporting me meanwhile. When at length the bandage was removed, several broad strips of dressing were disclosed, which, upon removal, revealed a ghastly great jagged wound stretching right across my chest, the edges of which had been very neatly drawn together by a number of stitches. Then, for the first time, I remembered the violent blow on the chest which I had received when the bows of the *Kasanumi* were destroyed. The wound was intently examined by the entire staff, pronounced to be healing most satisfactorily, and then, after being thoroughly sponged with warm water, was re-dressed, and a fresh bandage applied. Meanwhile, I had made the discovery that my head also was enveloped in bandages, and when I asked why, was informed that I had received a scalp wound, which, however, was of no serious consequence. When this also had been re-dressed, the entire operation occupying the best part of half an hour, I felt considerably easier, although much exhausted. While the wound in my chest was being dressed, I had seized the opportunity to look round the ward, and saw that several of the beds were occupied, one of the patients, who appeared to be suffering from a broken arm, being a man whom I appeared to know. As I sat staring at him he turned his head and our eyes met, whereupon, to my amazement, up went his uninjured hand to the salute.

"Who is that man?" I demanded. "I seem to recognise his face."

"You do?" remarked the Chief. "Ah! no wonder. He is one of the survivors of the disaster by which you so nearly lost your honourable life. He was one of the crew of the *Kasanumi*."

"One of the crew of the *Kasanumi*!" I repeated. "Of course; I remember now. How come he and I to be here?"

"You were both, with the rest of the crew of your ship, rescued by the *Akatsuki*, which ship was happily at hand when the disaster occurred," replied the Chief.

"Ah, yes, the disaster!" I remarked. "Yes, I am beginning to remember all about it now. What was the nature of the disaster, doctor? Was that ever ascertained?"

"According to your friend, Captain Ito, who brought you here, there is no doubt that your ship struck a mine," was the reply. "Of course she went down, though not so quickly but that the entire crew were saved, together with most of their personal effects. There was time, indeed, to save most, if not all, of your belongings, Captain, and they are now here, awaiting your convalescence."

"Thank you," I said. "And, pray, when did the disaster occur?"

"Just a week ago, last night," was the reply.

"A week ago!" I exclaimed in consternation. "Then, have I lain here all that time, unconscious?"

"You certainly have," replied the Chief. "Now, however, that you are happily conscious once more, we must do our utmost to keep you so, and to assist your recovery. Therefore, no more conversation, if you please, until I give you permission. What you now have to do is to remain perfectly quiet and free from all excitement, pleasurable or otherwise. Rest, sleep, take such food and such medicines as I shall order for you, and recover strength as rapidly as possible. Then, when you are sufficiently well to receive visitors, I will permit a few of the many who are now eager to see you, to do so. No, not another word!"

And therewith the little fellow and his staff turned away and proceeded to overhaul the rest of the patients.

The nurse whom I had at first seen upon recovering consciousness appeared to have been specially told off to look after me, for upon the departure of the staff she came and knelt by my bedside, as is their fashion, instead of sitting.

She was just within the range of my vision, as I lay, and I suppose I must have stared at her pretty intently for some time, for presently I saw her colour rising, which at once brought me to my bearings. Thinking to put her at her ease, I said to her:

"Nurse, what is your name?"

She coloured still more, and after regarding me steadfastly for a moment, answered:

"My contemptible and insignificant name, illustrious Captain, is Peach-blossom."

"Peach-blossom!" I repeated. "And a very appropriate name, too, by Jove! See here, Peach-blossom. The Chief Surgeon seems to have forgotten that I said I was thirsty. Do you think you could find me something to drink? Two or three tumblers of cold water, now, eh? I have an idea that they would taste particularly good."

"I will speak to the Chief, noble Captain, and if he consents I will honourably let you have it," she replied.

The Chief evidently consented, and a few minutes later I was quenching my thirst with the most delicious draught I had ever tasted. It was only pure, cold water, but as I slowly imbibed it I told myself that at last I really understood the full meaning of the term, "nectar."

Well, there is no need for me to dwell at length upon my sojourn in the hospital. I was given to understand that I was making a splendid recovery, yet although I was brought back to the Elliot Islands and admitted to the hospital on the morning of 20th June, it was not until nearly three weeks had passed that I was permitted to receive visitors, the first of whom was that fine fellow Ito, to whom I owed my life.

I shall not readily forget the little chap's delight when, upon entering the ward, he discovered me sitting up in bed, reading, propped up by cushions and a bed-rest. He sprang forward, his eyes fairly snapping with pleasure and excitement, and seizing my welcoming hand, shook it with such energy that good little Peach-Blossom felt constrained to spring hastily to her feet and rescue me from his too strenuous demonstrations of joy. At her vigorous remonstrances, however, he dropped my hand as though it had burnt him and, sinking into a chair by my bedside, proceeded to apologise with almost abject contrition, and would not be comforted until I had assured him, not quite truthfully, I am afraid, that he had not hurt me. Then, in answer to my questions, he proceeded to tell me what he knew of the matter.

It appeared that at the moment when the explosion occurred, the *Akatsuki* was so close to the *Kasanumi* that the two craft were all but touching each other, although, from the *Kasanumi's* bridge, where I was then standing, I could not see the other destroyer. It also appeared that at the moment when I ordered the course of the *Kasanumi* to be altered, the *Akatsuki* was close astern of us, and broad on our port quarter, the consequence being that the shifting of our helm carried us so close athwart her bows that she all but touched us when crossing our stern. It was at this moment that the explosion occurred; and Ito, instantly divining what had happened, at once manoeuvred his craft in such a fashion as to lay her alongside the fast-sinking *Kasanumi*, so that the crew of the latter were able to transfer themselves directly from one ship to the other without using boats. Meanwhile, the helmsman and signalmen on the *Kasanumi's* bridge had seen me tossed over the rail by the force of the explosion, and, although themselves severely shaken, had instantly flung themselves down upon the turtle-back, where they found me lying bleeding and insensible. To pick me up and carry me aft was the next thing to be done, for they realised at once that their own ship was sinking, and they did it, transferring my senseless body to the *Akatsuki* the moment that she got alongside. I was at once taken below and temporarily patched-up, while the crew of the *Kasanumi* were being transferred, together with such of their belongings as they were able to save, my cabin steward with the utmost devotion concentrating all his efforts upon saving the most valuable of my belongings, regardless of the loss of his own.

It was at first thought that possibly the *Kasanumi* might be saved, and Ito did his utmost in that direction, working for more than half an hour upon the stricken craft. But the damage was too serious, and despite collision mats and pumps the craft continued to settle until at length, recognising that all efforts were useless, he ordered all hands aboard his own ship, and cast off, the *Kasanumi* foundering almost before the *Akatsuki* could back off clear of her.

Ito made no attempt to attack the ships in Port Arthur roads single-handed, but at once shaped a course for the Elliot Islands, running clear of the fog half an hour later. Arrived at our base, he lost no time in having me conveyed ashore to the hospital, where, as already recorded, I lay for a week in a state of alternating delirium and coma before I recovered my senses.

The doctors assured me that I was making a splendid recovery; yet to myself my progress appeared to be horribly slow, and it was certainly not accelerated by the knowledge that while I was lying there helpless, big events were happening which had all the appearance of leading up to still bigger events in the near future. For instance, there was the second sortie of the Russian squadron from Vladivostock, in the middle of June, lasting over a fortnight, during which it inflicted great loss and damage upon the Japanese. It was a most risky thing to do, and must certainly have resulted in disaster had not poor, unhappy Admiral Kamimura been morally chained down, and prevented from taking effective measures against the raiders, by a stringent order that he was to hold the Strait of Korea at all costs. Yet, such is human inconsistency, notwithstanding the above stringent order, which bound the unfortunate admiral hand and foot, and effectually precluded his pursuit of the raiding ships, he was so severely blamed by "the man in the street" for the damage done that a mob actually attacked and wrecked his house! This, of course, was most unjust and cruel treatment of a thoroughly capable and zealous man who, hampered though he was, did all he could to bring the raiders to book, and indeed, but for a sudden change of weather at a critical moment, would probably have brought them to action and given them a severe punishing.

Then, there was the abortive sortie of the Port Arthur fleet, three days after the destruction of the *Kasanumi*. True, the ships were only at sea for about twenty-four hours, and did nothing, narrowly escaping capture only by Togo's over-eagerness to engage them, thus discovering himself to the Russians in time to allow the latter to make good their retreat back to Port Arthur; but, all the same, I felt that I was losing much in not being present. To me it seemed that our plucky little Admiral had missed a splendid chance over this last event; for we did the enemy no perceptible damage, and only succeeded in driving him back to his lair. As a matter of fact the only injury sustained by the Russians was that which happened to the battleship *Sevastopol*, which struck one of our mines as she was returning to Port Arthur anchorage, and was only got into the harbour with the utmost difficulty.

Chapter Seventeen
Unexpected Promotion

Among other naval customs which the Japanese had copied from the British, was that of trying by court martial all officers who were so unfortunate as to lose their ships; and on the day when I first received permission from the doctors to take a short turn in the open air, I also received an intimation that my trial for the loss of the *Kasanumi* would be held, a week from that date, on board the flagship *Mikasa*, which would then be in harbour.

Of course I was still very much of an invalid, for although the ghastly wound in my chest had so far healed that it no longer needed dressing, I was warned that even very trifling exertion might cause it to burst open again, while I had by no means recovered my former strength. Nevertheless, on the day appointed, I made shift to walk down to the beach, supported by the arm of an orderly, and, with the same assistance, to climb the flagship's side ladder when I arrived alongside her in the steam launch which had been sent ashore to fetch me.

There is no need for me to describe at length the proceedings of a naval court martial; it has been admirably done by Captain Marryat; and as it was in his day, so it is to-day, in all essentials. Of course the trial was the merest formality, for there could not be the slightest shadow of doubt that the craft had been lost through collision with a mine, while under way in a dense fog, and that it was one of those incidents of war for which nobody but the enemy can be held responsible; and accordingly I was honourably acquitted, and my sword was returned to me amid the congratulations of the Admiral and the officers who had constituted the court.

Five days later I received a visit from Togo himself, who seemed to have conceived rather a liking for me. After making most friendly inquiries as to my health and the progress which I was making toward convalescence, he repeated his congratulations upon my acquittal by the court martial, and then asked me how much longer I thought it would be before I should again be fit for active service. I was happily able to assure him that, unless anything quite unforeseen happened, I hoped to be quite ready for duty in a fortnight, or even less if my services were urgently required, and I remember that I gave the answer with considerable eagerness, for there was a certain subtle something in the tone of the Admiral's question which somehow suggested that events of importance were in the air.

"Good!" ejaculated Togo. "That is excellent news, my friend, for if what I hear be true, it would appear that the time is drawing near when I shall be in urgent need of all the assistance which my officers can give me. I will say no more at present—except that I hope you will take the utmost care of yourself, and get quite well again as quickly as possible—for at present my information is too vague to permit me to make a definite statement. Meanwhile,"—putting his hand into his breast pocket and producing a long, official-looking document—"it affords me the utmost pleasure to hand you this, which is your appointment to the command of the *Yakumo*. It has been my pleasant duty to mention your name in my dispatches, in connection with many services meritoriously rendered, the latest having reference to the very valuable assistance rendered by you prior to and during the battle of Nanshan; and this appointment is the outward token of the authorities' appreciation of those services. I am looking forward with much interest to the moment when you will take up this new command, for, as you know, the *Yakumo* is a very fine ship, and under a smart and enterprising captain I shall expect great things of her."

"And by Jove! sir, you shall not be disappointed if I can help it," I exclaimed, springing to my feet in a paroxysm of delight and grasping the hand which the Admiral kindly extended to me. "I don't know how to find words in which to express my profound gratitude to you, sir, for all your kindness to me, from the moment when I presented myself before you, an utter stranger," I continued huskily; but Togo interrupted me, reaching up and patting my shoulder in a very kind, fatherly way.

"There, there," he murmured, soothingly, "say no more about it, my dear boy; say no more about it. I want no wordy expressions of gratitude; you should know that by this time. And if you really feel grateful to me for anything I have done for you, you shall show your gratitude in deeds, rather than words, when the strenuous times arrive which I already see looming in the distance."

And therewith, affording me no opportunity to reply, the fine little fellow, well named "the Nelson of Japan," hastily shook me by the hand and effected his escape, while I sank into a chair, almost overwhelmed at the extent of my good fortune.

Captain of the *Yakumo*! I could scarcely credit it. As the Admiral had said, the *Yakumo* was a very fine ship; she was indeed one of the finest armoured cruisers which Japan at that time possessed. Her waterline was protected by a belt of Krupp steel seven inches thick amidships, tapering off to five inches thickness at bow and stern; she mounted four 8-inch quick-fire guns in her two turrets, and fourteen 6-inch guns on her broadsides; she could steam twenty-one knots, when clean; and she carried a crew of five hundred officers and men! A rather different craft from the little *Kasanumi*, with her single 12-pounder and five 6-pounders, eh? I felt that, in command of such a ship as that, I could dare and do almost anything. My delight must have proved an important factor in aiding my recovery, for from the moment when I received my appointment, my strength came back to me so rapidly that, instead of the fortnight which I had allowed myself in my conversation with the Admiral, I took only nine days to qualify for my discharge from the hospital, and to report for duty.

It was a proud moment for me when I stood on the spacious quarter-deck of my new command and, in the presence of all hands, mustered for the occasion, read my commission appointing me to the command of the ship. The vacancy had occurred in consequence of the death of her previous captain, and when I boarded the craft, I did so fully prepared for a certain coldness of reception on the part of the officers, for naturally, in the ordinary course of events, the command ought to have gone to the senior officer, one Commander Arisaka. But not so; on the contrary, as I finished reading my commission, folded it up, and put it in my pocket, the Commander approached, shook hands in the most friendly way, expressed the extreme gratification felt by himself and the rest of the officers of the ship at finding themselves under the leadership of one who—as they were kind enough to put it—"had so brilliantly distinguished himself"; and then proceeded to present to me the rest of the officers in rotation, in strict accordance with their rank, all of whom found something pleasant and complimentary to say. By way of response, I made a little speech to all hands, crew as well as officers, in which I expressed my gratification at finding myself in command of so fine a ship, manned by so fine a crew, and voiced the hope that, not only should we be able to all work comfortably and harmoniously together, but also that the Admiral would speedily afford us an opportunity to add fresh laurels to the *Yakumo's* fame; a speech which elicited a quite enthusiastic storm of "Banzais."

Agreeable relations with my officers and crew being thus satisfactorily established, I took up my quarters onboard, and forthwith proceeded to "learn" the ship—that is to say, I made myself intimately acquainted with the localities and purposes of the numerous engines and pieces of machinery with which she was fitted, the number and positions of her magazines, and their contents, the number and situations of her torpedo tubes, the uses of the many fitments to be found in her conning tower, and in fact everything connected with her working, so that in the hour of action I might have every detail firmly fixed in my memory, ready for use at a moment's notice. And wherever I found anything capable of improvement, I unhesitatingly had that improvement carried out, although I feel bound to say that I found very little anywhere needing modification. In this way, and by continually exercising the crew at such evolutions as could be carried out with the ship at anchor, I very soon became perfectly familiar with my new command and, as my strength steadily returned, began to long for the opportunity to test myself as well as my ship and crew. For during the whole of this time the *Yakumo*, with several other cruisers, and our four battleships, had been lying at anchor at our rendezvous at the Elliot Islands, not idle by any means, but, like the *Yakumo*, "tuning up" for a certain eventuality, the approach of which we all seemed to sense in some mysterious way.

And yet, after all, I do not know that there was very much mystery about it, for our Secret Service agents—of whom there were several in Port Arthur—informed us that, from the moment when, on that memorable Sunday, 7th August, one of the first twenty shells fired at the stronghold by the investing Japanese, fell aboard the battleship *Retvisan*, lying at anchor in the harbour, and seriously damaged her, there had been a general outcry that the Russian fleet ought to go to sea and fight, rather than remain in harbour and be ignominiously destroyed without striking a blow in self-defence.

It was known that Admiral Vitgeft, and Prince Ukhtomsky, his second in command, were utterly opposed to such a course, their freely expressed opinion being that the Russian ships, already more or less seriously damaged by the attacks to which they had been subjected from time to time during the progress of the war, were totally unfit to meet and engage the Japanese fleet, which, they had every reason to believe, was in first-class fighting trim. There were certain officers, however, whose mortification at their enforced inactivity blinded them to the soundness of this judgment. "If the ships must be destroyed, let them be destroyed at sea in the act of inflicting as much injury as possible upon the enemy," was their contention; and it was certainly a reasonable one. It was broadly hinted that the leader of this faction found means to convey his contention to the ear of Admiral Alexieff; for, strange to say, the following day brought a wireless message from the Commander-in-Chief to Vitgeft, ordering the latter to take his whole fleet to sea and proceed to Vladivostock, fighting his way thither, if necessary. Every effort was of course made by Vitgeft to keep this order a profound secret; but it was necessary to communicate it to the captains of the several ships and other officers whose duties required that they should possess such knowledge, and the delight of some of them at learning that their long-cherished desire was about to be granted was not conducive to secrecy. Moreover, the sudden, feverish hurry and bustle of preparation was a sufficient advertisement of what was impending; and that very night the news was signalled to the blockading squadron in the offing, from which it was as promptly transmitted by wireless to Togo, among the Elliots. The news was confirmed on the following morning by our patrol vessels off the port, from which came the information that a tremendous state of activity was discernible among the Russian ships, and that all indications pointed toward an almost immediate sortie.

The news arrived by wireless, about an hour after sunrise; and immediately upon receiving it the signal was made for all captains to at once proceed on board the flagship. Some such signal had confidently been expected, after the news of the preceding day; we were in fact all waiting for it, and its display was equivalent to the starting signal for a race, for no sooner did the flags break abroad than they were read, and the next instant the shrill piping of many boatswain's whistles was heard in the calm morning air, the crews of the captain's gigs were seen rushing along the booms and dropping recklessly down into the boats, and in less than a minute the mirror-like waters of the harbour were being churned into foam as the flotilla of gigs darted away from the ships' gangway ladders, each striving to be the first to arrive alongside the *Mikasa*. I was not the first to reach the goal, for the battleships were all lying together, with the cruisers some distance outside them, but my boat was the fourth alongside, beating the *Asama's* gig by half a length, to the intense disgust of Captain Yamada, who occupied her stern-sheets.

"Never mind, Yamada, old chap," I exclaimed, as we shook hands and ascended the *Mikasa's* side ladder together; "perhaps you will get the pull of me later on. But I'll bet you a case of champagne that the *Yakumo* scores a hit before the *Asama*, to-day."

The bet was eagerly accepted, and, chatting gaily, we passed along the flagship's deck and entered the Admiral's state cabin, where we found Togo and the captains of the four battleships already assembled and conversing eagerly. The Admiral shook hands with both of us, complimented me upon my rapid recovery, and then turned to welcome the other captains who were fast arriving, while we joined the little but quickly swelling group of officers who had already arrived; for of course Togo would say nothing until everybody was present.

We were not kept waiting very long, however, perhaps a matter of ten minutes after my arrival, and then Captain Ijichi, of the *Mikasa*, who as each captain arrived, had been ticking his name off a list, announced that all were present, and rapped sharply on the table with his sword-hilt for silence. The next moment, to use a common expression, one might have heard a pin drop. Then Admiral Togo stepped forward, unrolled a chart and spread it open upon the table, and stood for a moment looking round the crowded cabin with a curiously intent and eager gaze.

"Gentlemen," he said, "the wireless message which has this morning arrived from the blockading squadron off Port Arthur, entirely confirms the news of yesterday, to the effect that the Russian fleet is about to put to sea, probably with the intention of making for Vladivostock. I imagine Vladivostock to be its destination for the simple reason that there is no other port open to it; moreover, as we are fully aware, there is a dry dock at Vladivostock large enough to receive a battleship; and I conjecture the intention of the enemy to be to take his damaged ships there for the purpose of repairing them, so that they may be in condition to reinforce and assist the Baltic fleet upon its arrival in these waters.

"Gentlemen, if that be the enemy's intention, it must never be carried out; we must prevent it at all costs—short of the loss of our own battleships, which we *must* preserve in order that we may be able to meet the Baltic fleet upon something like equal terms, when it arrives. Now, the question of how best to meet the Port Arthur fleet without unduly risking our own battleships is one that has greatly exercised my mind ever since the moment when it first became apparent that the Russians were meditating a sortie, and I have formed a plan which I will now lay before you, and upon which I shall be very grateful to receive your frankly expressed criticism and opinion.

"Taking it for granted that the purpose of the Russian Admiral is to make for Vladivostock, I propose to proceed to Encounter Rock, which, as you are all aware, lies directly in the track of ships bound from Port Arthur southward past the Shan-tung promontory,"—the Admiral pointed out upon the chart the positions of the three places mentioned as he spoke— "and there await the arrival of the Russians, who will by that time be so far from Port Arthur that I trust the measures which I propose to take to prevent them from returning may be effective.

"I need not remind you that my instructions are, and have been throughout the war, to risk our battleships as little as possible, since upon them depends the safety of Japan—a fact which I believe we all fully realise; I therefore intend to fight the forthcoming battle at long-range, trusting to our superior gunnery to enable us to inflict the maximum amount of injury upon the enemy with the minimum amount of injury to ourselves.

"I purpose to proceed in the following manner. The *Yakumo* will lead the fleet to sea, followed by the *Kasagi, Takasago, Chitose, Takachiho, Naniwa,* and *Chiyoda*, in the order named. These will be followed, at a distance of three miles, by our six armoured cruisers, in the wake of which will follow the four battleships, with the remaining cruisers and the destroyers bringing up the rear. Further orders I cannot give at present, since my plans are necessarily subject to modification according to the reports which will no doubt come to me from time to time from the blockading squadron, a portion of which will follow the Russian fleet, reporting upon its formation, the course it steers, its speed, and so on. The only thing further which I have now to say is, that the duty of the destroyer flotilla will be to keep the Russian destroyers so fully occupied that the latter will have no opportunity to approach our big ships, while every opportunity must be seized to attack the Russians, especially their battleships. That is all I have to say, gentlemen, except that the fleet which we shall have the honour to meet to-day *must be destroyed*, and I look to each of you, individually, to give me your best assistance in the accomplishment of this purpose. Now, has any officer any suggestion to offer? I shall be most grateful for any helpful hint."

Nobody spoke, but all eyes wandered round the cabin, searching for a possible speaker. The Admiral's eye met mine, and I thought there seemed to be a question in it. As nobody else seemed inclined to speak, I decided to answer that questioning glance.

"There is just one remark which I should like to make, sir, if I may be permitted," I said. "I had not the good fortune to be present when the Japanese last met the Port Arthur fleet, less than two months ago; but from all that I have heard with regard to that meeting, I gather that there would have been no Port Arthur fleet to-day, had not you, sir, been too eager to meet them, revealing your presence to them at such an early moment that retirement to Port Arthur was still possible for them. If that be the case, the obvious lesson to be learnt seems to be that we should on no account show ourselves until the Russians have run too far off-shore to get back again before we can intercept them; and I would also suggest the desirability of taking steps to effectually cut off their retreat."

Togo nodded and smiled.

"Gentlemen," he said, "you have all heard Captain Swinburne's remarks. Have any of you anything to add to them, or any comment to make upon them?"

For a moment there was silence. Then Captain Matsumoto, commanding the *Fuji*, stepped forward.

"I should like to say, sir," he said, "that I entirely concur in what Captain Swinburne has said. Unlike that gentleman, I had the honour to be present on the occasion to which he refers, and I believe all present—including yourself, sir—will be inclined to agree that the honourable captain has put his finger upon the two causes which then combined to render the escape of the Russian fleet possible."

A low murmur of assent followed; and when it died away, Togo spoke.

"I thank you all, gentlemen," he said, "for the expression of opinion to which I have just listened. I agree that a mistake was made upon that occasion, and it was I who made it. But that mistake will not be repeated, you may rest assured. I recognised my mistake when it was too late to amend it, and I have now made my plans accordingly. Has any one else any suggestion to offer?"

There was no response.

"Very well, then, gentlemen," resumed Togo. "Our conference is at an end. Return to your ships, and get your anchors at once. We will proceed to sea forthwith; and may Hachiman Sama," (the Japanese god of War) "be with us to-day and crown our arms with victory!"

A moment's silence followed, and then the cabin rang with the exultant shout of "Banzai! Banzai Nippon!" instantly taken up by the crew out on deck, who heard it, and as instantly repeated by the crews of the other ships, as the sound of the cheering reached them. Then, one after another, we filed past the Admiral, who shook hands with each of us as we passed out of the cabin; and ten minutes later the harbour was resounding with the clank of chain cables being hove in through a fleet's hawse-pipes and stowed away below.

Chapter Eighteen
The Battle of the Yellow Sea

It was still quite early—half-past six o'clock in the morning, to be exact—when a gun from the *Mikasa* and a string of flags, drooping from the end of her signal yard in the breathless calm of a hot August morning, gave the signal for the Japanese fleet to go forth to battle.

In accordance with the Admiral's instructions, the *Yakumo* was to lead the way to sea, and it was a proud moment for me when, standing upon the cruiser's navigating bridge, I personally rang down the order to the engine-room, "Ahead, half-speed, both engines!" And I considered—and still consider—that I had every reason to be proud; for here was I, a lad not yet quite nineteen years of age, captain of one of the finest and most formidable cruisers in the Japanese navy. And I had attained to that position—I may say it now, I think, without laying myself open to the charge of being unduly vain—solely by my own exertions and without a particle of favour shown me, excepting that, when my own country contemptuously dispensed with my services, the aliens whom I was now serving received me with the utmost courtesy and kindness. Ah, well! thank God, that bitter period in my life is past now, and I can bear to look back upon it with equanimity, but the memory of it often swept down upon me like a black cloud in the days of which I am now writing.

But there was no thought of my unmerited disgrace and ruined career in my own country to interfere with my happiness or humble my pride upon that glorious morning; I enjoyed the satisfaction of knowing that my innocence had been made clear, that the stain of guilt had been removed from my name, and I was as happy just then as I suppose it is ever possible for mortal to be.

And indeed, quite apart from matters of a purely personal nature, it would have been very difficult for any normal-minded individual to have been otherwise than buoyant upon that particular morning, for everything conspired to make one so. The weather was glorious; the sky, a clear, rich sapphire blue, was, for a wonder, without a cloud, the air was so still that until we got under way and made a wind for ourselves the signal flags drooped in motionless folds, and their interpretation was largely a matter of guesswork. Then there was all the pomp and circumstance of modern war, the ships already cleared for action, and each of them decorated with at least two enormous battle-flags—wrought by the dainty fingers of Japan's fairest daughters—flaunting defiantly from her mast-heads. It must have been a magnificent sight to behold that proud fleet steaming out to sea, ship after ship falling into line with machine-like precision and keeping distance perfectly, first the squadron of cruisers, led by the *Yakumo*; then the other five armoured cruisers, with the *Asama* in the van; then the four battleships—accompanied by the *Nisshin* and *Kasuga*, which were powerful enough to take their place in the line of battle—and, finally, the swarm of heterogeneous craft composed of the older and less important cruisers and other vessels, and those wasps of the sea, the destroyers.

The *Yakumo* had scarcely begun to gather way when the flagship signalled "Course South-West by South; speed twelve knots."

As our signalman ran up the answering pennant, I entered the chart-room and, approaching the table, upon which a chart of the Yellow Sea lay spread out, requested Mr Shiraishi, the navigating lieutenant, to lay down a South-West by South course upon the chart, that we might see where it would take us. He did so, and I saw with satisfaction that it would take us some twenty-five miles to the eastward of Encounter Rock, that unfortunate spot near which the Japanese fleet had too prematurely revealed its presence upon the occasion of its previous encounter with the Russians. Twenty-five miles! That was excellent. If we held on upon that course we should cross the bows of the Russians at such a distance as would enable us to pass unseen, and then come up from the southward in the enemy's rear, so cutting him off from Port Arthur and rendering it impossible for him to avoid a fight.

Shortly after clearing the harbour, the *Asama* and her attendant cruisers parted company with us, striking off to the westward, with the object of working round in the rear of the Russians, and again I mentally complimented Togo upon his astuteness.

Nine o'clock came, and a few minutes later there arrived a wireless message from the Admiral for our squadron to change course thirty-four degrees to the westward. I wondered what this might portend, for we had been receiving almost continuous wireless messages from the squadron off Port Arthur, the latest of which told us that the Russians, although undoubtedly intending a sortie, had not yet started. I again visited the chart-room, and with Shiraishi's assistance discovered that our new course would bring us within about seven miles south-east of Encounter Rock about noon.

"Four bells" had just gone tinkling along the line of the Japanese ships, informing those whom it might concern that the hour was ten o'clock in the morning, when a fresh wireless message came from our blockading squadron, informing us that at last the Russian fleet was actually steaming out of Port Arthur harbour, with battle-flags flying, bands playing, and the ship's companies singing the Russian National Anthem, with the battleship *Tsarevich*, Vitgeft's flagship, leading. As the message was decoded and the news spread throughout the Japanese fleet, an almost audible sigh of relief escaped the breasts of officers and men; the Russians were not only coming out, but actually meant to fight; and the fateful hour which had been so long and so eagerly awaited was now at last at hand. A great cheer arose, passing along the line from ship to ship, and officers who had already assured themselves that all preparations for meeting the enemy were complete once more went the rounds, to make assurance doubly sure.

The Japanese blockading fleet gradually closed in behind the Russian ships, compelling Vitgeft to send back his gunboats, mining craft, and reserve destroyers, as our boats were threatening to cut them off; and about eleven o'clock we got a message informing us that the fleet which we should have to meet consisted of six battleships, four cruisers, and seven destroyers, an eighth destroyer, believed to be the *Reshitelny*, having contrived, by her superior speed, to give our boats the slip, and steam away in the direction of Chifu. Meanwhile, the glass was falling, great masses of cloud came driving up from the eastward, and a little breeze from the same quarter sprang up, rapidly freshening and knocking up a sea which soon set even our battleships rolling and pitching ponderously. "Well, so much the better for us," we told each other. Our gunners were by this time quite accustomed to shoot from a rolling and pitching platform, while the Russians had had no such profitable experience; and the heavier the sea, the greater would probably be the superiority of our shooting.

It was nearing noon when at length, broad on our starboard bow, a great cloud of black smoke began to show on the south-eastern horizon; and shortly afterward a forest of masts, from the truck of each of which flaunted a great white flag bearing a blue Saint Andrew's cross, began to rise above the sea-line, followed by numerous funnels belching immense volumes of black smoke. The two fleets were nearing each other fast, it was therefore not long before the ponderous bulk of the *Tsarevich* topped the horizon, with the *Retvisan, Pobieda, Peresviet* (flying Rear-Admiral Prince Ukhtomsky's flag), *Sevastopol*, and *Poltava* following. Then came our old friend of the five funnels, the *Askold*, followed by the *Pallada* and *Diana*, with a hospital ship, flying a Red Cross flag, bringing up the rear but well astern. On the port beam, but well to the rear of the line of battleships, was the cruiser *Novik*—easily distinguished by her three funnels with a single mast stepped between the second and third funnel—and seven destroyers.

Up fluttered a signal aboard the *Mikasa*, and scarcely had the flags broke out when away went our destroyers at top speed, like hounds released from the leash, to attack the enemy. And a stirring sight it was to witness their dash, for it was now blowing quite fresh and a nasty, choppy sea had arisen, through which the plucky little boats raced, like a school of dolphin chasing flying-fish, now throwing a third of their length clean out of the water, and anon plunging into an oncoming wave until the water foamed and hissed over turtle-back and bridge and poured in torrents down upon the main deck and overboard. But the Russian Admiral was not going to tamely submit to a torpedo attack in broad daylight; he allowed the boats to get well within range of his guns, and then opened a brisk fire upon them, driving them off for the moment. Nevertheless, although the boats never actually scored a hit that day, they were of the utmost assistance, hovering on the enemy's flanks and rear, dashing in upon him from time to time, and distracting his attention at many a critical moment.

Encounter Rock now bore north-west from us, seven miles distant, and was broad upon the port beam of the Russians, at about the same distance; and had both fleets held on as they were then going the Russians must very soon have cut through our line—provided, of course, that we had permitted them to do so. But the attempt evidently did not appeal to Vitgeft, for the *Tsarevich* suddenly starboarded her helm and led away from us in a north-westerly direction, while Togo, perhaps afraid that this was the preliminary to a retreat on the part of the Russian fleet, feigned a nervousness that he certainly did not feel, and shifted his helm, heading South-South-West, at the same time forming his battleships in line abreast. The result was that, for a time, the two fleets were actually steaming away from each other, the Russians being upon our starboard quarter. After steaming a short distance in this direction, our formation was altered back to line ahead, and the course was changed to South-West, apparently with the object of getting the ships well in hand.

It was close upon one o'clock in the afternoon when our Admiral, having put us through one or two further manoeuvres and apparently satisfied himself that he had strung us up to the necessary pitch of alertness, finally formed line ahead and changed course to East-North-East, at the same time hoisting the signal, "Engage!" The signal was greeted with a terrific outburst of cheering from every ship, and faces that had begun to look gloomy as the distance between the two fleets increased, once more became wreathed in smiles. Speed was increased, and we began to rapidly overhaul the enemy, the spray flying high over our bows as we pushed our way irresistibly through the rising sea. And now the horizon all round from north, west, and south showed dark with smoke as the Japanese cruisers began to close in from those points upon the Russians.

It was the *Tsarevich* which at length opened the ball, by bringing the 12-inch guns in her fore-turret to bear upon the *Mikasa*. There was a brilliant double flash, a big outburst of white smoke that for a moment partially veiled the great ship ere it drove away to leeward, a huge double splash as the ponderous shells hit the water about a mile away, and then came a crashing *boom* as the sound of the explosion reached us against the wind. The shots had fallen short. These two shots appeared to be regarded by the rest of the Russian battleships as a signal to open fire, for they immediately did so, the flashes bursting out here and there all along the enemy's battle-line, first from one ship and then from another, as though each ship were striving which could first get off her shots, while projectiles seemed to be falling everywhere excepting aboard the Japanese ships; true, two or three shells flew, muttering loudly, high over our heads, but the rest fell either wide or very far short. Our anticipations, it seemed, were proving correct, the roll and pitching of their ships was playing the mischief with the aim of the Russian gunners. Then the big guns of the flagship and the *Asahi* spoke, just four shots each, coolly and deliberately fired, one shot at a time, to test the range. This was found to be too great for effective practice, and the fire thereupon ceased.

But although not one of those eight ranging shots had actually touched a Russian ship, they all fell much closer to their mark than had the Russian projectiles, and close enough, at all events, to make Vitgeft nervous, for their immediate effect was to cause him to haul up to the northward, so that it looked as though he were seriously contemplating the advisability of doubling round Encounter Rock and retreating back to Port Arthur. It was a moment when everything seemed to be hanging in the balance, when a single false move would ruin everything, and the chance that we had been so long waiting for would be lost. Port Arthur was still close enough under the lee of the Russians to permit of their reaching the shelter of its batteries without very serious loss, should they elect to make the attempt. It was a moment demanding both boldness and astuteness of action, and, gambler-like, Togo resolved to risk everything upon a single throw. Instead of making the signal to close with the enemy and immediately bring him to battle, the Admiral signalled, "Change course sixteen points east," which meant that the whole fleet, now steaming in line ahead, parallel to the Russian's course, and heading in the same direction, must swerve round upon a port helm and go back over the ground which it had just traversed, that in fact it must turn tail and run away from the Russians! The manoeuvre was executed in splendid style, and two minutes later the Japanese fleet was heading south-west, while the Russian fleet, now some nine miles distant, bore about two points abaft our starboard beam.

The object of the manoeuvre was of course to impress the Russian Admiral with the conviction that we were as little anxious to put our fortunes to the touch as he was; and apparently the ruse was successful, for almost immediately the Russians shifted helm, heading about south-east and standing across our wake, with all their funnels belching great volumes of smoke, showing that a tremendous effort was going to be made to give us the slip.

For what seemed to us all an interminable half-hour, the astute little Japanese "Nelson" permitted them to lay the flattering unction to their souls that they were going to succeed, for during that half-hour the Japanese fleet plugged steadily away to the south-west, every moment increasing the distance between themselves and the enemy. Then, at last, judging from the respective positions of the two fleets that our superior speed must certainly frustrate any further attempt at escape on the part of the enemy, up went the longed-for signal for us to swerve round and give chase.

This manoeuvre of ours was the signal for another shift of helm on the part of the Russians. They had been heading about south-east, but now, seeing us coming straight for them, they swerved away until they were heading almost due east, as though even now anxious to defer the evil moment as long as possible. But they must speedily have recognised the impossibility of escape, for now, with carefully-cleaned furnace fires and a full head of steam, our ships were racing along through the fast-rising sea at a speed which would enable us to rapidly overhaul the chase, notwithstanding that they were plunging until they were buried to the hawse-pipes, and their fore-decks were smothered with spray.

The two fleets were now running upon converging lines, the enemy, about a point before our port beam, steering east, while we were steering east-north-east, and visibly gaining as the minutes slipped by. At last it looked as though the fight could no longer be delayed, and a thrill of excitement passed through me as I now began to fully realise that I was about to take part in a great naval battle, fought under modern conditions in ships protected by ponderous plates of steel armour and furnished with all the most modern engines of destruction. What would such a battle look like, and how would it end? Meanwhile the day was passing, and although the two fleets had been within sight of each other for more than two hours, nothing had thus far been done.

Both fleets were now steaming in single line ahead, the battleships leading, and the cruisers following closely, the Russian fleet being slightly ahead and steaming surprisingly well, considering the condition of their ships, though we were rapidly overhauling them.

Five bells (half-past two o'clock) in the afternoon watch pealed out, and at the same moment the *Asama* and *Yakumo* received orders to haul out from the fleet and heave-to, holding ourselves ready to deal with any enemy ships which might attempt to break back toward Port Arthur. So we were not to be allowed to take part in the fight, after all! It was positively heart-breaking, and for a moment I felt inclined to imitate Nelson at Copenhagen and turn a blind eye to the signal, but the sight of the *Asama* promptly sheering out from the line brought me to my senses. I knew that poor Yamada would be just as bitterly disappointed as myself; yet there he was, obeying the order with the same promptitude that he would have displayed had he been ordered to attack the enemy single-handed. I nodded—rather savagely, I am afraid—at Arisaka, the Commander, who was regarding me with eyebrows raised questioningly.

"All right," I growled. "Hard a-port, sir, and sheer out of the line."

We swept right round in a wide semi-circle, finally stopping our engines when we arrived at a spot about midway between the rears of the two fleets. Our engines had just stopped, and I was on the point of opening a semaphore conversation with the *Asama*, hove-to about half a mile distant, with the purpose of making some sort of arrangement for coping with certain possible eventualities, when a vivid flash and a great cloud of smoke burst from the *Mikasa*, and was immediately followed by similar outbursts from the rest of our battleships, which were opening fire upon the Russian rear as the ships came within range. To give them their due, the Russians were by no means slow to reply, and it was presently evident from the number of shells falling round her, that they were concentrating their fire upon the *Mikasa*. The first hit was scored by one of our ships— the *Shikishima*, we afterwards learned—which landed a 12-inch shell under the *Askold's* forward bridge. We saw the flash and smoke of the exploding shell, but could not, of course, tell what damage was done. The next second another shell hit the same craft about her waterline, and within a minute huge volumes of smoke were seen pouring from her, seeming to indicate that she was on fire. But with ourselves at a standstill and both fleets steaming away from us at high speed, they soon passed beyond our range of vision, and all that we knew about the fight was that there was a terrific cannonading going on, while the eastern horizon bore a dense veil of smoke which came driving rapidly down upon us before the rising gale. The cannonading continued with tremendous energy for about three-quarters of an hour, and then began to slacken, until by seven bells—half-past three in the afternoon—it had ceased altogether.

What had happened? Was the fight over? It might be so, although I could scarcely believe that the Russians had been utterly beaten in the short space of an hour; for although their ships were in anything but first-class condition, the men were brave, and were scarcely likely to yield so long as the merest ghost of a chance of success remained to them. We were not doomed to remain very long in suspense, however, for just as eight bells was striking a wireless message arrived from the Admiral, ordering the *Asama* and ourselves to rejoin forthwith, and giving us our course, east-south-east.

I believe our engines were the first to move, but the *Asama* was now nearly a mile to the eastward of us, we standing higher out of the water than she, and therefore drifting to leeward faster, consequently she really had the best of the start. But I wasn't going to let her get into action before me, if I could help it, and I called down the voice-tube to Carmichael, our Engineer Commander, explaining the state of affairs, and begging him to do his best. Unfortunately for us, however, the *Asama's* "chief" was Scotch, too; it therefore at once became a race between the two ships, all the keener because of the friendly rivalry between the two Scotchmen. It was generally conceded that *Asama* had the advantage of *Yakumo* by about half a knot; but when at length, shortly before four bells in the first dog watch, we rejoined the line, the two craft were running neck and neck.

The battle recommenced about a quarter of an hour before we were able to resume our former position in the fighting line, the *Poltava* opening fire with her 12-inch guns upon the *Mikasa*, against which ship, it appeared, the Russians had concentrated their efforts during the earlier phase of the fight. The *Poltava* was the sternmost ship in the Russian battle-line; and as though her shots had been a signal, the fire instantly ran right along the Russian line from rear to van. The din was frightful, for our ships at once returned the Russian fire, and in a moment, as it seemed, the sea all round about the *Mikasa* on our side, and the *Tsarevich*, *Peresviet*, and *Retvisan* on the side of the Russians, was lashed into innumerable great fountains of leaping spray which shone magnificently, like great showers of vari-coloured jewels, in the orange light of the declining sun. And presently, as the gunners got the range, there were added to the deafening explosions of the guns the sounds of the projectiles smiting like Titan hammers upon the armoured sides and other protected parts of the ships, and the crash of bursting shells. Great clouds of powder smoke whirled about the ships, hiding them for a second or two and then driving away to leeward upon the wings of the increasing gale. Splinters of wood and iron, and fragments of burst shells swept over the ships like hail, and prostrate forms here and there about the decks, weltering in their blood, proclaimed the growing deadly accuracy of the fire on either side. The pandemonium of sound was such that the human voice could no longer make itself heard, and the officers on the bridges were obliged to give their orders in dumb show. Even the shrieks of the wounded went unheard in that hellish babel of sound. As the distance between the contending ships decreased one began to realise the terrific character of the forces employed by man for the destruction of his fellow-man, for now it could be seen that the *Tsarevich*, ponderous as was her bulk, literally and visibly heeled and swayed under the tremendous impact of the enemy's projectiles. But we were by no means getting things all our own way, for when the fight had been raging for about half an hour, the *Mikasa* was struck upon her fore barbette by a 12-inch shell which shook the ship from stem to stern as it exploded, and put the barbette, with its two 12-inch guns, out of action for a time through the jamming of its turning machinery. The damage, however, was speedily repaired, and meanwhile the fight went on with ever-increasing fierceness and determination.

At length the superiority of the Japanese fire began to make itself apparent. The speed of the Russian ships steadily fell, and it could be seen that many of them, particularly the battleships, were in great distress. Especially was this the case with Vitgeft's flagship, the *Tsarevich*, upon which much of the fire of our own battleships had been concentrated. She had a great hole in her bows, about ten feet in diameter; her anchors were shot away; and her hawse-pipes had vanished—to enumerate only her more apparent injuries. Then a 12-inch shell struck her fore-turret, wrecked its interior and, as we subsequently learned, glanced off, entered the conning tower, killed everybody in it except two, destroyed the compass, and killed the man at the wheel, who, as he fell, jammed the helm hard a-starboard, causing the ship to swerve sharply out of the line and wheel round in a wide circle, completely upsetting the formation and seriously imperilling many of her sister ships. A few seconds later another shell fell aboard her, hitting the foot of her foremast and causing it to totter, though it did not actually fall. This same shell, we afterward learned, literally blew Admiral Vitgeft to atoms, also seriously wounding several of his staff, and throwing the ship into a perfect chaos of confusion.

This was the beginning of the end; shells now literally rained upon her, doing frightful damage both on deck and below, while it was patent to all that she was completely out of control. Her erratic movements produced the utmost confusion in the Russian battle-line, which broke up and became a mere disorganised mob of ships, upon which the Japanese ships at once closed, determined to avail themselves to the utmost of the opportunity to bring the engagement to a speedy end.

And, indeed, the end appeared to be near; for serious as was the plight of the *Tsarevich*, that of some of her sister battleships was even worse. The *Peresviet*, for example—the flagship of Prince Ukhtomsky, who, in consequence of the death of Admiral Vitgeft, was now in supreme command—was a perfect wreck, so far as her upper works were concerned; both masts were destroyed, her funnels were battered and pierced, and she was on fire; while the *Poltava* had two of her 6-inch guns smashed and the containing turret jammed.

At the moment when the confusion created by the erratic movements of the *Tsarevich* was at its height, the *Peresviet* displayed a signal from her bridge and, sheering out of the mêlée, headed away back in the direction of Port Arthur, followed by the *Sevastopol* and *Poltava*, while the *Askold*, Admiral Reitsenstein's flagship, followed by the cruisers *Diana, Pallada,* and *Novik*, broke away from the rest of the fleet and, under every ounce of steam that they could raise, headed away in a south-easterly direction, followed by the *Asama* and six other cruisers. As for the *Pobieda* and *Retvisan*, apparently animated by the same desperate resolve, they suddenly shifted their helms and steamed straight for our battle-line, as the mortally wounded lion will sometimes turn upon the hunter and, with the last remains of his fast-ebbing strength, slay his foe before perishing himself. It looked as though both meant to use the ram, the successful employment of which might cost us the loss of at least two of our treasured battleships; and they were accordingly received with a terrific fire from every Japanese ship present. The *Retvisan*, being slightly in advance of her companion, received the heaviest of our fire, and under it she seemed to crumple up into an almost shapeless mass of wreckage. It was not possible for mere mortals to continue to face such a devastating hail of shells, and as suddenly as she had started toward us she now swerved away, instantly followed by the *Pobieda*, both steaming hard in the wake of Prince Ukhtomsky's division, which they rejoined just as the dusk of evening was turning to darkness.

With the flight of those two ships the battle came to an end; because for some reason, known only to himself, Togo failed to follow up his advantage and complete the destruction of the Russian fleet. Some of us were of opinion that he felt himself handicapped by the stringent orders which he had received not to risk the loss of any of our precious battleships, one or more of which might easily have been destroyed in the darkness by mines dropped by the flying enemy, or by torpedoes launched from the decks of daring and enterprising destroyers. And if he was influenced by such considerations as these who shall blame him, or say that he was wrong?

Yet people were not wanting who complained that the battle was an indecisive one, because no Russian ships had been either captured or sunk in the course of the fight. But although this assertion was undeniable, the grumblers forgot a little group of very important facts, the chief of which was that the five Russian battleships and the protected cruiser *Pallada* which succeeded in regaining Port Arthur harbour were so desperately damaged that they were practically reduced to the condition of scrap iron, inasmuch as that, despite all the efforts of the Russians to repair them, none of them was again able to leave Port Arthur until they fell into the hands of the Japanese when the fortress surrendered. As for the sixth Russian battleship, the *Tsarevich*, she took advantage of the darkness to separate from the rest of the fleet, and made for Kiaochau, where she arrived on the following day, and where she was of course interned. The same fate befell the cruisers *Askold* and *Diana*, the former of which sought shelter at Shanghai, while the latter succeeded in escaping as far south as Saigon. The destroyer *Reshitelny*, which separated from the Russian fleet immediately after its departure from Port Arthur, escaped the Japanese destroyers and duly reached Chifu, whither she had been sent with dispatches from Admiral Vitgeft, requesting that the Vladivostock squadron might be dispatched to assist him in his proposed passage through the Korean Strait. Her mission accomplished, her commander agreed to assent to the demand of Sah, the Chinese admiral on the station, that she should disarm and surrender certain vital parts of her machinery. The Japanese, however, had their doubts as to the power of the Chinese authorities to enforce this demand, and accordingly Commander Fujimoto took matters into his own hands and, late on the night of 11th October, entered Chifu harbour and, after an altercation with the commander of the Russian vessel, calmly took the *Reshitelny* in tow and carried her off. This was of course a violation of neutral territory, and led to a little temporary friction, but it ended in the destroyer being added to the Japanese navy.

Chapter Nineteen
The Fall of Port Arthur

I have said nothing as to the part played by the *Yakumo* in the battle of the Yellow Sea, for the simple reason that there is nothing particular to relate; but that we played a not altogether unimportant part in the fight is evidenced by the fact that only two of the Japanese ships, namely, the *Mikasa* and the *Nisshin*, had a heavier list of killed than ourselves, although the *Kasuga* scored one more in wounded than we did.

The fact is that, in a general engagement such as that referred to, after the initial movements of the various ships have been noted, one becomes so utterly engrossed in one's own particular share of the work that there is little opportunity to note more than the most salient incidents of the battle. Moreover, the din of battle, the continuous roar of the guns, the crash of bursting shells, the deafening clang of projectiles upon armour, the screams of the wounded, the suffocating fumes of powder, all tend to benumb one's powers of observation, so that the captain of a fighting ship has little opportunity to note anything more than the movements of the particular ship which he happens to be engaging at the moment.

The importance of the defeat of the Port Arthur fleet, indecisive as it had at first seemed to be, soon began to be realised when our secret agents in the fortress sent us complete and carefully ascertained information relative to the condition of the ships which had succeeded in regaining the shelter of the harbour. From this information it at once became apparent that, as fighting units, none of them could again be made of service until the conclusion of the war, and Japan heaved a great sigh of relief, which was intensified when, on the evening of 14th August, the news was flashed through the country that the gallant and sorely tried Kamimura had at last been granted his long-cherished wish to meet the Vladivostock squadron, and had defeated it. True, the defeat, like that of the Port Arthur fleet, was not as decisive as could have been wished; for of the three cruisers—the *Gromovoi, Rossia*, and *Runk*—which sallied forth from Vladivostock, under the command of Admiral Jessen, in response to Admiral Vitgeft's call for support in his last desperate sortie from Port Arthur, two of them, the *Gromovoi* and the *Rossia*, succeeded in regaining the shelter of Vladivostock harbour, while only the

Rurik, the least formidable of the trio, was sunk. But again, as in the case of the Port Arthur fleet, although the bulk of the Russian force contrived to escape either capture or destruction, it had been so severely handled as to be rendered innocuous for many months to come, and Japan was at last free from the continual menace of it. The destruction of the fast cruiser *Novik* in Korsakovsk harbour on 21st August, by the Japanese ship *Chitose,* drove the last nail in the coffin of Russia's naval power in the Far East; and from that time forward, with the exception of maintaining the effective blockade of Port Arthur, the Japanese navy had little to do except prepare itself at every point to meet the menace of the Baltic Fleet, which at this time was beginning to materialise and take definite shape.

Meanwhile, after almost superhuman struggles against enormous odds, and in the face of frightful sufferings and losses, Japan's land forces were beginning to make progress. During the last days of July General Kuroki's forces fought and won the battles of Towan and the Yushuling Pass. On 3rd August, General Oku seized Hai-cheng and Newchwang old town, which is situated some twenty miles inland from the port of Newchwang; and then there came a pause, during which the final preparations for the advance upon Liao-yang were being completed.

Liao-yang promised to be a very tough nut to crack, for General Kuropatkin, fully recognising the possibilities of the position, had determined to make his stand there and inflict upon the Japanese such a crushing defeat that all further capacity for taking the offensive would be driven out of them, after which, the subjugation of a beaten and disheartened enemy should prove an easy task, rendered all the easier, perhaps, by the fact that the great assault upon Port Arthur by the Japanese had failed disastrously, with frightful loss to the assailants. The defences of Liao-yang were of great extent and enormous strength, including not only formidable forts and earthworks armed with powerful guns, and mile upon mile of most carefully and elaborately constructed trenches, but also with innumerable pitfalls, each with its sharpened stake at the bottom, as in the case of the Nanshan Heights defences. These pitfalls were arranged in regular lines, interrupted at intervals by patches of mined ground, while outside these again there ran a practically continuous girdle of barbed wire entanglements, the wire being charged with an electric current powerful enough to instantly destroy any one who should be unfortunate enough to come into contact with it. Liao-yang defences were, in fact, a repetition of the defences of the Nanshan Heights—where the Japanese suffered such appalling losses—except that they were of an even more elaborate and deadly character.

The attack upon Liao-yang was indeed in many respects a repetition of the attack upon Kinchau; for, as in the case of Kinchau, there was a formidable hill position—that of Shushan—to be first stormed and taken. This task was entrusted to the Second Japanese Army, under the leadership of General Oku; and they accomplished it on 1st September, after three nights and two days of desperate fighting, in the course of which the heroic Japanese suffered frightful losses. On the same day, the Russians began to withdraw from Liao-yang under a heavy fire from the Japanese artillery. On the following day the Japanese captured the Yentai mines; and a few hours later, General Nodzu, at the head of the Fourth Japanese Army, entered the town of Liao-yang unopposed.

Meanwhile, what was the state of affairs on land before Port Arthur?

As has already been said, the great general assault upon the land defences, which began on 19th August 1904, resulted in disastrous failure with frightful losses for the Japanese. Yet that failure, terrible as it was, was not by any means complete; its blackness was irradiated by a gleam of light here and there which sufficed to keep alive that spirit of hope and indomitable resolution which no misfortune could ever quite quench in the breast of the Japanese, and which was undoubtedly the determining factor in the campaign. To particularise. On 14th August the 1st Japanese Division was ordered to capture the five redoubts on the crest of the ridge west of the railway, known as the Swishiying redoubts. These redoubts were taken on the following day, and their capture paved the way for the general assault, four days later. This began with the furious bombardment of the height known as 174 Metre Hill, which was stormed and taken at the point of the bayonet, later in the day, by the 1st Division, which immediately pushed south-east, with the object of gaining possession of Namaokayama, or 180 Metre Hill. This hill was protected by, among other devices, an intricate barbed wire entanglement charged with a high-tension electric current, the penetration of which proved to be a task of almost insuperable difficulty; nevertheless, it was eventually accomplished. On the morning of 22nd August, by a splendid act of heroism and self-sacrifice on the part of fifty Japanese, West Panlung fort was captured, and this cleared the way for the capture of the East fort. But the superhuman efforts made by the Japanese in capturing these positions completely exhausted them, with the result that the assault ended in failure, since the majority of the defences remained in the hands of the Russians.

On 23rd August, the battleship *Sevastopol*—which, it will be remembered, was one of the ships which contrived to make good her escape from the Japanese fleet after the battle of the Yellow Sea—having been patched-up, as far as the resources of Port Arthur dockyard would allow, got under way and, steaming round to Takhe Bay, proceeded to shell the Japanese lines in the neighbourhood of Ta-ku-Shan and the Panlung redoubts. It was a rather daring thing to do, for there was not a ship in the harbour capable of supporting her, while the Japanese blockading squadron in the offing was close enough in to be clearly visible from the heights. Included in that squadron were the new armoured cruisers *Nisshin* and *Kasuga*, purchased from the Argentine just before the declaration of war; and no sooner was it seen that the *Sevastopol* had actually ventured outside the harbour, than these two powerful craft steamed in and opened fire upon her, and also upon the Laolutze forts, which were supporting her. The approach of the Japanese cruisers was the signal for a hurried retirement on the part of the Russian battleship, and she lost no time in effecting her retreat to the harbour. But while entering, she struck a contact mine, which exploded beneath her bows, inflicting such serious damage that it was only with very great difficulty she succeeded in returning to her berth, with her bow almost completely submerged. This was the last straw, so far as the *Sevastopol* was concerned, and she was practically put out of action for the remainder of the war.

A week later our cruisers and destroyers effected a *coup* which, there is every reason to believe, must have materially hastened the fall of the fortress. This consisted in the capture, off Round Island, of a great fleet of Chinese junks, bound from Wei-hai-wei to Port Arthur, conveying to the beleaguered city vast quantities of food, clothing, ammunition, explosives, and supplies of every imaginable description. The junks were taken into Dalny, where their cargoes were declared to be contraband of war, and confiscated by the Japanese.

These several successes, comparatively unimportant though they were, coupled with the practical destruction of the Port Arthur and Vladivostock fleets, put new heart into the Japanese for a time; but with the arrival and passage of the month of September, during which no appreciable progress was made in the operations before Port Arthur, even the unexampled patience and superb stoicism thus far displayed by the Japanese as a people showed signs of the wear and tear to which they had so long been subjected, and murmurings at General Nogi's apparent non-success began to make themselves heard. The casualty lists seemed to grow ever longer with the passage of the days, without any visible result, except that Nogi contrived to retain possession of the few unimportant positions which he had gained, and a black cloud of pessimism seemed to be settling down upon the Island Empire.

Meanwhile, however, in its silent, secret, undemonstrative way, the Japanese army had been making preparations of an important character, among which were included the construction of concrete emplacements for eighteen 11-inch howitzers, from which great things were expected. They fired a 500-pound projectile charged with high explosive, and had a range which enabled them to command the entire area of the fortress, including the harbour.

On the 1st October the first six of these howitzers opened fire, in the presence of General Baron Kodama, who had crossed to Port Arthur from Japan to administer, perhaps, a fillip to the officers and the army generally. North Kikwan fort was the first recipient of the new guns' delicate attentions, one hundred shells being poured into it. Huge clouds of dust and smoke at once arose from the fort; but it was enormously strong, and no very important results were apparent. On the following day and for a few days afterwards the howitzers lobbed shells upon the fleet, and the *Pobieda*, *Poltava*, *Retvisan*, and *Peresviet* were all struck, and their crews driven out of them, after which they were moved to the East harbour, where they were hidden from the sight of our gunners by the intervening high ground.

Meanwhile the Japanese engineers were resolutely and industriously pushing their saps ever closer up to the Russian forts, in the progress of which task the most furious and sanguinary hand-to-hand fighting with bayonet and bomb was of daily, nay hourly, occurrence. The slaughter was appalling, few of the combatants on either side surviving such encounters.

Yet, although the advantages were all on the side of the defenders, the patience and heroism of the Japanese steadily told, and on 4th October they attacked a work at Yenchang, near Takhe Bay, and destroyed the two machine-guns with which it was armed. This success was followed up by the capture, on 16th October, of an immensely strong Russian position on Hashimakayana Hill. Ten days later, the Japanese troops stormed and took, after hours of sanguinary fighting, the two important positions of Erhlung and Sungshushan, on the northern and north-western salients of the old Chinese Wall; and these successes were considered to have cleared the ground for the general assault which had been ordered from headquarters in Japan.

For four days—27th, 28th, 29th, and 30th October—the Russian works were subjected to such a terrific bombardment as, up to then, mortal eyes had certainly never beheld. It reached its height about eight o'clock on the morning of the 30th, and continued until about one o'clock in the afternoon, during which the din was terrific and indescribable. Shell and shrapnel fell upon the Russian works at the rate of one hundred per minute, the forts resembled volcanoes in eruption, from the continuous explosions of the shells which fell upon them, and the entire landscape became veiled in a thick haze of smoke. At one o'clock the preparation was thought to be complete; and ten minutes later the great assault began—to end in complete and disastrous failure! The Russian forts, supposed to have been silenced by those four days of terrific bombardment, were as formidable as ever; and as the stormers dashed forward they were met by so furious a rifle and artillery fire that they were literally annihilated. The second grand assault upon Port Arthur had failed, as completely and tragically as the first!

To have incurred such tremendous losses for such insignificant results was a terribly depressing experience for Japan; but the benumbing effect of the blow began to pass away when, in the first week of November, the news arrived of General Oku's splendid success upon the Shaho; and with renewed hope, and that indomitable patience and courage which is so marked a feature of Japanese character, the troops before Port Arthur set to work to repair their disasters.

Their first success was achieved in the middle of the month of November, when they gained possession of the little village of Kaokiatun, thus securing the command of Pigeon Bay. This success was followed, on the 23rd of the month, by an attempt on the part of the Japanese to capture the Russian trench on East Kikwan Hill. The attempt resulted in failure, with a loss of some three hundred slain, to say nothing of wounded. This was followed, on the 26th, by an attack upon Q Fort, North Kikwan, Erhlung, and Sungshushan. This too resulted in failure for the Japanese, with awful slaughter; the failure in this case, however, being tempered by the capture of the trench on East Kikwan Hill. This capture was of very great importance to the Japanese, from the fact that it commanded the approach to the fort on the summit of the hill; and the Russians, recognising this fact, fought madly to regain possession of the trench, finally succeeding toward midnight. The fighting on this occasion was most disastrous for the Japanese, their wounded alone totalling over 6000, while it was estimated that in dead their losses must have exceeded 10,000!

The result of all this sanguinary fighting was to convince the Japanese Staff, at last, that the defences on the eastern slope were impregnable to assault, and must be captured by other means. They accordingly next turned their attention to 203 Metre Hill, which was the key to the eastern defences of Port Arthur, and determined to take it by assault.

This was a particularly tough proposition, and after the tremendous losses which Nogi's army had already suffered in its disastrous assaults upon the eastern defences, the Staff might well have been excused had it hesitated to undertake such a herculean task. For the position was so immensely strong that the Russians regarded it as impregnable. The merely natural difficulties of the adventure were great, for, as its name indicates, it was a lofty hill, with steep, almost precipitous slopes, to scale which, even unopposed, was no light task. But when to this difficulty was added the further one that the hill had two summits, each crowned by very strong earthworks constructed of sand-bags, timber and steel rails, connected by tunnels with bomb-proof works on the rear slope, and that it was further protected by two lines of trenches, themselves protected by strong barbed wire entanglements, and that the works on the summit mounted several machine-guns and some heavier pieces of artillery, the reader may be able to form some slight idea of the obstacles which the Japanese undertook to surmount, as well as the indomitable courage which possessed them to make the attempt.

It must not be supposed, however, that the attack was about to be made on the spur of the moment and without any previous preparation. On the contrary; for two whole months the Japanese had been steadily sapping from the north and north-west, day and night, in face of the most vigorous and determined opposition on the part of the Russians, first constructing a parallel about a hundred yards from the first line of Russian trenches, and, from this parallel, driving saps which pierced the wire entanglements and in two places reached to within fifty yards of the Russian line. And while this was being done, four of the new Japanese 11-inch howitzers concentrated their fire upon the works on the twin summits of the hill.

The assault was ordered for the evening of 27th November. Supported by a heavy bombardment from the howitzers and batteries in their rear, the troops chosen for the assault broke cover and rushed the first line of Russian trenches, bayoneting the occupants almost before the latter had time to open fire upon them. Then followed hand-to-hand fighting of the most ferocious and sanguinary character, which lasted all night. Morning found the assailants still in possession of the trench which had been won; and now, strongly reinforced, the Japanese proceeded to push forward to attack the summit and Akasakayama battery. Immediately, the Russian guns in the neighbouring forts opened fire upon the stormers with shrapnel and heavy shell, and in a very few minutes the entire scene was so completely veiled in powder smoke that it was impossible for anyone to tell exactly how the fight was going. Four times the Japanese stormed the crest and were beaten back; and it was not until three o'clock in the afternoon, when they delivered their fifth assault, that they at last burst through the wire entanglements and reached the crest. For a time they held it; but the Russian fire was too hot for them, and at length they were not only driven off the crest but also out of the trench which they had won on the previous night.

The attack was resumed the next day, and again resulted in failure.

Then the Japanese Staff put its foot down and declared that both hills *must* be taken, at all costs! The cruisers *Sai-yen* and *Akagi* were ordered round to Pigeon Bay to co-operate with the troops by covering the assault with their fire; but, unfortunately, as the *Sai-yen* was getting into position on the 30th, she struck a mine and sank, not far from where the old *Hei-yen* disappeared some two months earlier. This put an end to the plan for naval assistance, and the land forces were obliged to rely entirely upon themselves. Fighting of the most desperate and sanguinary character proceeded all through the afternoon and night of 30th November, but it was not until the next day that the indomitable courage and persistence of the Japanese were rewarded with success; the western summit of 203 Metre Hill being taken by them and held all day, despite the most desperate efforts on the part of the Russians to retake it.

This was the beginning of the end, so far as Port Arthur was concerned. On 5th December the eastern summit of the hill also fell into the hands of the Japanese, and next day they secured possession of Akasakayama, thus obtaining command of the entire Metre range.

These important positions in their possession, the tide of war at once turned in favour of the Japanese, for the heights commanded not only the town but the harbour of Port Arthur; and the big 11-inch howitzers, as well as a battery of naval 6-inch and 47-inch guns, were at once brought up, and the bombardment of the Russian warships was begun. On 6th December the *Poltava* was sunk by the Russians to save her from destruction by the Japanese fire. Next day the *Retvisan* met a like fate, while a fire broke out aboard the *Peresviet*, and on the 8th she and the *Pobieda* were at the bottom of the harbour, while the *Pallada* was obviously following them. On the following day the *Bayan* was hit no less than twenty-two times, bursting into flame shortly before noon and burning until shortly after four o'clock in the afternoon, while the *Sevastopol* was seriously damaged. The mine-laying ship *Amur* was also hit and sunk. The dockyard sustained serious damage, yet, strangely enough, all through this bombardment the Russians did little by way of reply; they seemed overwhelmed and paralysed at the misfortunes which were now befalling them—or else, as some of us began to shrewdly suspect, their ammunition was at last exhausted. On the 9th of the month the *Sevastopol*—the only Russian battleship still remaining afloat in the harbour—moved from her moorings and sought refuge behind a big boom under the guns of Mantushan fort, on the Tiger peninsula, where, a few nights later, she was energetically attacked by our destroyers. These attacks were repeated nightly, with considerable loss to our side, until the night of 15th-16th, when the ship was successfully torpedoed. Her end was so evidently near now that we ceased our attacks; but nothing could save her, and on the 20th of the month her captain took her out into deep water, opened her Kingston valves, and sank her, so that she might not fall into the hands of the Japanese.

Meanwhile, North Kikwan fort was captured by our troops on the night of the 18th, after a fight which cost us close upon a thousand men. Two days later, we took a battery close to it; and on the 28th, the formidable Erhlung became ours after a tremendous fight. Success after success on our part now followed each other rapidly, each additional capture firing our troops with renewed courage and determination. The last day of the year saw Sungshushan fort fall to us, and the first day of 1905 saw the New Panlung and H batteries in our hands, the Chinese Wall breached, and the Japanese flag planted well within the Russian defences. Wangtai fort was stormed and taken on the afternoon of the same day, and as twilight was closing down upon the scene a Cossack, bearing a large white flag, was seen riding out of the Swishiying valley, followed by a Russian officer.

The officer was the bearer of a letter from General Stoessel to General Nogi, inviting the latter to open negotiations with the writer "to determine the conditions of surrender" of Port Arthur. Needless to say, the Japanese general gladly, yet without undue haste, acceded to Stoessel's proposal; and at noon of 2nd January 1905, Major-General Ijichi met Major-General Reiss at Plum Tree Cottage, a miserable little hovel situated in the village of Swishiying, and the negotiations were opened which resulted in Port Arthur passing into the possession of the Japanese on the evening of that day, although the Russian evacuation did not take place until the 5th of January.

Chapter Twenty
The Battle of Tsushima

Meanwhile, what had become of the Japanese navy, after the battle of the Yellow Sea?

So far as the *Yakumo* was concerned, we were in the very thick of the fight when it was at its hottest, and when at length the battle came to an end with the flight of the *Retvisan* and *Pobieda*, we were one of the ships which had been so severely mauled that extensive repairs were necessary before we could undertake further service. Accordingly, we were ordered to proceed forthwith to Sasebo to refit; and since we were by no means alone in our plight, we had to await our turn. Hence it was the middle of January 1905 before the *Yakumo* was again ready for sea; and in the meantime I had ample opportunity to cement my friendship with the members of the Boyd family, who had acted the part of Good Samaritan to me when I first made acquaintance with Sasebo.

The day before the *Yakumo* left Sasebo for our rendezvous at the Elliot Islands, news arrived that the long talked-of Baltic Fleet had reached Madagascar and was at anchor in Passandava Bay, refitting, provisioning, and generally enjoying the hospitality of the French nation. This, of course, was not the first news that we had received of it; we had been duly apprised of its departure from Libau on 15th October and had also heard—with surprise on the part of the Japanese, and with bitter mortification and shame on my own part—of its subsequent unprovoked and unpunished attack upon the Gamecock fleet of British trawlers; but nobody was in the least disturbed by the news that this formidable fleet was at last actually at sea, for as a matter of fact we in Japan regarded its departure as nothing more than a move on the part of the Russian Government intended to encourage the garrison of Port Arthur to continue its resistance. For, to speak the plain truth, nobody seriously believed that the voyage would ever be continued far beyond the western extremity of the English Channel, for we could not see how it was going to be done. But *now*, when it was apparent that France was openly ignoring and outraging all the laws governing neutral nations, in favour of Russia, it behoved Japan to take serious notice of what was happening, and she not only protested vigorously against France's violation of neutrality, but set to work in earnest to prepare for the new menace which was gradually creeping closer to her shores.

For a month after the arrival of the *Yakumo* at the Elliots, I and half of my crew formed a portion of that busy multitude who toiled in Port Arthur harbour to raise the sunken ships which cumbered it, and to clear the entrance channel; but on the 10th of February the naval contingent rejoined its ships, and on the 14th the Japanese battle fleet disappeared from human ken, and for three whole months was no more seen, save by a few who were made clearly to understand the vital necessity to remain absolutely silent.

Not so, however, the Japanese cruisers. It was our mission to generate a feeling of uneasiness and anxiety in the mind of Admiral Rojdestvensky and those of his officers and men; and with that object squadrons and single ships were directed to show themselves suddenly and mysteriously, and as suddenly to disappear again, in those waters through which the Russian fleet would have to pass on its voyage to Vladivostock. And we did this so effectually and with such excellent judgment that very soon the various telegraph cables grew hot with the number of messages transmitted through them, telling the most marvellous stories of enormous Japanese fleets seen in various parts of the world at the same moment, and of huge and incredibly strong fortifications erected on the Formosan coast and elsewhere.

"Bluffing" was not confined to our side, however; French newspapers were permitted to fall into our hands, in which the news was circumstantially set forth that, in consequence of the fall of Port Arthur, Admiral Rojdestvensky had been recalled, and that he was taking his entire fleet back to Europe by way of the Suez Canal—with the exception of four of his best battleships, which, it was hinted, had foundered at sea. On 20th March, however, reliable information reached Japan that the 1st and 2nd Divisions of Rojdestvensky's fleet had left Madagascar on the 16th of the month, steering north-east. Two days later, news reached us that the Russian fleet had been sighted in the Indian Ocean, still steering north-east; and a week later the first of our scouts—a smart and fast steam yacht, flying German colours— apparently bound westward, passed within four miles of the armada, took careful count of it, and reported by wireless its exact position and the fact that it consisted of forty-three ships, seven of which were battleships, while of the rest, ten were cruisers and seven were destroyers.

From that moment our scouts, under every conceivable guise except that of warships, never for a moment lost touch with the Russians. We knew that they passed Singapore on 8th April; we knew that they touched at the Anamba Islands and coaled there before the Dutch warships could arrive to prevent them; and we knew that on 14th April the fleet arrived in Kamranh harbour, in French Indo-China, where, while awaiting the arrival of Admiral Nebogatoff's squadron,—which was coming out via the Suez Canal,—the Russians proceeded to make good defects and generally prepare for the fight which they knew awaited them.

Of course the Japanese Government vigorously protested against this flagrant violation of the law regulating the conduct of neutrals, and France replied with polite assurances that such violation should not be repeated. This was followed by an order to the Russians to leave Kamranh harbour, which they obeyed at their leisure, moving on first to Port Dayot and then— when ordered from there in response to fresh Japanese protests—to Honkoe Bay. Thus, with the connivance of the French authorities, a very pretty game of hide-and-seek was played by Rojdestvensky, until 8th May, when Nebogatoff joined with his nine craft, and the now completed fleet entered Hon-koe Bay and calmly proceeded to complete the task of refitting, coaling, and provisioning prior to its great attempt to force its way through to Vladivostock. As for the Japanese Government, it speedily recognised that France had quite made up its mind to ignore the laws of neutrality in favour of Russia, and accordingly ceased to lodge any further useless protests.

A week later—on 14th May, to be exact—the entire Russian fleet left Hon-koe Bay, steering northward; and although the French authorities suppressed the news of the departure for two whole days, Togo, who was now with his fleet in Chin-hai Bay, on the southern coast of Korea, received the news by wireless the same night. Thenceforward its progress was carefully watched and reported daily, so that at any moment Togo could put his finger upon the chart and indicate the position of the enemy, within a few miles.

Meanwhile, Togo was busily engaged in the preparation of his plans for the great battle toward which we had all been looking forward for so long. In this work he was of course hampered by his lack of knowledge as to the intentions of the Russians. There were two routes by which they could reach Vladivostock: one—much the shorter of the two—by way of Korea Strait and up through the Sea of Japan; and the other, via the east coast of Japan and La Perouse Strait. Also, should Rojdestvensky choose the shorter route, he could pass either to the east or to the west of Tsushima Island. Togo solved the problem by preparing a plan of battle for each of the three alternative routes.

On 26th May the Russian fleet was reported as being south-west of Quelpart Island, off the entrance of Korea Strait, and its position rendered it practically certain that it was Rojdestvensky's intention to take the shorter route up through the Sea of Japan.

It was shortly before sunset, on 26th May, that the fateful wireless message—"Enemy in sight, fifty miles west of Torishima,"—came in from one of our scouting cruisers; and two minutes later a signal was flying from the *Mikasa*, summoning the Japanese admirals to a council of war.

The council was a brief one, lasting barely a quarter of an hour; then the admirals returned to their respective flagships, and the latter at once signalled the captains of the several squadrons to meet in the cabin of the admiral of that squadron. The *Yakumo* formed part of the armoured cruiser division, under the command of Admiral Kamimura, and accordingly it was in the cabin of the *Idzumo* that the six captains of that division presently assembled to receive our instructions.

These were concise enough, and of such a character as to indicate that Togo had given this long-expected battle a tremendous amount of consideration, and had finally settled all the details with almost mathematical precision. In the first place, for good and sufficient reasons, the battle was to be fought in the eastern strait, and, as nearly as possible, off the northern extremity of the island of Tsushima. To ensure this, the old *Chin-yen*, the *Itsukushima*, *Matsushima*, and *Hashidate*, of the protected cruiser squadron, accompanied by one division of destroyers, were to act the part of lures, approaching the Russian fleet on the following morning, as it neared the Straits, alternately attacking and retiring in the direction of the eastern strait, thus inveigling Rojdestvensky into a pursuit in that direction. The ships told off for this duty were to proceed to sea at once, as the *Chin-yen*—the slowest craft of the quartette—was only good for thirteen knots at best, and it was not desired that any ship should be pushed to the limit of her powers until the engagement should become general. The remainder of the protected cruiser division—fourteen in number—were to proceed to sea with the main fleet on the following morning, parting company when all were fairly at sea, and then find the enemy's rear, closing in upon it and harassing it as much as possible, acting according to circumstances, quite independently of the main fleet, and each captain using his own initiative. As for us of the armoured cruiser division, we were to have the honour of forming part of the battle-line. This was sufficiently gratifying intelligence, but that which followed was even more so: the former tactics of engaging the enemy at extreme range, in order to preserve our precious battleships from injury, were to be abandoned; this was the battle for which they had been so carefully hoarded, and in it they must be made the fullest use of, their utmost value must be exacted; in a word, they were to be fought for all that they were worth, closing with the enemy to within effective range, and firing slowly and deliberately, so that every shot should tell.

There was also a general order issued, in the highest degree illustrative of Japanese thoroughness. It was that every man throughout the fleet was to wash himself from head to foot most carefully and thoroughly, and to put on clean clothing, in order to reduce to a minimum the risk of septic poisoning of wounds, also to don woollen outer garments, so that their clothing might not be set on fire by bursting shells.

Nor had the ships themselves been forgotten. In turn each had been dry-docked, repaired, defects made good, down to the tightening of a loose screw, machinery overhauled and parts replaced where thought necessary, bottoms cleared of weed and coated afresh with anti-fouling composition, and hulls repainted, until each ship looked as though she had just been taken out of a glass case. And now there they all lay, in Chin-hai harbour, with boilers chipped clean of deposit and filled with fresh water, flues, tubes, and furnaces carefully-cleaned, new fire-bars inserted where needed, fires carefully laid and ready to be lighted at a moment's notice, and every bunker packed with specially selected Welsh coal, purchased for this very purpose, long ago.

Furnace fires were at once lighted and steam raised; and before midnight the old *Chin-yen*—looking very spruce and fit, despite her age— and her three companion cruisers quietly got their anchors and proceeded to sea, while aboard the ships still in harbour the crews were busily engaged in making the preparations referred to in the general order, before retiring to what was for some of them to be their last night's sleep on earth. As for me, I sat in my cabin, far into the night, writing long letters to my friends at home, so that, in the event of anything untoward happening to me, they might know that loving thoughts of them were in my heart up to the last.

In Chin-hai harbour the morning of 27th May 1905 dawned bright and clear, and at five o'clock the crews of the Japanese ships partook of a substantial meal before proceeding to the task of clearing for action. They were still partaking of this meal when a marconi-gram arrived from the *Shinano Maru*, one of our scouts, informing us that the Russian fleet was in sight, entering the eastern strait; that it was impossible as yet to say how many ships were present, as the atmosphere was misty; also that there was a high sea running in which the Russian ships were rolling heavily.

This was the news that Togo had been anxiously awaiting; and now that he had it, and knew that the enemy was making for the precise spot where it had been planned to meet him, the little Admiral gave vent to a great sigh of relief, and ordered the signal to be made for the protected cruiser squadron to weigh and lead the rest of the fleet out to sea.

This order was at once carried out, quietly and deliberately—for there was plenty of time on hand, the *Chitose*, Admiral Kotaoka's flagship, and her four consorts leading, followed by the *Kasagi* and her four consorts, under Admiral Dewa; these being followed in turn by the *Akitsushima* and her three consorts, under Admiral Uriu. These three squadrons, with that which had proceeded to sea some hours previously, under the leadership of the younger Togo, to draw the Russians into the eastern strait, constituted the protected cruiser division, to which had been assigned the duty of attacking and harassing the enemy's rear.

Following these went the main battle squadron, with the *Mikasa*, flying Togo's flag, proudly leading, followed by the battleships *Shikishima*, *Fuji*, and *Asahi*, with the new and powerful cruisers *Kasuga* and *Nisshin* bringing up the rear. Then, at a short interval, followed the *Idzumo*, flying Admiral Kamimura's flag, and the *Iwate*, *Yakumo*, *Adzuma*, *Asama*, and *Tokiwa*, in the order named, every ship flaunting two big battle-flags in the morning breeze. Once clear of the harbour, we parted company from the protected cruiser division, which headed away South-South-East, to get in the rear of the enemy, while we of the battle-line steered a trifle to the south of east for the battleground which Togo had selected. On the port side of the line steamed a flotilla of Japan's fastest destroyers, told off by Togo to act as dispatch boats, in the event of the flagship's wireless apparatus being put out of action, or her masts shot away.

Once clear of the land, we soon ran into an atmosphere of haze and a rising sea which set the long line of ships rolling ponderously; and as the vessels rolled and plunged, flinging heavy showers of spray over their weather bows, each captain stood in his chart-room, with a chart of the strait spread open on the table before him, anxiously awaiting the next news of the enemy. These charts had been, for convenience' sake, carefully divided up into a series of numbered squares; and about nine o'clock the expected message arrived. It ran—"The enemy is in two hundred and three," that being the number of the square on the chart occupied by the Russian fleet at that moment. No sooner was the message decoded and its purport made known than mutual congratulations were exchanged; for even as the fall of 203 Metre Hill into the hands of our soldiers had been the prelude to the surrender of Port Arthur, so now the fact of the Russian fleet being in square 203 on the chart was accepted as an omen of another victory.

The fine weather of the early morning had by this time completely deserted us; the sky had become overcast, Tsushima's conical summit was hidden by a great bank of heavy, louring cloud, the grey, dreary-looking sea was running in confused, turbulent, foam-flecked surges through which the big ships wallowed heavily, flinging great combers of yeasty froth from either bow, while the little torpedo craft, smothered in spray, were tossed about like corks. Yet, despite the gloomy aspect of the weather, the Japanese fleet presented a magnificent and inspiriting sight as it ploughed steadily through the leaping, mist-flecked sea, each ship keeping station with the most perfect accuracy, with her two—and in some cases three—great battle-flags snapping defiantly in the freshening breeze.

It was shortly after six bells in the forenoon watch when we at length received a message which must have removed a load of anxiety from our little Admiral's mind. It came from the *Izumi*—one of the ships which had been dispatched on the previous night for the purpose of luring the enemy into the eastern channel—and reported that at length her captain had succeeded in ascertaining the full force of the enemy's fleet, and that it consisted of eleven battleships of the 1st, 2nd, and 3rd classes, nine cruisers, nine auxiliary cruisers, and nine destroyers. These were heavy odds to face with our four battleships, eight armoured cruisers, and eighteen protected cruisers; yet never for a moment did we shrink from the encounter, for we were, one and all, *determined* to conquer. Moreover, the weather, gloomy as it was, was in our favour, for our ships, having been painted the peculiar grey tint that had been found so effective in the atmosphere of the Sea of Japan, were scarcely visible at a distance of four miles, while the heavy sea would probably give our own gunners a great advantage over those of the enemy.

It was about a quarter to two o'clock in the afternoon, and we were steaming in line ahead, with the *Mikasa* leading, our course being about South-South-West, when, the fog thinning somewhat, we suddenly saw, away on our port bow, a great cloud of black smoke, underneath which we presently discerned several large ships approaching in two lines, their black hulls and yellow funnels showing up with remarkable distinctness against the light grey background of fog. Instantly every telescope and pair of binoculars in the Japanese fleet was levelled at them in an endeavour to identify the craft in sight—for we were intimately acquainted with the characteristics of every ship in the enemy's fleet—and presently we recognised the big, three-funnelled craft at the head of the port line as the *Oslabia*, while the two-funnelled battleship leading the starboard line was undoubtedly the *Suvaroff*, Admiral Rojdestvensky's flagship. Astern of her followed the *Alexander Third, Borodino*, and *Orel*; while in the wake of the *Oslabia* we were able to identify the *Sissoi Veliki, Navarin*, and *Admiral Nakhimoff*, with a long string of other craft at that moment too far distant for identification.

While we were still endeavouring to identify some of the more distant ships, the *Mikasa* made the general signal: "The fate of our Empire depends upon our efforts. Let every man do his utmost!" It was greeted with a great roar of "Banzai Nippon!" which swept along the line of the fleet like the rumbling of distant thunder. The crews of the ships had, of course, been at quarters, and the officers at fire-control stations, for some time, and now we began to receive from the range-finders the range of the *Oslabia*, the leading Russian ship. "Fifteen thousand yards," "Fourteen thousand," "Twelve thousand," came the reports in rapid succession as the two fleets rushed toward each other.

At a distance of twelve thousand yards the *Mikasa's* helm was shifted and the course of the Japanese line altered four points to the eastward, as though our purpose was to pass along the Russian line to port, exchanging broadsides as we passed; and so the enemy evidently understood, for he came steadily on. But we knew differently. Already every forward gun in the fleet was bearing steadily upon the *Oslabia*, and when, in obedience to a signal from the flagship, the speed of the Japanese fleet quickened up to fifteen knots, we knew that the great battle was about to begin.

It began a few minutes earlier than we anticipated, for our range-finders had just given the distance of the head of the Russian column as nine thousand yards, when two bright flashes, followed by a great cloud of white smoke, broke from the *Oslabia's* fore-turret, and presently we saw two great fountains of foam leap into the air some distance beyond the *Mikasa*. As though this had been a signal, the *Suvaroff, Alexander Third*, and *Sissoi Veliki* instantly followed suit, and a second or two later we heard the loud, angry muttering of 12-inch shells hurtling toward us. But some flew over, and others fell short; not one touched us; and as the heavy, rumbling *boom* of the reports reached our ears, the *Mikasa* signalled another shift of helm a further four points east, and before the Russians fully realised what we were about, the Japanese fleet was "crossing the T," — that is to say, passing athwart the enemy's course.

Every gun which the Russians could bring to bear upon us was now being loaded and fired as rapidly as possible, so that in a very short time the enemy's ships were enveloped in whirling wreaths of powder smoke, yet not a single Japanese gun had thus far spoken.

"Six thousand yards" was presently signalled by the range-finders; and at the same moment three shots roared forth from the turrets of the *Mikasa, Shikishima*, and *Fuji*. We knew at what target they were aimed, and those of us who happened to have our glasses at our eyes saw a bright flash and a cloud of smoke suddenly burst into view on the *Oslabia's* conning tower. One of our 12-inch shells had found its mark, and—as we subsequently learned—instantly killed Admiral Folkersam! This instant success told us that we might unhesitatingly rely upon the accuracy of our range-finders, and at once every ship in the Japanese battle-line opened fire, first upon the *Oslabia* and then upon the *Suvaroff,* our manoeuvre of "crossing the T" enabling us to bring every one of our broadside guns upon the enemy, while he, in turn, could only fire a few of his fore-turret guns, the rest being blanketed by the ships leading the line.

The careful, deliberate fire of twelve ships upon two could have but one result; the *Oslabia* and *Suvaroff* both received a most fearful punishing; the unprotected portions of their hulk were blown to ribbons, dense columns of dark smoke poured from the *Oslabia,* and presently it was seen that she and the *Suvaroff* were on fire and burning furiously. Both ships, as though instinctively, swerved away to the eastward, anxious not to shorten the distance any farther between themselves and the Japanese, and presently both the *Oslabia* and the *Suvaroff* fell out of their respective lines and dropped to the rear, with both their own lines between them and the enemy.

Then came the turn of the *Alexander Third,* which was now leading the Russian starboard line; and she got even more severely peppered than her battered sisters in misfortune, for the range had now dwindled to four thousand yards, and every shot of ours was telling with terrible effect. It must not be supposed, however, that while the enemy was being punished so severely, we were going scatheless. We were not; very far from it, although we were giving a good deal better than we received. Shells were by this time falling pretty thickly all around us, while hits were becoming steadily less infrequent. The first to come aboard the *Yakumo* was a 12-inch shell which struck our fore barbette on the starboard side, glanced upward, striking the conning tower and exploding, the fragments wrecking a couple of ventilators, a boat, and freely puncturing our fore funnel, while one piece swept my cap off my head and overboard. The *Asama,* however, next but one astern of the *Yakumo,* suffered very much more severely than we did, three heavy shells hitting her abaft in quick succession, throwing her steering gear out of action, and causing her to leak so badly that she had to drop out of the line and be left astern, executing temporary repairs.

By this time—that is to say, shortly before six bells in the afternoon watch—the two fleets were heading about East-South-East, running in parallel lines, our own line leading that of the enemy by about a mile, while the *Alexander Third* was, like the *Oslabia* and *Suvaroff,* in flames and blazing furiously. A few minutes later it was seen that the *Sissoi Veliki* was also on fire, she being now the leading ship of the Russian port line of battle, and, in accordance with Togo's tactics, the object, with the *Navarin* and *Admiral Nakhimoff,* of the concentrated fire of our battle-line. Meanwhile, our protected cruiser squadrons had come upon the scene and were harassing the Russian rear so effectively that, aided by the vigorous attack of our battle-line upon the Russian van, the enemy's line was breaking up in confusion.

Togo now gave the order for us to close in upon the enemy's van, himself leading the way in the *Mikasa*, with the result that the leading Russian ships, in order to avoid being crossed and raked, were compelled to continually bear ever more and more away to the southward, until finally they swept right round and were all heading north once more, with the *Alexander Third*, *Suvaroff*, and *Oslabia* all out of the line and practically out of action.

It is difficult, nay more it is impossible, for the captain of a ship taking part in a general action to note and remember every phase and detail of such action; he is so intensely preoccupied in the task of fighting and manoeuvring his own ship that only certain detached incidents of the engagements impress themselves upon his memory strongly enough to be permanently remembered; thus I am able to recall that about this period of the battle I came to the definite conclusion that we had won, notwithstanding the fact that several of our ships, including the *Yakumo*, had suffered severely. The *Asama*, for example, was at least temporarily out of action, while the *Kasuga*—one of the two new cruisers purchased from the Argentine just before the outbreak of the war—had all three of her heavy guns rendered useless.

By this time our protected cruiser division had crept up on the starboard quarter of the Russian line, and was vigorously attacking in that direction, while our battle-line, to port of the Russians, was as vigorously pounding the enemy's front, thus bringing the Russian line between two fires. It was about this time that one of those brief interludes of comparative inaction which occur in most battles afforded me an opportunity to look round a bit and obtain my first comprehensive view of the battle since its commencement.

The wind, which had been blowing fresh during the earlier part of the day, had been gradually dropping, and was now little more than a mere breathing, but the sky still continued overcast and gloomy, its shadow, falling upon the sullenly heaving but no longer breaking seas, causing the tumbling waters to look almost black where they were not veiled by the drifting smoke wreaths or slowly moving patches of fog. It was the obscuration caused by this combination of smoke and fog that had produced the interval of comparative inaction of which I have spoken, for it rendered accurate firing difficult, and our ships, in accordance with Togo's determination not to waste ammunition, were only firing occasional single shots, when the hull of an opponent became distinctly visible, although the Russians were blazing away at us as recklessly as ever, thus enveloping themselves in an almost continuous veil of smoke, which was renewed as quickly as it drifted away.

It was now that the *Asama*, having effected temporary repairs, came up and resumed her place in our line of battle, which was thus once more intact, our ships keeping station with the most perfect regularity with the Russian line, such as it was, some four thousand yards distant about a point abaft our starboard beam. The roar of the enemy's artillery was incessant, the continuous crashing *boom* of the guns reminding one, as much as anything, of a tremendous thunderstorm, while the flash of their guns, seen through the gloom of the louring afternoon, not altogether inadequately represented the accompanying lightning.

I looked round to see if I could discover either of the silenced Russian battleships. Yes, there they were, all three of them: the *Oslabia* about three miles away, broad on our starboard quarter; the *Suvaroff* about half a mile astern of her; and the *Alexander Third* about a mile astern of the *Suvaroff*, all astern of their own line, and all being vigorously attacked by our protected cruisers. The *Oslabia* was low in the water and had a heavy list to port; the *Suvaroff*, still apparently on fire, had lost both her funnels and her foremast; and the *Alexander Third*, from which clouds of smoke, were still rising, also had a heavy list and was steaming ahead very slowly, although she, like her sisters in misfortune, still replied with the utmost gallantry to our fire.

But, so far as the *Oslabia* was concerned, her race was evidently run, for even as I watched her it became apparent that she was fast settling in the water, while with every roll her list to port became stronger, until at last I found myself holding my breath in momentary expectation to see her roll right over. The catastrophe was not long delayed. There came a moment when, having rolled heavily to port, she failed to lift again, but heeled steadily more and more until, watching her through my powerful glasses, I saw a number of objects go sliding away off her decks into the water with a heavy splash; over she went until her masts and funnels lay along on the water, her two after-turret guns spoke out defiantly for the last time; and down she went in a great swirl of foam, while the Russian destroyers closed in upon the spot to save such of her crew as might contrive to remain afloat.

I now turned my attention to the *Suvaroff*, and was just in time to witness a very plucky attack upon her by a squadron of our destroyers, which, notwithstanding her disabled condition, she beat off in most gallant fashion.

Next, I turned to have a look at the *Alexander Third*. Her crew appeared to have extinguished the fire aboard her and got her back into something like her former trim. She was now heading to rejoin the Russian line—which was re-forming after a fashion, and presently I saw her drop into third place in the line, between the *Orel* and the *Sissoi Veliki*, which latter also seemed to have extinguished her fire. Meanwhile the mist had thickened into fog, which rapidly became so dense that we presently lost sight of the enemy altogether.

Shrewdly suspecting that the Russians would seize this opportunity to effect their escape, Togo now led his battle-line round in a sweep from North-East to South-West, and then to south for a distance of some eight miles, during which we sighted and shelled the enemy's cruiser squadron and some of his auxiliary ships heading to the south-west. At this point Togo decided to turn northward again, but before doing so he detached the six armoured cruisers—of which the *Yakumo* was one—under Admiral Kamimura, with orders to pursue and destroy the ships of which we had just lost sight.

This was about four o'clock in the afternoon. By this time the wind had dwindled away to a mere nothing, and the sea had so far gone down that our torpedo craft could keep pace with the larger craft without being swept by seas from stem to stern; still, the weather continued to be very dismal and dreary, the sky still lowering and overcast, not a solitary gleam of sunshine, and the fog gathering so thickly that it was difficult to see anything beyond a two-mile radius. The heavy gun-firing had by this time died down to nothing; but a pretty lively cannonade of lighter weapons down in the south-western quarter told us that the engagement between our cruisers and those of the enemy was still proceeding briskly although nothing could be seen. Accordingly, the *Idzumo* led her five armoured sisters in that direction, at a speed of fifteen knots.

Suddenly, as we pushed along, guided on our course by the sounds of the firing, the thunder of heavy guns, easily distinguishable from the sharper report of the lighter weapons, burst forth ahead, to our amazement, for we fully believed that the whole of the enemy's battleships had fled northward. Clearly, however, we were mistaken in so believing, and Kamimura at once recognised that capricious fortune was unexpectedly holding out to him the opportunity to wipe off some of the utterly undeserved opprobrium that had attached to him earlier in the war, because of his failure to bring the Vladivostock squadron to book, and which his later success had by no means effaced; accordingly, he signalled the squadron to increase speed to eighteen knots, which was supposed to be the maximum attainable by the *Asama* and ourselves, although the others were capable of an extra knot. This inferiority of speed on our part had always been rather a sore point with me, and I had had many a talk with Carmichael, the *Yakumo's* Engineer Commander, about it, who had felt the reproach as keenly as I did, and had assured me that if ever the worse came to the worst, he would undertake to get the extra knot out of the ship, although it would be at the peril of what he elegantly termed "a general bust-up in the engine-room." So now I called to him down the voice-tube, begging him to speed her up as far as he dared; and a few minutes later I noticed that we were gaining upon the *Iwate*, our next ahead, while the *Asama*, our second astern, was also stoking up. Thereupon I signalled the flagship that we had speed in hand, if required, and the order was at once given to increase speed by half a knot.

It was not very long afterward that we had ocular demonstration of the value that extra spurt of speed might prove to be; for while we were still plugging along in the direction of the firing, we suddenly sighted two craft coming slowly in our direction. They proved to be the *Kasagi* escorted by the *Chitose*, making for the Japanese coast, the former being holed below the waterline and making so much water that it was doubtful whether it would be possible to save her. She signalled that matters were going badly with the protected cruisers, eleven of them being then hotly engaged by twelve of the enemy, one of which was a second-class battleship, while three others were battleships of the third class! Admiral Dewa, who was on board, concluded his communication by urging us to hasten to the rescue.

The steadily increasing distinctness with which the sound of the firing reached us, proved that we were rapidly overhauling the contending squadrons, and some twenty minutes later we sighted the rearmost ships on both sides, blazing away at each other "hammer and tongs." Our own cruisers were to the southward of the Russian line, therefore Kamimura led his force to the northward of the enemy, thus placing the latter between two fires, at the same time signalling us to concentrate our fire upon the four Russian battleships, which we did with a vengeance, and within five minutes we were all enveloped in a roaring tempest of flame, smoke, and bursting shells.

But the precision of our fire was infinitely superior to that of the Russians. They fired at least three times as rapidly as we did, but whereas every one of our shells reached its mark, the bulk of theirs flew wide. They were rapidly growing demoralised, and when the fight had been in progress some twenty minutes, their line suddenly broke up into little groups of twos and threes and made off to the northward at top speed, those of us whose speed permitted, following them and keeping up a brisk fire with our forward guns.

Suddenly, as we pursued, two ships were sighted ahead, evidently in difficulties, and a few minutes later we identified them as the Russian battleship *Suvaroff* and the repair ship *Kamschatka*. Immediately, Kamimura signalled, ordering their destruction. Then, while we were in the very act of training our guns upon them, another battleship was sighted in the distance. She, too, was evidently in a parlous state, so much so, indeed, that we scarcely had time to identify her as the *Alexander Third* when she capsized and sank!

Then we opened fire vigorously upon the other two ships, while our destroyers closed in upon the *Suvaroff*, now listing so heavily that she was almost on her beam-ends. But although she was in such a sorry plight her crew displayed the utmost gallantry, defending themselves from the torpedo craft with the only gun which they could bring to bear. It was a hopeless fight, however; our boats dashed in, time after time, discharging torpedoes at her, and at length two of the missiles got home, one under her stern, and the other in the wake of her engine-room, blowing a great hole in her side. This last finished her; the water poured into her in torrents, and a few minutes later she rolled right over and disappeared. The *Kamschatka* followed a few minutes later.

Meanwhile, the ships which we had been pursuing had disappeared in the fog, heading northward, *in which direction we knew our battleships had preceded them.* Therefore, since the hour had now arrived when, according to arrangements, our torpedo flotillas were to take up the game, Kamimura signalled us to reduce speed to ten knots and to shape a course for our appointed rendezvous near Matsushima Island.

The night which followed was an anxious one for all hands, for we were steaming through a dark and foggy night, with all lights out. Nothing untoward happened, however, and with the appearance of dawn on the following morning a little air of wind sprang up and swept the fog away.

It was shortly before three bells in the morning watch (half-past five o'clock a.m.) of 28th May, and the six ships of the Japanese armoured cruiser division were steaming northward in line abreast, when the *Tokiwa*, which was the easternmost ship, reported smoke low down on the eastern horizon. At once the course was altered eight points to the eastward, and the ships proceeded in line ahead, closing in upon the *Tokiwa*—the leading ship—as they did so, while Kamimura reported the circumstance by wireless to Togo, who, with his battle squadron, was some sixty miles away to the northward of us. Some twenty minutes later, after a lively bout of signalling by the wireless operators aboard the Japanese ships, it became certain that the smoke seen must proceed from enemy ships, and all our dispositions were made for dealing with them, the instructions of the armoured division being to close slowly in upon the enemy from the westward, while the battleships rushed down at full speed from the north, and the protected cruisers did the same from the south.

The result was that, a few hours later, four Russian battleships, namely, the *Orel, Apraxin, Nicolai First,* and *Seniavin* found themselves completely hemmed in by our ships, while the light cruiser *Izumrud,* availing herself of her superior speed, just managed to escape by the skin of her teeth.

I will say this for them: outnumbered though they were, and hopeless as was their situation, with their ammunition running short, and their crews almost in a state of collapse from nerve strain, those four ships made a gallant defence, and it was not until they were reduced to the very last extremity that Admiral Nebogatoff ordered the white flag to be hoisted over his squadron in token of surrender. Prize crews were at once put aboard the prizes, and they were ordered south to Sasebo under an escort of cruisers, of which the *Yakumo* was one. The *Orel* was such a wreck that she was incapable of steaming more than eight knots, consequently we did not arrive in harbour until the afternoon of the following day, when, our wireless messages having prepared the inhabitants for our arrival, we received such an ovation as it thrills me yet to remember.

Chapter Twenty One
Reinstated

It was not until nearly a fortnight later that the full results of the battle of Tsushima became known; then, tabulating the intelligence that came to hand from various points, we were at last in a position to realise the surprising character of the Japanese Navy's achievement.

Briefly and baldly summarised, it amounted to this: Of the eleven Russian battleships which went into action on that memorable 27th May, four were captured, while the remaining seven were sunk. Of nine cruisers, five were sunk. Of nine auxiliary cruisers, four were sunk and one was captured; while, of nine destroyers, one, the *Biedovy*, was captured with Admiral Rojdestvensky, seriously wounded, on board, and four were sunk. Twenty-six of the thirty-eight craft which composed the much-vaunted Baltic Fleet were thus accounted for. Of the remaining twelve, three — the small cruiser *Almaz* and the *Grosny* and *Bravy*, destroyers, succeeded in making their way to Vladivostock, while the remainder escaped to Manilla, Shanghai, and Madagascar, where — with the exception of the auxiliary cruiser *Anadyr*, at Madagascar — they were duly disarmed and interned.

I had fully made up my mind that with the destruction of the Russian Baltic Fleet the war must of necessity come to an end. But I was mistaken; no overtures of peace were made by Russia, and it was not to be expected that, after her signal triumphs on land and sea, Japan would jeopardise her prospects of securing a satisfactory settlement by being the first to open negotiations; therefore, in pursuance of their land campaign, it was decided to attack the Russians from the north by way of the great river Amur, which the Japanese had ascertained was navigable by light-draught vessels for at least a thousand miles during the late spring, when the thaw and the spring rains caused the river to run full. But in order to utilise the Amur it was imperatively necessary that Japan should have control of the island of Sakhalin; accordingly, on 24th June a fleet of warships, under Admirals Kataoka and Dewa, assembled at Yokohama, from whence a few days later they sailed, convoying a fleet of transports, aboard which were one of the newly raised army divisions, under the command of General Haraguchi.

My ship, the *Yakumo*, was one of the warships detailed for this expedition, and naturally I went with her. Space does not permit of my giving the details of this expedition, which was not at all of an eventful character; suffice it to say that it attained its object, Sakhalin becoming ours on 31st July 1905.

Meanwhile, however, after the result of the battle of Tsushima became known, President Roosevelt decided that the time had arrived when the friendly intervention of a perfectly disinterested Power, such as the United States of America, might be welcome to both belligerents; accordingly, on 8th June, he opened negotiations by dispatching an identical Note to the Emperor of Japan and the Tsar of Russia, offering his services as mediator. His offer was accepted by both; and on 9th August the plenipotentiaries of the two nations met at Portsmouth, in New Hampshire, U.S.A. The negotiations were of a protracted nature, and were several times in danger of falling through in consequence of the uncompromising attitude of Russia's representatives. Ultimately, however, thanks to President Roosevelt's masterly diplomacy and the conciliatory spirit of the Japanese, an agreement was arrived at, and the Treaty of Peace between Japan and Russia was signed on 5th September 1905.

Of the terms of the treaty it is not necessary for me to speak here, since they in nowise affect the fortunes of the present historian. The conclusion of the treaty, however, of course put a stop to all hostilities on both sides; and the end of September found me and my ship back in Sasebo, where the latter, among other ships, was paid off. Previous to the paying-off, however, Togo had sent for me, and at the interview which followed, inquired most solicitously what were my plans for the future, at the same time assuring me that if I cared to remain in the service of Japan I might absolutely rely upon continuous employment and further promotion. I had, however, long before this quite made up my mind as to the course of action I would pursue upon the conclusion of the war; namely, to return to England and endeavour to secure my rehabilitation in the British naval service, and I explained this to him at length. When he had heard all that I had to say, he admitted that what I had decided upon was undoubtedly the right thing to do. Then, learning that I proposed to return home by way of San Francisco and New York, he dismissed me for the time being, only to inform me, two days later, that, learning I was about to resign my commission as Captain in the Japanese Navy, the Emperor had expressed a desire to see me prior to my departure from his dominions, in order that he might personally thank me for the services I had rendered to Japan.

The interview took place four days later, in the Imperial Palace at Tokio, with most satisfactory results, so far as I was concerned; for His Majesty, after making the most flattering references to my services—full particulars of which he seemed to have at his fingers' ends—was graciously pleased to decorate me with the Star of the Grand Order of the Rising Sun, and to present me with a magnificent naval sword, the hilt of which and the mountings of the sheath being of solid gold, exquisitely worked.

The afternoon of the first Sunday in December witnessed my arrival in the Mersey; and somewhat late the same night I found myself once more in London.

I was, of course, anxious to see Uncle Bob and Aunt Betsy again without delay; but, being in London, I could not deny myself the pleasure of calling upon my friends the Gordons. In the first place I paid my respects to Sir Robert at his office. As it chanced, he was so overwhelmingly busy that he could only spare me a bare ten minutes of his time, just to welcome me home again and insist upon my dining with him and his wife that evening. I did so, and received such a welcome as went far to compensate me for many a lonely hour among the storms and fogs and bitter cold of the Japan and Yellow Seas. To my amazement, I then learned that my name had become tolerably familiar to such Britons as had been taking more than a merely superficial interest in the progress of the Russo-Japanese War, some kindly-disposed newspaper correspondent having kept the British public pretty well posted as to my doings. The result of this, I was informed, was that, in the event of my choosing to make application for restoration to my former position in the British Navy, the authorities would undoubtedly be willing to regard such application with considerable favour.

This I soon afterwards found to be true; for although there were several formalities to go through, while the onus of proving my innocence of the charge which brought about my dismissal rested entirely upon me, I had no sooner done this than I received the intimation that the Lords Commissioners of the Admiralty, having given due consideration to my representations, had been pleased to reinstate me as Midshipman in the British Navy!

It was not long, however, before I received my commission as Sub-Lieutenant; and now I am a full-blown Commander aboard a super-Dreadnought, eagerly looking forward to the dawn of a certain Day which, unless appearances are curiously deceptive, cannot be very far distant.